The Rule of Thumb

A.J. Paterson

Copyright © Alexandra Paterson 2015

All rights reserved

Without limiting the rights under copyright reserved above, no part of this publication may be reproduced, stored in or introduced into a retrieval system, or transmitted, in any form or by any means (electronic, mechanical, photocopying, recording or otherwise) without prior written permission of the copyright owner

The right of Alexandra Paterson to be identified as author of this work has been asserted in accordance with sections 77 and 78 of the Copyright, Designs and Patents Act, 1988

This book is a work of fiction. Names, characters, businesses, organisations, places, and events are either the product of the author's imagination or are used fictionally. Any resemblance to actual persons, living or dead, events or locales is entirely coincidental.

This Edition Published by Stanhope Books, Essex, UK 2016

www.stanhopebooks.com

Cover design by Perry Martin © 2015
Interior Artwork by Lynn Grech © 2015

ISBN-13: 978-1-909893-31-3

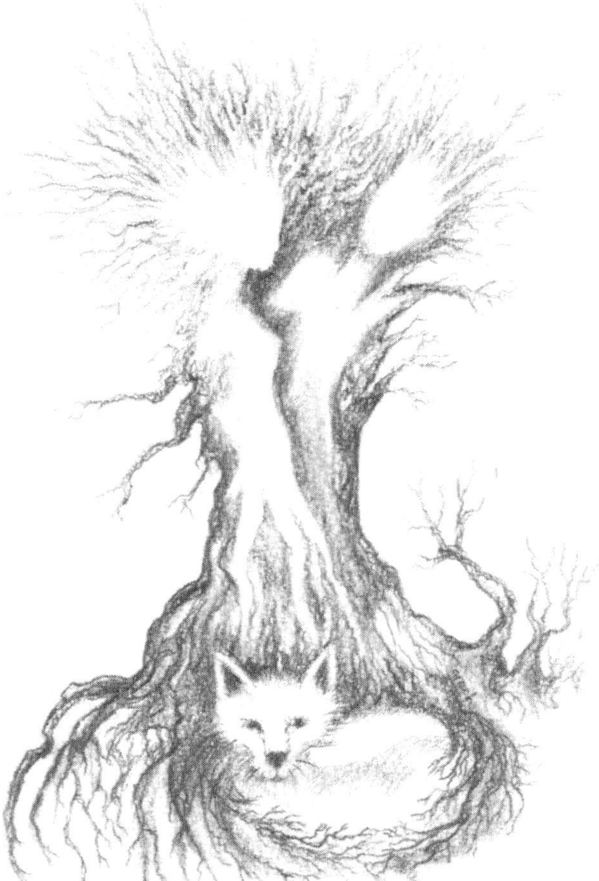

For Nana

Chapter 1

I thought back to when I was a child, eight to be precise, just before the event that changed everything. I was so young and naïve – running around the gardens like there wasn't a care in the world. Things seemed so simple and everyone seemed so happy; I know that I was. I had my friend and at that time there was nothing and no one that could have torn us apart. My father used to watch over us as we carelessly ran around him as he tended to his work.

"Emmy," he called out. "Time to come and help me!" It never bothered me that he wanted me to help him – in fact I really enjoyed it and it made me feel special. I loved being outside and playing with the mud; it was fair to say that I was never a typical little girl. I didn't care about dresses or pretty bows in my hair – by the end of the day I would always be covered in dirt anyway. My job was to work on the flower beds; I would carefully dig up the soil to make sure they all stayed fresh and when the new ones needed planting that was also down to me – with the supervision of my father of course. He never said it but I knew he just didn't think that I was big enough yet. I would take on the tasks with full concentration, lips pouting as all my effort went in to making sure it was done absolutely perfectly: the same expression that you would expect to see when a little girl is dressing her doll.

My father tended to the two gardens that sat either side of the main house. As a child it was the biggest house I had ever seen – I couldn't have imagined any other building being able to beat that. Although the house is still very large compared to the humble cottage that we live in and any of the houses in Sussex, it doesn't seem so overwhelming now. There was a long winding lane that led from the village directly to the house, though not all the land belonged to the Barrow family; there were a few small homes dotted along the way, our cottage being the last one before you reached the house. From the lane you could see the grey brick outline of the house stretching across the top of the hill. Its stone arms reaching out to invite you in. Although it was only one building, the structure of it gave the impression that it was constructed of five different parts. Countless windows filled the walls to let in the light, the huge black door the focal point of the centre building. What I always found most impressive however was that they had ten chimneys – who needs that many chimneys? To this day I still haven't set foot inside the house, not even into the servants' quarters. I live and breathe the life that I have outside which has left me slightly scared of those walls that would keep me enclosed.

We would spend the whole day outside, wake up with the birds and go in with the sun. Now that I can look back at things with an open mind I know that a lot of the reason was to make sure that I stayed out of the house and, most importantly, away from my mother. At the time I was none the wiser, just relished the idea of being allowed to play outside for the whole day and because of that, I got on so well with my father.

Edward came running over to join me. My father would always chuckle whenever Edward asked to help and would say something like, "You don't want to be getting dirty Master Edward." Or, "Isn't it time that you got back to the house, don't want your parents wondering where you are do we?" The little girl that was playing with the dirt was always a little disappointed that her friend couldn't join in – sometimes she even tried to argue it. That disappointment only ever seemed to last a few moments though, it was only a matter of minutes before it was like it had never happened. When I look back at it now I can tell that there was more to it when my father would say no to the little lord; it was like he didn't

That particular day, August 15th 1910, will always be engraved in my memory. Every detail. Every sound, every smell – all those tiny moments stay the same, never changing no matter how hard I try; the ending is always inevitable.

The day started the same as any other; I woke up early and ran outside with my father to set to work. That morning he was trimming the bushes which was one of my favourite things to watch; he always made pretty shapes or animals and I liked to try and guess what each one was going to be. It was just after midday - I know this because my father and I had just finished our little picnic - when Edward came bounding round the corner. I didn't even have to ask if I could go play, it was the same routine every day. He just smiled down at me to let me know it was okay. For the next few hours the day continued to play out as it always did. Edward and I ran around the gardens, climbing trees and playing our made-up games until my father called me back to help him and Edward's nanny came looking for him.

We were just finishing up in the gardens when James, the stable boy, came racing towards us. "Thorne, Thorne!" he spluttered nervously. "Come quick!" Father didn't wait to find out what the problem was and just ran after James. I guessed it was a grown up thing, sometimes they don't need to say things to know what they mean. I didn't really understand the urgency of the situation so I didn't run after them straight away. Instead I packed up the gardening tools – which took me a fairly long time as I could only hold two things at a time - and wheeled them into the shed, bolting the door like my father had taught me. It was only then that I followed them, running down the path with a spring in my step. When I look back at that day now one of my main regrets is that I didn't run with my father; if only I had then I may have had the chance to say goodbye.

I spotted the crowd as I turned the corner that led to our little home. What should have foretold me that something was seriously wrong instead awoke the little girl that loved to be the centre of attention, so it was that little girl that went hurtling into the centre of the grieving crowd. It wasn't until my father placed his weathered hands on my shoulder and I turned to see the tears falling steadily from his eyes that the smile was wiped off my face. I didn't know it then but it was the next four words he spoke that changed my life in a way that had never been expected. I walked in the door to find my mother laying on the bed perfectly still. Those few steps I took towards her seemed to stretch a mile. I placed my mud streaked hand on top of my mother's marble-like one and stared at her sleeping figure.

"Mama, you can wake up now." I whispered, softly shaking her like she did to wake me. She didn't wake up, she didn't move. Just stayed as still as she was when I had walked into the room. "Papa, why won't she wake up?" My father tried to answer me but choked on his words.

I didn't cry then. I didn't cry at the funeral when people stroked my hair and looked down at me pitifully. I still haven't cried. I don't think I have ever fully understood what happened on that day so I don't know how to grieve. The only thing I am sure of is that growing up without a mother can affect someone in more ways than you would have ever thought possible.

Chapter 2

8 years later ...

The chirping of the birds signalled the start of the day. I rolled out of bed, threw on my clothes adding an extra jacket to protect me from the chilly autumn air, and padded into the kitchen to make breakfast. As I was eating the bowl of oats I noticed that my father was sprawled out on the rug showing no sign of movement. The smell that filled the room confirmed that he had been out drinking again. I gently prodded him with my foot even though I knew it was a pointless effort, so when he didn't even stir I threw the tatty blanket over him and walked out into the cool morning air.

Brown curls were escaping from the pins that I had carefully placed this morning and flying into my face. It was pointless trying to tuck them away so instead I half-heartedly blew them out of my tired eyes. Even though the wind blew against my face leaving a crisp coolness on my cheeks the darkened skies were clear telling me that the sun would soon be shining. The grounds were empty as they always were at this time; I was the first to work every day. As I turned the corner I noticed the state of the shed; the rickety hut was falling down around its contents, the roof was gradually peeling away, there were ever-growing holes in the dated wood and the door was barely hanging onto the hinges. Inside was no better; cobwebs covered every inch of empty space and everything was covered in dust that seemed to appear from nowhere. I know that I should probably care more but I didn't want to spend my day cleaning a shed that was likely to fall apart at an unfamiliar touch.

There were guests arriving to stay at the main house on Friday so there was a lot that needed to be done. I made a list in my head, trying to organise it practically as I went. The grass tickled my ankles as I walked across it, but with the weather as unpredictable as it was at this time of the year it was best to make that one of the last jobs otherwise it would most likely just need to be done again at the end of the week. As I couldn't really decide what to do I settled on walking round the gardens to see how the flowers were growing.

This was my favourite time of the day – the grounds were void of all man-made noise, only the natural sounds of the outside world could be heard. The birds were singing their morning song, the crickets chirped as they jumped from leaf to leaf and the soft patter of feet could be heard as rabbits made their way out of the burrows that lined the tree edge. The air smelt fresh from the dew of the night before, the scent of the plants at their finest. The fog that filled the morning was covering the house that stretched along the length of the walled gardens, its temporary absence making me feel completely at home. The light that shone through the mist, signalling the presence of the indoor servants, woke me from the solitude of the morning. I knew it was time for me to start getting some work done before I was spotted wandering around without a tool in my hand.

The sun was starting to wake casting a refreshing light across the early morning. Through the rising fog came Oscar the new stable boy. I hadn't any time to get to know him yet but from his attitude I felt that he wasn't too fond on me. "You having some trouble there?" he asked as he spotted me trying to pull the wheelbarrow out of the shed. In my head it sounded like he was smirking at me but I wasn't looking at his face so I couldn't be sure. I chose to ignore him and continued to try and manipulate the wheelbarrow around the countless tools that had been carelessly strewn across the floor.

"Where's your father? Should you be doing all of this on your own?" I dropped the spade and shears into the wheelbarrow and turned to stare at him.

"He's unwell, not that it has anything to do with you. And I am more than capable of doing this." My frustration at the situation seeping into my words. I started to walk away from him when I heard my mother's voice telling me to be polite no matter what I was feeling so I threw a quick thank you in his direction. I didn't need some know-it-all telling me that I wasn't good enough to do this; it was hard enough tending to the entire land by myself – especially when I was trying so hard to make sure no one noticed that it was all being done by me.

I got as far away from the stables as I could and started turning the soil in the flower beds. This was always the way to relax myself, but as I felt the tension leave me I couldn't help but feel that I may have been a bit harsh on Oscar. When I replayed the conversation in my head it was obvious that he really hadn't said anything bad at all, I had just jumped to the worst conclusion because I was so on edge; allowing my defensive attitude to take over as it always did.

There was no point fretting about it though so I tried to push it to the back of my mind and it wasn't long before I had forgotten all about the morning and was singing away to myself when Toby came bounding up to me; tongue flapping and tail wagging. I laughed as the big Labrador flew at me knocking me flat on the grass.

"What you doing here buddy?" I scratched behind his ears as he excitedly tried to lick my face. We wrestled for a few minutes before I finally managed to get free of the playful tyrant. I found a stick for him and threw it as far as I could so that I was able to tidy the mess he'd made as he had scrambled across the freshly turned flower bed. Toby came running back to me with the slobbery stick firmly grasped between his teeth. He dropped it at my feet ready to play again when he was distracted by the calling whistle that sounded from across the garden.

As I watched the dog run away from me the realisation of how lonely I was struck me hard. I missed the days when I used to spend all my time with my father helping him do what he loved. It was only over the last five or six months that he had started spending more time at the small pub in town and less time getting up in the mornings. To start with he had still been sporadically coming to work but he hadn't touched a wheelbarrow or shears in a month now. I could never fault him for stepping up after my mother's death – he did the best job he could in trying to stop me feeling the void that she had left behind. I guess it got too much for him though, and as soon as he felt I was old enough to look after myself I found that I was spending more and more time on my own. When the start of the war was announced I couldn't help but notice the way he was acting; whenever someone was called up he would look disappointed, as though he was jealous that he wasn't in the same position. It was recently that he even took himself down to the closest enrolment office only to be told that he had a heart murmur;

there was no way he would be able to leave. It was after he received that news that the drinking took over his life.

I was so lost in my thoughts that I almost didn't notice the person trying to sneak up behind me. It was the crunching of leaves that gave them away, making me snap back to reality and jump around. Edward was standing there smiling sheepishly at me. "Thought you might be hungry, you haven't stopped in hours," he said as he offered me one of the sandwiches he had brought out with him. At the mention of food my stomach started rumbling as though it had been starved for hours. I looked for a clean spot on my clothes to wipe off my dirty hands. Edward laughed at me as he pulled out a handkerchief, taking my hands one by one to wipe away the dirt; the pristine white cloth tainted by my touch. I gratefully accepted the food and greedily bit into it.

"How'd you manage this?" I asked, or at least that is what I would have said if I didn't have a mouth full of food. Luckily Edward was so used to me that it didn't faze him.

"Just told Mrs Rook that I was going to take Toby for a long walk and have a little picnic so she packed me an extra."

"That's not why she packed you an extra." I remarked raising my eyebrow at him. It was widely known that everyone had a soft spot for Edward- from the local village girls to the household cook – and I guess it was perfectly understandable. Not only did he come from money but he was one of the most attractive young men in Sussex. He was tall and lean; all the time he spent outside growing up had given him a naturally athletic build. His blonde hair flopped charmingly into his deep blue eyes and his cheeky boyish smile lit up his face, making it impossible for anyone around him not to smile back. It was that smile that got him whatever he wanted and ensured that he was never in trouble; it always had. Even though there was only six month between us he seemed to be comfortable in his body, making him seem a lot more grown up than I did; there was no carelessness to him anymore. Compared to this practically perfect person I looked a complete state. My mass of curly brown hair had almost completely worked its way out of the ponytail and was sticking out at all angles – gathering twigs and leaves along the way. My permanently tanned skin was smeared with the dirt off the ground and I was dressed in old tattered clothes that were fast becoming too small for my growing body.

"Close your eyes," whispered Edward, his hand resting on my cheek.

"Why?" I questioned, my heart thumping uncontrollably.

"Just do it." He smiled that irresistible smile and my eyes closed on demand. He gently grazed my cheek with his finger sending goose bumps down my arm.

"Your eyelashes are ridiculously long," he remarked examining his finger. He looked straight into my eyes. "You have really nice eyes – so big and green. I never noticed that before." He said it in such a conversational tone that I knew it didn't mean to him what it meant to me. He had no idea of the effect that those words had on me or how I was holding my breath for the ten seconds he was scrutinizing my eyes; he was completely oblivious to what was going on inside me and that was how it should be.

"Make a wish." I was so engrossed in his eyes that I didn't realise he was talking to me. "Hey Emily," he nudged me, "I'm speaking to you."

I snapped out of my fantasy. "Sorry."

"Make a wish." He held his finger inches away from my lips. I closed my eyes and blew lightly. "What did you wish for?"

"If I tell you then it won't come true!" *More like you'll never talk to me again,* I thought. But instead I smiled and shoved him playfully bringing it back to a more comfortable dynamic.

"I better get back to work, your house doesn't look this beautiful by itself," I joked. Edward smiled but it didn't reach his eyes so I knew that something was wrong before he spoke.

"Emily." He paused as though what he had to say next was really difficult. "I know you think that we haven't noticed you doing everything on your own, but we have. They only haven't said anything because I managed to persuade them not to." I looked up at him, worry glinting in my eyes.

"I don't know how much longer I will be able to stop them though. Where's Thorne?"

I sighed. Edward never referred to him as my father, he was very proper in that way. I desperately wanted to tell him the truth but I couldn't put him in that position. "He's hurt his back so he can't do anything at the moment, but he is starting to get better." I lied, averting my eyes away from his suspicious gaze. "Everything's fine, honestly." It hurt more than I thought to lie to him but there was no choice. He stared at me for a moment with concern written across his face.

"Just as long as everything is okay," he muttered. I smiled with as much feeling as I could muster. "Guess I better actually walk Toby before someone notices that he has been wandering around without me." He pushed himself up and ruffled my hair as he walked past. I tried to convince myself there was a reluctance to his tone but I knew that it was all wishful thinking. There was a longing in my chest that ached as I watched him walking away from me, hoping more than anything that he would just turn around. How could it be that he could occupy my thoughts so entirely for hours and days together, that he could be the first notion that crossed my mind in the morning and the last niggling worry at night, when – it was perfectly clear to see – I did not so much as wander across his consciousness from one day to the next.

Chapter 3

After what Edward had said I knew it was time to talk to my father and I was dreading it. I'd been putting it off for so long, just getting on with things because I knew how it was going to play out. The rest of the day blurred together, my stomach knotting tighter the closer it came to going home.

I walked down the little path as slowly as I could, trying to think of the best way to broach the topic. I still hadn't come to a decision when I walked through the door but I wasn't to worry as he was still fast asleep – he had just moved from the floor to the sofa. I say that but he was dangling half on to the seat whilst the rest of him dragged across the floor, the furniture not really big enough to accommodate his horizontal body. His soft snoring upset me more than I cared to admit; igniting an angry fire that was burning a hole inside of me. I resisted the urge to nudge him forcefully as I walked past and instead went about making dinner – possibly a little louder than was necessary but the child inside of me wanted her father's attention. It wasn't until he smelt the eggs cooking that he finally stirred, his grunt of disappointment when he realised where he was signalling his return to the real world.

He stumbled over to the table and plonked himself down. The unshaven, unwashed mess that sat across from me was a ghost of the handsome man he had once been. His dark hair was lined with grey, desperately in need of a wash as was the rest of him. His once loving eyes were red rimmed with dark bags underlining them. His clothes were torn and covered in stains and his face had a strange yellow tint to it. I waited until he had nearly finished stuffing food in his face before I said anything – at least this way I knew that he wouldn't be going out with an empty stomach.

"Papa, when are you going to go back to work?" I asked as nonchalantly as I could manage.

"You know that my back is bad, I can't work until it is better, and it will only make it worse." he spouted, refusing to look at me. "Plus, you're doing just fine. It's good for you," he added. With that remark I built up the courage to speak to him with more confidence.

"Yes, I can do it but it is a lot of work to do by yourself!" I retorted.

"You think I don't know that?" he spat at me.

"No. But I have always tried to help you and now I'm the one that is working completely alone." I held my hand up to stop him interrupting me. "And not only that, it's your job. Not mine!"

He silently stared at me from across the table, his face turning a deeper shade of red with every word I spoke, my defiance only fuelling his anger. I knew that I was going to cause a problem but now I had started I couldn't make myself stop.

"I've been trying to cover for you so that no one says anything but I can't keep lying."

"You aren't lying. I'm ill."

"You're not ill," I shouted back, "You're just going to the pub every night instead of getting up and going to work. You need to sort this out because I won't keep doing this. Edward told me that …"

"Edward!" he shouted interrupting me. "What are you doing talking to that boy? You know what I have told you about that."

As soon as I mentioned Edward I knew that it was a mistake, it meant that everything I had finally built up the courage to say would now be overshadowed by my father's dislike for my childhood friend.

"I will not take this from you, you are my daughter and you will do what I bloody well tell you." He pushed his chair back with such force it flew back into the wall. He towered over me with menacing eyes, silently daring me to utter another word. I felt the slam of the door from across the room, confirming that nothing was going to change.

I couldn't understand why my father disapproved so strongly of mine and Edward's friendship – I mean it wasn't like he knew how I really felt about him. Thankfully Edward showed no sign of going away, it just meant that our meetings took place away from watchful eyes. Now that we were getting older he was expected to take on a lot more responsibilities with the house, especially since his older brother Thomas – who it should have fallen upon – had left to go and fight in the war, so our time together usually consisted of passing greetings and hidden conversations.

The sad thing was that it was the few fleeting moments during the day that I saw him that seemed to make everything else okay. I missed the days where we could happily run around the gardens every day; people so enchanted by our childish innocence that there were no rules to our friendship. I missed the days where no feelings were involved. Where I was just happy to have a friend and nothing more. I was still happy to have that friend, but it would never be the same. I wanted more and I knew that would never happen; he needed a lady and I was simply a girl.

I tidied the food away and set about boiling the water to clean myself. As much as I loved to be outside, it was always refreshing to wash away the dirt that covered me like an extra layer of skin. I was in the process of washing the twigs from my hair when there was a knock at the door. I jumped upright, flinging water all over the room.

"One minute." I called out, grabbing a robe to throw over me, rapidly trying to dry my hair with a cloth as I walked over to the door. I positioned myself behind the door to ensure my legs were covered and opened it a crack to see who was there. There was a man that I didn't recognise standing with his back to me.

"Hello?"

He turned at the sound of my voice. "Sorry to disturb you young lady, I'm looking for a Mr Alfred Thorne."

"He left about an hour ago, I'm not sure where he went," I half-lied. "Shall I pass on a message?" The stranger looked appreciatively at the small part of me that was peeking from behind the door. My wet hair was dripping down my back and into my eyes, but I daren't wipe the drops away in fear of revealing myself.

"Could you tell him that Mr Griggs stopped by? Charlie Griggs that is. He'll know what it is about." He said, tipping his hat at me before turning down the path.

I quickly shut the door and watched him through the gap in the curtains to make sure that he had left. The unexpected appearance had left me feeling slightly vulnerable yet I wasn't sure why. In my head I could see his dark beady eyes looking me up and down in a way that I had never seen someone look at me before. He didn't look like he could be trusted and it worried me that he had some kind of business with my father. I tried to push it to the back of my mind, I figured it was no use worrying about something I didn't know. I wrapped myself up in some warmer night clothes and grabbed my pencils and paper from under my mattress where I hid them from my father. I inspected the pencil that was now more tip than anything else – I desperately needed a new one but even though I was doing all the work my father was drinking most of the money away and leaving hardly any of it for me. I continued with my most recent sketch as best I could. Highlighting the shape of my mother's body as she lay like a statue on her bed.

The dim lighting of the candles that flickered around the room were making my eyes heavy so I decided to call it a night. I drifted off to sleep to the strangely comforting smell of candle smoke. It got to midnight, when the crash of my father's arrival would usually wake me, but instead there was silence. It was that eerie silence that struck me; it made the emptiness that surrounded me so much more apparent. The coldness of the night crept up to me and I had never felt so alone. I closed my eyes in the hope that sleep would take the worry away from me but the sinking feeling in the pit of my stomach wouldn't go away. I lay there staring at the ceiling, watching the morning make its appearance. The birds told me it was time to get up. There was still no other movement in the house. I got ready as quickly as possible hoping that I would give myself a little extra time to run down the lane.

The mist was thicker this morning making it impossible to see more than two feet in front of me. "Papa!" I called out as I jogged down the lane. My calls became more frantic the further I got and when I reached the end of the lane with no response I was feeling sick with panic. My father may be out all night but he was always back by the morning, always. I didn't have time to go and look any further, someone had to do the job that he wasn't.

As I turned the corner that led to the little shed I could hear the soft banging of the door. I started to wonder if I had shut it properly but I knew that I had, I was very particular about it which meant only one thing. I held my head high and swung open the door with a forced confidence ready to confront whoever or whatever would face me. It took a moment for my eyes to adjust to the darkness. As it did I was gradually able to make out the figure of a man propped up against the wheelbarrow.

"Papa?" I choked out, desperately hoping it wasn't him even though I already knew the answer deep down. The grunt that answered was too familiar to leave any doubt in my mind. Any worries that I had previously had quickly vanished and were fast replaced with disappointment. I didn't even bother asking him what he was doing there; I didn't want to know. I roughly pushed him to wake him up. "You need to get out of here before someone sees you. I won't be able to explain this one away." He didn't respond, just briefly opened his eyes then rolled them in the opposite direction. His refusal to help me at all was quickly starting to get on my nerves; I didn't have the time to deal with this. I picked up a bucket and stormed out of the shed. I ran round the corner knowing there was very little time left before someone would find us. I filled the bucket from the hose by the stables as quietly as I could. I accidentally kicked a pebble and the clang against the metal seemed to fill the silent morning – I was sure that was the end of it but when no one turned up after the minute I waited with baited breath I knew I was safe. For now.

I walked back to the shed as fast as I could and wasted no time in sloshing the contents of the bucket over the sleeping figure. As soon as the ice cold water hit his face he jumped bolt upright.

"What are you doing?" he shouted at me.

"If you don't plan on working then you need to get out of here before someone sees you." I stared at him, ready for the argument that he was geared up to have. When he didn't come back at me I added, "Plus, it's about time that smell was washed away."

With that comment he turned around, his face inches from mine.

"You will not speak to me like that," he spat, "Treat me with respect." He stormed out the shed and back down the lane.

"You don't deserve my respect," I whispered at the disappearing figure. I waited until I knew he wouldn't notice me and followed him to make sure he made it home. As I watched him walking away from me, tears threatened to form. I stopped, closed my eyes and took in a deep breath refusing to give in. I felt the cool morning wind blow over my face, as comforting as a person's touch.

Chapter 4

Over the next few days I kept myself as busy as I could to avoid thinking about what had happened. It wasn't hard considering there was so much to do in preparation for the guests that were to arrive on Friday. I had trimmed all the hedges, weeded the entire garden, re-potted plants and straightened out the flower beds. This was usually a two person job; but those two people would have been me and my father. Since he wasn't here I was taking on the responsibilities of both the head gardener and the under gardener. I had tidied up the trees, collecting up all the fruit that had fallen off the branches and had dropped it off for the cook. It was now Thursday morning and I was just completing the task of raking up the leaves, knowing that I would probably have to do it again in the morning. As I was wheeling the piles of leaves to the compost heap I spotted Edward riding across the hills with his younger sister Anabelle in tow. I hadn't spoken to him since he had mentioned my father. I had been going out of my way to avoid him and even though I felt terrible for it I knew that I wouldn't be able to lie to him again. I also knew that it would only be a matter of time before I had to face him – after all, I didn't actually want to be away from him.

My next task was to mow the gardens and the land closest to the house. Though this would usually be one of my favourite tasks, as I love the smell of cut grass, today I was dreading it. Not only because it was going to take me the entire day but also because I knew that there would be no chance of hiding that it was only me out there. Lord Barrow had treated my father to a new lawnmower last winter and it had been his pride and joy ever since. The whole house would be expecting to see him out there when they heard the motor turn. I wondered if I could maybe get away with it if I just used the old one like I always did, that way no one would think I was replacing him. The only problem with that was that the old mower was falling apart and took a lot longer to get anything done. I was making the last journey to the compost heap when I heard the sound of hooves behind me.

"Emily!" called out Edward as he jumped down from his horse, his smile stretching across his face. He quickly tied Silver's reins around a hanging tree branch then gathered me in his arms and swung me off my feet. The sudden action took my breath away, my face had turned a deep shade of red by the time he had set me back on my feet.

"Sorry I haven't seen you, my father is making sure that I know about everyone that is coming. It really is the most boring task but he hasn't let me out of his sight."

Edward's apology threw my concentration slightly as I was all set to try and come up with some excuse as to why I'd been avoiding him. I happily accepted his misguided apology and smiled at him.

"Anyway, I used Annabelle as an excuse as she was dying to go out on the horses. I had just taken her back to the stables and I thought I would come and say hello before you escaped." The whole time he was speaking he held my hand in his making my heart skip even though I was pretty sure he didn't even realise he was doing it. I could have listened to him all day but if there was any chance of getting everything finished by tomorrow I knew that I had to leave him.

"Are you excited for the weekend?" I asked as I couldn't bear the thought of saying goodbye yet.

"Not overly. It's really just my father's way of introducing me to all his important friends." He rolled his eyes impatiently making me snigger. As I looked at his smiling face I saw the appearance of the cheeky little boy who had been my most favourite childhood friend. It warmed me to know that this whole nasty business of growing up had not completely changed him.

"Enough about me, what are you doing for the rest of the day?" He leaned against the tree like he was ready to settle in for a long conversation, absentmindedly stroking Silver's nose as he waited for me to answer.

"I have to cut the grass," I said before I put any thought into it. "I mean, my father is letting me do it. He says that I'm ready to do it by myself now. I'm really quite excited although a little bit nervous considering it's such a big job." I stuttered, falling over my words trying to make the excuse believable. Edward walked towards me and rested his hand on my shoulder. I was convinced that I had messed up and he was going to ask me what was going on again. I was wrong. He gently grasped my shoulder and bent his head so it was level with mine.

"You will do brilliantly, you always do. Now I better be off before I get told off. I'll try and sneak out to see you in the morning since I won't get a chance over the weekend," he said. He expertly jumped up onto his horse and trotted back towards the stables.

"I miss you," I whispered once I knew that he was safely out of ear shot, forcing a smile when he turned back round to wave goodbye.

I couldn't believe that Edward had believed what I had said, and as I set to my final task I breathed a little easier knowing that when someone was to say something about it Edward would be able to vouch for me. There was also hope that everyone else would be as busy as I was, which meant that they wouldn't even have the time to notice.

As the day came to an end the grounds were looking much tidier. I was pleased with how I had managed to complete it all but the thought of going home was making me anxious. There had been silence between my father and me since I had found him in the shed and it was becoming more uncomfortable as the days went on. Last night he hadn't even looked at me during dinner and had left without a word whilst I was still eating.

From what I could see there was no light showing through the windows. This did not necessarily mean that anything was amiss considering that my father could either still be sleeping or just hadn't felt the need to get up and do anything about the lack of light. I was proved right in my thoughts when I walked in to find him sprawled across the table. I made a show of slamming the door in order to wake him up and was successful in doing so. He went to say something but just managed to stop himself when he remembered that he wasn't talking to me. I ignored the childish behaviour and broke the silence.

"I cut all the grass tonight; I thought it looked pretty good." I looked at him, my eyes pleading for approval. He stared at me in silence for such a long time that I was sure he was going to pursue with his silence. "What you doing that for?" he asked eventually – not quite the response that I had been hoping for.

"I, erm, there are people here over the weekend so everything needed to be done," I stuttered dejectedly.

"Well they're not going to be impressed with the gardens then are they?" With that spiteful comment he left the house, showing absolutely no regret for the way that he was treating me.

I was hanging the freshly washed clothes over the make shift line when there was a knock on the door. The unexpected interruption shot through my body and I found myself instantly on edge. I didn't know why but that knock gave me a feeling that something was wrong and I strongly considered not opening the door, but if anyone was to look through the window they would see me standing there which would only make things worse.

"I know you're in there," came a slurred voice. I backed into the corner, wrapping the knitted blanket around me tighter. I took in a deep breath and told myself that everything would be ok. I didn't get a chance to see who was at the door because as soon as I turned the lock the visitor came barging in, flinging the door into me.

"Where is he?" he shouted.

From my position on the floor I could now make out the details of Mr Griggs - he was adorned in the same suit that he had been wearing a few nights previously and I recognised the tufts of brown hair that were sticking out from under his hat. I stood up as fast as I could, trying not to look as disturbed as I felt.

"He's not here," I squeaked, coughing instantly to clear the fear from my throat. Mr Griggs turned around and looked at me. I could feel his eyes running across my body. As he walked towards me I tried to back away but I only managed to block myself in.

"You must be his daughter," he said as he edged closer to me. "What are you, sixteen, seventeen?"

"Sixteen," I managed to choke out – well I almost was, but it was easier just to agree with him.

"Old enough then," he whispered into my ear. He slowly wrapped one of my curls around his finger as he tried to move his other hand up my waist. I slapped it away but he grabbed my hand as I pulled it back.

"Feisty, aye? Lucky for you I like that." His body was getting closer to mine, the stench of alcohol on his breath making me gag. He moved his head forwards to kiss me and when his lips went to touch mine I bit down on his bottom lip as hard as I could. He yanked his face away from me causing my teeth to tear against his lip leaving a fresh taste of blood on my tongue. He screamed out something incomprehensible through the hand that was covering his mouth. His lip was swollen and blood was starting to fill his mouth, staining his teeth. As he pulled his hand away he noticed the splotches of blood that covered it. The look on his face instantly changed from one of desire to irrefutable anger. He roughly grabbed my arm grimacing at me. He drew his free arm back and it came flying forwards so swiftly that there was nothing I could do to stop it. The full force of his swing hit me square in the eye knocking me back off my feet, his ring crashing against my cheekbone. He spat blood down at me as I lay there sprawled on the floor reeling from the force of the punch.

"Let that be a message to your darling father," he scowled slamming the door behind him.

Pain shot through my eye as I tried to push myself up. My body was too weak from the shock, there was no fight left in me, so I gave up and slumped back to the floor. I lay there amongst the dust and the dirt, my clothes felt like they had been laid loosely over my naked body; covering the shame and the secrets I carried. I felt the warmth of liquid against my cheek so I reached out to brush it away with the back of my hand. Here's what I now know about blood: it is brighter than you could imagine; the colour of the deepest rubies, until it dries sticky and black.

Chapter 5

The next morning I rummaged through my belongings to try and find something that might be able to help cover some of the very noticeable purple bruising that decorated my eye. All I could find was a hat, so I tucked my hair under it and tried to pull the peak down as far as it would go. It would keep my eyes shaded if anyone saw me from a distance but if they got up close there would be no disguising it. All I could hope for was that everyone would be too busy this morning to be wasting any attention on me. I got through the first part of the morning without any disturbances but as the sun started to rise more of the outside servants appeared. I waved to the chauffer and the stable master without them giving me a second glance – the war had claimed a lot of the male servants that worked on the Barrow Estate, leaving behind only those that were too young, or too old and weak. It meant that those few that passed me that morning paid no attention to the fact that there was a young girl doing a man's work. I started to think that perhaps I would be able to get through the day without anyone noticing my injury when I spotted Oscar walking towards me and I had a feeling that he wouldn't be as satisfied with a wave.

"Morning cabbage patch," he called out.

"Morning," I called back, trying to busy myself so that he wouldn't feel inclined to stop and say anything else. Unfortunately for me he seemed to be in quite a chatty mood this morning which meant that there would be no getting rid of him as easily as I had hoped.

"You nearly finished everything now? I have to say that it is looking really good." I was so shocked by the unexpected compliment that I forgot all about trying to keep hidden and looked straight at him. "Woah, what happened to you?" he gasped, looking genuinely concerned.

"I stepped on the rake yesterday and it whacked me in the eye," I lied, shocked by how easily it came to me.

Oscar eyed me suspiciously but nodded as if to say he wouldn't press it any further.

"I better get to work," he said as he started to walk off. "Emily, if you ever need anything then I'm always happy to try and help." He muttered, smiling awkwardly at me.

"Thank you," I smiled at him even though it hurt me to do so. Now that the bruise had come out it was much more painful to move my face; it was only now that I realised how hard it was to avoid doing just that.

Oscar's unexpected behaviour made me feel a little better but it also meant that I let my guard down slightly, which turned out not to be such a good thing. About half an hour or so later, true to his word, Edward came to visit. But, he came sneaking up behind me so quietly that I had no idea he was there, so when he placed his hands over my eyes I jumped away, fear knotting my stomach. At first

Edward looked upset by my reaction but it only took moments before that look was replaced with one of deep concern.

"Emily, what happened?" he whispered, reaching out to stroke my eye but I stepped back so that he couldn't reach me, leaving his hand hanging between us.

"Sorry, it just hurts to touch."

"Are you going to tell me what happened?" he asked once again.

"It was just an accident, I trod on a rake and it hit me in the eye." This time the lie didn't sound as convincing and if I had really thought about it then it wasn't the most believable lie as a rake was unlikely to be able to conflict as much damage as a fist had done.

"I don't believe you," Edward said bluntly, "Tell me the truth." I debated whether or not to try and come up with another lie but it would only seem strange if I said it was something equally as harmless. Plus, I knew that he wasn't going to stop until he heard the truth. I sighed and looked down at the floor.

"Someone came looking for my father and I got in the way." I figured the fewer details there were the less angry Edward would be, besides technically I wasn't lying anymore.

"Someone did this to you?" He questioned even though I had just provided him with the answer.

"Yes, I don't know who he was though," I muttered. Edward paused for a moment, breathing steadily as though he was trying to calm himself. The next time he spoke his tone was a lot softer.

"Are you okay?"

"I ... yes, it's just a bit sore is all."

"What did he look like?" Even though Mr Griggs' face was clear in my mind I still couldn't bring myself to describe him.

"It was really dark, I didn't manage to get a proper look at him." I knew that he didn't believe one word of what I said; that much was made clear by the way he was looking at me.

"Emily, you need to go to the police. You can't let this man get away with it."

"No. Really, there is no need for that. It just happened once. I mean he seemed pretty drunk, I don't think he really meant it. I don't want to be causing a fuss." I was desperately trying to make him listen to me even though I was disgusted with myself for defending the man. I knew that I definitely couldn't tell him the rest of what had happened last night - partly because I knew that he would then force me to go to the police and partly because I felt somewhat to blame. My whole body was tingling with worry that something was going to be said, words that could only lead to my father getting in trouble. Edward watched me closely as I was speaking and I think that he sensed the desperate tone in my voice.

"I guess if you don't remember him then they won't be much help. But I have to tell my parents."

My heart sank with those words. "Please, there really is no need. I'm fine, I don't want to cause any trouble. Plus, you aren't supposed to be out here. What are they going to say when they find out you were with me?" My words caught in my throat as the emotion of the situation started to take control.

"Emily, I have to." He replied ignoring my desperate attempt to stop him.

"Please?" I begged, my green eyes big with worry.

"What's the real reason you don't want them to know?"

"I just don't want any trouble." Every word I spoke was making it harder for me to fight off the tears that were desperately trying to free themselves from my eyes. I didn't understand why it was so difficult, I had been fine up until now, but for some reason seeing Edward look at me like he was made me want to break down.

"Emily, you need to talk to me," he said softly, taking my hands in his. Just as the tears started to spill down my cheeks the clouds cried for me, disguising the sadness running down my face.

"You better go," I whispered, but Edward showed no sign of moving. "You have to go." I repeated.

He slowly nodded. "I'll always be here for you, no matter what," he whispered into my ear as he hugged me tightly.

I watched him running towards the house with a feeling of regret. I wished so much that I could have told him the truth; the truth about everything. I finished raking up the last of yesterday's fallen leaves then trudged back to the shed, letting the splash of rain wash away the salty trails of my tears. I decided to sit in the shed as the thought of going home now was not a pleasing one. The idea of starting to tidy the shed even flitted across my mind, but if any guests arrived and saw a mess outside then I would be in trouble. Instead, I found the small trimmers and started to carve into the wooden frame – after all it was going to need replacing anyway. As I was digging into the wood a very wet Oscar stuck his head round the door.

"Saw you sitting in here and I thought you might like a hot drink?" he asked somewhat nervously. "I'm just going to fetch some tea from the main house." I was all ready to turn down his offer when it struck me that this was the first attempt that any of the other servants had made at spending time with me.

I nodded. "That sounds nice."

"I can come get you on the way back if you don't want to get wet," he offered.

"It's okay, I like the rain."

"So do I," he said smiling, some of the nerves falling away.

We walked up to the main house in silence. It wasn't an awkward silence though, it was comforting to have someone there, plus we both seemed to be enjoying the rain. We walked across the gravel and round to the back of the house towards the servants' entrance. Like a true gentleman, he opened the door for me and I nearly stepped in when it struck me that it probably wasn't the best idea. I stood back and shook my head.

"I'll just wait for you here." I didn't bother trying to think up an excuse and luckily he didn't ask me for one either. "I won't be long, promise." He ran into the house and was back in no time at all.

The rain was starting to let off leaving behind the fresh smell that only the first proper rainfall can. I closed my eyes and breathed in deep. When I opened them Oscar was looking at me with a strange smile on his face.

"Yes?" I questioned curiously.

Oscar opened his mouth to say something then shook his head. "Nothing." Part of me wanted to push it until I found out what he was going to say but I definitely didn't know him well enough. Plus, I didn't want to ruin whatever it was that he was trying to do. I tried to think of something to talk about in an attempt to diminish the silence but my brain went blank.

"So, er, you like horses?" As soon as the words escaped my mouth I knew that it was a stupid question and when I heard Oscar chuckle I could feel my cheeks burning. "Erm, I mean, of course you do. I meant what's your favourite?" I spluttered making an even bigger fool of myself. I looked at him hopefully, praying that he would pull me out of the mess.

"Yes I do like horses," he said with a smile. "And as for my favourite, you're probably expecting me to say Silver. He is the most impressive but I think I would have to say Arabella is my favourite. She's the softest ya know. Have you ever met them?"

The truth was that a few years ago Edward had secretly taught me to ride. He would ride Silver down to the lake, which was out of sight of the house, and I would run down to meet him. At first I rode behind him, arms wrapped around him tightly as he galloped around the lake. After a few months I was riding alone, the wind tangling up my curls as I felt like I was flying across the ground. It was an experience that someone like me should never have been given the opportunity to have, so it was for that reason that it would always have to remain mine and Edward's secret.

"I've seen them out, but no, I haven't met them."

"Would you like to?" He asked eagerly, hoping for the chance to show off what he knew.

"I'd love to!" I exclaimed with a genuine smile. "Plus it will give us a chance to dry off a bit." Oscar's face turned a light shade of pink making me realise that the clothes had moulded to the shape of my body. I giggled shyly as I looked down at my soaked clothes.

"I've got a top you can borrow," he said. "Come up with me." I followed him up the old wooden ladder that led to the rooms that some of the outside servants shared. This is where my father would have been living but when the family found out that I was expected they allowed my parents to rent the little cottage that was now our home. He led me over to the far corner where there was a small bed and chest pushed up against the wall.

"Nothing special, aye?" he muttered as he sorted through the chest pulling out a top and handing it to me. "I'll go boil the kettle," he said politely.

I waited until I was sure he was down the steps before I struggled to pull off the soaking wet top. In my struggle I stumbled, stubbing my toe on the corner of the chest. I just managed to stop myself from shouting out in pain. Even though I was wearing shoes they were flimsy from age and the pain still shot through my foot as though they had been bare. I quickly pulled the dry top on before I allowed myself to momentarily give in to the pain – I didn't want to risk anyone coming up and seeing me half naked. I silently screamed the pain away as I limped over to the ladder. I foolishly jumped the last few steps, forgetting my recent injury, but was promptly reminded when my toe slammed against the hard floor.

"Aaagghh," I grimaced unable to stay quiet this time.

"Still hurting yourself I see," chuckled Lenny. I had known Lenny since I was tiny, he had always been one of my father's closest friends, helping him out a lot when my mother passed away. He was the stable master and ever since I was a child he had always seemed like a magician to me when it came to the horses. As far I was aware he had been working at the estate for as long as my father had, which must have been nearing on thirty years now – I remember my father telling me that they had arrived together when they were young lads. His snow-white hair showed his age but he had the same youthful smile shining on his tanned face. "Let's go get our tea little lady, it's been far too long since I've seen you." he said, ruffling my hair.

It was true, I'd been so busy trying to get everything done by myself that I had completely forgotten about the few people that actually cared about me and for that I felt very guilty.

"And are you going to tell me what happened to your eye?" he asked.

"No." I replied cheekily.

"Wrong answer. Try again."

"She got in a fight with a rake. I saw it," pitched in Oscar. In that moment I don't think I had ever been so thankful for someone. I nodded to discreetly say thank you.

"It's true. Wasn't paying attention to what I was doing." I shrugged nonchalantly as if to say that was all on that matter. Lenny laughed and I could tell from the look on his face that he was going to launch into some embarrassing story that he had stored up about me.

"It's funny you say that, I remember when you were, oh this high," he said raising his hand just above the ground." You were trotting around after your father …"

"You owe me a proper explanation now," whispered Oscar as he set the steaming cup of tea in front of me. Lenny was none the wiser that neither of us weren't really listening to him; he was happy swimming in the memories of his past. Since I had heard the story so many times before I was able to nod enthusiastically at him and pull shamed faces in all the right places.

"Not now," I whispered back.

"Later," came his one word demand and I sighed when I realised that I wasn't going to get away with it this time. I nodded slightly to show that he had got his way and went on pretending to listen to the story. While I was sitting there, smiling in all the right places, it was like I noticed Oscar properly for the first time. It wasn't until this moment that I realised that his dark brown eyes seemed to hold mysteries that I wanted to take the time to solve, his smile was charming though it never reached his eyes making me wonder what it was that stopped him from really letting go. Even though he wasn't as obviously handsome as Edward was there was something intriguing about his dark features and the way he carried himself.

"So, how is old Bertie? I haven't seen him around recently."

It took me a moment to realise that he was asking about my father. "He hurt his back so he hasn't been able to do much."

"Oh what a shame. Who is doing the gardens then?"

"I am," I muttered sheepishly. "It's alright though."

Lenny nodded slowly. "You always did have your father's green fingers, was only a matter of time before you took over. Perhaps I should stop by and see how he is …"

"No, no, really. He's not up for visitors at the moment but I shall tell him you were asking about him," I interrupted hastily. The last thing that was needed was for someone to see him sprawled across the floor in the middle of the day or to not see him there at all. I had worked too hard at keeping the truth hidden and I was desperately hoping that my father was going to snap out of it very soon so that everything could get back to normal. Lenny looked hurt so I quickly added, "But as soon as he is better I will let you know so you can come see him." It didn't seem to make much difference though as it was clear that his previously sunny spirits had been dampened by my selfish behaviour.

"Well I better get on with it. Nice to see you little lady," he muttered as he got up from the table.

"Bye Lenny," I replied sadly feeling even guiltier than I had earlier.

Oscar must have sensed how I was feeling because he pulled me up and dragged me along behind him.

"Come on, I know what will cheer you up." I gently pulled my arm from his grip but continued to follow him all the same; after all I had worked so hard this past week that there wasn't much for me to do now. Nothing of the utmost importance anyway. He led me out to the back of the stables where all the horses were neatly lined up in their stalls. I momentarily forgot myself when I saw Silver, softly stroking his nose when he bowed his head to greet me.

"That's strange, he doesn't usually like anyone but Master Edward," he observed. "I'm sorry, I'll leave him alone," I responded trying to ignore the statement. I stepped back from the horse who whinnied in protest. Oscar shook his head to say that it didn't matter.

"Perhaps you just have a way with them," he muttered staring in wonderment at the horse. Oscar had been right when he said Silver was the most impressive; he was a tall Thoroughbred, from the looks of him I would have said about 16 hands high. His coat was a light grey that shone silver in the light. He was a truly remarkable horse, his attitude as well as his appearance making him stand apart from the rest.

"I thought that I would walk Arabella, maybe you want to stay and help? Then you would get a chance to meet her." He seemed to be quite excited about the prospect and when I saw him with her I could understand why. As soon as he swung open the door Arabella went straight up to Oscar rubbing her face against his. Arabella was a shadow of the horse next to her, barely measuring up to his height, but she was a beautiful horse all the same. Her brown coat was groomed perfectly – clear that Oscar was taking particular care with this one – and she looked as though she was wearing socks; three black and one white.

Before we got a chance to take her outside one of the younger stable boys came running in. "Oscar, Lenny said you need to help him with the hay." Oscar looked disappointed but we both knew there was no arguing with Lenny.

"I better get back to work anyway," I said even though there wasn't anything to do. "Thanks for the tea."

"No thank you," he called back. I didn't know what he meant by that so I just smiled and waved as I walked away.

Chapter 6

As I was leaving the stables I noticed that the guests were starting to arrive. The cars were slowly making their way down the lane towards the main house, the procession of vehicles looking like a group of children playing follow the leader. From where I was standing I could just make out the figures of the hosts and the servants lined up waiting to greet them. The hosts were covered from the rain by umbrellas held by some of the servants, the others standing off to the side waiting to provide the same service to the new arrivals. If I stared hard enough, squinting my eyes, I was able to see Edward standing next to his mother. It was easy to imagine that he would be whispering inappropriate remarks about the days ahead if I was standing beside him but when the first of the guests arrived he looked like a natural from what I could see.

I remained by the stables, hidden from unfamiliar eyes as I watched each of the guests arrive, seeming more elaborate the further down the line they got; the first car contained who I assumed to be a Lord accompanied by his wife, the next few cars contained men arriving solo and the last car contained Duchess Moorely – Edward's Godmother. I was all ready to leave when I noticed another figure exiting the car. All I could see was a petite young lady, blonde hair flowing free of the hat that was pinned to her head. I desperately wanted to be closer, not only so that I could see more of her but also so that I could see Edward's face as he greeted her. It didn't seem to me that he was paying her any more attention than he had done to the other guests but when he turned to his father I felt a pain in my heart as I imagined him nodding his approval. It was in that selfish moment that I realised how hard the situation must be for Edward, the absence of his brother always the more apparent at times like this.

I had to force myself to turn away from the house so that I wouldn't just stand there staring at what I would never have. Unfortunately I was at a loss with what to do with myself considering I had done so much in the last week; also I had grown used to my father telling me what it was that needed to be done next. All I knew was that I needed to keep myself busy or my mind would keep wandering to things that would do me no good. In the end I decided that perhaps it would be a good idea to start sorting out the shed after all; it wasn't likely that anyone would be coming outside in this weather. The idea may have seemed brilliant but the problem was that I had absolutely no idea where to begin. I just stood staring at it like it was a completely foreign object. I knew that there wasn't really much point in tidying it all when the structure needed so much work in itself and in order to do that I was going to have to empty the majority of the contents. Though this wasn't exactly the biggest problem – that would have been the fact that I had no idea how to go about fixing it. I was a gardener, not a carpenter.

As I set about doing the best that I could with the mess laid out in front of me my mind started to wander. No matter how I tried not to think about it I couldn't turn my brain onto any other subject – I needed to know what was going on with my father. I stayed with my task for the next couple of hours but my heart really wasn't in it and it didn't feel like I was making any real progress so I ran back to the house, wasting no time getting straight to the point.

"I need to talk to you," I called out as I ran into the cottage. I was fully prepared to have to repeat myself to gain my father's attention; however, what I wasn't prepared for was to see my father already awake, sitting on the chair opposite the door.

"Oh, you're awake."

He didn't respond just slowly walked over to where I was standing by the open door. He gently turned my face into the light and stared sadly at the bruise that adorned my face.

"It was just an accident Pa."

"You don't need to lie to me, I know what happened." There was no emotion in his voice so I couldn't tell if he was mad at me or if he was mad at himself, perhaps he wasn't even mad at all. I wanted to say something but instead I just stood there watching my father as he scrutinized my face. He sat back down holding his head in his hands.

"I'm sorry you got hurt Emmy."

It took a moment to process the words as he was talking to the floor, but when I finally understood what he had said I was shocked, not because he had apologised but because it was the first time that he had called me Emmy in months. I stood there, open-mouthed, as he continued to speak.

"I know I haven't been around much lately and I hate myself for putting you through that. But I hate myself more for doing that to you." He pointed at my face and looked at me sadly waiting for my reply. The light from the windows was shining on him and for the first time I could see the state that he was in; his eyes were red raw as though he had been crying and I could see his hands shaking as he nervously ran them through what little hair he had left on his head.

"You didn't do anything," I muttered avoiding eye contact. "I'm the reason that you have that bruise on your face. Don't act like I'm not."

His voice was growing louder but he checked himself before he started shouting. "Sorry. Look, I'm going to change. I will be better. Promise."

My heart ached as he spoke those words but I couldn't let myself give into him so easily. His words would be empty until he was able to prove that he meant it and if I was honest with myself then I wasn't expecting much from him. I remained silent and when my father didn't say anything else I was sure that he had interpreted the real meaning of that silence. Even though I had been wanting to have this conversation for the last few months, now that it was happening it was the last thing that I wanted. I started busying myself with pointless tasks so that he wouldn't bother me: re-cleaning pans, straightening blankets and wiping the same spot over and again; anything that didn't need to be done.

"What did you need to talk to me about?"

"What?" I had no idea what he was going on about.

"You came running in like you were on a very important mission. So, what did you need to talk to me about?"

"Oh. That. Just wanted to say that the shed needs fixing and I was wondering if there were any tools anywhere that I could use."

"I could help you." He made it sound like a question, his hopeful eyes looking across at me. Part of me didn't want to accept his offer but I couldn't decline every effort that he made, that would only push him away again.

"Okay, I don't know what I'm doing anyway," I said trying to sound as casual as I could.

The rest of the day dragged. Our home was tidier than it had been in a long time since I was spending my time here even though my body was itching to be outside. I had taken the sheets off my small bed and cleaned them along with the blankets that my father flung over himself when he stumbled home. They were now hung over the string that stretched from wall to wall forming small puddles on the floor as they dried. Our cottage was almost completely opened out which made it hard to get any privacy. The tiny bathroom, only big enough to hold the toilet and sink, was tucked into the corner – its' only shelter was the handmade wall that my dad had built out of discarded bricks.

I had hung a spare sheet from the ceiling to section off a small area to make into my room. I could have sat in there but it was too cramped to do anything anyway. There wasn't much more to our home – the kitchen was small but it was enough for the two of us and we had a small wooden dining table with two chairs tucked underneath. Our living space consisted of an old rocking chair that used to belong to my mother and a tattered sofa that faced the fireplace – the best feature of the house. I was so insistent on avoiding my father that I even cleaned the fireplace, sweeping out all the soot that had been discarded by the burning coal. When I finished everything, my father was still at home as well trying desperately to strike up the conversation that he had missed the whole time he had been too intoxicated to care. His attempts were awkward and my reluctance to engage with him didn't make the situation any more comfortable. It was still light outside and there was nothing else to do – I couldn't sit inside any longer.

"I'm gonna go check everything is alright. Won't be long." My leaving was probably not the wisest move as it meant that he would now be at home with nothing to do. For that reason I wasn't expecting him to be there when I got back and I wasn't sure how I felt about that. No matter what, I loved my father and of course I wanted everything to be okay but I couldn't bring myself to believe his promises, not after all that had happened recently – my face served as a painful reminder of that. I walked around slowly, with no purpose other than trying to get my head around what was going on. It was times like this where I needed a friend, one who wasn't busy having dinner with a group of people that he didn't know, one that I could rely on to be there for me no matter what. And I was starting to realise that maybe Edward wasn't that person anymore – he was too busy for me. Even as I thought it I didn't really believe it; after all he still saw me whenever he could despite what his parents thought. Also, it wasn't really his fault that he had to do all these things, it was expected of him, he had been born into it. Plus, I knew that it didn't matter what it was that I thought I needed, I would always want to be near him and that was out of my control.

The grounds were eerily quiet as I wandered on my own; the usual hustle and bustle of the land had been put on hold for the guests. As I neared the house I knew that it was an entirely different story inside. I could hear the servants running around to get dinner prepared and making sure that everything was in place. I guessed that it was about the time that everyone would be changing for dinner – something that I had never quite been able to understand. I would always remember the first time Edward had told me about that; we were playing when he was called in, his nanny saying that it was time to change for dinner. I mean, I was always told to wash my hands and face but I had never had to change – I didn't have enough clothes to be able to do that. Edward didn't come and play with me for two days after that because I had laughed at him.

I was so lost in my thoughts that I hadn't even realised that I had walked back down to the stables.

"Emily, what are you doing here?" Lenny walked around the corner carrying a large bale of hay on his shoulder.

"I wanted to apologise for earlier, I was selfish and I never meant to upset you."

"It's fine little lady." He shuffled the bale of hay onto the other shoulder.

"Pa said that he is going to help me with the shed so I think he is feeling better. Maybe you could go see him sometime?"

"I'll see what I can do."

I wanted to talk more but I could tell that he wasn't interested so I smiled at him and walked back down the path.

When I walked back in the door I wasn't expecting the sight that greeted me. Not only was my father still at home but he was standing over the stove, spoon in hand.

"What's this?"

"I thought you deserved a break."

When he turned I could see that he had made an effort with his appearance; he had shaved which made him look more like the man that I had grown up idolising.

"Thank you."

I sat at the table, unsure how I was supposed to react and waited patiently to see what I would be presented with. My father laid a plate of sausages and potatoes in front of me, decorated in the way that it had always been when I was a child. He had cut the sausage up to make a face and laid the potato out for the hair, fresh green peas smiling up at me. I couldn't help but smile back at the dinner that had always been my favourite. I enjoyed every bite and felt better for it afterwards, starting to feel myself begin to give in to what was happening with my father. When he got up from the table

I felt my stomach knot thinking that things were going back to normal already. I watched with baited breath, ready to see him walk out the door, but instead I watched as his hand reached out and took away the empty plates.

I spent the rest of the night on edge, constantly waiting for my father to get bored of this act and walk out the door. Even once we had said our goodnights I stayed awake expecting to hear him sneak off when he thought that I had drifted off to sleep. But he didn't go and I could still hear his snores when I got up the next morning, tired from a sleepless night. I snuck out, pulling the door closed as quietly as I could so as not to wake my father. For some unknown reason I didn't want to be there when he woke up so I wanted to make sure I was out of the cottage and busy if he was to come looking for me.

I was jammed into the corner of the shed trying to dig out buckets that were stuck when I heard footsteps coming up the lane. No one came in so I assumed it was just a passer-by, it wasn't until I heard the roof being peeled off that I tried to manoeuvre my way out of the shed. In my rush to leave it wasn't as smooth an exit as I had hoped it would be and my shins came out slightly more bruised than they had been when I had started.

"What do you think you're doing?" I shouted out before I had managed to get out the shed, unaware of who I was even shouting at. Surprisingly it was my father's face that greeted me from atop the roof where he was perched precariously.

"You said you needed help. I'm helping," he said as he continued to pull the roof apart. "Why didn't you wake me?"

"I, erm, I thought you wanted to sleep," I muttered. I could tell that he wasn't happy with my response but he didn't push it any further.

"If we get this roof off first then we will be able to mend the rest and see if there is anything that needs replacing."

It felt like I was a child all over again, doing what my father asked of me, eager to assist. It was a great feeling but I knew deep down that it wouldn't be able to last; my life was constantly changing, nothing seemed to stay the same anymore.

Chapter 7

For the rest of the day we continued with our project as though nothing had changed. There were still times when he looked like he wanted to be elsewhere but he never strayed; not that I was aware of anyway. As we neared completion I found myself wondering what it would all be like when we were finished, whether or not he was going to be taking on his old responsibilities.

That evening there was a knock at the door and my father opened it to find his old friend standing there.

"Bertie! Good to see you up and about again." came Lenny's voice.

"I was going into town and wondered if you wanted to join me."

I could sense the atmosphere change as the temptation was laid in front of my father. It wasn't Lenny's fault: he had no idea what a problem this could potentially cause. If anything it was my fault for keeping it hidden from everyone. My father didn't say anything, he didn't have to; the sound of the door shutting behind them was all that needed to be said. Surprisingly I wasn't as upset as I thought I would be, in fact I found that it took me no time at all to settle back into being alone. I almost relished the fact that I was able to sit there and draw, letting myself get lost in the picture instead of the thoughts that were racing through my head. Perhaps I even would have enjoyed it if the reason for my being alone hadn't been such an upsetting one.

I was still awake when my father returned, but I feigned sleep all the same. When I heard him stumble through the door I knew straight away that he was drunk and I didn't want to face him. As soon as I knew that he was back home and that I no longer had to worry about him sneaking out I fell straight to sleep.

The next morning I woke up later than usual and had to rush to get out the house. Unsurprisingly my father was still asleep but this time I didn't bother trying to stay quiet, I wanted to make sure that he knew how much he had let me down. What upset me most was seeing the finished shed; it looked so much better now that the wood had been realigned and the roof had been re-patched. Even the inside was tidier, organised so that I was able to get what I wanted without a battle. It was going to forever serve as a reminder that my father had broken the promises he had made to me.

"Looking good."

I turned to see Oscar standing behind me.

"You were working on it with Mr Thorne, right? Where is he now?"

I couldn't bring myself to speak so I just shrugged and went to unlock the shed. I thought that he would take the hint and walk away but when I felt his hand lightly graze against my wrist I knew it wasn't going to be as simple as that.

"Emily, what's wrong?" He turned my face towards him and I lifted my eyes, wet from the tears that lined them. My bruise had matured to a yellowy-green colour and it was nowhere near as painful as it had been a few days ago. There was something about Oscar that made me think that he could be trusted but I still stopped myself from saying anything. I didn't know him well enough which meant that I couldn't be sure he would keep it to himself.

"You heard anything about any of the guests?" I asked trying to change the subject.

Oscar sighed at me as he realised exactly what I was doing but he still went along with it. "Some of them are saying that Master Edward is being set up with the Duchess's granddaughter. Victoria I think her name is."

It took all my control to stop myself from asking anymore questions; if I came across too eager then Oscar would start to suspect something.

"Yeah think I saw her when they arrived." I tried to sound as casual as possible but I could feel my voice catching.

"Emily, I was wondering, well you got tomorrow off right?"

"Yeah." I welcomed the change of subject readily.

"Well, erm, well I was gonna head into the village and I wondered if maybe you wanted to come with?"

I didn't even need to think about it, it was a brilliant excuse to be out the house, plus I hadn't been able to enjoy a day off in a long time.

"I'd love to."

"Great," beamed Oscar. "I'll pop up to get you in the morning."

"Okay." I replied without thinking about the state my father was likely to be in. "Actually, why don't I meet you here?"

Oscar seemed a bit put out, probably thinking that I didn't want my father to see me with him.

"I'm looking forward to it," I added in the hope that it would make him forget about it. When he smiled I knew that it had been forgotten.

"I better be off then, see you tomorrow."

For the first time that day I allowed myself to smile properly, it felt nice to know that there was actually someone that wanted to spend time with me – and it didn't have to be a secret.

Today I had decided that I was going to work on the flower garden by the house. As I made my way up there I noticed that there were two people walking towards me. I couldn't make out who they were from this distance but as my eyes started to adjust to the moving figures I could make out Edward's frame – almost as familiar to me as my own. I didn't want to run into him but if I moved now then it would be obvious that I was trying to avoid him, which his companion would think me rude for doing. Instead I kept my head down and greeted him appropriately.

"Morning sir." I muttered as I quickly sauntered past. It felt strange to be so formal but it was the only option in that circumstance. I caught a glimpse of the blonde haired beauty that walked alongside him, her gloved hand tucked into his arm; they looked like the picture perfect couple. As I was walking away I heard the conversation that struck up.

"A female gardener. Who does she think she is?" The snotty tones grabbed my attention and I slowed my pace so that I could hear the response. I listened intently, waiting to hear Edward sticking up for me, but instead what I heard hurt me more that the stranger's comment.

"I know, she'll never get anywhere looking like that all the time."

They both chuckled as they walked further away unaware that their conversation had been overheard. It wasn't like I had expected him to greet me like a friend; I'd had years to get used to the fact that it would be frowned upon if our friendship was known. However, I still wasn't prepared for him to talk me down, especially not so that he could impress someone else at my expense. My previously good mood had been wiped away and I went about my day with a sad heart; the blue skies seemed grey and the flowers looked dead. It wasn't jealousy that broke me; it was the confirmation that I would never be good enough.

I did the work that I had to do with no real enjoyment then headed home. My father was awake when I walked in, looking at me with a very guilty expression.

"Emily, I couldn't say no. It won't happen again."

"Forget it." I wasn't in the mood to deal with him as well, I wasn't sure that my head could take anymore. I couldn't be bothered to do anything, I just wanted to sleep and pretend that it had all been a dream; that I would be able to wake up a different person with an easier life.

The next morning I still woke up bright and early even though it was my day off, this morning however my mood was a lot brighter knowing that I wouldn't have to spend the day here. It didn't take me long to realise that the only clothes I owned were all torn and covered in grass stains. I wasn't vain enough to think I needed a best dress but I knew that it wasn't right to be going out dressed like that – people would think even less of me than they already did. My huffing and puffing must have woken my father because I heard his footsteps creeping up behind me.

"What you looking for Emmy?"

I hadn't planned on telling him any of my plans for the day, and I certainly hadn't wanted his help but I somehow forgot myself in my current state and blurted it all out anyway.

"Oscar asked me to go into town with him but I haven't got anything that isn't stained from working!" I sighed exasperatedly. He chuckled at my whiney tone and walked away.

"Oh, thanks for helping!" I called out sarcastically. I went back to the futile task of digging through my clothes even though it was a complete waste of time. My father returned a few minutes later to find me flinging useless material all over the place.

"I reckon this will fit you now." He was holding up a navy blue dress that had a daisy print dotted along the hem line. I sat there staring at it, not only because he had potentially solved my problem but also because I recognised the dress even though I couldn't think why.

"It was your mother's," he whispered, answering my silent question. There was a longing to his tone and an unspoken sadness in his eyes that said everything he didn't. I knew how much he missed her even though I think part of me had started to forget that recently, focussing on what was happening rather than the reasons why.

"I had to sell most of her things but I couldn't bring myself to get rid of it all so I kept some. I told myself that I was saving it for you but I have kept putting it off. I guess now is as good a time as any."

He took my hand and led me through to where the wooden chest that usually sat in the corner lay open, making me wonder why I had never given any thought to its contents before. I knelt next to it and delicately pulled out each item, taking my time to inspect them separately. Each piece of clothing smelt as sweet as I could remember my mother being, the familiar smell of soap and lavender warming me. The books made me smile as I pictured her sitting in her chair reading to me. As I was breathing in the scent of the dresses I felt the coolness of gold being laid against my neck.

My father pinched the clasp together then picked up the delicate chain with his clumsy fingers to show me. There was a small dove with a flower grasped in its beak gracefully floating along the chain.

"I bought this for your mother when we found out that we were expecting you." His eyes twinkled with the tears of the memory. I flung my arms around his neck and felt his tears slide onto my shoulder. I guessed that he wouldn't want me to see him cry so I allowed him to wipe away the tears before I let him go.

"Now, go get ready. You don't wanna keep the young lad waiting." I ran off with the bundle of clothes in my arms, gently laying them across my bed so that they wouldn't get ruined.

I settled on a simple green cloth dress that fit perfectly, making me feel much more presentable. I fought with my curls until I managed to pin them back from my face, which was as good as I was going to get it. I grabbed my jacket off the floor and walked back out. The look on my father's face said all I needed to hear – he looked like he was proud of me and that made me happier than anything else.

"You look just like your mother," he whispered as I walked over to him. "I don't have much but this should be enough to get yourself something." He handed me some coins from his pocket and I gratefully slid them into mine.

"Thanks Pa. I won't be back late." I laid a light kiss on his cheek before I went running out the door.

Chapter 8

Oscar was already by the shed waiting for me, looking around in anticipation. When he spotted me he smiled and walked over.

"Morning," he called out.

"Morning," I replied. "Sorry I'm late, have you been waiting long?"

"Not at all. It's a nice day anyway, I didn't mind waiting."

We walked down the lane in silence though I could tell from the way that he kept looking at me that there was something he wanted to say. I took the silence as an opportunity to really look at him, that is without all the extra unwanted accessories that came with working outside. He had made the effort with his appearance dressing in an old suit and even though his tie was slightly awry it only served to make him seem even sweeter. He had wet his hair so it wasn't sticking up and he was wringing his hat nervously in his hands. I noticed that he was wearing brown leather gloves that were worn from constant use. As I was staring at his hands I realised that every time I had seen him he was wearing them – I suppose it wasn't completely out of character for an outside worker but he didn't even take them off when we were inside.

"You clean up very nicely," I said when I caught him looking back at me.

"You look lovely," he muttered at the same time.

I felt my cheeks blush at the compliment and for once I felt that perhaps I really could be pretty. Even though I had picked the dress mainly because it was the plainest – I hadn't wanted to come across as trying too hard – I was also aware that the colour really brought out my eyes, the two shades of green complimenting each other perfectly.

"What did you want to do today?" I asked quickly trying to change the subject.

"I thought we could look around the market and then maybe head back and have a picnic. That's if you want to that is?"

"Sounds lovely."

The sun was warming the air and I soon found myself getting too hot beneath the jacket. I loosened the buttons allowing the breeze to swim in around me. It wasn't long before we reached the village that was bustling with shoppers. We headed straight towards the stalls that were set up at the far end alongside the church.

As we were walking along I noticed a few people glancing back at me, mainly people who knew of my father. I couldn't tell if they were looks of pity or if they were just surprised to see how much I had grown up. No one stopped to say hello or showed any sign of acknowledging me; not that it bothered me, I was getting used to being invisible. I was also receiving some disapproving looks from young girls which I didn't understand until it struck me that they were probably jealous of my company – simply put there was a death of men. And as I watched Oscar smiling charmingly at the old woman running the book stall I could certainly see the appeal of him.

All his work with the horses had made his arms muscular which suited his tall frame. His magnetic black eyes drew me in and when he smiled his whole face softened which made him very approachable. What I found most appealing though was his manner, he seemed so caring – a true gentleman – not at all how I had imagined him to be. It struck me that my first impressions of people had been way off recently, making me realise even more that I was wasting my heart chasing after the wrong person.

Oscar lightly touched my arm bringing me back to reality and I allowed his hand to linger.

"Do you read much?" he asked.

"I never really have time," I said shaking my head. "I do like to draw though." As soon as I said it I was shocked that I had revealed that information, it wasn't something that I had ever told anyone.

"That's brilliant, maybe I could see your drawings some time? I don't seem to have an artistic bone in my body." I nodded my head, not committing to anything. My drawings were personal to me and I wasn't sure that I wanted to start parading them around. "You like reading then?" I asked taking the conversation back to the previous topic.

He nodded eagerly. "Yeah, but I've read the few books I have so many times that I know the words so well I can recall the story without reading."

"I have some at home that you're welcome to look at. I'm not sure if they're any good though." It felt nice to be this comfortable around someone and I found myself wanting to make as much of an effort as possible. As we were strolling along I saw a flash of something glinting in the sunlight that caught my attention. I walked over to the stall and noticed that it was the sun reflecting off a brooch, a green stone embedded in a lace of gold winking up at me. It was the most beautiful thing I had ever seen but I knew there was no way that I would ever be able to afford it so I set it back down reluctantly and walked away.

After we had finished looking around the stalls we set back off down the lane towards the house.

"Hey Oscar," called out a female voice. I turned to see the owner, the young kitchen maid Sarah. She was beaming from ear to ear as she ran over to where we were standing.

"I didn't know that today was your day off. What are you doing here?" she gushed, completely ignoring me.

"I'm here with Emily," he replied, gesturing towards me.

"Oh." She sounded disappointed as she looked me up and down judgementally. "Mrs Rook said you're to bring new vegetables." She spoke down to me as though she were far more important, it was like she didn't approve of me having a life outside the house. I wanted to shoot back that it was also my day off so I didn't need her orders, but I somehow managed to hold my tongue.

"Are you going back now? Perhaps we could walk together Oscar?"

"No, actually we have a few things to do first."

"Right, well have a good day Oscar." She skipped off down the lane, completely oblivious to the obvious rebuff. It wasn't what she said that had bothered me; I was well aware that none of them were particularly fond of me. I just felt more embarrassed that Oscar had witnessed the way in which she had spoken down to me.

"You okay?" he asked seeming concerned.

"I'm fine," I replied waving it off. "Think she is a bit keen on you." I laughed. Oscar blushed and turned to me with a worried expression written across his face.

"I don't feel the same, you know that right? I mean she is a nice enough girl but she's not who I like." He met my eyes to make sure that I fully understood and I could tell from the look in his eyes that he desperately needed me to believe him. I nodded and then dropped the subject deciding that I wouldn't be bringing that up again.

"It seems to be clear now, shall we get going?" I asked indicating that there was no longer anyone else on the path. He led me back to the stables where he quickly popped in to grab a basket.

"I was hoping you would say yes to the picnic." He winked cheekily at me as we walked along.

"Where we going?"

"You'll see."

I was trying to think of all the places he could be taking me. I was almost certain that I knew the land far better than he did but I didn't want to come across as arrogant so I let him lead the way. He took us past the house and down across the hill that led to the farmers land at the bottom of the estate. We kept going past the old farm house and wound through the trees where he stopped and turned to me.

"Close your eyes," he said smiling at me.

I eyed him suspiciously and shook my head. "Why?"

"Because I want it to be a surprise. So close your eyes, or do I have to blindfold you?"

He laughed - a pleasant sound that I didn't hear from him too often. I sighed dramatically as I closed my eyes allowing him to take my hand as he led me further along, the feel of his gloves seeming to take any intimacy away from the situation. My foot caught on a root that was sticking out the ground and I stumbled forwards. I felt myself falling and I was sure that I was going to hit the floor but strong arms caught me and pulled me back upright. I didn't open my eyes, just stayed motionless in Oscar's arms feeling his breath against my face.

"You alright?"

I nodded, not daring to speak a word.

"We're about here now, I guess you can open your eyes."

From the smell of the air and the sounds of the running water I could tell that this wasn't somewhere that I had been before and as I slowly opened my eyes my suspicions were confirmed. The small stream ran through the rocks, flowing down from the lake that sat directly above it. Full green trees hiding the spot from prying eyes.

"It's beautiful." I had known about the lake, but this little hidden sanctuary was something completely new.

He had laid out the red blanket and was emptying the contents of the basket. There was bread and ham, a pot of jam and a slice of fruit cake – I wouldn't be surprised if Mrs Rook was also keen on Oscar. I could tell from his expression that he was pleased that I hadn't known about this place and I was too – it made it seem more special that there was something about this estate that could remind me of someone else.

The sun was beating down on us so I took off my jacket as I sat myself on the blanket, the sun catching the gold chain that hung around my neck.

"I like your necklace." Oscar leaned towards me, eyes on mine as he reached out to take it between his fingers. He toyed with it for a moment before softly letting it full back against my chest.

"It was my mother's."

"Was?"

"She died when I was young. My father gave me a load of her stuff this morning."

"I'm so sorry." Oscar seemed annoyed with himself for mentioning it.

"It really doesn't matter, you weren't to know." I smiled at him slightly to show that there was no harm done but his expression was void of happiness.

We ate in silence for the next few minutes which worried me because I didn't want Oscar to be feeling uncomfortable but I had no idea what else I could say to make him realise that it was all okay.

"I didn't know about your mother, I'm sorry." he repeated breaking the silence.

"I wouldn't have expected you to know so please don't worry." I paused for a moment. "It was Spanish Flu, I think. I'm not really sure though, no one ever really spoke to me about it properly. I think they always thought that I was too young to know the truth but I remember her being ill, she could never get out of bed and she always looked so pale. I remember my Pa talking to the doctor when he had to come and check that I wasn't ill as well. I find it difficult to remember what she was like now though, is that bad? Sometimes I am sure that I still breathe in her scent when I walk around the cottage but I'm sure that is just my imagination." I looked up to see him staring at me intently. "Sorry, I didn't mean to go on."

"No, please do."

However, now that I had stopped talking I couldn't think of what else to say. It felt strange to be talking about her, I had never really had the opportunity to do so. It didn't make me sad though, instead it warmed me to know I was still able to remember things about her, no matter how bad the memory was. The more I thought about her the more images flew into my head: images of her in her dresses, flouncing around the kitchen as she made meals for me and Pa and the way she would always kiss my father sweetly as he came in from work. I could even picture her as she would tuck me in at night, singing to me softly as my eyes grew heavy – the words escaped me but I could hear her humming the tune in my head.

I smiled to myself as I thought of her and even though it felt good to remember I didn't want to start getting into that story so I swiftly changed the topic of conversation.

"So, what brought you here then? To the estate that is."

Oscar looked at me intently for a moment as though he was sizing me up to see if I could be trusted with the answer; I could tell all this from a look as I knew that I did the same thing.

"When I got back from France I wasn't sure what I was going to do but I knew that I wanted to be working outside. When I was in the army I had grown fond of the horses and was always eager to help in whatever way I could so when I saw the advertisement I jumped on it straight away." He stopped and I could tell that he wasn't sure whether or not to continue.

"I didn't know that you were a soldier."

"Was. I got shot so I had to return home." He held up his gloved hand to tell me where his injury was.

"Well that answers my question about the gloves," I said before thinking about it. My hand flew up to cover my mouth when I realised the mistake I had made. "I'm sorry, I didn't mean it like that."

Oscar chuckled, shaking his head. "The injury is still a bit sore and I don't want to risk an infection working outside, but I don't need to wear them. I just do it for myself really."

"You must be older than I thought then?" I hadn't thought that he was older than me, but then again I hadn't really thought about it. Now that it had been brought to my attention I guessed that he did look and act older; the mystery of his demeanour seemed to be unravelling before my eyes.

"I enlisted when I was fifteen. My brother was called up and I didn't want to be left behind. Seems like a childish reason when I think about it."

As we were talking I felt a sudden change in temperature and couldn't stop myself from shivering. I rubbed my arms to warm them up, forgetting about the jacket that was laid next to me.

"Shall we head back before it starts to rain?" Oscar asked, his head pointed in the direction of the dark cloud that was heading in our direction. I helped to pack up the picnic and folded the blanket, noticing that he seemed almost relieved for the distraction from his story.

"Did you find it hard growing up without a mother?" he asked as we were walking back. I paused for a moment thinking about the answer to that question.

"I don't really know. I always seemed to spend most of my time with my father anyway so I'm not sure I really noticed the difference if I am perfectly honest." I think somehow I did miss the presence of there being that important female in my life, but because it had happened when I was so young I didn't grow up feeling like something major was missing, mainly because I didn't know any better. I knew that was bad and I knew I probably should have been more upset about the situation but I couldn't lie to myself about how I felt.

"My Pa never made me feel like I needed more, he did the best he could to give me everything I wanted and I could never fault him for that. I will always love him, no matter what has happened."

"What happened?"

I hadn't realised the mistake I made until Oscar picked up on it. Luckily, at that moment Toby came bounding towards me giving me the perfect excuse to not answer the question.

"What you doing here buddy?" I said scratching behind his ears as his paws rested on my shoulders. I could feel his hot breath on my face and I had to keep pulling back to get away from the tongue that was so desperately trying to lick me. The appearance of Edward at the top of the hill answered my question. I felt the tension in my body tighten as I spotted him. I really did not want to see him, not after what I had overheard him saying. Plus, I was enjoying being with Oscar; I didn't need Edward to ruin that. I hoped that he would just walk past and ignore me like he had done the previous day but there was no such luck.

"Afternoon Emily, I was just looking for you." It seemed strange that he was happy to acknowledge me today, but then again there was no one around that he needed to impress. "What you doing out here?"

"It's my day off." I answered bluntly. Oscar seemed shocked that I had spoken to the young lord like that but he didn't say anything to stop me.

"Out with the stable boy I see." There was an edge to his tone that I couldn't quite figure out but I didn't like it anyway.

"Yes sir, it is also my day off. I hope that's not a problem."

"Of course it isn't Oscar." I said before Edward had the chance to make another comment. "We best be off, we don't want to get in your way." I bowed my head as was deemed proper and bid him goodbye.

"M'lord," I muttered mockingly.

I could feel Edward's eyes burning into my back as we marched up the hill. I felt exhilarated knowing that I hadn't given into Edward as soon as he had paid me the slightest bit of attention; for once I felt that it was me that had got the better of him.

"Won't you get in trouble for speaking to him like that?" asked Oscar once we had made it to the top of the hill.

"Oh. We used to play together as children. Sometimes I forget myself now." It was true, I did forget that when I was around others it was expected for me to be polite and address him as all servants did. I made a note in my head to be more careful in the future if I was to ensure that no one thought anymore of it.

"You still friends?" He asked curiously.

"Wouldn't call it that," I muttered trying to bring the conversation to an end.

"It just seems a bit strange, I've never seen him talk to anyone else like that. He barely even greets us when he comes to get Silver." My heart sank as I listened to him. I had known that Edward was going to ruin it all somehow.

"I'll leave you alone then," I suggested dejectedly.

"No, no I didn't meant it like that." He grabbed my arms and pulled me back next to him. "Let's just forget about it and enjoy the day, aye?"

I smiled sadly and nodded, hating myself for letting my attitude rule my head as it always did.

As we neared the stables I stopped to say goodbye to Oscar but he kept on walking past me. I had to run to catch up with him and when I did I noticed that he had a playful smile on him lips.

"What?" I asked a bit too bluntly.

"Wouldn't be very good if I let you walk home alone now would it?"

"But it's only down there, I'm fine! I do it every day."

"Well I'm not ready to leave you yet."

I felt my cheeks burn and I quickly turned my head so he wouldn't see. The last few minutes of the walk that led to my cottage were spent in silence, partly because I was too embarrassed to speak and partly because he seemed proud of himself for making me blush. Oscar took my hand just before we turned the corner and pulled me to a stop.

"I just wanted to say that I had a lovely day, thank you for coming with me."

"Maybe we could do it more often?" I suggested. I looked up at him but his eyes were focussing on anything but me. His thumb was softly tapping against my hand and I found myself wanting him to take off the gloves so that I could feel his skin. When he didn't say anything else I spoke again.

"Well goodbye then, I'll see you soon." I went to walk away but he pulled me back once more, this time closer to him. He pressed his lips lightly against my cheek, his face so close to mine that I could feel the flutter of his eyelashes as his eyes closed. I closed my eyes as I smiled, but when I opened them again expecting to see him standing before me instead I was greeted with the image of his back walking away.

Chapter 9

The next day Edward found me in the vegetable garden. I could tell from the way that he walked towards me that he had a purpose but when he spotted my father it seemed to completely throw him off guard.

"Oh, good morning Thorne. Good to see you back on your feet."

"Thank you m'lord. Is there anything we can help you with?" My father remained calm and positive towards the young lord even though I could tell by the look in his eyes that he was suspicious of Edward's motives. As I watched them together I made a mental note to make sure to ask what the reason for this dislike was, because as far as I was concerned nothing major had happened.

"No, it's nothing." he replied. He started walking away when he quickly turned back. "Actually, I came to speak to Emily, there was something important that I needed to ask her."

"Go ahead." My father's response seemed to surprise both of us, I couldn't remember the last time he had been so dismissive of us spending time together; it wasn't like him to be so lenient.

The shock seemed to render Edward motionless so I took the lead; I placed the last of the vegetables in the straw basket and heaved the weight up as I got to my feet.

"I need to take these to the kitchen, walk with me?" I made it sound like a question so as not to come across too demanding, although I wasn't too enthralled with the idea of the inevitable conversation.

He waited until we were out of sight and sound before he grabbed my arm and pulled me to the side; causing me to lose my grip on the basket scattering vegetables everywhere.

"What were you doing yesterday?" he snapped at me.

"I went into the village with Oscar. It was my day off." I replied bluntly. He looked directly at me and for a moment there was a look in his eyes that I had never seen before, but it passed too quickly for me to decipher what it meant.

"I wasn't even aware that you were friends." His tone had softened slightly but I could tell that there was much more to this than he was letting on.

"Since when has it mattered who I am friends with?"

"Well, I thought you were my friend. And you weren't there when I came to see you. You're always there," he muttered sheepishly sounding like a spoilt child.

"And I thought you were mine." I threw the words back at him refusing to break eye contact. "But I guess I was the fool to think that was ever going to last."

"What are you going on about?" He seemed genuinely oblivious to what I meant and I nearly found myself giving into him when I caught the broken look that had taken over his face.

"I heard what you said. Friends wouldn't say stuff like that."

His stare remained blank but I refused to say anything else; if he really didn't know what I meant then he was even worse of a friend than I had originally thought. I stared back at him waiting for the ball to drop. I didn't have to wait long, it only took a few moments until I saw that confident sparkle leave his eyes.

"I didn't mean anything by that."

"No, you were just trying to be funny right?"

There was no response; he just stared at me guiltily. "If there is nothing else that you need to say then I need to get on," I said.

"Fine." He walked away without another word and I could tell that I had just uncovered a sore spot for the spoilt lord who was used to getting everything his own way. I chose to ignore him and knelt down to gather up the vegetables.

From my spot on the ground I saw feet approaching before I realised who they belonged to.

"Everything alright?" asked Oscar.

"Yeah, just clumsy."

"Emily, I saw you. I know this wasn't exactly your fault so it would be easier if you just told me the truth otherwise you are going to end up owing me two explanations." This time it was my turn to look blank and when he spotted the expression he added, "I told you I wouldn't forget." It was only then that I realised I still hadn't given him the real story behind my black eye and since I had genuinely forgotten about it I didn't feel as bad as I probably should have.

"I lost my grip when he pulled me to the side. That's all it was."

"He shouldn't be treating you like that."

"I probably shouldn't have spoken to him like I did yesterday. I had it coming."

He knelt down beside me to help collect up the runaway goods his arm resting against mine. To my surprise I could feel myself blushing at his touch.

"Thank you so much for helping me but I really have to get these to the kitchen. I'm probably going to be in trouble for being late already."

"Maybe I'll see you later?"

"Hopefully," I called back as I rushed towards the house.

It was Sarah who met me at the door, roughly pulling the basket out of my hands as I offered it to her.

"We've been waiting for these," she said in an accusing tone.

"I'm sorry, it took longer than I thought," I apologised.

"Too busy thinking about Oscar? You know he won't really be interested in you. You're not his type." She looked me up and down as if to prove her point, I could feel her eyes burning into me and I resisted the urge to pull my cardigan across my body. Her judging look was making me feel incredibly self-conscious; I felt almost as exposed as I would have done had I been naked.

I didn't stay about any longer than needed, scurrying off to find my father. I scanned the grounds looking for him and it took me a moment to spot him up a tree, precariously perched on the ladder leaning against the trunk.

"Should you be doing that?" I called up, it made my stomach turn seeing him up there; I didn't want there to end up being a genuine back injury. At the sound of my voice he made his way back down and I found myself holding my breath until his feet were firmly back on the ground.

"I can't pick the last of the apples, the ladder won't go up high enough."

I was already halfway up the tree before he had a chance to argue. I expertly rested the basket he handed me between two of the sturdier branches and pulled myself up higher to where most of the apples were nestled. I twisted my left leg around the branch to give myself some sense of stability and started to pull the dusty red apples free of their leaves.

"So, what did Edward want?" my father called up. I was prepared to ignore him or come up with some white lie that would cease the questioning but I didn't seem to have the energy to lie anymore.

"He wanted to know what I was doing with Oscar yesterday." Contrary to any beliefs it was actually the truth that seemed to stop any further questions. I jumped back down with a basket full of apples just managing to regain my balance after my stumbled landing.

"Why do you always have to do that?" he asked, chuckling.

"Do what?"

"Jump down from everything. You're going to hurt yourself one day."

I chose to ignore the comment, mainly because I knew he was right but I didn't want to give him the satisfaction of knowing that.

"Can I ask you something Pa?"

"Of course."

"Promise you won't get mad." I looked up at him through dark eyelashes, my green eyes nervously pleading. He was silent for a moment too long making me think that it had been a bad idea to say anything.

"Promise."

I toyed with how best to word what it was I wanted to say, but even though I tried to think it over I still just blurted it out in the bluntest way possible.

"Why don't you like me being friends with Edward?"

"I've told you before, it's just not proper anymore."

"No. I want the real reason."

He looked down at his hands and sighed a defeated sigh as though he had known this moment was coming.

"How about I tell you over some tea?"

"It all started just after your mother died," he started as he set the mug in front of me. "The Lord and Lady approached me to voice their concerns about the relationship that you two had. Now, you have to remember that I was still very upset and I didn't really appreciate them telling me what I should be doing with you. I told them that you were both still so young that it couldn't do either of you any harm to have a friend. That time it was left and they allowed you to keep playing together even though I'm sure it wasn't without a few muttered comments."

"What were their concerns?" I interrupted.

"I'm getting to that. It was a few years later, I think you were about eleven or twelve, when Lady Barrow came to see me. This time on her own. Maybe you remember? I gave you an errand to run or something to get you out of the way."

I vaguely remembered, but if I was perfectly honest most of my past memories tended to merge into one.

"Once you were gone she wasted no time in getting to the point. She told me it was inappropriate that the two of you were friends and now that you were growing up there were certain expectations in place for Edward, I believe her exact words were 'he can't be seen frolicking with the help'. As much as I wanted to, I knew that there was no arguing with her. I had known how it was going to end from the moment you had started playing together. I guess I had been waiting for the day since they had first approached me. She continued to tell me that I needed to stop you from playing with him and that if the friendship was to continue then I may find my job in jeopardy."

"She threatened you?" I cried out in shock.

"Believe me; I was as surprised as you. It was completely out of character, I had never expected her ladyship to act in such a manner, but I guess she was just doing what she thought best for her child and that's not something I can blame her for. So there you have it. Although that's not the only reason." He paused, looking down at his hands. "Part of me did it for you, though I'm sure you won't ever see it like that. I didn't want to watch you get your heart broken when he decided that you were no longer good enough for him. I know he was your friend and I am very sorry for that, but you have to know I never disliked him. In fact I will always be grateful to him for helping you after your mother died; he made you happy like I never could." I could see a sadness in his eyes as he recounted the tale and it was easy to tell that every word he said was from the bottom of his heart. As I got up to clean away the mugs he laid his hand on my arm.

"Emmy, I know how stubborn you are and I don't believe for one second that me telling you not to do something would ever stop you. Just please be careful."

I nodded at him and gently grasped his calloused hand to show that I meant it. Part of me wondered whether Edward had ever known this, if his parents had ever given him a reason why he had to stay away from me. When we were younger we had just thought they were trying to keep us busy, though I guess we had some inkling that they were really just trying to keep us apart. I also wondered how much my father actually knew; was it possible that he saw the way that I looked at Edward? It hurt me to know that I would now be causing my father's heart to break as well as my own.

Chapter 10

The seasons were changing; blustering winds blew in pushing away the warm summer breeze, rains poured almost constantly keeping the sun hidden away. The change in weather also brought with it a change in mood – as much as I loved the smell of rain it was never fun to be standing outside in it for the whole day. Not only that but it meant the birds hid in the trees and the presence of other people was somewhat scarce.

A few days into the bad weather I found myself starting to work alone once more. As far as I was aware my father hadn't been going out but I could easily have been wrong. I had a feeling that I couldn't shake but I couldn't place a finger on what it was. Even though my father couldn't always be found with me I would always find him there when I eventually made it home, sitting by the ready-made fire he would have going to dry me off from the rain that would soak me through. Luckily, by the end of the week the rain seemed to be easing off which left me to enjoy the muddy puddles that had remained.

The one positive the rain gave was that I got to sneak into the stables to see Oscar and the horses. Lenny seemed to have softened up towards me once more so there wasn't any tension between us, in fact he seemed to appreciate the extra hand – especially with Silver.

"Ah, glad you're here little lady. Silver won't leave the box," called out Lenny as I was shaking off the rain. The sky was covered in menacing grey clouds so I could understand why the horses were getting restless; I recalled someone saying that animals had the ability to predict the weather which made me think that perhaps the worst was yet to come.

I slowly approached the middle box where Silver had backed himself into the corner. I moved cautiously, not wanting to startle him; I knew that even though he was comfortable with me his behaviour right now was very unpredictable.

"Hey Silver." I spoke softly, mimicking the tone Edward would use whenever the horse got spooked. The large horse's ears pricked up at the sound of my voice and he began to whinny nervously.

"It's okay," I muttered as I continued to approach the wooden fence. I held my hand out in front of me giving Silver the opportunity to approach me first. He was just about to nuzzle his nose into me when the loud rumble of thunder sent him rearing up. Even though I was trying my hardest to remain calm - I didn't want him to smell my fear - I couldn't help but jump at the sudden movement; the sight of such a large creature looming over me was terrifying. Oscar came into the stable at the same time as the horse spooked and he came running straight to me.

"Silver, down," he shouted.

"Don't yell at him, it's not his fault." I said grabbing his arm to get his attention. "Don't scare him more."

I didn't notice that Oscar had his arm draped over me protectively, pulling me further away from the scared animal.

"I always knew they could sense the weather," I muttered to myself.

"What was that?" asked Oscar, pulling me out of my trance.

"The thunder. That is why they are so worked up."

Oscar stared at me in amazement. "How did you know that?"

"I didn't really, I've just heard it mentioned and realised the truth in it now. I think we should try to make them as comfortable as possible, perhaps bring in extra hay?" I directed my question at Lenny warily. I wanted to help but I didn't want to tread on anybody's toes. He didn't say anything but he did nod and smile before leaving the stables. The next task wasn't going to be as simple as that. Silver needed to be calmed down, but a creature that size and in such a temperament was not going to be as easy to deal with.

"I'm going to have to go in," I said shrugging Oscar's arm off my shoulders.

"Emily, it's too dangerous. I'll do it." Even as he said it I could tell that he knew as well as I did that there were only two people that stood any chance of calming the horse down, and I was the only one that was present that the moment.

"I'll be careful, I promise." I held his hand tightly as we slowly walked back towards the horse. I inhaled my nerves in deeply and slowly blew them away. Silver was facing away from me but at the creaking of the gate he turned his head sharply in my direction.

"Hey Silver, I've just come to see how you are." I silently prayed that there would be no more thunder claps whilst I was standing there or I would find myself lying on the ground.

"It's not very nice out there is it?" I continued to speak in soothing tones as I shuffled my feet, gradually closing the distance between us. The horse's eyes were on mine, watching my every move intently. I continued to breathe deeply, trying to keep myself calm. After what seemed a lifetime the horse eventually started to move towards me and I found myself having to force myself to breathe as he approached.

"That's it," I whispered as he nuzzled his long face against my shoulder. I continued to whisper reassuringly in his ear as I stroked his soft coat. Oscar silently handed me the brush so that I could continue to calm him. Lenny came back not long after with extra bundles of hay and set to replenishing the horses' boxes as quietly as possible so as not to spook them.

Without even looking outside I could tell that the weather was getting worse by the dark shadows that were being cast into the barn. As if to confirm my thought a flash of lightening lit the sky followed by a low rumble of thunder. My heart quickened in unison with Silver's and I felt his frame shudder against my arms. He whinnied loudly in my ear and I buried my face into his neck.

"It's okay, it's okay," I repeated, as much for me as it was for the horse.

I could feel everyone's eyes on me, anxiously watching every second that ticked by. I could feel the horse's heartbeat start to slow so I knew that he was staring to calm down again.

"Should we close the doors?" I asked without turning away from the horse. The click of the lock answered the question. It wouldn't shut out nature's noises completely but I was hoping that it would mask them enough to keep the atmosphere calmer.

"Oscar, could you push the bale of hay over?" I asked as I walked backwards towards him. I felt for the hay and took it without turning my head and gently placed it down.

"You're doing brilliantly," whispered Oscar. I smiled at his compliment and I found those three words instilled a new confidence in me. I pulled apart the hay and scattered it across the floor. I then reached into the pocket of my apron and found the apples that I had sneaked in to give to my favourite horse.

"There you go, you've been so good." Silver munched the treat greedily. When the next round of thunder sounded without a reaction from the horse I finally felt comfortable enough to leave the horse to his own devices. I lightly kissed him on the nose and praised him one last time before leaving. Securing the gate, I turned to find Lenny and Oscar staring at me in disbelief.

"You're welcome," I remarked cheekily taking a mock bow. They waited until we were away from the horses before they slapped me on the back in congratulations, almost knocking me off my feet.

"Think we need to keep you around," said Lenny as he ruffled my hair.

We sat by the little table, one of us popping our head round the door every time there was a noise. Thankfully there didn't seem to be any sign of Silver, or any of the other horses, spooking again. Although they would protest against the disturbance they seemed comfortable enough – perhaps our presence was keeping them even more settled.

"I may have to have words with your father. Tell him he's got you doing the wrong job," joked Lenny.

Even though I loved the horses, I couldn't see myself doing anything other than the job I did now – I didn't even consider it as a job because I enjoyed it so much. Since I was still young perhaps I should have had bigger dreams for myself but I always seemed to find myself incapable of aspiring to be anything more. I already found myself in a position professionally that would have been unthinkable just a few years ago, and though people may stick up their noses at my being a young woman doing what was essentially a man's job, I now found myself not caring what they thought; as long as I was happy why should it matter?

"So did you have a good day on Sunday, Emily?" asked Lenny, a huge grin plastered across his face. "Oscar certainly seemed happy when he got back."

I noticed Oscar's cheeks turning a deep shade of red at that comment and I couldn't stop myself from mimicking his embarrassment.

"Yes thank you," I replied, keeping the answer short and sweet.

"Perhaps you'll be doing it again then."

Neither of us responded to that, but from across the table I felt Oscar's eyes searching for mine as though the answer could be communicated through a glance. I looked up to see his dark eyes looking at me expectantly and when I smiled bashfully it was for the first time I saw those deep brown eyes sparkle. I liked the mystery of what was happening between us; I enjoyed spending time with him but I still found myself thinking about Edward and wondering what it would be like if he was sitting across from me instead; to have those sea blue eyes searching for me. I knew that I needed to forget about him - it was never going to happen and I couldn't spend my whole life feeling unrequited love. At the same time I knew it was wrong to take advantage of the first, and only, person to show any interest in me. What confused me however was that I wasn't sure I was taking advantage at all; surely my stomach wouldn't twist and turn when I saw him if there was nothing there.

It was times like this that I was sure it would be much easier if my mother was here. I could never talk to my father about it, but perhaps a mother would be more clued in on matters of the heart.

"Em, you alright? You're very quiet." They were both looking at me.

"Sorry, just in my own world." It was true, I was in my own world – wrapped in a story of fantasy and confusion where the ending was still yet to be written.

Chapter 11

I noticed that my father was becoming more and more subdued. I'd come home to find him sitting in front of the naked fire staring blankly ahead of him. Surprisingly he didn't sneak out at night which was what his manner had led me to believe was going to happen; he simply just sat there. It was this that worried me more than anything. I could tell that there was something wrong, something that he wasn't going to tell me unless I managed to force it out of him – but that was what I wasn't sure how to go about doing.

I tried to push the thought to the back of my mind and just get on with things, and now that I was working alone again I found that there was plenty to keep me busy. It was always lunchtime that I looked forward to the most: the hour that I got to spend with Oscar. We took it in turns to bring the food, either going down to our spot by the lake or huddling in the barn depending on what the weather would permit. I found myself feeling closer and closer to him, genuinely looking forward to the time we got to spend together. At the moment he was reading out loud as I lay on my back letting the rare autumn sun beat down on me. His deep voice was soothing and I nearly found myself falling asleep at times – having to force my sleepy hands to stretch and discreetly pinch my side to try and wake myself up.

"Why don't you read for a bit?" he asked, breaking the flow of the story.

"No, you're much better than I am," I responded not opening my eyes. The truth was that I was not a strong reader and I didn't want to embarrass myself as I stumbled over the words that would jumble before my eyes. I certainly wasn't going to admit this to Oscar though, I was convinced that as soon as he realised I wasn't as smart as he was then he wouldn't be interested anymore. He continued to read for a little longer then stopped again.

"I've got to stop, my voice is going." The raspy catch in his voice confirming that. I sat myself up and grabbed the bottle of water I had brought with me, topping up the cup he held out towards me. As he sat there staring out at the rippling water I couldn't help but wish that I had my sketch pad with me. The way his eyebrows furrowed as though he were in deep thought and his eyes, so dark they were almost black, made me wonder what he was thinking about. His features seemed to be in perfect proportion with his face; his nose was perfectly straight coming to a neat point, his lips had a nice fullness to them and I could see the shadow of his long black eyelashes on his cheeks every time he blinked. I squeezed my eyes tight hoping to commit the image to memory so that I would be able to draw him later. When I opened my eyes I found him looking back at me, a quizzical expression dancing on his face.

"What exactly are you doing?" he asked with a hint of a smile to his tone. I shook my head in reply unable to think of anything to say. He continued to look at me as though I was very strange then chuckled to himself.

"We better get going anyway, Lenny won't like it if I'm late."

Even though I knew that I would see him again tomorrow I always hated having to say goodbye, there was never anything else to look forward to once that hour had passed.

I was slowly walking back to the gardens when I spotted Edward walking just before me. I slowed my steps more not wanting to catch up to him or make him aware that I was there. I hadn't spoken to him since he had confronted me about Oscar; in fact it was the longest that we had ever gone without talking to each other. Although I hadn't made the effort to approach him I also hadn't hidden myself away so he was just as much to blame for the lack of communication. To be honest I wasn't even sure if I missed him or not; I missed the person that he had used to be but everything seemed to have changed in such a short period of time so I was pretty sure I didn't miss the person that he had recently become. I watched him walking away, oblivious to the fact that I was watching him, as I thought back over the friendship we had shared and what was happening to it now.

The sun was beginning to set, casting a blood orange glow across the sky; my shadow following me as I trundled along the lane. The emptiness of the lands and the silence that was engulfing me gave me the feeling that there was something not quite right. I quickened my steps at the thought, overcome with the sense that I needed to be at home. I heard a crunch behind me which made my heart stop, my head snapped round to find only the darkness. Relief turned my legs to jelly but my hands were trembling, warning me that I couldn't afford to relax. I turned the corner to see the cottage in darkness, and I was just able to make out the figure of a man pounding on the deaf door. I stopped in my tracks, my body telling me that I shouldn't go any further. I forced myself to inch forward, walking on the balls of my feet to avoid crunching the stones with my steps – every tiny sound echoing through me. I pressed myself up against the tall oak tree that stood guard over our home, the sound of my heart thumping in my ears.

"I know you're in there, you can't hide from us forever." The gruff voice shouted at the door, the angry tones slicing through me. With one final shove at the door he turned and walked towards me. I took in a deep breath and pressed my body tight against the tree hoping the darkness would camouflage me. Tears leaked from the corners of my eyes and I blinked them back. I held tighter to the tree that was just wide enough to conceal me. I held my breath, counting the footfalls as they came closer. I counted ten steps when he stopped. Even though I couldn't see anything I could tell that he was standing next to me, the tree the only thing between us. I was sure he knew I was there, and even if he didn't he would now as I slowly had to let out the breath that I had been holding for far too long. I was about to step out and confront the intruder when the scent of cigarette smoke tickled my nose and the crunch of gravel put a stop to the pounding of my heart. I waited until I heard the feet turn the corner before I went running to the cottage. I pushed at the door only to hit my body square against it. I wasn't sure why I thought it would be open, not after what I had just witnessed. The only problem was I didn't have a key, I never thought to carry one with me. I absentmindedly rubbed the bump that was forming after my collision with the door as I thought about what to do.

"Pa, it's me." I said, tapping lightly against the window. The curtains were drawn so I couldn't see inside but I was pretty sure that he was in there. "Pa, please let me in." I tried again, this time a bit louder. I could understand if he was hiding from someone else but he had no right to keep me out here, after all it was my home too – it wasn't like I had anywhere else that I could go. The shuffle of his bare feet echoed through the silence, the removal of the chain seemed to ring louder than anything I had ever heard. It felt like an eternity before the door eventually cracked open and I pushed it wide to enter into the dark room. I immediately went to the windows to let in what little light was left outside.

"Don't!" shouted a voice abruptly from across the room. I wouldn't usually have listened to him but there was a tone to that single word that made me move away from the curtains.

"What's going on?" My eyes had started to adjust to the dark so I could just about make out his stooped figure propped up against the hard wooden chair. He whispered something but I was unable to make out the mumbled response. I stumbled across the room, hands held out in front of me to act as my eyes, until I was stood opposite him.

"What's going on?" I repeated.

He stared straight at me and even though I couldn't see his eyes properly I could tell that they would be bloodshot as the overpowering stench of alcohol hit me.

"You've been drinking again," I retorted, instantly on the defensive.

"I knew that it wasn't going to last, I was stupid to think that anything was going to change." I was so busy babbling, so wrapped up in the sound of my own voice that once again I missed my father's whispered words.

"I'm in trouble!" he had to shout over me. I instantly froze, all words halted on my tongue.

"What? What do you mean?"

"I'm in trouble," he repeated, lowering himself back into the chair and burying his head in his hands. I grabbed hold of his arms and shook him.

"Talk to me!" I could feel the anger in my voice. I couldn't stomach his pathetic form sitting there feeling sorry for himself. He was the adult, the parent, and he needed to start acting like it. I was fed up with him putting it all on me, expecting me to be the grown up and just come up with a magical solution to all his problems. I knew that only this morning I had been hoping that he would tell me what the problem was but I was already starting to regret that thought.

"Stop feeling sorry for yourself and talk to me!" To my dismay I could feel tears prickling under my eyelids; the constant battle of emotions inside of me threatening to spill over and show the world. I was glad of the darkness so that I was able to brush away the unfallen tears unnoticed.

The silence wrapped around us, strangling us with its tight grip. I stood there staring at him as he watched the floor, unsure of what to say next. I had no fight in me anymore; there were no answers.

"I owe people money."

"How much?" I didn't waste any time with sympathy.

"Too much. They want to hurt me."

The thought of my father being hurt tugged at my heart but I refused to feel sorry for him, after all he was the only one to blame for the mess that he had gotten himself into.

"Well pay it back then, before it comes to that," I responded naively.

He wrung his hands through his silvering hair, nervously pulling at it.

"It's too late, it's already there."

I could tell by the defeat in his voice that it was true, that he had run out of options and this was the final one.

"No, there must be something that we can do." I was suddenly filled with a need to help him regretting everything that I had recently thought or said. He was my father; I needed him.

"There's nothing Emily. Nothing! So forget about it." He towered over me as he jumped up from the seat, the heat radiating from his body was all that was needed to tell me how angry he was. I felt myself crumble as fear raced through every nerve in my body. The look that shone in his eyes mixed with the alcohol running through his system told me that I needed to be out of his way.

I stepped away from him and quickly made my way to the door. I opened it, checking that the lane was empty before I made my way out into the setting sun. The lock of the door clicking behind me sounded through the empty night; I had been locked out of the only place I had ever called home.

The darkness crept towards me, closer and closer, as I delicately made my way across the field. I hadn't really thought about what I was doing or where I was going; my feet were leading the way. I neared the tall trees that enclosed the lake and kept walking even though I knew that it was a bad idea; I wasn't thinking straight. I used my hands to guide the way, brushing my fingertips against the bark and gliding my feet through the long grass. I could hear the rippling of water as the wind rushed through it and I let the sounds guide me to my final destination.

The moon shone down eerily over the lake, the wind pushing the clouds across the sky. Goosebumps appeared on my arms as the coolness of the night set in making me wish that I had thought to grab a jacket before my departure. I sat in silence, the crescent moon my only friend. I gathered my legs up to my chest and wrapped my arms tightly around my knees – cocooning myself in my own embrace. I didn't bother to even try to sort out the jumble of thoughts that were running riot through my head, instead I just let the tears spill freely down my cheeks. I cried away everything I felt about Edward, I wept about all the pain my father had caused and I washed away all the emotions that had been tangled up inside me for so long. I don't know how long I sat there for, there was no change to tell me that any time had even ticked by at all.

I stretched out my stiff arms and wiped my wet cheeks dry. I pushed myself up, my bones creaking in complaint from the cold that had set in. I slowly stretched my body out, lifting my legs one by one to work out the knots. I lifted my left leg and as I did so I felt my right knee buckle under my weight throwing my body forwards. With my arms holding my bended leg behind me I couldn't reach my hands out to break my fall fast enough causing me to go tumbling head first into the water. My head scraped against the side of a rock as I stumbled into the darkness. The force of the impact mixed with the sharp coolness of the water made me gasp, drowning my lungs in icy water. The breeze whisked around me as I struggled to regain my balance, pulling me further out. I fought to reach the surface, arms and legs flailing as I tried to pull myself up. I held in what little breath I had left and blinked my eyes open to try and find an escape yet only darkness surrounded me. I could feel its arms reaching out to grab me, long black fingers rubbing against my ivory skin as I felt the life begin to drain away from me. Hands gripped my arms and pulled me – I couldn't tell if I was going up or down – I fought for a moment, trying hard to hold onto what little life I had left in me but my captor had too much strength; pulling me in until the darkness held me close.

Chapter 12

The wind looped wildly making the water that clung to me sink into my body. I willed my eyes to open but there was no fight left and I felt myself go limp on the cold, hard ground. The pressure pushing down on my chest was all the confirmation I needed to tell me that my heart was no longer doing its job and when I felt cold lips press against mine I knew the life was being sucked out of me. I was finally allowing my body to rest when I felt a bubble catch in my throat, fighting hard against my resistance to escape. As the cold lips left mine and the pressure pushed against my chest, harder this time, I spluttered feeling the water trickling down my chin as I choked on the life that was spreading through me. My body shook as it heaved out the water that had filled up inside me. I coughed uncontrollably, unable to catch my breath between the mixture of sobs and lake water that were desperately trying to escape my body.

"Emily, Emily. It's me. You're okay, it's all going to be okay." The familiar voice sounded distant even though I could tell they were right next to me by the strong arms that were wrapped around me protectively. I let myself sink into the embrace, unable to hold my own body upright. The firm arms gently pushed me away from the warmth of the body.

"Emily can you look at me?"

I slowly opened my eyes, my vision blurring the face that was only inches from mine. As I regained my senses I saw first those unmistakable blue eyes; a blue so bright you could almost see through them.

"Edward?" My voice was raw, scratching against my dry throat.

"Oh Emily, thank goodness. I was so worried." He didn't take his hands off me, just kept holding onto me like his palms were glued to my shoulders. "We better get you into the warm, can you walk?"

He pulled me onto my legs letting me place my entire weight onto him. My legs wobbled unsteadily beneath me as I took a step. The prospect of the long, daunting journey back up to the house filled me with dread and I was convinced that I wasn't going to make it all the way but Edward kept his arm steadily around me, almost carrying me over the tree trunks and stones that lay in my way. As we made slow progress up the hill I could feel myself slipping in and out of consciousness, the light from Edward's torch the only thing that kept me awake.

"I need to sit down," I croaked.

"We're nearly there, only a little bit further." I could hear the concern seeping through his words which made me try harder to keep battling on.

Edward guided me around the back of the house and half carried me down the long hallway that led to the servant area downstairs. The lateness of the hour meant that the rooms were deserted; there was no other creature present but for myself and Edward. He carried me through to the dining area where he lifted me up and lent me against a chair; my body sank into the cold hard material as though it was as welcoming as a warm bed. I was shivering uncontrollably and even though I was now inside I could feel the aftermath of my experience more fully now that I knew I was safe. Edward ran out the room, I tried to call after him but no sound escaped my mouth. I felt my eyes go heavy and I struggled to fight against the overwhelming urge to sleep. Through heavy eyelids I made out the figure of Edward hurrying back into the room. I felt, rather than saw, the soft material of blankets draping over me as he wrapped the warmth around my body. He pulled me in close to him and laid my head against his chest. The steady beating of his heart and the feeling of his fingertips dancing across my skin as he pushed away the wet hair that clung to my cheek, made my eyes drift shut.

I dozed for a while before Edward gently woke me.

"You'll have to get going soon, the servants won't long be up."

Even though I was wrapped tightly in blankets my bones still felt like ice and I really didn't want to move from the comfort of Edward holding me close to him. I tried to stretch through the aches but my movement was very limited and I couldn't take the pain of it. He handed me a glass of water which I sipped slowly; the liquid refreshingly cool against the dryness of my throat.

"What happened?" I croaked out after I had drained the glass.

"I was hoping you could tell me that."

I looked at him blankly, unsure what to say. I remembered going down to the lake but after that my mind went blank. My vacant stare must have told him what I was thinking because he sighed with a frown on his face.

"I saw you walking alone so I followed you, I thought that it would be a good chance to talk to you but by the time that I got out of the house I couldn't see you anymore so I just started walking in the hope that I would find you. I was walking down towards the lake when I heard a loud splash, so I ran. I could just about make you out as you were struggling but by the time I got there you weren't moving anymore, well I couldn't even see you that is. I was sure that I was too late but I dove in and grabbed you, pulled you out and tried to get you to breathe again. Guess that pretty much brings us to now." He looked sad as he had to tell the story of what had nearly befallen me.

It was only when he said that he had jumped in that I realised that he was also still slightly wet which made me wonder why his body had seemed to warm to me.

"Why were you out so late?" he asked.

"I had an argument with my father." I decided that since he had just saved my life the least he deserved was the truth.

"What about?" The look in his eyes convinced me that he cared, that he was still the same person I had fallen in love with all those years ago. Because of that look I found myself unable to hold back anymore.

"He's in trouble. But it is his own fault. He started drinking ... all the time. That is why he was never at work. And tonight he told me that he owes people a lot of money, too much for him to pay back. It seems that it is being left to me, once again, to solve his problems but I don't know what I am supposed to do. He won't give me all the information so how can I be expected to help him?" I blurted out. Edward's stunned expression stared back at me.

"I'm sorry," I muttered sheepishly.

"No, don't be sorry," he said shaking his head. He stood there in silence and it made me uneasy. I was sure I had said too much. I used my weak arms to push myself up, my head swimming as I stood. It took a moment for the contents of the room to stop spinning, by which point my legs had started to shake unsteadily again. I wasn't sure that they were going to be able to carry me all the way back to the cottage but I needed to leave. I slowly took the blankets off my cold shoulders and started folding them.

"What are you doing? Keep those around you?" He bustled about me like a concerned parent, wrapping the blankets over me once more.

"I'll walk you home." He took my hand and started walking with me. "If you're struggling just put your weight onto me."

As we stepped outside the air hit me and I started to shiver uncontrollably. I gripped the blankets tighter and kept my head down as we made our way down the lane. The sun was just starting to wake up by the time we made it to the corner that led to my little cottage. The walk had pretty much been done in silence except for a couple of moments when Edward had asked how I was feeling. It felt good to know that he still cared though I couldn't help but worry that what I had told him was going to be a problem, and if I had paid a bit more attention I would have noticed that he hadn't responded to what I had blurted out.

"Thank you. Well for saving me I guess."

"You're not home yet. I said I was taking you home and that means right to your door."

I would have argued but I wasn't sure that I was even strong enough to make it the few feet to my door. True to his word he marched me straight to the door and to my horror he turned the handle to let us in. As the door creaked open the emptiness of the house greeted us like an old friend.

"Where's your bed?" he asked.

I pointed in the right direction, exhaustion taking away my ability to speak. He left me leaning against the door and walked over to my bed. He pushed open the make-shift curtain and turned back the bed. He walked back towards me and pulled the blankets away from my cold body.

"Take those clothes off and get into bed," he said assertively, blowing out the candle he had lit on the way in - engulfing us in darkness.

I obeyed, shaking hands peeling off the clothes that had dried to my body. Shivering and exposed I climbed onto the hard mattress and pulled the sheets up to my chin, making sure no part of my body other than my head was on show. Without even looking I could tell that my hair was now an unruly mass of curls where I had fallen asleep with wet hair, but it was the least of my worries – even though it was Edward that was sitting next to me. He relit the candle and laid the blankets over the top of me.

"You need to get some sleep," he whispered soothingly. "I'll come and check on you tomorrow." His lips pressed lightly against my forehead making all the feelings I had buried deep come bubbling back up to the surface.

"It's all going to be okay, you are safe now," he spoke as he stroked my hair reassuringly making me drift off to sleep.

"I love you," I muttered unable to control the words that escaped my mouth. My confession was met with silence. If my eyes weren't already closed I would have seen the shocked look that jumped onto Edward's face and if I had been more aware of what was going on the sound of the door closing would have told me all that I needed to know.

Chapter 13

I awoke the next morning feeling as though a ton of bricks had fallen on me; my chest was tight making it difficult to breath and whenever I attempted to move a limb it sent excruciating pain running through my body. I was supposed to be working today but if it was causing me this much trouble just getting out of bed then I knew there was no chance of that happening.

I lay back down unsure of what to do. From the silence that blanketed the little cottage I could tell that I was still alone. Rather than being worried I was more annoyed by the fact that my own father wasn't here to look after me when I needed him, even though there was still that little voice in the back of my head asking where he could be. There was nothing to do but sit and wait until Edward came to check on me like he said he would. After an hour ticked by and there was still no sign of anyone coming to my rescue I knew that I was going to have to get on with things by myself. My stomach was growling in protest to the lack of attention it was receiving. I struggled out of bed, moaning as my feet hit the floor. I shuffled along unsteadily wincing at every movement until I finally made it to the kitchen. I placed some bread on a plate and filled a glass with milk unable to muster the energy to do anything more extravagant; the movement of simply pouring from a bottle was enough agony for the moment.

I sat myself on the chair, the hardness of the wood an enemy to my aching muscles, and stared at the door waiting for any sign of movement. Another hour ticked by slowly and I could feel myself growing restless – I was used to constantly being up and doing something, the inability to move was getting to me already. I ran my tongue across my teeth, disgusted by the fuzzy sensation they left behind. I filled my cup with water and took a mouthful, swishing the liquid round my mouth in the hope it would wash away some of the dirt. Since I was up I decided that I was going to take on the battle with getting myself dressed. So far I had only managed to throw on a robe and I knew that would probably be slightly awkward when Edward did eventually show up. I thought back to the night before unable to really piece anything together – it all seemed a blur. I remembered walking back to the cottage but I couldn't recollect how I had gotten into bed – it was as though I had been walking in my sleep.

I pulled on the first pair of trousers that I could find, wincing as I bent down to pull them over my legs and slowly pulled a jumper over my head grateful for the extra warmth that it provided me. I had come to realise that my father must have supplied me with men's, or rather boys, clothing since I had never seen another female walking around with trousers on – I always made a point to wear skirts or dresses outside of the house or work though; I didn't need people thinking worse of me than they already did. I couldn't make myself get onto the floor to look for anything to cover my feet so I left them bare; I knew that even if I was able to make it down there it would be highly unlikely that I would be getting up again. As I was walking away from my room I noticed the pile of clothes I had discarded last night and frowned at the bitter memory they left behind.

I wanted to draw to take up some of the time but there was no way that I would be able to lift the mattress, no matter how light it was. It was baffling that even though there had been no real physical damage I was still in so much pain, but there was no arguing with my muscles. Instead I made my way to the sofa. Just before I sat myself down I noticed the pile of books that had belonged to my mother beckoning me from their place by the fire. I grabbed one off the top and sat down, pulling the tattered blanket over my feet to keep them warm. I turned the book so that the cover was facing me and read the title for the first time.

"The Wind in the Willows, by Kenneth Grahame," I spoke quietly to myself. The binding of the cover was well worn and the edges were fraying. When I turned the pages they cracked unappreciatively so I made sure to turn them as daintily as my clumsy hands could manage, worried they would dissolve beneath my fingertips. I started to read, wishing that Oscar was here to read to me, the sound of his voice always brought the stories to life. However, as I was reading it wasn't his voice that I heard, instead it was my mother's and I could picture a distant memory of her reading these somewhat familiar words out loud as I lay on this same sofa listening to her melodic tones. To my surprise I found myself getting engrossed in the book and I was slightly miffed when a knock sounded at the door.

"Come in," I called out, sure that it would be Edward. I had finally made myself comfortable and I didn't want to have to face that chore again by moving. I turned my rigid neck expecting to see blonde hair and smiling blue eyes where instead I found black hair and a frown.

"Are you alright?" asked Oscar as he rushed over to my side. "I hadn't seen you out all morning and when you didn't turn up for lunch I got worried. I hope you don't mind that I showed up here."

"Of course I don't!"

"So, what's happened?" he asked, looking my fragile body up and down. As far as I was aware there were no visible remnants of the night before but I guessed that it was pretty clear from my inability to move and pale demeanour that something had happened – not to mention that I hadn't even tried to tame my wild curls. I didn't see any reason not to tell him what had happened so I started the tale of what had occurred the night before.

"I went out last night, which I know was idiotic before you say anything, and went and sat by the lake. From what I can remember I was trying to stretch myself out when I fell in. I guess the shock of the fall and the fact that I wasn't prepared for it meant that I struggled to get myself back out. The rest I don't really remember apart from it was dark, very dark. And so cold." My voice drifted off towards the end as the memory of what had happened started to fail me. As I recalled the night I felt my body starting to shiver uncontrollably once again. Noticing this, Oscar pulled the blanket further over me, leaving his gloved hand resting on top of mine.

"Edward said that he pulled me out and got me breathing again. Then he took me back up to the main house to get me warmed up, then I think he walked me home. I'm still not entirely sure how I got here though." I tried to laugh it off but the look of concern that was plastered across his face told me that it was no laughing matter.

"I'm okay though, just a bit sore. That's why I'm not at work today," I added to try and reassure him. After what felt like a lifetime of silence he eventually spoke.

"But why were you out on your own at night?"

"I had an argument with my father and I was too scared to stay here," I answered honestly.

"Really?" he seemed shocked.

"There's a lot that I haven't told you," I admitted reluctantly. "My father has been drinking for a long time, that is why I was working on my own so often, and when I got home yesterday there was a man banging on the door. I asked my Pa what it was about and he just said that he owed people a lot of money. That's all I know, when I tried to ask him more he got mad. And I haven't seen him since." I gestured at the empty house to back up my point.

"Emily I had no idea, why didn't you tell me earlier?" The look of pain in his eyes made me feel bad but I knew that my reasons were justified.

"I didn't know you well enough. I had to be sure that I could trust you."

A slight hint of a smile danced across his lips.

"So you trust me?"

"Completely," I uttered, nodding vigorously before realising how much it would hurt. I managed to cover up the pain before he noticed. I could tell that my answer was not what he had been expecting but it was true – I had grown to know him well and I felt that he could be trusted.

"Then we are going to sort this out together. I'm not going to let you do it on your own anymore. Now, are you hungry?" he whipped a bag from behind his back with a cheeky smile.

"Starved."

"Will you be okay on your own? I don't want to go back but I have to. I can come back as soon as we're done. Make you dinner if you like?" I was touched by how much he cared.

"That would be lovely." Usually I would have said no because of my father but I just didn't care what he thought; not anymore.

"I'll see you later then," he said as he made his way to the door. "Oh by the way, your father stayed at the barn last night. I meant to tell you earlier. Shall I tell him that you asked for him?"

"No, please don't." I hoped he would stay there, stewing in his own temper so that he could think about what he had done.

Chapter 14

When the sun started to set I realised that Edward wasn't going to show. I was sure that he had said he would come and check on me but maybe I had been wrong, after all there were chunks of the night missing from my memory. It wouldn't have surprised me if I had imagined the whole conversation. My body seemed a little less heavy now so I made myself get up and walk around. I was so bored that I even tackled the mattress to get my sketching stuff. I sharpened the pencil with a small knife and lit a candle so that I could see the picture I had started more clearly; Oscar stared away from me on the canvas, gazing out at the unknown. I took myself back to that day at the lake and focused intently on the far away gaze in his eyes. I wanted to capture that look as best I could. I was so engrossed in my drawing that I didn't notice Oscar enter. The creak of the door caused me to jump and I had just enough time to cover the sketch before he was at my side.

"Sorry, shouldn't I have let myself in? I did knock but you didn't answer and I thought you may have been asleep. I didn't want to disturb you, sorry."

"It's fine, I was just in my own world. So tell me about your day, I need some entertainment."

As he was talking I watched his face and decided that my original description of him still held good. He wasn't quite what you would call handsome but he was definitely interesting. Close up the angular lines of his face didn't seem so pronounced, his nose was slightly softer and his lips more inviting which all served to make his face more welcoming. But it was still those eyes that held my attention; the magnetic black eyes that drew me in close. What surprised me most about them though was the depth of sensitivity I saw hidden within. My fingers twitched over the sketch beneath my palm as I found myself wanting to add those details to the unfinished picture. The look in his eyes was completely different to the one that I had seen that day; those sensitive features would have softened the dramatic visage that I had given him.

"Are you listening to anything that I'm saying?"

The answer was obviously no, I had been too focused on looking at him to listen to a single word.

"Yeah, was about horses," I replied cheekily.

"Lucky guess. What was so interesting that you tuned me out?"

Your eyes, I thought but I daren't say that.

"Nothing."

The drumming of my fingers against the table must have drawn his attention to the paper I had been trying to unsuccessfully hide with my arm as he reached out to try and sneak a peek.

"Have you been drawing?" he asked curiously. "Can I have a look?"

I started to panic, not wanting him to know that I had been drawing him but I didn't know how I was going to disguise it as all the other sketches were beneath it.

"It's not finished yet," I muttered in an attempt to put him off.

"That doesn't matter, I still want to see," he said with a smile.

Reluctantly I loosened my arm and let him slide the paper from beneath it, I really didn't know what other option I had – it would have seemed very suspicious if I had just said no and tried to keep them from him. I could feel my cheeks begin to fill with embarrassment before he had even had a chance to see the subject of the drawing. He remained silent as he stared at the picture in his hands, his eyes darting over the pencilled lines as he took in every detail that I had put on paper.

"There was more that I wanted to add, it really isn't finished yet. I didn't, well I know that it isn't really that good …"

"Emily it is amazing," he spoke, interrupting the stream of excuses I was throwing at him. "I had no idea that you were so talented."

Even though it felt incredible to hear someone comment on my hobby in such a manner I was still shamefully embarrassed to have him know that I had been sketching him. I didn't know what I could say to explain the reasons behind it though so I just remained silent, staring down at my hands with abashed eyes.

True to his word Oscar made me dinner and I was surprised by how good it actually was. The steak and kidney pudding was rich with the juice from the meat and the potato was so creamy it melted in my mouth.

"How are you feeling?"

"A little better, I reckon I should be at work tomorrow." I couldn't bear the thought of spending another day like this; I was determined to get back no matter how much pain it would cause.

"It's Sunday tomorrow," he said with a smirk.

"Really?" I seemed to have completely lost track of the days in the week.

"Hand on heart," he replied solemnly even though I could see his eyes laughing. "And because I am so nice I will even let you decide what we do."

I hit him across the arm playfully. It made me realise that we didn't even ask to see each other anymore, we just assumed that it would happen and that was a relationship that I had never expected to happen for me.

"Why don't we go for a swim?" I joked. The smile instantly vanished and I immediately regretted saying it. "I'm sorry, too soon."

"Clearly your head has been affected as well so maybe I should just decide." I could tell that he was trying to joke with me as well but his voice was slightly too stern.

"Good idea, when you picking me up?"

"Is eleven okay?"

"Perfect."

He took the empty plates and went to start clearing up. I stood, too quickly, jarring the muscles that had taken all day to regain normal function and slumped back against the chair. Oscar was at my side before I had even fallen back onto the seat.

"What happened? What hurts? Are you okay?" he fired the questions at me hastily, looking me over to make sure that I was alright.

"I am fine," I laughed. "Just trying to stop you waiting on me. Now help me up."

When he saw me laugh he seemed to relax and placed his arm around my waist to pull me up. The closeness of his arm against me made my body tingle.

"What's this?" came a voice from the doorway. We both spun around to see my father standing there, the glowing moon illuminating his stooped figure.

"I was just leaving Mr Thorne," came Oscar's reply, his arm briskly leaving its place at my waist. I steadied myself against the table as I unwillingly watched him leave.

"Since when do you invite people into the house?" he asked gruffly.

"Since I needed someone to help me and you weren't here." The tension in the room made the pain in my head start swimming around. I needed to be horizontal, not having another pointless argument with my poor excuse of a father.

"Where did you go last night?" he spat at me.

"What do you mean where did I go? More like where did you go? This is the first I have seen of you since last night." He seemed to collapse under my stare and the words that I shot at him.

"I felt bad so I went looking for you, I thought you would be at the barn but when I got there Lenny said that he hadn't seen you. I guessed that you must have come back here, and I didn't want to disturb you. So, well, Lenny offered me a drink and I ended up staying there with him." He sounded like a child attempting an awful lie to get out of trouble.

"You didn't really look very hard did you, guess the temptation of alcohol must have been too much for you." I was disgusted with him, but more so I was disgusted with myself for expecting anything else of him. I didn't feel the need to explain to him what had happened, he obviously didn't care and I was in no mood to receive the fake sympathy from him that now meant nothing to me. I didn't even bother to excuse myself, just turned and walked to my room pulling the curtain closed behind me. I slumped onto the bed and closed my eyes, trying to push away the pain that was seeping through my body once more. As I lay there I tried to work my way back through the week so that I could figure out where I was again, I worked out that it was now October the nineteenth which meant that tomorrow was the twentieth; my birthday. Not that anything special was going to happen, no one was likely to remember especially if I couldn't. I drifted off to sleep with no expectations for the day that loomed ahead.

Chapter 15

I didn't wake up with that bubbling excitement that most people have on their birthday, to me it was just another day. Nothing exciting would happen; there would be no parents waiting eagerly with presents for me to open, and no friends waiting to celebrate the day with me. Thankfully my body seemed to be functioning normally today and I was able to get up and out of bed with no real struggle. I was about to get dressed when I realised that I was still yet to wash the lake water off of me. I got the water hot and relished the feel of the clean water trickling down over my body from the sponge I squeezed over my head. I washed the knots from my hair and prayed that the soap would somehow control the disobedient curls that so furtively ignored me. I chose the navy blue dress with the daisy print and rooted through my possessions until I came across some warm black tights to protect my legs from the cold. I also managed to find an old, black knitted cardigan that seemed presentable enough so I threw it on for an extra layer along with my black boots.

I was just clearing away the remnants of the porridge I had made for my breakfast when there was a soft knock at the door. The noise made my father stir from his position on the floor but he didn't wake.

"I'll just be one minute," I called out. I ran my fingers through my hair to see whether it was dry or not – the ringlets were still slightly weighed down with water but for the most part it was dry. I opened the door then doubled back to grab my jacket, forgetting that Oscar could see everything from his position in the doorway. I turned to see him looking straight at the crumpled heap that passed for my father.

"Sorry about that," I muttered grabbing his arm to escort him out of the door. I was waiting for him to ask about what he had seen but he remained silent. I found myself unable to think of anything to say and for the first time I felt awkward around him.

"How's your morning been so far?" he asked pleasantly and I felt myself relax with his tone.

"Nothing exciting, yours?"

"Just been getting some stuff sorted." There was a smile on his lips that made me curious. He must have seen the look on my face because he chuckled to himself before adding, "And before you ask I'm not going to tell you what." He cuffed me on the arm playfully but it didn't work to dampen my curious nature.

"Oh," I sighed dramatically, turning down my bottom lip to try and make him feel bad.

"Not going to work cabbage patch, but nice try," he said winking at me. I felt a burning in my chest at the sign of affection creating a new found tension between us.

"You not going to ask where we're going?"

I hadn't even thought about it, I had just followed him assuming that we were going to the village like we usually did. We were walking in that direction as well so I couldn't understand why he seemed so concerned about it.

"We're just going to the village aren't we?"

"Well, no, I had some special things planned for you." He genuinely looked hurt by my response which made me worry.

"I didn't mean anything by it," I exclaimed guiltily.

"Don't be silly, you didn't say anything wrong."

The conversation came to an end as we walked into the village, I thought it was surprisingly busy for this time of year when I realised that the church fete was coming up so the villagers were all running around trying to prepare for the event.

"Can you wait here for two minutes please?" asked Oscar, his eyes pleading with me. I nodded and he was running off before I even had the chance to ask him what he was up to. I stayed glued to the spot watching people bustling past me as they went about their errands; mothers pulling along their children as they chatted to their friends, old couples shuffling along hand in hand as they went from one market stall to the next. As I was looking around I spotted Oscar walking back towards me trying to sneakily fit an object into the inside of his jacket.

"Shall we get going?" he asked acting like he hadn't been up to anything.

"Where exactly are we going? You still haven't told me."

"Follow me and you will find out." He took my hand and gently pulled me along after him.

We walked slowly past the row of shops displaying their goods on tables outside the windows. My eyes glided across the table of books, the collection of fruits and vegetables that my eyes knew so well and settled on the enticing scent of freshly baked bread. My fingers twitched longingly as the smell tickled my nose but I tried not to let it show. Oscar started to slow, perhaps feeling the graze of my fingertips against his forearm where they were resting, but I made a point to keep moving. I wasn't going to allow him to waste his rations on me and I was certain that was what was going through his mind at that moment. I saw his body visibly stiffen when we neared the recruitment office, automatically on the defensive as though he was waiting to be reprimanded for not fighting for his country. We hurried past, his head bowed low as if to try and disguise himself. I noticed the sadness in his eyes; darkness clouding over as his past life watched him walking away.

"So, where are we going then? We are just walking away from everything now!" I exclaimed, trying to pull him away from whatever thoughts may be haunting him.

"It's a secret." He winked at me, a slight smile gracing his lips, but the sadness was still there. I decided it was best just to leave him to it and instead focussed on the walk, taking in surroundings that should have been familiar to me.

As we got further away from the village it got quieter, the sound of busy voices barely a whisper to my ears, and I could hear the music of the wind gliding past the leaves. The tall trees decorated the dirt road that led us away, glimpses of the expanse of land could be seen through the gaps. I knew that this path would take us along the outskirts of the estate and to the bottom fields where the farmers kept their land, but I didn't remember there being anything of significance along the way.

The path started to climb and as we got to the point where the skyline met the dirt, Oscar gently tugged my arm so that my body turned with his. He guided me through a gap in the trees and across the open field before stopping at an old wooden bench, indicating for me to take a seat. The decaying wooden planks didn't look like they would hold my weight but I was intrigued as to what would follow so I gingerly sat down, leaning hard against the cold, hard arms to support me.

I was about to speak but Oscar reached out and laid a gloved finger against my slightly chapped lips, his hypnotic eyes stealing my words.

"Just look," he directed. I pulled my gaze away from his and looked out over the view before me. The estate house looked magnificent from this angle, not because it was the most flattering way to view the house but because you were able to see all the beauty that surrounded it. The gardens stood symmetrically, mirroring each other in size. I could see the tops of the trees, speckles of colour shining where the fruit hid and though I couldn't physically see behind their walls, I knew that the flowers would be pushing out of their beds and reaching out towards the sunlight. I breathed in the comforting scent of the fresh, clean air and let myself lean back against the comfort of Oscar's arm. I watched over the fields, enchanted by the movements of the insect-like horses that moved in the distance, as Oscar's eyes kissed the freckles on my cheeks.

"Lenny said that we can take one of the horses out for a bit. They aren't being ridden enough and he doesn't want them forgetting the feel of it. Plus he thought that you would enjoy it." Oscar spoke, pulling me out of my trance.

Even though I was excited about the prospect I couldn't shake the gnawing in the pit of my stomach; I had already ridden a horse and he would be expecting me to be a complete amateur. I was going to have to pretend that I had no idea what I was doing but I wasn't sure how to do that; how do you forget what you have been taught? It didn't take away from the fact that this was yet another opportunity that I wouldn't have usually had the chance at: it was uncommon that we, as servants, would be allowed to ride the horses. It was

Oscar's job to care for them but even that was unlikely to give him the privilege, so I don't think that either of us had any intention of passing on this opportunity.

We passed my cottage as we walked closer to the estate and I caught a glimpse of my father through the opened curtains. He was leaning against the kitchen table, his head burrowed in his hands like he was deep in thought. His eyes latched onto mine as I walked away, I was unable to tear myself away from the desperate gaze that was searching for me.

"Did you want to go in? You can come meet me later if you would rather." Oscar asked, pulling my attention away from a situation that I really didn't want to be involved in.

"No, no. Sorry. What were you saying?"

"It really wasn't anything important and it clearly can't have been very interesting if you weren't even listening to me."

I over-dramatized a pout to communicate how bad I felt but it didn't come across as sincere as I had hoped.

"For that you can wait out here," he stated nonchalantly.

"You're going to leave me out here in the cold?" I forced a shiver to feign my sadness.

"Let me think …" He stroked his chin and looked up to the sky, smirking as he humoured me. "Yes!" He chuckled as he shut the door behind him, leaving me standing there staring at the closed door.

My mouth dropped when he didn't return straight away and for a moment I thought he was actually going to leave me standing out there. The soft sound of approaching footsteps made me quickly regain my composure, turning my back to the door so he wouldn't catch the expectant look on my face.

"You didn't think I would really leave you out here did you?" asked Oscar's attentive voice.

"Yes," I answered honestly, no dramatics involved this time.

"I just had to check something but we can go in now."

"Maybe I don't want to," I said stubbornly.

"Yes you do, come on." He took my hand and pulled me towards him, ignoring my arduous attitude. I resisted at first but that only served to make him take hold of both of my arms and pull me with more force. This time I was no match for his full strength and I found myself flying towards him. He caught me masterfully, holding me just inches away from him. I could taste the cinnamon on the air as his breath misted around me. Close up his eyes were even more intriguing; long dark lashes framed his eyes making them look even darker than before. They were simply arresting, making me want to delve into his soul.

"Are you going to walk or do I have to carry you in?" He didn't move his face away from mine and I could almost feel his lips moving as he spoke. I found myself wondering what it would be like to kiss him as he moved his lips close enough to touch mine. He was holding me up so that our eyes were on the same level, my feet swaying inches above the ground.

"I can walk," I whispered.

He slowly lowered me down his body until my feet were back on the hard mud. He kept hold of my hand and pulled me along after him. I followed him into the barn to find it empty which was unusual for a Sunday. "Where is everyone?"

"Erm, they're busy." He didn't make eye contact with me and there was something about the way he was acting that seemed very shifty.

"What are you up to?"

He beamed down at me then he excitedly pulled out the little box that I had seen him hide in the inside pocket of his jacket; forgotten about until he presented it to me.

"Happy Birthday Em."

I froze, unable to believe what he had just said. He unravelled my fingers and placed the box in my hand.

"Wh ... but ... how did you know?" I stuttered in disbelief.

"Lenny told me. Are you going to open your present?"

My fingers were shaking as I covered the box with my hand, tears threatening to fill my eyes. I couldn't remember a birthday where someone had given me a present just for me. I slowly opened the lid, anticipation tingling in my stomach. Inside the little black box there was a velvety black cushion. Laying on that soft black cushion was the most beautiful brooch I had ever seen. The emerald green stone seemed even more spectacular than the first time I had seen it as I ran my finger across its cool surface, the gold lacing that decorated it even more intricate.

"It's beautiful," the emotion caught in my throat. "Thank you so much."

He took the brooch out of its box and gently pinned it on the collar of my cardigan, smiling to himself with what I thought was a mixture of relief and success.

I stood on my tiptoes and delicately kissed his cheek, my lips brushing over the corner of his mouth as I moved away.

Chapter 16

The brooch kept catching my eye, I couldn't stop admiring it unable to believe that it was mine. Once Oscar had given me the present we walked through to the stables where everyone was not so hard at work.

"Happy birthday little lady," called out Lenny as he walked over to give me a hug.

"Thank you. I can't believe you remembered!"

"I'm not likely to ever forget that. You always made a pretty big deal out of it when you were younger. I remember the countdown that started months beforehand."

I giggled sheepishly. I wasn't used to people making such a fuss over me – or at least I had forgotten what it felt like. I was always doted on by Lenny and my father when I was younger, but a lot had changed since I had started to grow up.

"Arabella needs to be taken out. Not far though, I'd rather it was just round here." Lenny spoke to Oscar though there was really no need to explain much, it had been made clear that Oscar was more than competent when it came to the care of the horses.

"No problem boss." He then turned to me with a smile and added,

"Come on then cabbage patch, let's keep up with the celebrations." He took hold of my hand once more and like always I wanted to pull those gloves off so that I could feel his touch; longing to know the intimacy of his skin. I had a strong feeling that my inquisitiveness would make this a reality eventually but for now I would make the effort to keep a lid on my curious nature.

I watched Oscar as he prepared Arabella for her ride. He was completely at ease with the horse, moving around her like it had been part of his everyday routine for years. He knew exactly what he was doing and what made it even more endearing was that he seemed happiest when he was doing so.

"Do you want to go first?"

"No, you can. Maybe I can learn by watching a master at work," I joked. I decided that if I made out that I was reluctant to saddle up then I may be able to make it more believable when I said that I hadn't ridden before. He mounted the horse like a true rider and as I watched him trotting around the stables it was clear that he had done this numerous times before. Part of me was saddened by the knowledge that someone who loved these creatures so much would never be able to have one for his own; this would be the closest he ever got to these majestic animals. It was a shame that such expertise was wasted, especially when their masters showed no real interest other than to show off the skills they had acquired. I was so lost in my thoughts I didn't notice Oscar jumping off the horse next to me.

"Your turn," he whispered in my ear. He stood behind me, arms out ready to catch me, as I mounted the horse – not quite as gracefully as he had done.

"We'll just go slowly. If you want to stop at any point then just say."

He gently tugged the reins and Arabella started to move forward slowly. It was exhilarating to be back in the saddle but I kept my face totally dead pan and held tightly onto the reins, gripping until my knuckles turned white; partly for show and partly because it had been such a long time since I had ridden.

"Don't be nervous, she won't do anything to hurt you." It wasn't long before I had forgotten all about the façade and was just enjoying the ride. Oscar had let go and I was in complete control of the horse. Unconsciously my legs squeezed around the body of the gentle giant and I felt her speed quicken beneath me. I was overcome by a sudden urge to ride off into the horizon but I caught the bewildered expression on Oscar's face and I knew that the game was up. I expertly guided the horse to his side and came to a stop.

"You're better than I am." He reached his arms up to help me down and as his hands closed around my waist I couldn't help but compare the moment to the one I had shared with Edward years ago. Right now, in this moment, it felt natural like it was meant to be; that in some way his hands belonged right where they were. It made me wonder if what I had felt for Edward was real or if it was all simply because I knew that I couldn't have him. I shook the thought from my head and turned my attention back to the present moment. His hands stayed around my waist as he stared down at me.

"Perhaps I'm just a natural?" I shrugged nonchalantly.

"It seems that way. She certainly got her exercise anyway, we should take her back in now."

Together we walked the horse back round to the stable entrance. The sun was just starting to set turning the sky a relaxing shade of red. The air felt still, the temperature dropping with the sun but the cold breeze couldn't touch me. It felt like a chapter out of the books that Oscar read to me, making me one of the most content characters that had ever been written.

Oscar was filling me in on all the gossip from the household as we were walking back, he had just told me about the cook setting her apron on fire causing me to burst out laughing as I pictured it. I was still laughing when we walked in but that was soon brought to an abrupt stop at the sight of Edward. There was something about the gleam in his eyes that put me instantly on edge, it was like there was a terrible secret that only the two of us knew yet I couldn't remember being told. He was looking at me – through me – as though just the sight of me disgusted him. It was the complete opposite reaction to how he had been acting the last time we had been together; he had saved my life and then spent the entire night with me just to make sure that I was alright. As far as I was aware the last words that were spoken between us were by him declaring a visit that never happened. It was clear that there was something vital that I was forgetting. I urgently raked through the files stored in my memory to try and turn up the missing information but kept coming up empty handed.

"Where have you been? I've been waiting for far too long. I shouldn't have to be waiting at all," Edward snapped at Oscar.

"Sorry m'lord, it is actually my day off but I shall tend to you straight away." He hurried to put Arabella back in her box.

"That is no excuse. I can take that day away from you with a snap of my fingers if you don't get your job done properly."

Oscar bowed his head slightly towards Edward then ran off to get Silver saddled and ready for his master. I knew that I should have been more angered at the way that he was speaking to Oscar but I was still flummoxed by the way that he was looking at me; there was a malicious glint in his eye that made my throat tighten.

"What are you doing here?" he spat the words so viciously it hurt. He was talking to me as though he felt I was below him, and though that were true he had never made me feel like that before.

"I ... it's ... we took the horse out for some exercise," I stuttered suddenly nervous in the presence of the young lord. His eyes squinted closer together at my response.

"What's wrong?" I whispered.

"What's wrong? What's wrong?" he repeated, his voice raising with each word. Oscar turned his head at the sudden commotion but I smiled lightly to let him know that it was nothing. Edward had walked right over to me and was standing inches away, I could feel the anger radiating off of him.

"You told me you loved me." The spit from his words hit me across the face as what had been said slowly sunk in. "I can't believe that you ever thought I would feel that way about you, you have no idea what I was risking just being your friend and now you have ruined everything because of some stupid fantasy. You are nothing, why would I ever love you?" His voice was barely audible but it was the hushed tones that made it even more painful. I could just about recollect uttering those three words in my exhausted state but I couldn't be sure that it wasn't just my imagination playing with what he had told me. His last words echoed through my mind, the sting of hatred echoing through my body. I knew that I was nothing but to be told that by someone else was not something anyone ever wanted to hear.

"Are you done with that horse yet?" he shouted, spinning around sharply to face Oscar who was just leading Silver out of his box.

"Yes m'lord. Sorry again," he spoke humbly not showing any sign of defiance to the person who was speaking to him so disagreeably. I was in awe of the way he could hold his tongue and act professionally no matter what; it was a basic skill I was still yet to master.

Edward jumped on the horse and left the stables a little too fast. Oscar was back by my side in seconds, his presence instantly began to relax me.

"What was that about?"

"I have no idea," I whispered, shaking my head in disbelief. There was no chance that I was going to tell him what I had just learnt, as much as I trusted him there was still some things that he never needed to know.

"I thought he was your friend? That didn't seem very friendly," he persisted.

"No. Like I said before I wouldn't exactly call us friends," I sighed.

"Can we just forget about it please? I don't want to ruin the day."

"Of course."

We walked back into the barn where Lenny had set out some bread and cheese on the table.

"Just a little treat before you head home." He patted the seat next to him, inviting me to join him.

"Now I know that it's not much but I wanted to get you a little something," said Lenny as he handed me a small parcel wrapped in brown paper and tied with string. I hadn't expected anyone to know that it was my birthday let alone to be receiving any presents. I pulled at the string slowly until it loosened away from the parcel, the paper came away easily after that. I could feel two pairs of eyes watching me expectantly and it made me uncharacteristically nervous to be the centre of attention. When I pulled the paper away it revealed a small sketchpad and a new set of pencils.

"Oscar said that you like to draw so I thought this might come in useful."

"I love them, they are perfect," I exclaimed as I threw my arms around him. "Thank you so much."

Oscar walked me home a little later, my new possessions tucked carefully inside my jacket to protect them from the cold.

"Today has been the best day I can remember for a long time," I muttered as we walked beneath the twilight.

"Were you surprised?" he asked. I could just make out the smile playing on his lips.

"Completely. It was perfect." I wasn't sure how I could put exactly how I felt about it into words. He had made a day that had grown to mean nothing to me into something unbelievably special.

"I wish it didn't have to end," he said as we came to a stop just before the cottage.

"Then don't let it," I whispered as I edged closer to his body heat. His arms automatically wrapped around me and I lay my head against his chest; our hearts beating in unison. I don't know how long we stood there for, I didn't even care, I just knew that there was nowhere else that I would rather be.

"You better go in before you freeze," he whispered against my hair. He moved his head so that his lips pressed against my forehead and I counted three blissful seconds before he moved them away. He didn't move away from me though, instead he laid his head to rest against mine and I was almost sure that he was going to kiss me – properly this time. I closed my eyes and held my breath, waiting eagerly for that moment. I felt his head move away from me instead of closer and my heart sank with disappointment. It wouldn't surprise me if he didn't feel the same way about me, there seemed to be an awful lot of that going around after all. The look in his eyes said otherwise though, they told me that he wanted it as much as I did. I wanted to reach up and press my lips to his but the moment had gone, it was too late now.

"Why are you back so late?" were the words that greeted me as I walked in the door.

"I've been out," I threw back.

"What you got there?" he asked as he spotted the brooch and sketchpad as I removed my jacket.

"Why on earth have you got presents?"

I didn't respond straight away, just stared at him blankly. I don't know why it hurt, I shouldn't have been surprised that my father of all people would be the one to forget.

"Because it's my birthday."

Chapter 17

My unexpected birthday celebrations had temporarily wiped my mind of any of the problems surrounding my father, but they all came rushing back as soon as I was alone – along with the pressing matter of what I was going to do about Edward. Life went straight back to normal, my brain working double time as I tried to figure out a solution for both problems; neither of which was looking to be particularly easy. Stupidly I thought it would be easiest to deal with Edward first since I would definitely have to be dealing with this one alone. I spotted him as I was working in the gardens but as soon as he noticed me looking in his direction he turned and walked the opposite way. I would have chased after him but it would have looked far too suspicious, plus it was being made pretty clear that he wasn't going to cooperate easily.

I sighed and picked the spade back up. My hands were stiff from the crisp coolness that sat in the air, the gardening gloves that I usually wore had been destroyed beyond repair when I had unsuccessfully tackled a rose bush. I wrinkled my nose, or attempted to anyway, to see how my face was faring in the cold weather; the lack of movement answered that question. I could tell from the tightness that my nose and cheeks would be a bright pink though thankfully my mass of hair was proving to be somewhat useful in keeping my ears slightly warmer. It was abnormally cold for this month, perhaps winter was coming early.

I heard panting before I felt the golden Labrador jump on me. I quickly looked around me to check whether or not his owner was with him but there was no sign of another's presence, so I knelt down beside the playful dog who was patiently waiting for my attention. I was scratching his belly, his wagging tail thumping happily against my foot, when an angry voice filled the air.

"Toby I told you not to come here. Get back here, now," Edward demanded, whistling to get the dog's attention when he didn't respond. Toby padded back towards his owner, his head bowed solemnly. I could only imagine that he was disappointed that all the attention that was being lavished on him had been ended abruptly.

"In the future stay away from my dog." Hatred seeped out of every word he reluctantly spoke to me. I couldn't quite understand why he was acting in this manner; I had never expected him to reciprocate my feelings but then again I had also never meant for him to find out the truth about how I felt. He had said that I had ruined everything and I was well aware of that, it was the main reason I had forced myself to be content with what we were in the hope that at least that would stay the same.

"I'm sorry that I said what I did, I didn't even know that I had but I can't take it back. It can't be changed now. So why do you have to be like this?" My voice croaked as I struggled to keep up a calm front.

"You should never have even felt it," he spoke bluntly, turning to face me. There was no trace left of the Edward that I knew.

"I can't help how I feel, believe me I've tried to change things. Do you think I was happy about it?" He just stared at me, his face void of expression. "I never planned on saying anything, I never wanted you to know. I knew that nothing was ever going to happen. I just wanted to be your friend. But now that is all ruined."

"Yes it is, and it is your own fault. My mother was right, I never should have been friends with you." He looked me up and down and I felt naked beneath his stare, once again being reminded of the fact that I was beneath him. It didn't matter that it was the truth, Edward had always treated me like I was an equal; it had never mattered where either of us had come from, but that was all being proved differently now.

"What do you mean your mother was right?"

"She said you weren't good enough for me, that you would just become attached and create some ridiculous fantasy about us."

Even though I had been expecting the answer it still hurt. After the conversation I had had with my father I was well aware that Lady Barrow showed little affection for me, but I didn't think it went that far.

"Can't we just forget about it? Just be friends again. Nothing has to change," I begged. I couldn't bear the thought of him being like this with me.

"It can never be forgotten and we never should have been friends in the first place." His ice blue eyes stared straight at me, daring me to say anything further. I scrutinised his face for any sign of reluctance over what he was doing, but if there was he gave nothing away.

"But I don't want to lose you."

"You never had me in the first place." The words cut through me like a knife. As I watched him walk away I felt my body crumble as I knew that this time it was forever.

For the rest of the day tears pricked at my eyes every time I thought back to the conversation. I refused to let myself cry though, I wouldn't give him the satisfaction. I knew I had to be strong, there could be no sign of weakness so every time I felt the warm rush of tears approach I closed my eyes and breathed in deep. I told myself that it didn't matter, that there were far more important things and that it would all get sorted eventually. I knew I was lying to myself because the truth was an entirely different matter; I had just lost the one friend I had always had, the person I had always thought would be there. All because of some stupid feelings that were no longer even relevant, but he was never going to believe that, it was unlikely that he was even going to talk to me again.

I couldn't feel the cold anymore, I was numb. I was hardly aware of my body as I made my way back home, my feet guided me along the path as I stared straight ahead - oblivious to anything around me. I didn't even acknowledge my father as I walked in, just headed straight to the kitchen and filled a saucepan with water. I could feel his eyes on me, waiting for the first words that would break the silence that had grown between us once again. If he was expecting happy tales or kind words then he needed to re-think the situation. I had set myself a task and there was no point playing nice about it that never seemed to get me anywhere. I figured it was best to just throw all the disappointment into one day so that I could tackle the task of overcoming it at the same time.

I took my time boiling the water for my drink. Holding the warm mug tightly between my hands I let the aroma of the coffee beans blow into my face.

"You need to tell me exactly how much trouble you are in and why before I can even think about helping you."

It was clear from the stunned look that appeared on his face that he hadn't been expecting that. I sipped at the boiling contents of my mug whilst retaining eye contact with him. If either of us was going to break it was going to be him; there was no way that I was going to back down. If anything had been made clear over the last couple of months it was that I had inherited my stubbornness from my father.

"I owe a lot of money," he muttered reluctantly.

"Why?" I asked instantly,

He paused before responding, I could see him toying with the correct words.

"Gambling," he whispered through a sigh eventually. I probably should have been shocked but I wasn't, at least it explained why there was barely any money around; we were just about surviving on a pittance.

"It doesn't matter; there is no way I could ever get the money together to pay them back."

I wasn't going to argue with that it wasn't like we usually had a lot of money anyway.

"Who do you owe it to?" I hadn't moved from my spot where I was leaning against the kitchen counter. I knew my voice was stern but it seemed to be working. My green eyes were hard as they interrogated my father who was crumbling under my unforgiving stare.

"There's a few."

"Who?"

"Griggs, Porter and Lambert." The first name shot through me like a bullet. My instinct was to reach up and feel for the invisible bruise that had long since faded, the warmth of my fingertips sent pain tingling through the phantom injury. My father looked pained as he watched my reaction to the name, his grey eyes lined with worry as he also remembered what his only child had been put through for him. I guessed that one of the other names must have belonged to the unwanted visitor from a few nights previously, though neither of them sounded familiar to me.

"When do they want the money by?" I sighed; there was much less conviction to my voice now.

"Two weeks ago."

My father slumped into the sofa that looked like it would swallow him up. I noticed how unwell he looked; his skin had a greyish tint to it and you could almost see his bones. It was a shock to see this figure in comparison to the well-built man who had brought me up.

"What will they do now?" I asked dreading the answer that I knew was coming.

He shook his head refusing to say anything.

"Pa, what will they do?" I repeated. In spite of myself I could feel myself wanting to tell him that everything was going to be okay, that we would get through it together. But I couldn't.

"They said that what happened to you was nothing compared to when they are finished with me." His voice broke as he finally let it out and in the dim candlelight I could see the fresh tears that were trickling from his eyes. The sight of them made me well up but I knew that I had to remain strong; I had to fix this before anything bad happened.

His hunched shoulders started to shake as he gave into the sobs that escaped his broken body. I slowly made my way over to him, perching on the arm of the sofa next to him.

"I'm so sorry," he spluttered through his tears. I flung my arms around him and squeezed tightly. I sat there consoling my father knowing that it was the wrong way round, he should be fixing my problems. But I didn't care. I let him cry and swayed us gently just like he had always done for me when I was a little girl crying over the pain of a fall rather than a shattered life. I wanted to rewind time and change it all; bring my mother back so my father would never have taken up drinking or gambling to try and drown his sorrows, and I would have listened to my father when he told me to stay away from Edward so that I wouldn't now be nursing a broken heart.

Chapter 18

Oscar stared out at the trees as I told him everything I had learnt the night before. I had spent the entire night trying to come up with a solution but when the morning arrived and I was still coming up blank I knew that I wasn't going to be able to do this alone. Without even thinking about it I had hunted down Oscar and made him my new thinking partner.

"I know it's a lot to take in but do you think you can help?" I asked hopefully.

He nodded slowly but he didn't speak, just stared out in front of him like there was something mesmerising that was only visible to his eye.

"Did he hurt you?" His voice was barely a whisper and I had to strain to hear before the words were carried away on the wind.

"You know, your eye." He looked at me for the first time since I had started speaking, his dark eyes glittering with the information.

"No of course not. He would never do that," I insisted. It was important that he didn't think that, it was bad enough that he now had this new incriminating information about my father without adding that to the pile. I had spent so long trying to keep it all a secret that even though it was a relief to finally have someone to help me I couldn't help but worry about what could go wrong.

"Who did it then?"

I considered trying to stick with the rake story but my heart wasn't in it; it never really had been. Plus, I was almost certain that he hadn't believed it the first time either.

"One of the men that came looking for my father," I muttered, grimacing as I waited for his reaction.

"Did you tell anyone about it?"

"Well no, not really. Edward knows a little bit I guess." His name left a burning sensation on my tongue and I noticed Oscar flinch as I spoke it. Perhaps he knew more than I had suspected.

"What did he say?" He put particular emphasis on the 'he', a hint of jealousy seeming to come through in his tone.

"Erm, he wanted me to go to the police or tell his parents."

"Why didn't you?"

"How do you know that I didn't?" I asked trying to throw him off the topic.

"Because I know you. So why didn't you?" he persisted.

"I didn't really ..." I paused knowing that the excuse of not remembering wasn't going to work this time. "I didn't want to cause any trouble," I corrected.

"You should have gone to the police," he stated. "What was his name?"

There was a look in his eyes and a scowl on his lips that warned me not to say anything else.

"It really doesn't matter anymore, it was so long ago. Can we think about what we are going to do now? Please." I kept my tones soothing as I tried to calm Oscar down at the same time as trying to quickly change the subject. Even though there wasn't any obvious signs to say he was angry, the darkening of his eyes was all I needed to see to tell me what he was feeling. He didn't move, just turned to stare back out at the trees, the wind ruffling his hair was the only movement around him.

"I had better get back to work now anyway," I said sadly. I didn't want to leave him but I knew that my presence wasn't going to help, hopefully being alone would do what I couldn't. I walked slowly back up the hill, continually stopping to look back and see if there was any sign of him following me; but he didn't move. Even as I turned the corner and lost sight of him I could tell that he would still be rooted to that spot; as permanent as an aged tree.

"Hey Emily," said the guilty voice announcing itself behind me. I put down the small spade and pushed myself up wiping my hands down the apron before turning around.

"Hey," I replied, trying to add a smile to my voice. When I heard my voice sing out sadly I knew I had failed at that too. We stood opposite each other awkwardly, both of us looking anywhere but at the other. I didn't want to be like this but he had made it pretty obvious that I had said something to make him mad and I didn't want to make the situation any worse. As the silence grew longer the aching in my chest pulled harder.

"What did I do to make you mad?" I asked, the strain in my voice made it clear how I was feeling at that moment.

"You didn't do anything," he said humbly, stepping closer to me. "I just can't stand the thought that someone hurt you and then got away with it. It's not right, but it's not you. I'm sorry I made you think that."

He pulled me close to him and hugged me tight. I breathed in the scent of soap and horses; the mixture of scents a strange yet perfect combination. I reluctantly loosened myself from his grip and looked up at him with pleading eyes.

"Will you still help me? I mean, will you help my Pa?"

"Of course I will. I just don't know how yet." He brushed one of the fly away curls off my cheek and gently tucked it behind my ear.

"You nearly done here?"

I looked around at the mess I had created turning the flower beds and laughed to myself.

"I'll probably be a little longer, still got to repot some of the plants." I managed to keep a straight face as I gave my professional answer, even though I desperately just wanted to admit that I had been in my own world – making a huge mess that was going to take forever to clean up.

"Okay, come find me when you're ready and we can talk some more about what the options are?"

"Sounds perfect." Before I had time to think about it I had kissed my fingertips and blown the affection towards him. Even though I was now sure that I had mud smeared across my lips I was far more embarrassed by what I had just done. I caught the smile on his lips as I felt the shame running up my neck and I quickly turned back to my work so that he couldn't witness the full extent of my mortification.

I took my time finishing my jobs not knowing how I was ever going to be able to face Oscar again after that. The sun had long since set by the time I made it back to my empty home. Where I had once grown to enjoy the silence it now just sounded eerie to me instantly putting me on edge. I washed myself quickly and crammed some bread and cheese into my mouth before heading back out the door. I reached up to the edging of the door, running my fingers along the dusty ridge until I felt the coolness of metal. I locked the door behind me and checked the empty lane before jogging towards the stables. I hated the fact that my independence and confidence had been cruelly taken from me because of one man; I no longer felt safe in my own home. I was so busy checking the path behind me that I ran straight into Oscar, knocking the breath out of me.

"Why you in such a rush?" he laughed as he steadied me whilst I got my breath back. "Really that eager to see me?" he joked. I was thankful for the darkness that covered us as I felt my cheeks burn.

"Just knew I was running late that's all." I couldn't bring myself to admit that I had grown scared of my own shadow.

"I was actually just coming to find you. At least you saved me the walk. Coming in?"

I nodded, still a little out of breath. The dim lighting in the barn helped to calm me a little but when I spotted two figures sitting across the table from each other I felt my stomach tighten once more.

"Do you want to go somewhere else?" Oscar whispered in my ear. But it was too late, we had already been spotted.

"What are you doing here Emmy?" my father called out.

"I could ask you the same thing," I retorted unable to control my defensive attitude. I spotted the mug sitting in front of him, but when I caught the wisp of the steam I instantly relaxed, knowing that he wasn't up to his old tricks just yet.

"I needed to get out the house. Why don't you both come join us?"

Oscar and I glanced at each other hesitantly making our way over to the two men.

"Make yourselves a drink Oscar," said Lenny. "Then you can come and meet Albert properly." I could tell from the mischievous glint in his eyes that he was going to be enjoying this far more that I was.

We sat down opposite each other, sandwiched between my father and Lenny.

"So, Bertie. Have you met Oscar before?" Lenny asked with an interfering smile.

"Not properly, no," replied my father. To give him credit he was being a lot more amicable than I had been expecting. "Although I do know that he has been spending a lot of time with my daughter."

I couldn't imagine how Oscar was feeling, even I had squirmed at that remark and I had grown up with the two of them – whereas one was his boss and the other was, well, my father. I snuck a quick glance at his face but his expression remained completely calm.

"Yes sir. I think Emily is really quite special." My father smiled at the comment and Lenny nudged me playfully.

"And are you expecting more than just spending time together?" My father asked slyly.

"Pa!" I cried out in outrage. "I think that's enough of that now, don't you?"

They both laughed, clearly pleased with their attempt at interrogating us. I grabbed Oscar's arms and led him outside not wanting to put either of us through another line of questioning.

"Sorry about that. They think they are a barrel of laughs when they get together," I muttered once we were safely outside.

"That's fine ... Emmy." His smile shone in the moonlight as he tried to sneakily ask a question without actually saying anything. I commended his approach but I chose to ignore him anyway – he would have to remain curious. But his persistence shone once again as he continued with the teasing.

"So, Emmy. Where do you want to go now, Emmy? It's a bit cold to just be wandering around outside don't you think, Emmy?"

"Fine!" I exclaimed, trying to feign annoyance even though I couldn't stop my dimples forming. "I couldn't say my name properly when I was a kid alright! My father just kind of kept calling me it." I sighed knowing it was easier to just tell him in the hope that it would make him stop.

"Now aren't you just adorable, Emmy?" He laughed loudly when he saw my face drop. He tried to reach out for my arm but I was too fast for him, darting past his fingertips and running deep into the darkness. I blindly ran, the moon providing the only light to guide me; not that I needed it. I knew the land like the palm of my hand. I ran and ran, enjoying the rush of cold air against my naked cheeks. Just as I thought I had outrun Oscar he silently snuck up on me, grabbing me and spinning me round before dropping us both to the floor.

"You're no match for me, Emmy," he said even though he was panting for breath and his heart was racing. I dug him in the arm.

"Stop teasing me about it," I remarked seriously.

"Okay I'm sorry. I really do think it is quite charming though," he said nudging closer to me. The heat of his body spread through me and I smiled up at the moon as I lay my head against his chest. The stars were winking down at us from the clear night sky; looking over us with watchful eyes. We lay there cocooned in the silence of the night. The two of us – him and me – the only people left in that outside world.

Chapter 19

I got the fire going so we could both huddle around it to keep warm. The rain had decided to surprise us as we were laying happily on the grass, soaking us to the bone before we even got the chance to stand up. The heat radiating off the flames was welcomed as it started to dry up some of the rain water.

"Maybe we shouldn't choose that as a resting spot next time," I suggested. I couldn't help laughing at the situation; it was starting to become a list the amount of times I had been caught by the rain this past year.

"Agreed. The season isn't quite right for it. Perhaps indoors is more appropriate." His smile spread wide across his face so I knew that he wasn't bothered either. Once we had stopped shivering from the cold we sat back against the sofa and I pulled the old blanket down to cover our shoulders. Our arms and legs were touching sending sparks running through me.

"So what are we going to do about this problem," he asked, addressing the topic that we had been trying so hard to avoid. I stared straight ahead watching the flames dance with each other, licking the wood they passed gracefully. I knew the problem had to be dealt with but I had no idea what there was that could be done. Even though I didn't know exactly how much was owed my father had made it pretty clear that it was too large a sum to even consider finding the money. Since he had stopped going out I had started keeping the wages hidden in a pot under my bed, only spending sparsely on food and necessities.

"Emily?" his soft voice broke through my trance.

"I have not got a clue." I turned to look at him managing half a smile.

"I could help you to pay them back?" he offered. It was the little things like this that made me realise what a selfless person he was.

"Thank you, but no. I would never ask you to do that. I'm not getting you involved in this. Well no more that you already are."

He looked as clueless as I felt, I guess that it wasn't exactly a predicament that either of us had come across before; I certainly hadn't encountered it before anyway.

"We could go try and talk to them," I suggested. "Try and come up with another solution to get the money back or something?"

Oscar just stared at me, his expression unreadable.

"I mean, maybe they aren't as bad as I am imagining them to be," I said, quickly trying to change the atmosphere in the room.

"Do you not remember what happened last time you met with one of them? Clearly they aren't looking to just be talking things over."

There was a slight hint of anger in his voice which made me feel like an idiot for even suggesting it in the first place.

"I'm sorry," he muttered. "Of course you remember. I just can't stand the thought of him being near you." He moved his arm over my shoulders and gave me a gentle squeeze.

"It was probably my fault anyway," I breathed, absentmindedly shaking my head. It was as clear in my mind as though it had only happened yesterday; the taste of blood still tickled my teeth.

"It's definitely not your fault, why would you even think that?" he asked, turning to face me. His dark eyes held onto mine trying to draw out the secrets that were hidden within.

"It's just, well, he tried … so … I … oh, I don't know." I stumbled over the words unable to retell the more incriminating part of the night.

"Emily, what happened?" concern laced his words. I wanted to tell him but it was clear from the way he had reacted earlier how much it had affected him already; I didn't want him to go and do anything that he would regret.

"Don't say it was nothing, tell me the truth," he said before I had a chance to say anything.

I paused, watching him as he braced himself for what I would say. I took in a deep breath to ready myself for what was going to happen next.

"I don't know exactly what it was, he tried to kiss me or touch me or something, so I bit his lip and that was why he hit me." Even repeating the words made me feel dirty and I was ashamed to be repeating what had happened. My words seemed to echo through the silence in the cottage. Any trace of light had been distinguished from Oscar's eyes.

"He did what?" He spoke so quietly I struggled to hear him.

"Nothing actually happened, I mean I managed to stop whatever it was he was trying to do."

"That's not the point, he still tried it!" he exclaimed. "What does he look like?"

I could picture his beady eyes looking at me through the darkness, I could recall every tiny detail about him. Too much had been said already though, it had to stop before it got out of control.

"Oscar it doesn't matter. Let's just leave it, we can't do anything about it now. Can I get you a drink?" I asked trying to take his mind off it.

"Stop trying to change the subject. He can't get away with this."

"He already has," I sighed. His silence said everything. There was no way that anyone was going to pay attention to this now, not after such a long period of time had passed. I needed to lock up the memory of that night and destroy the key.

Even though we sat in silence for quite some time I didn't try to break it; I knew he needed time to digest what had been said and I wasn't going to be the one to disturb him. The flames had dithered into bright orange embers so I shuffled along the floor to poke the burnt wood around in the hope that it would reignite the fire. I waited until the flames started licking the wood before I made my way back to Oscar. He was staring down at his knees, his head stooped so I couldn't see his eyes, but I could tell from his slumped composure what he was thinking. I tucked myself under the blanket and gently leant my head against his shoulder.

"I'm sorry," I whispered. His arm moved around to my waist and rested there; the small movement all I needed to tell me that everything was okay.

"Hasn't your father worked here for years?" asked Oscar.

"Yeah, why?"

"Well he must have quite a good relationship with the Lord and Lady, right?"

I thought back to the conversation my father and I had shared about Edward and I was unsure how exactly to answer that. Especially considering I had no idea what Edward had said about the recent events that had taken place between the two of us.

"I guess it must be pretty good," I replied curious to see where he was going with this.

"Perhaps he could ask them to loan him the money until he can pay them back?" he asked. It was sweet of him to suggest it, and in any other circumstance it may have even been a decent idea, but somehow I didn't see any plausibility in it right now.

"I'm not sure that would work, I mean I don't even have a clue what exactly it is that he owes," I sighed.

"We shall have to make him tell you then. If he wants your help then he is going to have to be more help as well." There was a determination to him that made me smile, I had never heard him say anything remotely out of turn about someone else.

"Do you really think they would loan the money when they find out what it is for? It doesn't exactly make him the most reliable person around does it?" I didn't want to put down his idea, principally because it was the only real solution that either of us had come up with. But I could also imagine exactly what my father's reaction would be when it was placed in front of him.

"Good point. Couldn't we think of something else he would need the money for?"

"All depends on how much it is. And since he isn't willing to part with that information I am guessing that it is a rather large amount of money. Plus, Edward already knows the gist of what is going on and I don't think he will play along with our lie."

My green eyes moistened as the dreadful consequences of what was going to happen ran amok in my head. Evidently these men weren't just looking to get their money back anymore – now they were looking for blood. Maybe it would be better if the police were to get involved, it would mean that my father would be almost certain to end up in prison but at least that way he would still come back to me eventually. The problem was that there was no way I could be the one to do that to him and somehow I didn't think these men were in the situation to be going to the law for help either.

"It's going to be alright. We will think of something."

"But we need to think now, we've already ran out of time!" I bit down on my bottom lip to stop it trembling and tried to clear the unfallen tears out of my eyes.

"Okay. So you don't think paying it back between us is an option, no? Not even if we got Lenny to help as well?"

I shook my head, not trusting myself to speak.

"And I certainly don't think it is a good idea to go and speak to them," he stated, anger stringing his words together. "You really don't think Lord Barrow will lend the money?"

I shook my head again slightly more enthusiastically this time.

"See, we're out of ideas," I said now that tears no longer pricked my throat.

"No, just give me a minute."

I watched him sitting there deep in thought, ideas dancing across his face. After what seemed like forever he finally spoke.

"I know you said no to paying the money back, but what if we got enough money to help him run away?"

I stopped my head from automatically shaking as I let the words sink in. It really wasn't a bad idea, in fact it was quite a good one. I could see no reason why it couldn't be achieved.

"That's quite brilliant. I really think that perhaps that could work," I said, enthusiasm shining out of me.

I saw Oscar beam at my approval and for the first time I felt that we could actually fix this impossible dilemma we had been placed in. I leaned back against the sofa, closed my eyes and smiled up at the ceiling letting the warm feeling rush through me. It was short lived though as the realisation hit me that if we were to help him run away then that would leave me on my own. Surely I was too young to have no parents ... right?

Chapter 20

The flickering of the candles reflected in my father's dull grey eyes. He remained silent as I spoke, it seemed as though each word sucked a tiny bit of life from him.

"I can't think of any other option," I muttered dejectedly.

He didn't speak. He didn't move. There were no signs that he had even heard anything I had said.

"Pa?" I spoke his name anxiously. I didn't know why he was taking it so hard, I thought it was ten times better than the other schemes we had concocted.

"You want me to go away?" he whispered. When his eyes met mine I could see the world of pain they were sheltering. His grey eyes were no longer smiling, instead they carried the stress of what his life had become; worry lines burrowed deep into his brow and dark circles and heavy lids served as a cruel reminder of what life had done to him.

"No I don't want you to, of course I don't," I insisted. "It's just, well, it's the best idea we've got."

"This is my home. It's been my life," he choked through the silence.

I completely understood what he meant but it was really the only acceptable choice that he had so I desperately needed to make him see that.

"I don't know what else to suggest, Pa. I'll get the money together for you as quickly as I can so that you can leave as soon as possible. You'll just have to lay low until then."

"Where will I go?" There was a meekness to his voice that made him sound like a small, defenceless child.

"I haven't figured that part out," I said shaking my head. I fiddled with my fingers unconsciously, starting to wonder if perhaps this hadn't been such a good idea after all. "It can't be nearby though."

Oscar's first suggestion had been to write to family and ask for their help but as far as I was aware there were no other living relatives. I had never met grandparents or aunts and uncles – then again I had never thought to ask about them either. It was going to have to be a brand new destination, one where he knew nobody and that was the worst part; he was going to be completely alone.

"I'm sorry, Pa. I really am. But there is no other option. It has to be this." I watched his body crumble as the realisation of how bad the situation was hit him. I wanted to go and help him up when I saw him fold into himself but I couldn't keep doing it anymore; I wasn't going to be there with him for much longer.

I put my hand on the door and reluctantly let myself out into the harsh wind that blew the bitter tears away from my cheeks. I breathed in deep and composed myself.

"You need to be strong," I told myself. I let the wind wash the words over me and sink into my skin. I opened my now dry eyes and walked on to continue with life as I did every day.

"Have you heard the news?" Oscar ran up to me as soon as I walked into the barn at lunch time.

"No, what's going on?" I said, unable to suppress a laugh at his excitable behaviour.

"Edward proposed to Victoria." The words shot straight through me like an arrow. I felt my heart jolt at the impact. I don't think it was so much the news of the engagement that shocked me but more the hurtful reminder that he really did not want anything to do with me anymore since he hadn't even bothered to tell me himself.

"That's exciting," I managed to say with some conviction.

"I'm surprised you didn't already know," he speculated after a moment.

"What do you mean?"

"Well you said that you were friends. I thought he would have told you himself."

"Clearly he didn't think I needed to know," I mumbled unable to keep the resentment out of my voice.

Oscar stared at me as though he was trying to figure out what was really going on behind my emerald gaze.

"Anyway, I spoke to my father," I said trying to change the subject.

"How did it go" he asked, his eyes instantly softening.

"Not great, but what can we do? Just need to get the money together now and figure out where he is going to go." Something tickled at the back of my throat and I had to breathe deep to regain control.

"I've been thinking about that actually and there's something I need to talk to you about later." There was a hidden message in his voice that I couldn't quite uncover – reluctance maybe – but it made me worried about what he was going to say.

"What's wrong with telling me now?" I asked impatiently.

"Don't think now is the best time," he said indicating the hustle and bustle of the barn; the stable boys were walking in and out, rushing about in preparation for something I had not been clued in on. "Plus I really need to get back to work now."

"What's going on?"

"Victoria and her grandmother the Duchess are arriving here tomorrow, that and the family got back this morning so need to be on top of everything. I thought you would be pretty busy as well?" I could tell from the way his eyes kept flickering towards the door that he was eager to get on so I ceased with the questioning and allowed the conversation to come to an end.

"Okay. See you later?"

"Definitely," he called back before running into the stables.

I hastened my pace and made my way to the garden to start seriously on the work I should have been stuck into hours ago. My mind had been so preoccupied that I hadn't even been paying attention to anything else that was going on. To be perfectly honest I was disappointed in myself that I had let my priorities get so mixed up. I was usually the first to be out and working hard when there was a big occasion. It only served to remind me that the sooner this was all over and done with the better; then I could get on with my life how it should be.

Thankfully there wasn't too much that needed to be done as I had been keeping on top of things. I neatened the gardens and snipped the last of the flowers for Mrs Montgomery, the housekeeper, who swapped the dying stalks she held for the fresh adornments I handed to her.

"Good day, Emily," she uttered sternly and though it wasn't overly welcoming it was more of a greeting than I got from the others so I wasn't going to complain.

"Good day," I mirrored. I watched her walking back into the house; there seemed to be a world of difference between the two classes of servants. Just watching how she walked, how they all walked, said that they thought they were better than me, the way they spoke told stories of how much more important they were and the pristine condition of their appearance said more than anything else had to. But I didn't care, I never had. I loved being outdoors and I would never envy them for one second despite what they may think.

Once I had made sure the gardens were how they should be I made my way back to the main house to get it dressed in its best clothes. I trimmed the edges of the grass that surrounded the gravel and re-potted the plants that decorated the windowsills. I took my time with the final task even though I knew Oscar was waiting to talk to me, there was something, a feeling in my stomach, which was holding me back – it was as though I already knew deep down what it was that he needed to say. My mind wandered as the different possibilities stumbled though my head; at first I thought that he didn't want to see me anymore but he hadn't been acting like that was the case. I was pretty sure he had said it in relation to my father. I then thought he was going to tell me he wanted out of this whole situation, which I could completely understand since I had no right to get him involved in the first place. My thoughts were interrupted by a small robin that flew gracefully down onto the bush that sat next to me. He danced around, hopping from foot to foot – his luscious colours vibrant against the grey day. His silent movements mesmerised me, drawing me away from the dark hole I could feel myself falling deeper into. He chirped sweetly and shortly then flew back off and somehow I knew that it was going to be alright.

Lenny was dozing in a chair at the table when I walked into the barn, the wind pulled the door shut louder than I had intended causing him to jolt back into reality.

"Sorry Lenny, I didn't mean to wake you," I said sheepishly feeling bad for intruding on his rest.

"No problem little lady, Oscar is upstairs if you want to go straight up." He shuffled back down in his chair and fell back to sleep almost as quickly as he had been woken up.

I slowly climbed the ladder feeling somewhat apprehensive at the thought of being upstairs alone with him. I poked my head up through the hole in the floorboards and scanned the room to find him lying on his bed, his arms propping his head up – hands clasped behind his neck. He looked so serene and peaceful laying there that I didn't want to disturb him but there was an air about him that was drawing me closer, moving my feet towards him as though I were a puppet.

"Oh hey, Em," he muttered sleepily when an old board creaked beneath my weight. His coffee-brown eyes peered at me through half-closed lids as he ran his hands through his ruffled brown hair, stretching his long body out slowly.

"I didn't mean to fall asleep, must have been more tired than I thought."

"I should have let you be."

"Not at all." He swung his legs over the bed and patted the space next to him. "Come sit down."

It was then that I noticed the nakedness of his hands winking up at me. He must have noticed where my gaze fell because he quickly pulled his hand away and searched for those worn brown leather gloves.

"No, please," I whispered, sitting delicately on the bed. I reached my hand out and softly placed it on his left wrist. He looked at me warily, the ghosts of his past glittering in his eyes as I reached across him for the mysterious injury.

"It's okay." I nodded slowly and gently eased my fingers across the back of his hand. At first I was surprised by how soft his skin was, particularly for that of someone who spent all their time at work outside, but it then dawned on me that those gloves kept them protected from the elements. I even felt some shame at the thought of how dry and hard my hands would feel to him, I tried to keep my touches light and delicate but I wasn't sure I managed it properly. As I traced the skin on the back of his hand I could feel the raised edges of a circular scar in the centre on his hand. At first look you wouldn't have noticed anything unusual but as I studied closer I could see the colour differences – the scar much whiter than his already pale hands. I turned his palm towards me, almost in slow motion, knowing that what I would see next was going to be much worse. The middle of his palm was pinched together, intricate pink lines shooting out of the labyrinthine ball that covered his hand. I felt his breath quicken as my finger hovered over the maze of scars. As my finger traced his injury with the minutest of touches I felt his sharp intake of breath and I pulled my hand back, afraid I had hurt him.

"I'm sorry, I didn't mean to hurt you," I said, doubt lining my words.

"You didn't," he whispered. "I just, no one has ever touched my hand like that before." He spoke softly and I could tell how scared he was at that moment. He closed his eyes as he unclenched his fist to reveal the injury; the physical suffering that I could now see went deeper than just his hand. As we sat there in silence I could hear his fears radiating off of him; all those unspoken sadness's screaming out for help.

I continued to trace the numerous lines, committing the map of his hand to my memory; letting those beautiful scars tell me their story. I stole a glance at him to find his eyes still closed and his face perfectly undisturbed as though he had fallen back to sleep. In that moment I decided to take a risk in order to tell him that I was here no matter what. I gently raised his hand as I lowered my head, softly pressing my lips against his hand. He didn't pull away, he didn't tense. He just curled his fingers so they were resting against my cheek; the feel of his fingertips sent my pulse racing.

"You have nothing to worry about, it will all be okay," I whispered. And as my green eyes met his I knew that it was true.

Chapter 21

Eventually I freed his hand and though he instinctively reached out to cover his hands back up with those gloves he stopped himself and rested them back in his lap. I watched him for a moment as he anxiously twiddled his fingers, his eyes burning into the scar that the war had left behind.

"What is it that you wanted to talk to me about?" I asked. Even though I was wary about what was going to be said I knew that he needed to be focussing on something else.

"Oh, that. I had forgotten." He suddenly seemed nervous and I couldn't help but mirror his emotion. It occurred to me that perhaps I had been too hasty in dismissing the notion that he was no longer interested in me. I hardly dared to breathe as I waited impatiently for him to continue speaking.

"I've been giving it a lot of thought and I really think it's the best thing that we can do," he said, avoiding eye contact with me. I desperately wanted to interrupt, to tell him that there was no need for this, but I remained frozen; unable to utter a single word.

"I think once we get the money together we should just send your father off. We don't pick a destination and we don't ask where he is going. He just has to go." Sorrow filled his eyes as he told me his plan. At first I was filled with relief that it hadn't been the topic I was expecting but when I eventually heard the words that relief quickly changed to dread. Oscar must have seen my expression suddenly change because he reached out to reassure me.

"I know it's not ideal, but I think it is the safest option. This way no one can trace anything back to us and if someone was to ask where he has gone, which is likely to happen, then you can answer truthfully that you don't know." Even though there was a sadness to his voice there was also an underlying eagerness that was pleading with me to understand. Deep down I knew that what he was saying was right, I think that really I had known all along that this was going to happen and that was the reason that I had been so reluctant to try and come up with a solution myself. I couldn't be angry with Oscar, after all I was the one that had forced him into making the decision for me. Despite knowing this I could feel anger bubbling to the surface just like it always did when I didn't like what was happening.

I tried to speak but the words caught in my throat and I choked on them. It was probably for the best that the shock had rendered me so otherwise I would have ended up saying something that I would have immediately regretted. I got up off the bed and walked away without a word; the silence creating miles between us.

"Emily, please," he called out, the desperate tone making my heart crack, yet I still didn't turn back. I walked swiftly out of the barn and as far away from the words as I could manage. The further I went the more my heart ached, screaming at me to turn back and face reality. But I was too weak to face the truth; I wanted to continue in a false bubble where everything was normal. I wanted my father back and I wanted him to stay there forever.

I stumbled through the door, emotion claiming me as a victim to its power. I vaguely saw the blurred outline of my father through the tears that filled my eyes and perhaps he even spoke to me but I was temporarily deaf as I clumsily made my way to my bed. I collapsed onto the hard, thin mattress and curled myself tightly into a ball, sure that if I moved my world would tear apart at the seams. I started shivering, though I'm sure it wasn't from the cold. My father must have come to check on me because I felt my scratchy blanket being drawn over my body and the feel of chapped lips pressed lightly against my head. I heard him kneel down beside my bed and he reached out to stroke the hair from my face. "Go to sleep, Emmy. Rest your tired eyes," he whispered as he ran his fingers through my curls. Those words took me back eight years, to the night of my mother's death, where my father had uttered those exact words to calm me as I lay on his lap. I reverted back to the child-like state and allowed him to soothe me until I felt my eyes drooping and I was no longer aware of anything around me.

The sound of muffled voices woke me. I felt like I had been asleep for hours but when I looked out the window the sky was still not quite black enough for it to be fully night time.

"I'm sorry but she is asleep at the moment," I heard my father say in hushed tones. From what I could tell there was no disdain towards the visitor, there was just that fatherly concern for his daughter's well-being. I waited to hear who was asking after me.

"I shall wait out here until she is ready then sir. Please tell her that I am here when she does wake," replied the familiar soft voice. There was a slight pause before my father answered.

"You can wait in here, at least it is a little warmer." I could imagine my father standing there trying to seem in control though I knew his frail body and dull eyes would give him away.

"Thank you sir, that's kind of you."

I heard the door creak to a close softly and the timid patter of footsteps across the wooden floor. I lay there silently hoping to listen in on the conversation they would have; yet it was a conversation that didn't happen. I could imagine them sitting there awkwardly, unsure what to say to one another. Oscar would be perched on the sofa looking nervously down at his hands and my father would be sat on the old rocking chair – the ominous screech of the floorboards told me that – looking at Oscar, essentially sizing him up.

I waited a little longer before I decided it was time that I saved Oscar from the uncomfortable stare of my father. I rolled out of bed and drew back the make shift curtain; the almost silent swoosh of material trumpeted through the still air. Their heads turned in unison at the noise and I felt as though I could hear the sigh of relief that came from them both.

"We didn't wake you did we?" Oscar asked. I shook my head, supressing a laugh at how he thought there silence could have disturbed my sleep. I shuffled into the kitchen to get myself a glass of water. I caught my distorted reflection in the metal of the tap: my face was still warm from the pillow; my cheeks flushed with sleep, my dusty brown curls were plastered to the side of my face where I had been laying on them, the other half was sticking out at all angles and my wide vibrant eyes shone like green jewels in the shiny metal. I hastily ran my hands through my hair to try and tidy it up, but with little success – ultimately just making it worse. I could feel two sets of eyes burning into my back, expectantly waiting for me to join them and provide an end to their awkward silence. I sat myself next to Oscar on the sofa, leaving as much space as I could between us.

"Oscar came to see if you were okay and I must say that I was wondering the same thing," remarked my father. I drummed my fingers against the glass I held in my hand in an attempt to avoid their curious gaze.

"Are you going to tell us what's wrong then?" he asked when I remained silent.

"Nothing," I replied abruptly.

I could see my father's mouth toying with what to say next, though I could tell he wasn't going to push it and I knew that Oscar wasn't going to step in because he wouldn't want to be there when my father found out what he had suggested.

"I'm fine, just tired is all," I added to settle their interests. I turned my head slightly to glance at Oscar only to find his dark eyes already studying my face. It was clear from his furrowed brow and the distraught look written across his face that he desperately wanted to talk to me but he didn't dare to utter a word with my father in the room. Perhaps my father could sense it because he pulled himself up out of the chair and moved towards the door.

"I said I would go see Lenny. You don't mind do you, Emmy? I won't be long."

"That's fine, Pa," I muttered. His grey eyes reflected silver in the moonlight and I saw the kindness that dwelt within them; the colour of soft-silver melting.

Oscar waited until the door was safely shut and the crunch of footsteps had travelled out of hearing before he turned to face me.

"Emily, I'm so sorry if I upset you. I never wanted to do that which is why I was so unsure about mentioning it in the first place, but I do still think that it is the best option. I know you don't want to hear it, and I really am sorry, but you asked for my help and that is what I am trying to do," he spoke hastily, stumbling over the words that he had been rehearsing whilst he had sat there. The silence that sat between us was painful, made worse by the knowledge that it was my fault. I needed to speak, to close the distance that was growing between us, but the words wouldn't come to me.

"Please forgive me," he begged.

I shook my head before realising that he would interpret that differently, and the hurt look on his face told me that he had.

"I didn't mean that. You don't need to be forgiven, you haven't done anything wrong. I know that you're right, I just didn't want to hear it," I reassured him. His body relaxed as soon as I finished speaking.

"I don't blame you, I wouldn't want to hear it either," he said.

"How am I supposed to tell him though? He will think that I don't want anything to do with him." I could feel my heart breaking at the thought of it, just envisioning the hurt in his eyes was enough to kill me inside. Oscar looked at me with pity in his eyes, not knowing what to say to make me feel any better. I was grateful though, I didn't want to hear words that meant nothing, I needed to hear the truth so that I could start to accept it.

"We need to figure out how much money he will need so that we can start getting it together and see if we need to ask Lenny for help," he muttered. I could tell that he didn't want to be adding to the upset but I knew that it was best to just get it all out there now. I nodded, deep in thought.

"We need to think about transport and money for food and rent. At least enough to keep him going until he can find work," as I said that it struck me that we had been missing one major detail. "What are we going to do about his job? Won't he need a reference?"

Oscar looked blank, the thought as new to him as it was to me. It was becoming clearer by the second that we were in way over our heads; there were all the tiny details that we had overlooked that were key to the success of the plan.

As we sat there staring at the near impossible road that lay before us I felt utterly useless. Somewhere, far down, I could feel an itch in my heart, but I made a point not to scratch it; I was too afraid of what might come leaking out.

Chapter 22

Oscar was gone by the time my father came back and I had made sure that I was safely pretending to sleep so as to avoid the conversation that I knew I needed to have. The next morning when the sun painted the sky a dark orange I was up and ready to get to work.

"Can you wait two minutes and I will come with you?" came a voice from the darkness. The shock of the statement made me obey. We walked out into the early morning sunshine in silence, not daring to face the harsh reality that was coming for us.

"Shall we trim the hedges today?" he asked, eliminating that silence. I simply nodded not trusting that the right words would leave my mouth. He stopped to pick up the right equipment, leaving me to stare up at the blossoming sky; the sun was gradually making its way up to the centre of the sky, pulling the clouds in on an invisible rope.

I sat on the damp grass watching as my father expertly trimmed and shaped the small green leaves; beautiful shapes starting to appear in the uniform, squared hedges like circular memories of my childhood. I didn't listen to the usual snip of metal hitting metal, instead my ears filled with the creak of the old wooden handles as they tried to keep up with the workload. I lay back and closed my eyes enjoying the sound of someone else hard at work, welcoming the rare chance to fully appreciate nature at its best; the air was fresh, the smell of forthcoming rain lingering on the breeze which blew lightly through the falling leaves. The branches were gradually becoming more naked as the seasons progressed.

"Is there something else you should be doing?" asked the voice breaking my solitude.

"I got a lot done yesterday so I am in no rush," I replied, feeling more relaxed than I had in a long time.

"You could always help me," he suggested though I could tell that he knew he wasn't going to get far, but I noted his effort.

"You're so much better at it than I am," I said cheekily even though it was actually true. It was a skill that I was still yet to master and when I thought about it I realised that I probably should be watching him more closely so that I could learn from the best. "Plus, thought it would do you good to get some exercise."

He chuckled to himself at my comment, playfully jiggling his non-existent belly. "That's fine Emmy, but you can't let anyone see you laying around like that or you'll end up getting both of us fired, so at least try and act like you are busy." There was a hint of the old Albert lurking behind those words so I chose not to argue it. I took on board what he said and made myself useful by starting to rake up a mixture of the fallen leaves and the discarded hedge, creating a pile of unwanted debris.

Hushed voices travelled through the maze of trees that I was standing in the middle of, safely hidden amongst the branches above the ground.

"You mean she actually told you that she loved you?" spoke the sickly sweet voice, painful words dripping from her tongue like melted caramel.

"Exactly that. I was disgusted," came the venomous reply. "And then she had the audacity to tell me that she wanted us to be together."

"I never said that," I said to myself outraged, somehow managing to keep the words confined to my head, curious as to what they would say next.

"How could she ever think that you would want to be with someone like her?" she managed to say through her laughter as though my shame was her greatest source of amusement. Anger started to swirl around my body and I had to fight the urge to jump down and defend myself against his lies. It was no shock that he had turned the distressing memory into meaningless stories to impress his friends, I wasn't even surprised that he was adding lies to get more laughs – he was just showing me his true colours and for once I was grateful that I had finally seen them. I looked down on two identically blonde heads as they unknowingly walked beneath me still laughing, oblivious to the pain their arrogance caused. At that moment the clouds poured over and karma came falling down on the rich mannequins. A girlish shriek escaped from the doll-like mouth of Victoria as she turned to run back to the house her entertainer running swiftly after her even though I had never known a spot of rain to bother him before.

The rain stopped almost as suddenly as it had started, though I could still see the pair of them running towards the safety of the walls. There was a part of me that hoped she would slip on the fresh mud and ruin her perfect hair and immaculate purple dress – not that I would have admitted this – but unfortunately she managed to totter back to the house unscathed.

"How can the tiniest bit of rain cause so much damage?" complained my father when he saw me walking towards him.

"You've been cooped up inside for too long, it's made you soft. You'll get used to it again soon enough," I said as I secured my wet curls to the top of my head with a pin. Even though the branches had shielded me from the eye line of the blonde duet they hadn't protected me from the sudden downpour of rain. Though I am sure if they had been more observant to anything but themselves they would have spotted me unintentionally eavesdropping on their conversation.

"I'm just saying that it's not so great when it is also so cold," he stated sulkily.

"Since when has that ever bothered you before?" I remarked a little more harshly than I had intended – apparently the overheard conversation had affected me more than I had previously thought.

"You're right, I'm being pathetic. Were there any apples left?" he asked, quickly changing the topic.

"No, they were bare," I muttered. I should have apologised for snapping at him but the opportunity seemed to have passed now. I couldn't shake the feeling that I was ruining what could potentially be one of the last days we got to spend together. As I was busy reliving the past moments Oscar came bounding towards us with basket in hand.

"Oh hello Mr Thorne, I didn't realise you were working today. Would it be okay if Emily came to have lunch with me?" he asked, suddenly very considerate of what he may think.

"Of course, don't let me stop your plans my boy." He smiled down at me like he had always done to let me know that it was okay to go out and play. Oscar and I started to walk away when I remembered that my father would be going without.

"Do you mind if I take something to him?" I muttered sheepishly, hand on basket.

"Of course not."

I unwrapped my sandwich and took out half, carefully refolding the paper over the top. I ran back to my father and handed him half the sandwich.

"Thank you little one," he said and I ran off to meet back up with Oscar.

"Everything alright?" he asked as we made our way to our usual spot.

Another lie was starting to grow in my mouth but I found it impossible to let it out. I said, "Not particularly," not a lie but also not revealing the whole truth. I decided it was easiest to let him infer the meaning for himself and then take it from there. He stopped and stepped in front of me so that it also stopped me from walking any further.

"Look, I know that you're upset by all of this but we are going to sort it out, I promise. I know it isn't ideal but it will be fine," he said reassuringly. He had interpreted my answer exactly how I thought he would but I couldn't help feeling disappointed that I hadn't taken the opportunity to tell the truth, nevertheless I'm sure it was for the best that he still didn't know what had happened. Instead I just nodded to let him know that I had heard what he had said even though his words had pretty much washed over me.

I was trundling back towards the gardens, in no rush to get back to work, when I noticed someone walking towards me. They were too far away for me to make out who it was so I chose to ignore them and continue on my way. However, after only a few more steps I heard a voice being carried away on the wind – too quiet for me to hear the words. This time I stopped and turned towards the fast approaching figure to make sure they weren't in any trouble. They had travelled a lot further than I had in those moments, their steps more urgent, so I could now see that it was Victoria that was walking towards me purposefully. I wanted to turn and run in the opposite direction but it was too late for she had seen me acknowledge her, so I now had no choice but to face the wrath of the perfect doll that was coming to confront me.

"You're the gardener right? Emily?" she called out before she had even reached me.

I stuttered over the words - suddenly paralysed by nerves – and I found myself unable to speak so I simply nodded, eyes wide like a startled rabbit. This was the first chance that I had been able to see her up close properly; her light blonde hair was pinned into a neat bun at the nape of her neck, not a strand out of place, her skin was as clear and smooth as a porcelain dolls and her eyes were a deep blue – so dark they were almost violet. She was beautiful, that was undeniable, but there was also a darkness that I could see beneath her perfect features that seemed to take away some of that beauty.

"I take it that you know who I am?" she asked expectantly.

I nodded again to respond and she scowled at me.

"Are you mute? Do you not know how to speak?"

"Sorry ma'am, yes I know who you are ma'am," I spoke, finding my voice.

"Then you will know that Edward and I are engaged to be married," she stated, a sly smile appearing on her lips.

"Yes ma'am," I uttered, unsure where this was headed.

"Then you need to know that you don't want to mess with me so I suggest that you stay far away from him. You don't speak to him, you don't touch him, and you don't even look at him!" she threatened. She had gradually got closer to me, her finger pointing at me vehemently, her rounded nail just inches from my face now.

"Someone like you has no right hanging around someone of his class so you need to forget anything that you thought was acceptable," she spat at me as she looked me up and down with a look of disgust.

"I'm not sure I know what you're going on about ma'am," I said feigning innocence. It would have been just as easy to nod my compliance and get on with my day but her threats had only refuelled my desire to defend myself. At first she seemed taken aback by my defiance and for a moment I thought that I had knocked her off her high-horse, but she managed to jump back on in the blink of an eye and her intimidating stare was back in place.

"You know exactly what I'm talking about. I told you not to mess with me, you will regret it if you do!" she exclaimed spitefully. With those final words she turned on her heel and stomped away from me like a child throwing a tantrum, leaving me standing there open-mouthed and stunned by the one-sided heated exchange.

Chapter 23

"Have you spoken to your father yet?" Oscar asked later that evening. It was definitely more of a reminder than a question since he knew that I hadn't.

"I will. I didn't want to ruin the day," I said truthfully, even though it was a poor excuse. I knew that as soon as those words hit my father everything was going to change again and I didn't want our last days together to be spoilt by pain and regret. There was another reason that I had been holding back, one that I couldn't tell Oscar, I had decided that I was going to try and talk to the men that were after my father; to try and grasp at the almost invisible threads of hope that I had left. I understood what Oscar had meant when he said that it was too dangerous to face them but I would never forgive myself if I didn't at least try. All I had to do was promise myself that I would be careful and if the situation seemed even slightly dangerous then I would get out as quickly as I could.

"What's going through your mind?" Oscar asked, pulling me out of my trance.

"Nothing," I answered probably too quickly. He didn't say anything but his eyes told me that he knew there was something that I wasn't telling him.

"Actually I should probably go now, you know, talk to my Pa before it gets too late," I muttered as I hurried to the door. If I had thought about it then I would have noticed that my behaviour was blatantly suspicious and I should have realised that Oscar knew me a lot better than I gave him credit for. Instead, when I made it outside with no interruptions I let out a sigh of relief as I leant against the wooden barn door, my nails gripping between the planks of wood.

I walked slowly into the village trying to think of what I was going to say. It hadn't even occurred to me how I was going to find them, up until now I had just assumed that they would be at the pub but if they weren't there then I would be left clueless as to where I was to turn to next.

"Griggs, Porter and Lambert," I whispered to myself, repeating the names over and over again until they were engrained in my memory.

I stared at the yellow lights that lit up the pub, watching the movement inside through the steamed windows. A crunch behind me caused me to snap my head round anxiously. The lane behind me was completely empty; unseen eyes watching me through the darkness. The naked branches reached out for me with twig-like fingers, the wind whispering my name as it blew past me.

"You're just being paranoid, Emily. There's nothing there," I told myself, forcing myself to turn back around and walk to the pub to face my fears.

The door seemed ten foot tall, looming over me as I stood before it. I placed my cold hands on the handle and threw my weight into it, pushing the heavy door open. I was overwhelmed by the stench of tobacco and beer that hit me as I entered the pub. Silence swiftly followed as drunken heads turned to face me.

"You can't be in here miss," said the man positioned behind the bar.

"I know," I said meekly. "I'm just looking for some people, could you help me?"

"Names?" he demanded as he wiped the dirty cloth over the sticky surface of the bar.

"Erm, G...Griggs, Porter and ..." my skin felt cold and clammy as I panicked as I tried to remember the last name. "Lambert!" I exclaimed when I remembered.

The bar man repeated the names with a deep chuckle. "What do you want with them?" he asked and I could sense the beginnings of a warning forming on his tongue.

"I need to talk to them," I muttered nervously. He eyed me suspiciously trying to figure out what a young girl like me could want with them.

"They're not in tonight," he stated, his lack of eye contact revealing his lie.

"Now, John, what are you doing lying to the girl?" a voice said before turning its attention to me. "And what do you want with them?" The man leaning against the bar was no taller than me with a bright burst of red hair that extended scruffily to his beard. As his shady eyes looked over me his lips spread into a slimy smile revealing several missing teeth.

"I just want to talk," I managed to stutter.

"Follow me then," he beckoned. My stomach was quickly filling with dread and the voice in my head was telling me that I needed to get out now but I stubbornly – and stupidly – ignored it and allowed my feet to follow after the stranger. He led us round the back and through a door that was hidden in the corner. He opened the door for me, acting the gentleman as he guided me into the smoke filled room, his hand creeping to the bottom of my back as I glided past him. It took all my strength to stop myself from slapping his hand away.

As my eyes adjusted to the smoky haze that decorated the room I saw the men that were huddled around the circular table, cigars hanging carelessly out the side of their mouths.

"What you got there?" asked an unmistakable voice that sent chills running down my spine.

"She said she wants to talk to us."

"Well have a seat then girl and do begin," Griggs said sarcastically. Either the smoke was camouflaging me or he didn't remember my face because he showed no signs of recognition. I nervously took the seat opposite him, trying hard to avoid his beady gaze. The smile that slowly appeared over his lips told me that he had now placed my face though he didn't reveal my identity to anyone else; as though I was his dirty, little secret.

"It's about my father," I started.

"Speak up!" called out the tall, dark-haired one. Porter or Lambert I wasn't sure.

"My father," I restarted, coughing to clear the nerves in my throat.

"He, erm well, he owes you some money and I wanted to see if we could think of some other way to resolve it." I felt like I was standing before a roomful of judges who were taking note of every word and sound that I made. Sweat seemed to be pouring from my trembling hands and I tried to wipe them on my coat inconspicuously. The three of them exchanged knowing glances, revealing their nicotine stained teeth.

"Thorne's daughter, right?" asked the red-headed one, inching closer to me.

"Back off, she's mine," Griggs spoke eagerly. The smell of danger was hitting me square in the face but their unfaltering gaze was leaving me motionless in the chair; my arms and legs were as useless as they would have been had they been strapped there. The sounds of fingertips drumming against the table thundered through my ears, the squeak of chair legs being pushed along the floor carved through my body.

"This was a mistake," I whispered somehow managing to push myself onto my shaking legs.

"Where do you think you're going?" asked Griggs. "If your precious father can't face us himself then we can tell you what we have been wanting to say to him."

I thought about calling out but it would have been no good; it was unlikely that I would be heard over the noise of the pub and even if I was there was no guarantee that anyone would come to my aid. The one thing I was sure of, however, was that I needed to get out of here, and now. The only advantage I had was that all three of them were standing the opposite side of the table to me, placing me closest to the door – though that wasn't to say that I was certain to make it there first. I watched them carefully as they stood there sneering at me, trying to calculate the best time to make my move. It was obvious that they were waiting for me to run but I had no choice other than to do exactly that, so I kicked the chair over with my foot, leaping over the upturned legs towards the door. I made the fatal mistake of pushing at the door impatiently shaking the handle to let me out. I figured out that I needed to pull just at the right moment, throwing myself out the door as a hand reached out for me, fingers grazing my shoulder as I fell past it. The commotion caused the punters to turn in my direction but no one made to help me. I gathered myself and hurried out the pub, letting the door slam behind me as I sprinted down the lane. The cold air was painful to take in but I couldn't slow myself so I continued to gasp down the iciness. I didn't look around, just kept running; each step I took echoed in the stillness of the night. I was convinced they were chasing me so I ran straight past the cottage knowing that would be the first place they would look for me. I kept going, hoping that my speed and the head start would lead me to safety before they could catch up. I sped towards the barn, flinging myself through the wooden door. I landed in a heap on the floor, only now allowing myself to stop. The creak of the floorboards above told me that someone had noticed the disturbance and was coming to check what was going on.

"Emily!" called out the voice, clearly struck by the crumpled head on the floor. "What happened? Are you okay?" he asked as he hurried down the ladder to reach my side. Oscar's hand lightly gripped my shaking arms to sit me up.

"I'm ... sorry," I said as I gasped for breath. I didn't want to explain and I didn't need to. He had known from the start that something was going on and it only took those two words to confirm his suspicions. It must have taken all his strength to hold back further questions in order to comfort me.

"They followed me!" I exclaimed, suddenly remembering why I had been running. Oscar instantly jumped up and was out through the door in no time. I waited nervously, breathing heavily as I sat there alone, anxiously awaiting the next move. Oscar walked back in shaking his head.

"There's no one there, Em," he said soothingly.

"No, I heard them. They must be hiding," I cried out meekly.

"There's no one there," he repeated, kneeling down to gather me in his arms. I allowed his strong, steady arms to wrap themselves around me as I silently regretted the mess that I had just created.

Chapter 24

My father's rusty silver eyes spilt over when I finally built up the courage to tell him what was going on.

"Why did you go there?" he asked quietly.

"I don't want you to leave, I thought I could sort something else out." I was still shaken up by what had happened but the realisation of what we were dealing with had stormed towards me with all its tricks and fancy shows. There was now a new darkness that surrounded me and it seemed like there was no light left to guide me home.

"Did you know she was going?" This time the question was directed at Oscar. I had forgotten that he was here with me; he had lifted my trembling body, gently coaxing me outside to fight the demons that were holding me down. He had bravely ignored my cries of anguish and insisted that it had to be done – now more than ever. By trying to help I had only managed to make things worse.

"No sir. The first I knew about it was when she showed up. I would have stopped her had I known," assured Oscar.

My father nodded to himself gradually taking everything in.

"We've got some money together though it is not quite as much as we had wanted. Lenny will help though," Oscar said.

"No, don't get him involved."

"Pa, there's no choice. There is no way we have enough to help you out and I'm not letting you go unless I know you're not going to fall into more trouble," I explained.

"Emmy, I can find a job. Even if it isn't in gardens I will find a job somewhere and I am sure that I can find somewhere to stay. You don't need to worry about me it's for the best that I go and I think it will be safer the sooner I leave." It was the most he had said on the matter - I had grown used to the stumbled answers and abrupt questions - but this time he sounded sure of himself as though in his head the matter had finally been settled. It was that new confidence that I heard in his voice that stopped me from arguing. I wanted to be sure that he was going to survive on his own but there was no way that I could have that assurance; I just had to let him go and hope for the best.

Oscar left, telling us that he would be back soon – I knew that he was going to talk to Lenny even if he didn't say it.

"He's good for you," my father said into the darkness. The scent of approval settled on the air and the true meaning of his words reached out to me; nestling between his words I heard him whispering that at least he knew he was leaving me in good hands

Those good hands arrived into the silence carrying a weight of help. He dropped the coins out of the bag onto the wooden table;

the chime of hope rang clear as they landed. I ran into my room, grabbing the can hidden beneath my bed. I pulled out the few coins that I would need to keep me going until I next got paid and proceeded to empty the remaining contents onto his ready-made pile. The mound scattered across the table and it looked like there was a sufficient amount there though I knew that some of the coins were almost worthless. Lenny remained an anonymous contributor, though I made a note to thank him later, and I couldn't help but wonder how Oscar had managed to save up so much and I felt bad that it was likely these were his savings from the terrible scars he had received in the war.

"This will be enough to get you there and get you set up," stated Oscar.

"Thank you," came the humbled reply. It was hard to imagine what was going on inside my father's head right now, his emotions must have been in turmoil, but on the outside he remained strong. He looked on at us with gratitude despite the tears and anger that he was desperately holding back.

"So, the last step is to decide when I leave." He said what we were all thinking but were too scared to say. It still twisted my stomach to hear it spoken out loud. I could feel the tears creeping up my throat and the room suddenly seemed too small for the three of us. My legs took control of the rest of my body and ran me out of the door into the refreshing night air.

"No, leave her," I heard my father say, stopping the footsteps from running after me.

Panic was taking over and I struggled to regain control of the ragged breaths that were shaking my body. Tears covered my cheeks and I let them sink back into my skin, no longer wanting to hide the truth of how I felt. I stared up at the motionless sky, the scattering of stars poking holes of light into the jet-black sky. The moon shone down on me providing a comforting glow and the smell of the fresh night air flowed through my veins. I could hear voices echoing beyond the closed door behind me but I blocked out the noise, wanting to be anywhere but there. Instead I stood alone in the colours of the night, hoping the breeze would twist around me and pull me away.

The door clicked softly in the distance and I could see the silhouette making its way to where I lay sheltered beneath the tall oak tree. He sat next to me without a word; there was no movement to disturb the peaceful bubble I had created. Though he didn't speak his silent words gathered around him, screaming out loudly. As bad as it sounded I didn't want to hear what he had to say but it was inevitable that it was going to happen.

"He's going to ask for his reference tomorrow," his whisper echoed loudly through the lonely night. "He will tell them that his sister is ill so he has to go and look after her and her children. They won't be able to argue that, not if he says the husband was killed in active duty," he continued, answering my unspoken question. There was a sympathetic edge to his tone which told me that it was all coming to an end. Whereas before he had remained focused and strong for my benefit it felt like it was all now being replaced by an overwhelming sadness; a sadness that foretold what was coming for me.

Chapter 25

I moved my work closer to the main house as I waited impatiently for my father to return. I had spotted him heading towards the house just after what the sun told me was eleven; his head held high as he went to ask for the acknowledgement he deserved. The minutes turned into hours as I absentmindedly toyed with the same plant, unable to concentrate on anything but the blank door that remained closed. I jumped up when I saw the door crack open and I had to hold myself back from running to greet him. My arms and legs twitched anxiously as I stood there willing him to hurry up. He eventually made his appearance, trudging towards me with a sad smile on his face.

"How did it go?" I made myself ask.

"I got the reference and a month's wages," he replied avoiding the question. I wished that I could have been in there with him, that I could have heard all their words and seen the expressions on their faces because I knew that I wasn't going to be getting all that information now.

"But what did they say?" I pushed.

"Nothing much, just that they were sad to see me go. Don't worry though, I asked them, well begged them, to let you keep your job."

It hadn't even occurred to me that my job may be in jeopardy, not because I was so arrogant I thought I would be safe but for the reason that I had been so concerned about what would happen to my father that I hadn't stopped to consider where my future lay. Did it mean that I would also have to be looking for a new job? And what about the cottage? I didn't think for one second that they were going to be letting me stay there on my own – not that I could afford to do so anyway.

"I'm going to head back to the cottage, start sorting things out," he muttered interrupting my stampede of unanswered thoughts. As he walked away I watched him taking in his surroundings; enjoying the imprint of nature. I'm sure he was thinking that it would be his last time, and that may have been true for these particular gardens, but the smell of the fresh grass and the birdsong would never leave someone who truly cared for it.

I came home to find my father slumped across the sofa, an empty bottle cradled against his chest. There was a crumpled note lying on the floor beside him, the black writing bold against the snow-white paper:

For Being A Friend. L.

I pried the empty bottle from his grasp and covered him with the blanket, feeling nothing over what lay before me. It did, however, make me wonder what Oscar had told Lenny as the offer of alcohol seemed inappropriate if he had known the whole story. For had he known it would have been insensitive to us both; firstly for providing my father with the gift of his downfall and secondly for rewarding me with the worry of what would happen next. If my father had so willingly accepted the enemy into his arms then how was I to know that all the hard work wasn't going to be thrown away again, this time in a secret town where there was no one to save him. His drunken snores reverberated off the walls and I found myself holding onto each one subconsciously knowing that I would miss them. He must have already been to the train station for the ticket stub was placed in the centre of the table, drawing my eyes to its print. He was leaving on Sunday. That was two days away, which meant tomorrow would be my last day with him. I was suddenly overcome by the urge to shake him awake so that we could spend time together but I knew that would only result in yet another argument, so I left him lying there untouched.

I tried not to sleep that night as I wanted to listen out for any sign of my father waking up but I must have drifted off at some hour as the house was empty when I woke. I was immediately filled with dread thinking that it had all been a decoy and he had already gone but once I had calmed down I was able to reason with myself; he would never have left without a goodbye. I dressed quickly and left the house earlier than usual to hunt for him. I scanned the empty lane trying to decide what direction to go in when I felt a magnetic pull telling me to turn left and away from the estate. As I was walking away I noticed lights coming from a cottage a little further down the lane, a strange sighting for this hour in the morning, and I knew in my heart that was where I would find him. Sure enough there he was; two greying heads flopped over the top of chairs as they snored in unison. I stood there watching them through the window, just taking in the simple scene of an everlasting friendship, when I heard laboured movement from inside. I made my exit, not wanting to face anyone else and instead headed off to work, filled with regret that so many hours would now be wasted away from the man who had raised me.

The day's tasks seemed meaningless only weighing against my heavy heart. I tried to finish early but the world was against me, either making the simplest tasks go drastically wrong or inviting what seemed to be the entirety of the estate to come and ask something of me. I somehow managed to finish whilst also keeping everyone else happy, but by that time the sun was setting on that last fateful day.

My head hung, my neck unable to bear its weight, as I made my way home in broken spirits. I entered the humble cottage and my heart broke when I noticed the emptiness. I had felt terrible all day because I hadn't been here, but that was out of my control. The least my father could have managed was to spend one measly night with me before he was gone forever. I slid down the wall and heaped myself on the floor, drawing my knees into my chest; I didn't want to be here alone but I guess that was something that I was going to have to get used to now.

"Emmy," a voice croaked above me.

I moved my head from the cave I had created against my knees and turned my green eyes to meet the desperate face.

"I just went to say goodbye to Lenny, I didn't think you would be back yet," he continued, reaching out a weathered hand to pull me up.

I thought you had gone, I wanted to say – desperate for the comfort of his arms – but I somehow managed to hold it in even though his eyes were screaming out for that same comfort. We stood apart from each other staring into the silence of our words.

"I'll make some dinner," I whispered.

We ate our last meal together in silence. There didn't seem to be any words. There was nothing that either of us could have said to make the situation any easier.

I was helping him to pack up his few belonging when he reached out and took the shirt I had been refolding from my tight grip; I struggled, not wanting to part with the memory of him. He pulled me close and held me against his chest, his pulse radiating through my body as we stood there. The silent action was all that was needed; any words would only have destroyed the moment.

The careful click of the door should have alerted me to the unwanted departure, but I just lay there oblivious to the warning, drifting back into a calm sleep. By the time I did eventually pull myself from the comfort of my bed it was too late; only the loneliness was there to greet me like an old friend. Tears were already fighting to be free as I ran out the door and down the lane, trailing the invisible figure of my father. My shabby night clothes were all I had to cover me, my feet bare on the gravelled ground and my legs left out for all to see, but I didn't care I just wanted to find the man that was already out of my reach. I stumbled and fell, the tiny stones and pebbles grazing my naked knees. I scrambled back to my feet but confusion took control and I was unsure of what way to turn. Reluctantly I headed back to the cottage with blood trickling down my legs and tears sliding down my face.

I wiped my nose and cheeks against the back of my hand and leant my head against the old door as I closed it behind me. It seemed somewhat bigger now, almost as though one person could get lost in it. As I was surveying the dusty interior my eyes scanned over, and then skipped back to, the folded piece of paper that was propped up in the middle of the table. My hands were surprisingly steady as they reached out for the note, unfolding it slowly to reveal my father's steady hand.

Emmy,

Sorry I left without waking you but I couldn't make myself say goodbye or I never would have left. It breaks my heart to leave you but I know you will be safer without me and that is what matters to me most.

I am so proud of the person you have grown into and I know your mother would be as well. You are stronger and more beautiful than I ever could have imagined. I only wish that you didn't have to become strong for me. You will never know how sorry I am for everything that I put you through, I should have been a much better father. You deserve better than that. I only have one thing to ask of you. Don't let my mistakes stop you. Be everything you want to be and don't let yourself be alone. There are people that love you and I hope that you will love them back.

I won't say goodbye because I will always be hoping that I will see you again. Be brave my beautiful girl. I love you.

Pa.

The ink smudged at the end, blurring the last words into one. I was unsure if the tears had come from the writer or the fresh tears that were cascading down my cheeks. I clutched the note close to me when the words became too much, uncontrollable sobs forcing me to the floor as my legs gave way beneath me; my whole world broken by the words that had been engraved on the paper.

Chapter 26

I cried until my body was completely empty of tears and only dry sobs heaved my body. Exhaustion sent me to sleep, curled up on the cold floor hugging the letter to me as though it were a comforting teddy bear. My dreams were empty; there would be no saviour. The crash of the door woke me, though my eyes did not do anything that shock normally describes. There was no starting or snapping; those things only happen when you wake from a bad dream, not when you wake into one. Instead my eyes struggled to drag themselves open, my body remaining motionless on the dusty floor. The light that snuck in with the open door made me squint. I didn't want a reminder that the world was still moving.

No words were spoken, there was no need to ask what was wrong; red eyes and exhausted movement said everything. He lay down behind me and placed a soothing arm across me, pulling me closer to the warmth of his body. A hot tear trickled out of the corner of my eye, sliding down onto his bare hands. His fingers twitched at the contact and they blindly came up to wipe the wetness from my cheek. His gentle touch only created more tears which came tumbling freely from my sore eyes. He held me tight, letting my tears fall, not letting go. When the tears finally stopped and I was only left with ragged drawn breaths and a running nose, Oscar carefully unwound himself for me and went in search of something to dry my eyes. He lifted me up, popping my heavy head against the chair so he could wipe my face.

"Tears always dry. No matter how many years they will always dry in the end," he whispered as he tried to wipe away my sadness.

"We need to wash your hair, it's covered in dust and dirt," he said quietly. Taking control of the situation he filled the metal bucket with hot water and brought it to my side. He draped a towel around my neck before going in search of the soap.

"Lean forward," he said gently, guiding my head over the bucket. The hot water flowed over me, the drips that fell from my hair washing away the salty tracks of my tears. He carefully tilted my head back so that he could work the soap through. The water had worked out the curls so my hair was long, trickling down my back. Once he was done he towel dried my hair until the curls came springing back to life.

"That's much better. Why don't you go get dressed? You'll be much warmer."

I hadn't even realised that I was only in my night shirt, perhaps I should have been embarrassed but I didn't have the energy to feel anything. I walked slowly in my zombie-like state and threw on whatever I could fine. Oscar was sitting on the sofa; book in hand, waiting for me. I shuffled over and automatically rested my wet head against his shoulder, breathing in his familiar scent. He draped my father's blanket over me and started to read from where I had left off in *The Wind in the Willows*. The fictional world swan around me and I kept my eyes squeezed shut in the hope that I could escape.

"Do you want to get some fresh air?" Oscar asked once he had finished reading. I nodded, hoping that perhaps it would pull me out of this stupor that I had fallen into. I found my shoes and coat then met Oscar at the door.

"Are you hungry?"

I shook my head in response, even though my stomach let out a loud growl at the same time. My stomach may have been empty but I didn't feel up to eating. Oscar may have doubted me but I knew that he wasn't going to push anything. Just before we left he ran back in and grabbed a hat off the coat rack.

"Your hair is still a little wet," he said as he tucked my hair beneath the hat. He took my hand in his, lacing his naked fingers between mine.

We walked in silence down to the lake, my voice still buried within. It was an inappropriately nice day; even though there was a chill on the still air it didn't threaten to bite. The sun was shining bright in the clear, cloudless sky and the plants were thriving in the light after a night of rain. The grass looked greener and the sky a softer shade of blue when I felt it should have been grey. It seemed that even the weather was no longer on my side. We sat staring at the motionless water, his hand still gripping mine. My life reflected back at me; a painful reminder of what I had lost.

"He's gone," I whispered to myself looking up to Oscar for clarification. His dark eyes mirrored my sadness and I watched him struggle to find the right words – his mouth opening and closing like a fish out of water.

"I'm sorry", he said, finally settling on the most commonly used words to try and comfort me.

"I can't believe he has really gone." The realisation of what this truly meant was slowly creeping up on me. I had been upset earlier but that was because of the written words, not due to the realisation. Now I wasn't upset though, nor was I angry. I was just empty. I felt nothing.

I could feel Oscar looking into my hollow eyes trying to decipher what I was thinking even though there was nothing; just the echo of loneliness resounding through my head. I knew it couldn't be classified as abandonment if essentially I was the one that had sent him away but that was how I felt; abandoned.

"I can't help but feel this is my fault," Oscar mumbled sadly. The words took me by surprise, I had been so busy blaming myself that I hadn't even considered how Oscar was feeling.

"No, you just did what I didn't have the courage to do. It needed to be done." The words were true though they didn't offer me any consolation.

"I know you think you are, but you're not alone. You have me," he paused before adding. "And Lenny of course. We're not going anywhere."

A small smile played over my lips even though it felt wrong. I had needed reminding that I still had people who wanted to be there for me, I just needed to remember to let them.

"It may not feel like it now but it will be okay," he assured.

"Yeah, it will just be … different."

"Different can be good. You're strong, you can do it." His eyes smiled at me. I was overwhelmed by a sudden surge of love that I felt for him. Was it just because he was being so kind to me or had I always loved him? I wanted him to kiss me, to drag my hand across and pull me over to him. It didn't matter where; mouth, neck, my cheek. My skin was empty for it.

"I know you said you're not hungry but your stomach seems to be in disagreement so I think we should probably find you some food." He let go of my hand, letting it fall to my side for the first time since we had stepped outside. My disappointment rose with it. Maybe it was for the best, I'm sure he wouldn't want to kiss me in my state. Some may have said that at that moment I only had a desperate need to feel loved but I would argue that; when I looked at him I knew that he was the only one I wanted.

"Mine or yours?" he asked as we reached the fork in the path. I didn't really want to see anyone else but there was a lack of food in my house and I had only left myself with a few pennies to keep me going until the next payday.

"I can just go in and rustle up some sandwiches and we can take them back to yours if you would rather?" he suggested reading my mind. I nodded and followed him to the door.

"I'll just wait out here," I said before he could invite me in. It was unlikely that Lenny would be there but I didn't want to run the risk of bumping into him. I leant against the wooden wall, unconsciously playing with the buttons on my jacket as I stared out at the gardens. I could hear horses coming up behind me and I turned to find Silver's face pressed against me. He nuzzled into me somehow knowing that I needed it.

"I thought he would cheer you up a bit," Oscar said, handing me the reins. "Can you take him back round for me, he's just out in the paddock at the moment." He didn't wait for my answer, just ran back to finish his job leaving me to care for the horse he had led to me. The silence of the animal was comforting, there was just the sound he made when he snorted out air, gently ruffling my hair.

"There you go," I said as I secured the gate behind me. His long nose reached over to my pocket nudging my hand in search of the apples I always treated him to.

"Sorry buddy, I didn't bring any today."

He turned his head away from me in defiance, no longer interested now he knew there was nothing in it for him. I couldn't help but laugh at how easy it was to buy an animal's affection.

Oscar was waiting for me when I got back to the front of the barn, a paper parcel of sandwiches tucked under his arm. My hand felt awkward at my side now that he wasn't holding it I wasn't sure what to do with it so I stuffed it carelessly into my jacket pocket.

Oscar tried to stifle a yawn but I caught him out the corner of my eye.

"You don't have to stay with me," I said.

"I know, but I want to. I don't want to leave you." His tired eyes looked on me with concern.

"I'll be okay," I lied. The last thing I wanted was to be alone but I guess that was something that I was going to have to get used to. This little cottage was too big just for me. He edged closer to me, until his arm was wrapped around me. With his free hand he stroked the hair out of my face and traced my skin with the back of his fingers; it was the lightest touch though he left a tingling sensation trailing in his path. He brought his face closer to mine until our lips were almost touching.

"You're beautiful," he whispered on a breath. His soft lips pressed against mine, lightly at first until he felt my lips respond. He increased the pressure, melting my eyes closed. My heart felt like it would burst out my chest as he slowly pulled away, leaving one last kiss lingering on my lips. I slowly opened my eyes to see those sweet lips spread into a broad smile. I was stranded by that softest touch. His eyes opened slowly, and I locked into their black depths, afraid to breathe and break the spell his touch had cast.

"I've been waiting to do that for a long time," he sighed, holding me close to him. He bent his head and laid a gentle kiss on the tip of my nose. The emptiness that had taken over my soul was now replaced with a growing warmth; he was gone but I wasn't alone.

Chapter 27

Out the corner of my eye I thought I saw someone peering through the window, a shock of yellow hair giving them away, but when I glanced back the glass was empty apart from a tell-tale circle of misted breath that got left behind.

"I think I better be going. Are you going to be okay?" Oscar asked through a yawn.

"I'll be fine," I lied. My heart racing as I wondered who had been watching us.

I walked him the few feet to the door, anxiety already starting to bubble in my stomach at the thought of being left alone.

"Tomorrow at the usual time?" he asked as he bent to press a kiss against my fleshy lips.

I nodded slowly, I had forgotten that life returned to normal tomorrow – I was only being allocated one day to grieve. I scanned the front perimeter of the house nervously, looking for any sign of movement or anything that looked out of place.

"Are you sure you're going to be okay?" Oscar asked when he noticed the worried expression on my face. "I can stay a bit longer if you need me to."

It would have been very easy to jump on the offer, I definitely would have at least a chance of sleeping if I knew that he was there, but I knew I couldn't let myself run the risk of getting used to his company. I would have to be alone at some point so surely it was best to just start now. He must have been able to read the expression on my face because he took my hand in his to try and reassure me.

"It can just be tonight, you shouldn't feel bad about it you have been through a lot."

I nodded slowly, leaning further towards giving in and letting him stay.

"I need to run back quickly, but I'll be back before you know it," he said before running off into the darkness.

Paranoia wasted no time in setting in once he had left, making me think that every rustle and whisper of the wind was someone coming after me. I was just about to turn back into the safety of the house when I felt a chill on the back of my neck; a sixth sense. There was something behind me. I turned around a dozen times but saw only the bare trees standing like sentries. Still my heart was racing. I inched closer to the cottage wondering if anyone would hear my screams. Then I heard it, the crunch of a twig, a break in the surface of the mud. I could run, but if I ran then whatever was behind me would chase me. I stood my ground and breathed out slowly, ready for the fate that awaited.

"You don't seem overly upset considering your father has just left," the voice sneered coolly.

I gulped down the fear and turned to face the scowling blonde-haired lord who had once been my friend.

"I'm surprised you didn't go with him to help take care of your sick aunt," he said before I had a chance to speak. There was a certain emphasis on his last words that told me he didn't believe the story my father had told; it was clear now that I had made a serious mistake when I had confided in him.

"There wasn't enough room for both of us," I muttered – the first excuse that came to my mind.

"Oh really? Nothing to do with him running away?" The evil grin that spread across his face made uneasiness settle over me.

"Of course not," I replied trying to remain as calm as possible.

Edward didn't speak, just kept looking at me through the darkness, his ice-blue eyes trying to pierce through my false confidence.

"What are you doing here anyway? I thought you weren't talking to me anymore." An unknown anger had come bursting to the surface with his unwanted appearance. I had already dealt with enough emotional turmoil caused by him, I didn't need to add to it. I had promised myself that I wouldn't let him hurt me anymore and I owed it to myself and my father to stick to that.

"Think you'll find that my family own these lands so I'm entitled to go anywhere I want," he retorted obnoxiously.

"Maybe, but I'm not sure that allows you to go snooping around other people homes," I bit back, snatching away some of his arrogant glow.

"I actually came here to warn you," he stated calmly, elaborating no further. It was that calm silence that worried me the most.

"Warn me of what?" I muttered nervously.

"My parents want to discuss your job with you. Looks like you should have gone with your father after all, maybe then you wouldn't be ending up jobless, homeless and alone," he spat at me. I stood there frozen, unable to register the words that had just been thrown at me. He turned to walk away, leaving me swimming in the shock of the news he had just delivered. I had wondered what was going to be happening about my job, I wasn't naïve enough to think that I would be left alone, but I hadn't thought for one second that they would toss me out like garbage.

"Enjoy your boyfriend while you still can," he added spitefully before falling back into the darkness.

"Have you been waiting out here the whole time?" Oscar asked once he reached me.

"Yeah, I just got distracted I guess," I replied not really lying.

"By what?"

"I don't know," I muttered. I re-entered the cottage leaving the questions outside.

There was a mixture of sadness and guilt as I handed Oscar the tattered blanket.

"Sorry it's not much. You really don't have to stay if you won't be comfortable," I said sadly.

"It's fine, stop worrying."

I would have rather had him sleeping next to me but I knew that neither of us was going to be the one to mention it. I sat myself on the sofa, suddenly wide awake. Perhaps the prospect of sleep was secretly terrifying. Oscar sat next to me, pulling me onto his chest.

"We can stay awake if you'd rather," he suggested, though the husk of sleepiness gave him away.

"No, I'll let you sleep," I said moving to get up.

"Stay for just a minute," he mumbled, his eyes already closed. It wasn't long before I felt the soft rise and fall of his chest, his heart beating steadily in my ear. The light snores that signalled his temporary absence were practically non-existent compared to what I had grown used to; the slight disturbance was strangely comforting though it wasn't enough to switch my brain off. Crazy thoughts and consequences of what would be ran uncontrollably through my head, making sure that every nerve was functioning in overdrive. So, when a new day dawned my eyes were still fixated on the nothing that surrounded me.

I gently removed myself from the protection of Oscar's arms and lifted away from him as quietly as I could manage. I wanted to wash away the stains of yesterday but I didn't want to risk waking him so I soaked a sponge with water from the tap, quickly washing with the freezing water. I hid around the corner so that Oscar wouldn't catch me if he was to wake. The sound of the kettle boiling made him stir but his eyes did not open, I made sure to grab it before it started to shriek. I left a bowl of porridge on the side for him and was just about to sneak out and leave the peaceful figure to his dreams when it dawned on me that he would also be expected at work shortly. I gently shook him awake.

"Wake up," I whispered. "You have to be at work soon."

Oscar's sleeping eyes jolted to life scanning the room in an attempt to figure out where he was, his hand gripping onto my arm.

"There's some porridge for you, I have to leave now but please help yourself to anything." I reached out and kissed him shyly on the cheek, unsure what to make of his reaction.

Most of the day was spent looking over my shoulder anticipating the arrival of a messenger come to tell me that my time was up. That messenger arrived when I had finally become engrossed in my work, announcing themselves with a somewhat anxious cough.

"Emily Thorne?" an early adolescent voice queried.

I turned to see a young boy standing before me, looking at me hopefully. I didn't recognise his face but there were a lot of workers that came and went without my knowledge, either I or them not being deemed important enough to be introduced to.

"Yes, that's me. How can I help you?" I asked, acting as though I had not been expecting his arrival. Was I doing myself or Edward a favour by doing that? I couldn't be sure.

"Mrs Montgomery asked me to come fetch you." His eyes blinked nervously looking all around me. I got the feeling that this was the first time he had been entrusted with such a task and I could tell how apprehensive he was feeling about it.

"Did you want me to come now?" I asked.

"Yes." He nodded enthusiastically and I followed on his heels as we walked mutely towards the house. The silence gave me a chance to take note of my appearance: mud stained my hands and I desperately tried to rub it off on my already filthy apron thinking that it could just be discarded; my clothes were also flecked with mud, permanent grass stains decorated the knees of my trousers and my hair was as wild and carefree as always. Though my face was clean it was plain, the after effects of a sleepless night making themselves apparent beneath my hollow green eyes.

The servants' door creaked loudly as it opened onto the long, daunting hallway. I wandered through the servants' hall where the butler was waiting for me, a disapproving look on his face when he noticed my attire.

"If you would please follow me, the lord and lady have requested an audience with you."

I could feel the stares of judgemental eyes on me as I was led to my inevitable decline.

Chapter 28

The old stairs creaked beneath our steps as I started what felt like an everlasting climb. Mr Yates opened the door into a new world of colour, carpets and curved staircases. The entrance hall was painted in a timeless cream, the walls reaching with nothing to stop them; the stairs curved around the majority of the room, its intricately carved bannisters also painted in that immaculate cream. I recognised some of my own handiwork in the plants and flowers that were sparsely placed on the few tables standing around with no other purpose. As I slowly followed the pompous butler through to the next room I spotted framed paintings lining the walls of the stairs but I didn't have enough time to appreciate them.

"Wait here please."

I rooted myself to the spot, staring up in awe at the spaciousness of the room.

"Miss Thorne is here my lord," I heard the announcement of my arrival through the door.

"Yes, send her in," the Lord replied dismissively causing my stomach to knot up. The butler beckoned me in with what I thought was a smug look on his face and waited for the nod before he walked out, leaving me standing completely alone. I felt small in the large, open room; the high ceilings making me feel trapped. This room was decorated in slate grey, though not much of the colour could be seen due to the wall-length bookcases that covered the room. There were two large sofas, both in the same shade of grey, sitting opposite the crackling fire where Lady Barrow sat. I looked around, unsure if this classed as a sitting room or a study. I wasn't used to there being so many rooms, and I only had one door in the cottage. When Lady Barrow noticed me looking around she stood to greet me.

"Emily, I'm glad you could join us. It is so lovely to see you again," she said falsely, irony seeping through her words. Lady Meredith Barrow would still be described as attractive with her dark blonde hair and blue eyes – the same physical attributes that her son had inherited – and she still stood tall and proud though there was a sternness to her face that took away any softness.

"Yes, ma'am," I replied, unsure of what else to say. The pristine condition of the room made me extremely self-conscious about the mud I was covered in, quickly peeking behind me to check that I hadn't left any muddy footprints on the carpet.

"We were sorry to see your father go," the Lord interceded. "How is your aunt doing?" His brown eyes asked me.

"Not good, sir." I lied.

Henry Barrow was everything that you would expect a Lord to be. His hair had greyed but it suited him as though it should have always been that colour. He was still in good shape, looking forever smart in his perfect suits and he carried himself with such confidence and superiority it was hard not to be in awe of him. He didn't look an age older than the man that I had constantly ran into as a child, the same man who had always ruffled my hair affectionately and sent us back off to play. His face was much more welcoming than his wife's and there seemed to be genuine concern over my personal problems. I found myself navigating towards him as the conversation began.

"Obviously his untimely departure has left us with a bit of a predicament as we no longer have a head gardener. This is what we asked you here to talk about," Lord Barrow continued. I felt my stomach tangle itself into more knots as I waited for what they would say next. I wanted to jump up and defend myself, list all the reasons why they shouldn't fire me but I knew that I had to control myself.

"Yes m'lord, I understand. I just want you to know that I do love my job and I really appreciate all the opportunities you have given me," I said, my voice shaking as I spoke. Shamefully I could feel tears starting to prick my eyes and my lips wobbled slightly as I spoke. I discreetly bit my lip to steady it and took in a deep breath to calm my nerves.

"Yes. The fact of the matter is that you are too young, and well …" she paused, looking me from head to toe "… inexperienced to run the estate gardens so we need to get someone else in." There was no hint of sympathy over what she was doing to me, her words almost as cold as her eyes. I wanted to tell her exactly what I had been doing for the last few months, to shout at her to look out of the oversized bay window behind her that overlooked the gardens I had been single-handedly keeping in the condition she ordered. The sight of the walled in gardens made me want to run out and hide between the safety of the old bricks; to shelter myself beneath the trees where I would be protected from their words, but I knew there was no escape for me.

"Does this mean I'm losing my job?" I choked out, feeling as though the floor had been pulled from beneath my feet.

"No, of course not Emily." The Lord seemed convincing but I still couldn't be sure what it all really meant.

"We are looking for a new head gardener as we speak but of course you will be staying on in your position, we wouldn't want to replace you," he assured me. "Losing one Thorne was bad enough, we don't want to lose both of you," he added with a soft smile. It was clear from her body language that it was not what Edward's mother had wanted and it was obvious that she was the one that had never approved of me in the first place; she must has been disappointed that she had missed out on this opportunity to finally get me rid of her son's life.

"Hopefully there will be someone in place by the end of the week. Do you think that you can cope with the work load until then?" We can always ask Yates to find someone to help if not," he added.

"I can manage, sir," I replied. A mix of emotions flowing through me.

"Very good, Emily," he said with a smile. I relaxed slightly with that show of friendliness but that was short-lived as the Lady chose that moment to interrupt.

"You must know that this all means that you can no longer stay in the cottage as that accommodation will be given to the person who is replacing your father. You will need to be out by the end of the week." The wretched smile that spread across her face made her pleasure quite obvious.

"Meredith, there's no need for that," Lord Henry whispered sharply to his wife. Quite out of turn in front of me I was sure, though I was too shocked to take much notice.

"Pardon?" I spluttered.

"I'm afraid that is the case. The cottage now comes with the job so you must find somewhere else to live. We will help you in any way we can of course," he said amicably.

I nodded unable to think of any words to say seeing as muttering *of course* back sarcastically was probably not the smartest move. It had never occurred to me that I would be losing my home.

"Now I believe that is all, unless there is anything that you would like to ask us?" he asked. I shook my head. "Very well. We shall let you know when a replacement is employed. Good day Emily," he said dismissing me in a friendly manner.

"Thank you sir. M'lady," I replied, bowing my head at each of them in turn. I wasted no time in scurrying out of the room and straight into the waiting butler.

"In a rush?" he asked in his deep voice.

"No, sir. I just need to get back to work," I said to my feet.

"As you were then," he said, using his arms to indicate the way.

I left the house, paying no attention to those watchful eyes, bursting through the door. I fell to my knees on the pebbled ground gasping for fresh air.

I wandered back to where I had left my wheelbarrow as though I was floating on a dream. I had foolishly let myself think that I was free of all those problems when instead I should have been thinking about what was going to happen next; I should have known that it wouldn't have been that simple. Perhaps I could ask for a room at the inn, but I knew that it was unlikely that I would have enough money for that. I thought that they may have provided me with a room in the servants' quarters, even though it was the rooms above the barn that were provided for the outside servants; a segregation I had never truly understood. I couldn't stay in a room full of young men though, that would be inappropriate not to mention unbelievably uncomfortable for me and probably them also. Maybe I would have to ask Mrs Montgomery if there was a spare room for me. After all there was no way I could afford the rent anywhere else. The fact of the matter was that I only had the week to figure it out, perhaps not even that, before I ended up homeless.

"Emily?" A voice asked breaking through my thoughts. I looked around to find Lenny standing before me. "I saw you coming out the house. Is everything alright little lady?"

"Yes. Well, erm, they are appointing a new head gardener," I replied uncertainly.

"You still got your job though right?" he asked through worried lips.

"Yes. But I need to find somewhere else to live. What am I going to do?" I blurted out pathetically, unsure how to look after myself anymore.

"Now there's no need to worry about that. We can figure something out. Why don't you pop in for some tea?"

"I can't, I really must get back to work," I said sadly.

"Then come by later. And try not to think about it until then you'll only end up making yourself ill with all this worry." He ruffled my hair lovingly before walking away, leaving me thinking that it was a lot easier said than done.

I finished up earlier than usual despite the long interruption I had incurred during the day. I couldn't set my mind onto anything I was doing and I knew it was pointless trying to achieve anything if I wasn't concentrating. This meant that Lenny and Oscar were still busy getting the horses back into their boxes when I arrived. I went around the back to join them with the intention of offering my assistance. As I neared the paddock I overheard voices in what sounded like a heated discussion, so I slowed my steps not wanting to intrude.

"How can they just kick her out of her home like that? It just shows that they really don't care for us at all," Oscar said angrily.

"You are not to speak like that. You'll get us both in trouble," Lenny demanded.

"So I get in trouble! They can't do that to her. Where is she supposed to go?"

"I know it isn't fair, but we will think of something. I get the feeling this has more to do with how you feel about the particular young lady in question than anything else though," Lenny suggested.

Oscar remained silent and in my eagerness to get closer to see his reaction I walked my shin into the hose which caused me to involuntarily call out in pain. A deepening silence seemed to fall over the men at my interruption and I had no choice but to announce myself before they discovered that I had been snooping.

"My fault, I wasn't paying any attention to where I was going," I said conversationally as I walked around the corner to greet their curious faces. "I know I'm earlier than I said I would be but I thought perhaps I could help you finish up here?" I added.

"Always welcome. How long you been here for?" Lenny asked.

"Just got here. Why?" I lied.

"No reason," he replied shaking his head.

"Will you get Silver? He's being stubborn today," Oscar said. His words were rushed and he looked embarrassed which told me that he was convinced he had been caught out. I allowed myself a small smile before remembering why I was here.

Silver looked magnificent against the setting sun. His mane was glimmering in the low light. As he heard footsteps approach he turned slowly in the opposite direction.

"I've got a treat for you," I called out reaching into my pocket, attempting to bribe him back towards me. His ears pricked at the sound of my voice turning eagerly to receive his gift.

"Sometimes I think it would be much easier to be you," I muttered as I let him sniff around my hand after devouring the carrots I held out to him. It was the most peaceful I had felt in a long time as we stood there, our heads pressed together as we watched the day turn into night.

Chapter 29

The expected proclamations of outrage were announced once I settled, though I paid little attention to them; as flattering as their concern was it wasn't going to help anything.

"Have you thought anymore about where you can go?" Lenny asked me sympathetically; a sympathy that I was gradually growing to resent.

"Perhaps I could ask Mrs Montgomery if there is a room spare in the house. I know it isn't how things usually work, but special circumstances and everything," I said dully.

"Good idea, I'm sure she will be more than happy to help you. And didn't Lord Barrow say that they would help? If Mrs Montgomery was to say no you could ask him to speak to her," he added enthusiastically, his naivety almost childlike. The suggestion made me recoil; there was no chance that I was going to start tattling to the lord, they didn't like me enough without adding that into the mix. If she said no, then she said no. There was nothing I could do to change that. A silence settled upon us as the seriousness of the situation took over.

"If there's no room for you then there are spare beds here," Oscar said hesitantly, indicating the unseen beds above us.

"Thank you, but I couldn't do that," I said quickly. Living in such proximity to Oscar would not be a good idea, plus it wasn't exactly deemed acceptable for me to be staying in amongst men that were of no relation to me.

"I understand, but if it comes to it then the offer is there," he said reiterating his point, this time with a bit more certainty. I ungratefully hoped that it wouldn't come down to that but at least I knew that I wasn't going to end up homeless at the end of it all; that at least was a slight relief.

"And I can ask Dorothy if you can stay with us. There's not much room but I am sure that we can make it work," Lenny added.

"I wouldn't want to put you out," I said although the suggestion was much more appealing than anything else that had been mentioned. I had met Dorothy a few times and she had always been welcoming and friendly enough, but only in the manner that it was as though she had been told to act that way. They had never had children of their own, for whatever reason, which is why Lenny had always treated me as one of his own though I am not entirely sure his wife reciprocated those feelings. I got the impression that she resented the attention that he had always lavished on me, sometimes sensing a hint of jealousy hidden in amongst her words and secreted looks. It was that notion that gave me the feeling she would find a reason to dispute the suggestion, but even so I would much rather be sleeping in a corner of their little house than anywhere else; I felt that would be the closest I would feel to home.

"If I don't ask then we'll never know."

The next morning I waited until after the occupants of the house would have finished with breakfast before I let myself in the servant's entrance door. The long hallway seemed never-ending as I shuffled down it in search of the housekeeper, the sound of voices guiding me in the direction of the servant's hall. I could see them all gathered around the long table; I hadn't thought that they would be eating now. I watched them from behind the doorframe, for some reason feeling incredibly nervous about stepping in there. Unfortunately before I got the chance to announce myself I was spotted by one of the maids.

"How long you been snooping around there for?" she called out brazenly causing all eyes to fall silently onto me. Her accent wasn't recognisable as being from around here and I had difficulty in understanding her. I couldn't help but wonder how she came to be serving in such a high house when everyone else always spoke so proper.

"I was just hoping to speak to Mrs Montgomery if possible." I stuttered feeling the shame of being caught creeping up my neck. Mrs Montgomery stood from her place at the table and nodded at me.

"Perhaps we will be more comfortable in my room," she said casting a disapproving look over the sniggering occupants of the table. Their reaction made me feel even more uneasy about what I was about to ask but I hadn't been left with many other options.

"What can I do for you, Emily?" she asked as she closed the door behind her.

"As I'm sure you already know my father has had to leave and I need to vacate the cottage. I know it isn't usually the way but I was wondering if there was a room available for me in here? I wouldn't ask but I have nowhere else to go." I spoke slowly, thinking over every word before I voiced it and even though I tried to remain calm I could still hear the desperation in my voice.

"Are there no beds at the barn?" she asked, making my heart sink.

"There is but I'm not really comfortable with the idea of staying there. Not when it is all young men." My green eyes pleaded with her hard brown ones, trying desperately to find some human emotion within them. I hoped that she would understand this plea but her stern face gave away nothing. Her dark hair was piled into an immaculate bun on top of her head, the hair pulled so tight it seemed to stretch her face back as well. Her hands were folded purposefully in her lap as she sat opposite me; my fate precariously placed within them.

"Please, I don't know where else I can go, I don't have enough money to go anywhere else. I won't ask for more than just a room, I can make my own meals and I won't get in anyone's way. I promise that you will hardly ever see me." I was practically begging, I may as well have been on my hands and knees' clutching at her skirts for all the good my forced calm was doing me. Her unblinking eyes stared back at me with no emotion; her silence stretching out for miles as I waited eagerly for her answer.

"Very well. I shall see what I can do. When do you need the room by?" she asked curtly.

"The end of the week."

"I will let you know, Emily. Is that all?" She stood and held open the door: my cue to leave.

"Yes, thank you for your time," I said politely as I hurried past. The few people that had congregated by the door quickly scampered as I rushed past; their judgemental smiles piercing my already shattered façade.

The thought of having to live here made me restless but it was better than the alternative. The expansive house already made me feel trapped and I was yet to spend longer than a few hours within its suffocating walls.

I got to work with mixed emotions, part of me resented the situation of my job and the other part relished the feeling of being alone; of being the one in control of what I did and when I did it. I needed to be making the most of the time that I had left to myself before someone new would take over. My father had been difficult over the last few months but before that he had undoubtedly been the best boss and I knew it was highly unlikely that was going to happen again; especially considering my recent luck. I also wanted to make a good impression though so I vowed to do some of my best work this week so that the new head gardener, whoever that may be, would know that I was more than capable at this job. Although I was hard at work I made a conscious effort to keep watch over the path that led to the house so that I could scout out any potential candidates. I wondered who would be conducting the interview in place of my father, it didn't fall under Mr Yates' jurisdiction but I'm sure his lordship wouldn't have bothered himself with it so I had to assume that it would be the butler filling in anyway. I couldn't help but feel slightly let down by the fact that they hadn't asked for my input, after all I had been here my entire life. Then again, it wasn't an extension that I should ever expect. The day passed without any visitors and I allowed myself a little hope thinking that perhaps no one would respond to the advertisement.

The day had been cooler and the night was turning even colder so I threw some logs onto the unlit fire. I grabbed the matches from the side and threw the lit stick onto the wood. The wind gushed down the chimney and blew it out before it had a chance to interact with the wood. I opened the matchbox once more and noticed that there were only a few left. I toyed with the idea of saving the rest knowing that I couldn't afford to buy anymore just yet when another gust of wind blew over me; my uncontrollable shivers settling the matter for me.

I scanned the room from my knees in search of anything I could use to cover the hole. I was just about to give up when I spotted an old newspaper hiding beneath cobwebs in the corner of the room. I scurried over on hands and knees to fetch it, opening it out to full length. I lit another match hoping that this time I would be more successful. I threw the thin stick in once more and quickly covered the hole with the outspread paper to protect the tiny flame from the overpowering draft.

I was too afraid to peak behind the paper so instead I listened intently for the sounds of crackling flames. Before I heard anything though I felt the heat of the flame that licked the paper hungrily. I let out a shamefully girlish shriek as I threw the paper into the fire to be eaten by the growing flames. I inhaled the smell of burning logs and sighed with pleasure; there was something very comforting about the woody scent.

When my stomach growled at me I realised that I hadn't eaten since my meagre portion of porridge that morning. I stood and went to search the cupboards that I knew were going to be empty. My stomach rumbled louder in agreement, knowing that it was unlikely to get anything overly substantial. The only edible contents of the cupboard that I could find was a pot of jam and a lump of bread that was bordering on being stale. I sliced it as neatly as I could, the stone crust making it an almost impossible task, and then carried it over to the fire. I stuck the prongs of the toasting fork through the first slice, accidentally sticking my finger in the process.

"Oh, crumbs," I muttered to myself, sucking my bleeding finger as I held the bread over the fire – the coppery taste taking over my senses. I wasn't sure how I was going to survive on the little I had until I got money on Friday, and I had so stupidly informed Mrs

Montgomery that I would feed myself – that was even considering that she allowed me a room. I curled up in front of the roaring fire, mesmerised by the flickering flames. They moved expertly and gracefully as they devoured everything in its way; only leaving a trail of destruction once it could eat no more. I couldn't help but feel jealous of that fire; nothing could stand in its way and though its light may go out it never truly died.

Chapter 30

Friday arrived with no news about a replacement or any word from Mrs Montgomery but I still had a feeling that someone would be coming to speak to me during the day — luck didn't seem to be my friend so I knew my prayers would go unanswered. I jolted at every sound, which was a lot considering the rain was falling — appropriately reflecting my mood. The drops of rain landing on the few leaves that adorned the trees surrounding me; the gathering wind sounding like a whisper calling out my name.

The time hit midday, signalled by Oscar's arrival, and there had still been no interruptions.

"Sorry I missed you yesterday, I was pretty busy," Oscar said once we had sat down.

"And because you wasn't sure whether to bother me or not, right?" I guessed, adding what else he had really wanted to say.

"No, well, yes. I thought you would want some times alone to do what you needed." He seemed ashamed, his voice sounding guilty even though he had no reason to be.

"It really doesn't matter. I don't expect to see you every day," I said with a laugh. It was true, I didn't expect anything from him despite how much I enjoyed the times that I did get to spend with him.

"That doesn't mean that I don't want to though," he said with a smile.

"You may regret saying that," I joked. I helped myself to the sandwich he had prepared for me, fed up and too hungry to be polite and wait for him to offer it to me. My stomach wasn't exactly my best friend at the moment considering I hadn't been doing my job and feeding it particularly well over the last few days. I was hoping this would keep it satisfied for a while.

"Hungry?"

"Mmm starved," I said through a large mouthful. Oscar waited until I had finished eating before he started with more questions.

"Did you speak to Mrs Montgomery?" he asked and the way he spoke told me that he had been wanting to know the answer for some time.

"I did, but I am still waiting to hear what she has to say about it. I was hoping that I would find out today at some point."

He nodded in response. "And have they told you who your next boss is going to be yet?"

"No, I've heard nothing. Can't help but feel like I am being kept in the dark with it all. Guess I just have to wait and see," I said with a sigh.

A flash of anger darted across his eyes but he managed to keep it controlled to just that glimpse of emotion.

"Why don't you go ask them what is going on?" he asked and I could tell that it was not what he had wanted to hear at all.

"I will wait until the end of the day at least," I said not wanting to have to go in and face the leering eyes unless absolutely necessary. As far as I was concerned no news was good news.

"Well please let me know when you hear," he pleaded.

"Of course."

As I was walking back it occurred to me that I had never thought to ask what would happen if they couldn't find a replacement. Was it possible that I could then keep the cottage and take on these extra responsibilities that I was already capable of doing? I was sure that they wouldn't get rid of me if they couldn't because then they would be left with no-one. I didn't want to get my hopes up as it was pretty clear they didn't want that to happen so they would keep looking no matter how long it would take.

It turned out – as I knew it would - that I was wasting my time with those thoughts. I knew there was news of some kind when I spotted the same young lad walking towards me that I had seen the other day; his brown hair waving at me in the wind. This time I took it upon myself to study him closer, deciding it was about time I started trying to get to know the other members of staff. I decided that he couldn't have been much older than twelve but then again looks could be deceiving. His face was young and still had some of that chubbiness that childhood brought with it and he walked with a skip in his step, obviously proud that he had been given such an important job yet again.

"Hello Emily," he said cheerfully, his dark blue eyes smiling up at me, not yet tainted with the hardship of growing up. His innocence was catching and I wondered if perhaps I could request his help if it was to come to it, after all he always seemed so eager to please.

"Hello," I replied turning and smiling at him. He wasn't far off my height, only about half a head shorter, but then again I wasn't exceptionally tall myself.

"Mrs Montgomery asked for you to come and see her when possible please," he said, his head held high as he related the message.

"I can come now. Want to walk with me?"

"Okay," he said cheerfully before remembering his new position. "I have to go back that way anyway."

I managed to keep my smile hidden at his eagerness to grow up, remembering that I had not been so different at that age. I could remember my father telling me that I should be in no rush to grow up and I had paid no attention, so I knew that if I was to repeat that now then I would get the same response.

"I feel rude, I don't even know your name!" I exclaimed in an attempt to strike up a conversation.

"My name is Bobby, I mean Robert," he corrected hurriedly, momentarily forgetting the new name that came with the job.

"Well hello Robert. Although I must say I think I prefer Bobby," I said trying to sound as casual as possible.

"You can call me Bobby if you like," he replied matter-of-factly as though it was a privilege for me to be able to do so.

"Thank you. So, what is it that you do?" I asked, thinking that he would appreciate the interest shown in him.

"I pass on messages and I help out whenever I'm needed. It's much more important than you'd think," he said, his eyes pleading with me to understand.

"Oh, I wouldn't doubt that," I said appealing to his new found ego.

"Do you know where to go or would you like me to walk you in?" he asked when we reached the door, acting like the true gentleman.

"Would you walk me in?" This time I wasn't just asking to make him feel important but more because I didn't want to go in there alone, at least this time I could make it look as though someone could potentially like me.

Bobby led me through to the room where I had met with Mrs Montgomery at the beginning of the week and knocked on the door politely.

"Emily is here to see you Mrs Montgomery," he called out at the closed door.

"Send her in please," the muted reply sounded.

I entered the room with a new apprehension, not wanting to hear what was going to be said. Alison Montgomery wasted no time with pleasantries, instead getting straight to the point.

"We were waiting for news about what was happening regarding the job situation before we made a decision about whether you would be staying here or not," she stated with little feeling or remorse. "As I'm sure you are aware a replacement has been found for your father and he will be starting on Monday."

"I wasn't sure of that, no," I interrupted, annoyed that I was apparently the last person to find out when I was the one that it most affected."You know now then," she said daring me to interrupt her again. I remained silent and just stared at her waiting dutifully to hear the next piece of news.

"Anyway, it has been decided that you can stay here for now. Though it is unlikely to be on a permanent basis as there are a limited number of rooms and we may need them for staff working inside the house. If that is the case you will need to vacate when we tell you and find somewhere else." Her dismissive tone told me that she wasn't overly pleased with the decision so I knew that I was going to have to stay out of her way; as well as everybody else's. It didn't look I was going to be making new friends any time soon.

I left the house with a mix of emotions; I was partly glad that a decision had been made, relieved that the waiting was over, but I was also nervous about the two big changes that were about to take place. I had until Sunday morning to pack up my stuff and vacate the house. It didn't give me a lot of time but thankfully I didn't have many possessions to my name; it was the cleaning that was going to be the most time consuming.

I quickly packed away the gardening tools I had been using for the day and walked over to the stables before heading back home. When I got there Oscar wasn't in sight and I didn't have the time to go looking for him so I asked the nearest stable boy to pass on a message and hurried on home to start another lot of work.

I started with the kitchen, if it could be called that, because I figured it would be the easiest to sort out and then at least I could say that I had tackled one area. There was practically no food so I didn't have to worry about that and the cookware was almost non-existent; I decided I would either offer it to the occupants of the barn or leave it here for the new inhabitants of the cottage. I gave it a thorough wash then and there knowing that I was unlikely to be using it in the remaining time I had here. I was going to move into the living room next when I realised that it would be best to wash everything that needed doing whilst I had the opportunity – also giving it the time it needed to dry.

I was elbow deep in soapy water, a pile of dirty washing to the right of me and a smaller pile of clean washing to my left when Oscar arrived. The temperature of the water had turned half of my arms red and my face was flushed from the heat, steam cementing curls to my forehead and cheeks. Oscar chuckled when he saw the state of me, making no move to come over and help.

"Is this why you asked me to come over? To do your washing! Because there is a limit to how much I will do to help you," he joked.

"Ha, ha. Very funny," I replied sarcastically. "I just have a lot to do so I thought you could keep me company whilst I was doing it. Plus you said you wanted to know when I heard anything."

"Good or bad news?" he asked eagerly.

"Not sure I'm going to tell you now," I muttered, purposefully paying keen attention to the washing rather than to him.

His mouth opened to respond but decided against it and instead he chose to go and sit on the sofa away from me. We remained in that playful silence for some time, mainly because I forgot and was too busy concentrating on the task at hand. It wasn't until I got up to hang the wet material out to dry that I broke the silence.

"There is someone new starting here on Monday so I have to be out by Sunday morning and Mrs Montgomery said that I can stay in the house for now, though it wasn't worded quite so nicely as that," I informed him.

"So, is that good or bad?" he asked again. I thought about how best to answer but I couldn't figure out how I did feel about it.

"I'm not sure," I said. "I can tell that I'm not really wanted in the house but I will spend as little time there as possible and obviously I have no idea what this person is going to be like. But I guess only time can tell."

He looked at me sympathetically though this time it didn't feel as patronising as sympathy usually did. I could tell that he felt bad for the situation I was in rather than feeling sorry for me – that he was empathising with me more than anything else.

Oscar didn't stay for long, I could tell that he was tired so I made him leave by pretending that I would never get anything finished if he was here, which wasn't a complete lie; he proved to be a rather large distraction even if it wasn't his intention to be so. I gathered up the few possessions from the living room, most of which consisted of my mother's books. I delicately placed them back in the chest they had originally come from and hoped that I would be able to fit the majority of everything else that I owned in there. My eyes were dry and itchy from tiredness and I had to make myself put down the old sponge I was using to scrub the floor and head to bed. I didn't want to finish now but I could feel my body fighting me and I knew it was time to give up.

Chapter 31

Sunday morning came and I left; a large chest and a small bag my only companions. The cottage was as clean as it had ever been and I was being forced to start a new chapter of my life without it, having to allow strangers inside my home. I walked slowly down the path counting the steps away from where I was meant to be. My possessions weighed heavier than they should have done and I struggled as I made my way down the path. I got about halfway and had to stop, using the chest to sit and rest on. From my resting point I had a perfect view of the estate and the gardens that up until now had felt like home to me. To some, winter may seem like a dull time with few flowers and bare trees, but to me it was something entirely different. In those naked twigs and empty soil I saw the opportunity for rebirth; that early struggle for something new to be born into this world. I loved to watch the old leaves fall, giving way for the fresh green ones to take their place and I couldn't think of anything more alluring than the frosted cobwebs that adorned the chairs and tables; magical and delicate in the undisturbed morning air.

The innocence of a child's voice rang out and grabbed my attention, pulling me away from my daydream.

"Papa, is this our new home?" it called out excitedly. I would have guessed that it was a little girl but I couldn't be certain.

"Yes it is petal. Why don't you take the baby from your ma and you can go in." The father, and who I assumed to be the new head gardener, had a kind voice but I wasn't prepared to judge him solely on that. I leant back and tried to see through the trees in an attempt to sneak a peek at them. I could just about make out some figures but the tree trunks were obscuring my view. I leant back a little further to try and see around it but I misjudged my position on the chest and went toppling off backwards – legs sprawled over my head in a very unladylike fashion. Thankfully that same tree that had been blocking my view also protected me from them. I got up as quickly as possible, which was difficult considering I had got myself caught in quite a tangle, promptly deciding that my rest break was now over. I found a new burst of strength and was able to heave the chest up to the main house with more determination.

I stood there for a moment just staring at the door, I was reluctant to turn the handle knowing that when I did there was no turning back. I didn't want to be living amongst a group of people that didn't like me but there was very little choice. I wondered if Edward knew about this new arrangement and how he would react when he was to find out. I hoped that there would be little to no chance of running into him because I didn't need any extra tension added to the situation.

I reluctantly let myself in and dragged my belongings in behind me, leaving them by the door as I went in search of someone to show me to my new room. I could hear movement from the kitchen but I didn't want to bother them as I knew it wasn't their job to attend to me, not that they were likely to anyway, so I turned in the opposite direction in search of the room where I had met with Mrs Montgomery the last two times. I knocked on the door nervously, afraid that I would be disturbing her. There was no answer so I knocked again, this time a little harder. There was still no response so I wandered back to the entrance door and sat myself down to wait for someone, anyone, to happen upon me.

I waited there for some time though I had no way of knowing exactly how long so it was highly likely that my mind had stretched out the time. I just sat there and stared at the wall opposite, studying the bumps and tears that covered the surface; details the usual passer-by would skip over. The image was now painted on my memory; I could tell exactly what sections needed covering up and the corners where cobwebs were beginning to gather dust.

"Emily, what exactly are you doing?" a voice called out breaking my daze. I turned to see Mr Yates standing at the end of the corridor staring at me in confusion. I jumped up and tried to straighten myself, realising that this would be the first time I had set foot in this house not covered in mud.

"I, er, I was waiting," I stuttered.

"Waiting for what exactly?"

"Mrs Montgomery," I stated, though it came out sounding more like a question.

"She's not working today, but perhaps I can be of assistance?" Even though there was no physical sign of it there was the hint of a smile to his voice that cast a new light on the otherwise straight laced butler. There could be no denying his professionalism; his suit was immaculately clean, his dark grey hair slicked back without a strand out of place and he made it perfectly clear that his job came first no matter what. He wasn't an overly tall man though his confidence made him appear larger and he would have been considered slim if it weren't for the slight belly that could be seen when he stood to the side. He had sharp features, though they were not at all disagreeable and his eyes were always watching you, taking note of everything that was going on.

"I was told that I would be able to move into the room today," I said.

"If you can hold on for one moment then I shall find out what room she has arranged for you." He expertly swivelled and marched off to complete his task. He returned with a solemn look on his face and I automatically jumped to the worst conclusion.

"I'm very sorry Emily but it appears that no one seems to know what room has been arranged for you, and as that is not an area that I usually deal with I can't be of much more help. However, Mrs Montgomery should return within the next few hours so she will me much more helpful. Until then I can keep your possessions in my room so they are out of the way and you are also welcome to sit in there to pass the time," he said politely. His first words had made me think that he was going to be telling me they had changed their minds but as he continued to speak my concerns were hushed.

"That's no problem, thank you though. And thank you for the offer but I can find something to keep me out of the way for a while," I said. I could tell that it was hard for him not being able to help so I made sure to be extra polite and grateful.

We carried my stuff through and then I wasted no time in leaving. I turned to smile and wave at the door before my departure. It could easily have been my mind playing tricks on me but I could have sworn I saw what would have passed for a smile in response.

Oscar was sitting facing the door as though he had been perched there waiting for me for some time.

"I wasn't sure that I would see you today," he said eagerly. "Are you all settled in? Have you met the new boss yet?"

"Not exactly," I replied before launching into the tale of my morning – he laughed when I recounted falling off the chest in an attempt to spy and his face turned grim when I revealed I was still yet to see my room.

"That's not very organised," he deemed unable to keep his annoyance hidden. "It's bad enough that you're in this situation without them having to prolong the stress of it."

"It really doesn't matter. Mr Yates was perfectly polite and it makes no difference to me if I have to wait for a few more hours."

"Still," he grumbled sulkily. I laughed at his persistence and chose to leave the conversation at that. The time passed quicker than expected and when I next looked outside the sky was darkening.

"Oh my, I should get going. They will be wondering where I am," I said. "Actually they probably won't be at all, but I should still get going otherwise I am going to end up with no room at all."

As usual I got my timing completely wrong and turned up as they were about to sit down to eat their supper. No one offered to make room at the table so I took the butler's earlier offer and went to sit in his work room to wait it out.

After what seemed like forever, Mrs Montgomery eventually came to show me to my room – leaving me to try and lug the chest up the stairs without any assistance.

"Everything you need should be in there, the bathroom is two doors down the hall," she said, offering me no words of encouragement before she made her hasty exit.

My hands were shaking as I reached out and grabbed the cold handle, turning it slowly in nervous anticipation of what lay beyond it. The door opened; no creaks or groans like I had grown used to. The room that greeted me was not large by any standards but it was still far bigger than anything I had seen. A single bed was pushed against one white wall with a small window hanging above it, there was a desk with a chair tucked neatly underneath, tight against the opposite wall and a chest of drawers stood proudly next to the door.

Where I was used to a tiny bed with piles of clothes surrounding me, I now found that I could walk through the room – even lunge – without having to watch my every step.

Although I still didn't particularly want to be staying here I was astounded by what had been provided for me and I felt that I would have little trouble in avoiding other members of the household. I unpacked my effects with room left over, my brooch taking pride of place on the top of the dresser. I cautiously left the room and scurried across to the bathroom which was thankfully vacant. I heard the distant approach of voices when I left but I managed to duck back into my room before anyone saw me; counting the doors as I hurried to make sure I was in the correct place. I tucked myself under the fresh crisp covers and let the warmth and comfort sweep me into a deep sleep.

I was up bright and early the next day prepared to make a good impression on the new head gardener. I was the first to wake so I tiptoed down the stairs, remaining on the balls of my feet until I reached the door. The door didn't budge when I pulled the handle, only occurring to me now that they would have locked up for the night meaning that I was now effectively locked in. Thankfully someone had more sense than me and had thought to leave the key hanging beside the door for me to let myself out – either that or that was where the key had always belonged. I placed my shoes on the floor outside and stepped into them one by one, sneaking out into the fog that had not yet lifted. It was so thick that I could barely make out my hand, fingers wriggling in front of my face, but I was fortunate that my feet knew where they had to guide me.

I was the first to arrive at the shed, and since I was still in possession of the key I unlocked it to check that everything was in order. I temporarily forgot myself and started collecting up the required instruments for the day ahead. It wasn't until the wheelbarrow was almost full that it hit me that I was no longer in charge of the day and was probably being presumptuous by doing so. I hurriedly put everything back in place before I got caught in the act. I returned to my spot by the shed and stood there, impatiently waiting for the day to start – I wasn't used to hanging around for somebody else. The fog was just starting to lift when I noticed the figure of a man walking towards me. From the distance he looked tall and proud – or maybe I was just saying that in comparison to what my father had become. As he drew nearer I could see that he was quite well built which meant he would have no trouble handling some of the jobs that I struggled with.

"You must be Emily," he said holding out his weathered hand to me. His warm face was welcoming, the lines showing his age creased with his smile and I felt some of my earlier anxieties start to slip away. He had neatly cut brown hair and a tanned face to match with the most unusual eyes I had ever seen; one was a blue so dark it was almost violet, and the other was a hazel flecked with gold.

"I'm Benjamin Morton, but please call me Ben. You'll have to be patient with me to start with as I learn my way around, but I've heard that you are more than capable so I'm sure I'm in good hands," he said happily.

I felt a swell of pride in my chest with his words, absurdly pleased that he had turned out to be him; from first impressions it looked like we would be getting on well.

"I met Lenny last night and he told me a lot about you. He speaks very highly of you I must say. How are you feeling without your father around?" he asked as we made our way to the walled gardens.

"I'm okay, thank you," I said politely not wanting to divulge too much information to this strange man.

We reached the first of the walled gardens which housed the vegetables, all contained within the crumbling brick wall. The weather beaten oak gate creaked open and we stepped beneath the archway, his head instinctively ducking, into a low maze of neatly trimmed rows and pots. I proudly showed him around each section, pointing to where the green buds would usually be poking through, to the neatly planted rows of carrots and beans that were hidden beneath the soil and the heaped mounds where the potatoes would appear before long. There were iron frames arching over the pathways where sweet peas would bloom, later scrambling up the climbing roses. I looked over the garden, hidden by tall trees that sprouted around the walls – a serene hideout – and I was overwhelmed by a sense of pride at what I had helped to create.

Chapter 32

I spent the rest of the morning giving Ben a tour of the land, showing him not only the land that we were to tend to but also to the other areas that surrounded the estate.

"You've done a really good job here," he said once we had made our way back to where we had started. We hadn't stopped talking the whole time we were walking and I had learnt that they had come from 'up north' as he put it, from the area of Manchester, with his wife, Ruth, and his two children; Lizzie who was six and Teddy who was not yet a year of age. The more he spoke, the more convinced I became that he was a genuinely good guy and that it wasn't going to be as bad as I had imagined it to be.

"Thank you, I try to do the best that I can," I replied bashfully.

"Where should we get started today? I figure you are more in the know about what needs doing around here than I am."

"There's some new fruit trees that need planting in the orchard and I try to see to the vegetable garden every day if I can just to make sure that it is all in order."

"That we'll do then, and I'll have a wander round to start looking at what needs to be done."

It took some time to heave the six new trees over to the orchard – two cooking apple, two eating apple and two pear – before we could actually start working. They had actually arrived at the start of the previous week but it would have taken me an entire day, and a very bad back, to do it myself so I had left them in their pots and tended to them as needed there. The almost continuous rain that we had been having meant that the soil was soft and easy to dig. It was so soft in fact that I could kneel down and dig with my hands like a dog. I caught Ben watching me out the corner of my eye with a quizzical expression on his face, leaning against the shovel he had been conventionally using to dig his hole.

"Would you rather I did it another way?" I asked, sitting up to speak to him. I wiped a strand of hair off my face, smearing a streak of mud across my forehead in the process.

"No, not at all lass. It's just that I'm used to my girl who will throw a fit if she even gets slightly dirty. Was kind of hoping this means she will grow out of it," he said with a chuckle. His laugh was deep and friendly and I found myself mentally adding it to the list I had been creating about him.

"I hate to break it to you but I have been out in these gardens since before I can remember. My pa had me digging in the mud and planting the seeds as soon as I was big enough." The memory warmed me even though there was a tug at my heart – the painful reminder that he was no longer there.

"But you still have your little boy, we can train him up to not be afraid of the mud," I added with a smile.

"Maybe you could still get Lizzie interested as well," he said hopefully. I laughed politely not wanting to be the one to tell him that it was unlikely that his little girl was going to stop being, well, such a girl, though I would have to meet her before I was to make any judgements.

"Why don't you go walk around? I can handle the rest of this," I said when I noticed that the day was getting on. It was nice to have someone to talk to, or even to just have them there whilst I was working but I already missed the peacefulness of working on my own.

I continued to plant the trees alone, enjoying the song of the wind whistling quietly above me. The mud was building up beneath my fingernails and I had to keep blowing away the curls that were relentlessly springing in front of my eyes. My knees were wet from the damp mud and even though I had been working non-stop I could feel the cold starting to seep into my bones. I patted the mud down firmly over the last of the freshly-planted trees and reached my arms up, stretching from my shoulders to the tips of my fingers. I pushed myself up and twisted the knots out of my back before heading off to the vegetable garden; I figured that Ben would be able to figure out that was where I would be. However, I finished up in there before he returned and I found myself unsure of what to do now that there was someone else in charge of me. I wandered back out through the creaky gate to see if I could spot him anywhere, but the land seemed to be deserted. I decided to go wash myself off whilst I was waiting for Ben to reappear, not wanting to go back into the house covered in mud. I darted unseen around the side of the stables where the tap was located and splashed the ice-cold water on my face and tried my best to brush away the mud that caked my hands. When I eventually drew my hands away from the falling water and spun the tap dry I noticed that my hands were now red raw from the temperature of the water I had been using to clean myself. I pulled my sleeves down and used them to cover my hands like gloves. I wiped the water from my face and headed back to the gardens.

I stopped by the shed to return the equipment that we had used that day, hanging my apron by the door instead of taking it with me. I locked the door and instinctively slipped the string around my neck for safe keeping, soon realising that I would have to pass it onto Ben when I found him. The sound of footsteps running up behind me announced his return, though I still couldn't stop myself spinning around nervously to check that it wasn't anyone else.

"Sorry to leave you alone for so long, I got a bit lost finding my way back."

"That's fine sir, I finished everything up."

"None of this sir business, just Ben!"

"Okay, sorry sir. I mean Ben," I corrected hastily.

"Are we all done for the day then?" he asked, laughing at my mistake.

"I would usually say so, I don't see much benefit of working when the sun has gone down."

"Completely agree. The wife is eager to meet you, would you like to pop in for some tea?" he asked. There was no way that I could refuse, he was being polite by extending me the invitation and the working relationship was still too new to risk by declining that offer. There were a few main reasons that were unsettling me about going with him; the first being that I was unsure how being back in the cottage would make me feel now that it was no longer mine, the second reason was that I was nervous about meeting his family since I knew they had to like me and the third, and possibly the most pathetic, was that I missed Oscar. Our lunch time meetings were now likely to become a thing of the past so I wanted to try and see him after work. I tried to brush the thoughts aside and just concentrate on trying to make a good impression. I pointlessly attempted to smooth out the permanent creases in my clothing and ran my fingers through my knotted curls, which only served to make them spring out even more. I don't know why I was trying to make an effort since my appearance was unlikely to improve even if I wasn't currently covered in mud, I was just thankful that at least I had had the foresight to scrub the main layer of mud away from my skin.

Even though it had only been a day since I had left it the cottage looked like a stranger to me; the old bricks seemed darker, the thatched roof seemed heavier and the small windows seemed brighter. The glow that the windows were emitting made the small home look like it was smiling; happy that there was once again a positivity closed within its walls.
"Papa!" the little girl called out as her father walked through the door, expertly catching her as she flung herself at him.

"Hello my little flower," he said happily planting a big kiss on her rosy cheek. He walked to the kitchen to greet his wife and placed an affectionate kiss on his sleeping son's forehead; they were the picture of a perfect family.

"And you must be Emily," said Ruth with a warming smile. She walked over and wrapped me in her arms, just how I imagined my mother would have done. I felt a lump form at the sentiment of the action and I had to swallow hard to get rid of it.

Ruth and Lizzie were the image of one another, both with long dark hair and dark blue eyes, their skin was milky-white and untainted by the sun without a blemish in sight. Teddy was still too young to have grown into his looks but he had the tufts of brown hair to match his father's and when he blinked his sleepy eyes open they were the same shade of gold to match that one of his father's mismatched eyes. Lizzie was looking up at me through long dark eyelashes, hiding behind her father's leg.

"Your hair is very curly, it's like my dollies hair," she said matter-of-factly. I smiled gently and nodded at her, unsure what I was supposed to say in response to the small child.

"Would you like to meet her?" she asked, unfazed by my lack of response.

"I'd love to," I said following her to her spot by the fire.

"You're staying for tea, yes Emily?" Ruth asked and I could tell it was more a statement than a question so I simply nodded politely in agreement.

"Teddy is small like a doll but he moves and makes a lot of noise. And sometimes he really smells which isn't very nice," Lizzie said, full of childhood innocence. I revelled in her imagination, playing games with her doll and hearing all about what she had been learning. After we had eaten I had a tentative hold of the baby, even though I was terrified of dropping him. He stared up at me with inquisitive eyes and gurgled happily at my worried expression. When I left I felt as though I had been welcomed into a new family and until I thought about it I hadn't even noticed my father's absence in the house that had once belonged to us.

The barn was dark and the doors were closed when I walked past on my way back to my room. I paused outside it for a moment just watching its stillness in the hope that there would be the slightest sign of movement to welcome me in.

I took my shoes off at the servants' door, not wanting to tread mud through the house, and walked quietly down the corridor. There was still some noise coming from the servants' hall and the distinctive sound of plates being washed up could be heard from the kitchen, but I was still set in my choice to remain as invisible as possible and succeeded in getting up the stairs without being seen. Unfortunately, I didn't make it into the safety of my room without being spotted by Lydia, the ladies' maid.

"Are you enjoying your new room?" it sounded like a perfectly innocent question but the sneer on her face told me that it was quite the opposite.

"Yes, thank you," I replied politely trying to discreetly sneak past her to avoid the conversation, but she stepped in front of me to block my way.

"We haven't seen much of you around," she continued.

"No, I'm trying to stay out the way."

"Don't you think that is a bit rude?" she questioned and I could feel myself getting annoyed even though I knew that her goal was to wind me up.

"Sorry, I am very busy at the moment though," I tried to keep my tone light but there was a hard edge to it.

"And you think we aren't busy?" she snapped back.

"I never said that."

"You just think you're better than us don't you? Because you've always been friends with Master Edward," she stated.

"No!" I cried, outraged. Though at least I knew now why they all had a problem with me.

"Bet you're jealous that he's getting married."

"Of course I'm not," I snapped back, and the truth was that I really wasn't; Edward hadn't even crossed my mind recently. She shook her head at me and started to walk away.

"You know that no one here likes you, right? How does it feel to be all alone?" she asked nastily, turning on her heels and leaving me to ponder that very question.

"Just great," I whispered to the empty corridor.

Chapter 33

The eleventh of November, 1918, started off the same as any other day; I woke earlier than the sun, tiptoed out of the house and set to work in the cold hours of the early morning. No one could have anticipated that today would be different to any other; that it would be a day to change the lives of so many.

The sky was overcast and grey though it hadn't spilt a drop of rain and the air was unusually still, hugging its iciness close to me. I was kneeling in the mud, my stiff, aching hands buried deep in the soil, working alone. Though Ben and I had appeared to bond early on, he believed that it was far more efficient to be working on separate tasks. I couldn't say that I didn't understand because I completely agreed with him, I just couldn't help but feel a little lonely, especially knowing that I now spent more time alone than amongst the company of friends.

The sun struck midday and I knelt up eagerly anticipating Oscar's arrival. I waited for some time, even stretching up to see if I could spot him walking in my direction, but there was no sign of him. I couldn't help but worry, it was very unlike him to miss our meetings, and he knew that I was working alone so he was always able to pop by even if it was just to say hello. I reluctantly settled back into my work, unable to focus properly on my jobs for the day due to the stampede of possibilities running through my head. There was no point rushing as it was down to Ben when I finished for the day, but my hands couldn't hide my eagerness to find out what the problem was.

As the day continued at a painstakingly slow pace I noticed that I didn't see anyone passing by; not the chauffeur taking anyone into town, not the footmen stepping out for a cigarette or the maids rushing to the village on an errand. I couldn't shake the unease that there was something of the utmost importance, but unfortunately I was stuck in the position where I could do nothing to find out what it was. The minutes ticked by languidly and it felt like a lifetime before I heard the crunch of footsteps on the gravel path announcing that the work day would soon be over.

"It's getting darker earlier, isn't it?" Ben commented as he approached. I looked up to the darkening sky and nodded my head in agreement. With the season changing to winter it brought with it shorter days and longer nights, taking away the cheeriness summer delivered.

"Everything been okay today?" he continued, showing me that he must also not have heard any news today, so either nothing had happened and I was imagining things or the news was yet to reach us. I hastily packed everything up and carried the pile in my arms to the shed. I quickly tidied it away and locked the shed behind me, my body eager to leave.

"There were no problems, I got everything done that you asked," I replied, eager to please him.

"I expected nothing less," he said with an approving smile. I started to shuffle my feet to try and subtly tell him that I wanted to leave but he seemed intent on carrying on the conversation.

"My family were won over by you, little Lizzie won't stop talking about you. And my wife has told me to let you know that you are welcome anytime."

The offer warmed me, it had been a long time since I had really felt included anywhere and it was a sensation that I wasn't used to; to actually know that I was wanted somewhere.

"Thank you, that is really kind," I said with feeling. "You have a wonderful family." There was a tiny part of me, hidden somewhere deep, that experienced a pang of sadness knowing that the ideal of that perfect family was something that I had unfortunately missed out on. I pushed that sadness far down, not wanting to appear jealous to people who had no control over their happiness. They had every reason to be happy; it wasn't their fault that mine had been tragically stolen from me.

"Well I shall let you get on, see you in the morning Emily," he said with a cheery wave. I watched him walk into the distance towards his warm home, before I grudgingly shuffled my feet towards the looming house.

"Emily!" called out the unmistakable voice. I would have recognised those deep tones anywhere, and my body tingled with anticipation as I turned to face the man that had been at the forefront of my mind for days.

"Sorry I missed you earlier, things have been rather hectic. Have you heard the news?" His voice was full of excitement but there was something missing in his eyes; there was a twinkle of disappointment and anger that could be seen if you looked hard enough. I shook my head and patiently waited to hear the news that had clearly affected the entire estate.

"The war is over. The fighting stopped at the eleventh hour of the morning."

"It's really over?" I asked, more for him than for me. I could only imagine how it must be affecting him though I was finding it almost impossible to read exactly what it was that he was feeling.

"All stopped," he muttered, and it was then that I heard the anguish that escaped with his sigh. I looked up into his dark eyes and saw that they were blurred by unfallen tears.

"What's wrong?" I asked gently, taking his hand in mine. He shook his head and stared up at the dark sky.

"I'm not sure. I should be happy that it's over, and I am. I just can't help but feel guilty that I wasn't there at the end. So many lives have been wasted, innocent lives, and so young. I was given the chance to continue with mine but I lost so many friends, and I'm not sure how many of them will get that chance to return home. I can't help but feel that the whole thing was just a waste of time and a waste of perfectly good men." He sighed and looked down at me, letting his fingers trace the edges of my cheek. "I envy you sometimes, Emily. You're one of the few that was saved from the war, you don't know how lucky you are to not have such disturbing images and memories carved into your brain. Your innocence is beautiful." He stared into my wide eyes as he spoke. I wasn't sure if I should be annoyed by his final comment, but I couldn't see a reason to disagree. As much as I thought I had problems they were no greater than anyone else's and they were certainly insignificant in comparison to the burdens the soldiers were carrying home with them. His words held no lies, I had barely noticed the war from my little cocoon, I had heard the news that was relayed to me and I had been shocked when I heard of all the blood and deaths, but I had been able to continue on with my life unaffected. How Oscar had entered into this world and functioned alone I had no clue, and I felt awful knowing that I had done little to help and I had been too selfish to ask how he felt.

"It's not your fault, you did everything that you could," I said in an attempt to make him feel better.

He stared down at his injured hand, the scars protectively hidden by his leather glove. He slowly pulled the fingers of the glove and peeled the material away from his skin.

"It was all because of this. A foolish mistake that meant I could no longer hold a gun," his voice cracked with emotion as he held those heroic scars up for me to see. It was easy to see the torture in that intricate maze: the lines of agony that he had experienced for his country. I was lost for words, caught up in his emotion.

"I was fed up of sitting in those cold, stinking trenches surrounded by dead bodies and those injured by the shells that were relentlessly thrown at us, so when the officer in charge said that soldiers were being sent across No Man's Land, I was taken over by a young burst of enthusiasm and volunteered to be a part of the front line. Some would say that I was doing the right thing to defend my country but I knew that I only did it out of boredom and it was because of that, that I could no longer fight." He paused as he remembered the event. "The enemy's bullet shot through my hand severing the nerves and any chance I had of returning. They said I was one of the lucky ones, that I could easily have been added to the body count but sometimes I wonder if I really am lucky."

I was shocked by his words, maybe I shouldn't have been surprised by his reaction to such a devastating event, but it was his disregard to life that hit me the most. I had no idea that he didn't value the life that had been handed to him and that worried me.

"I didn't know," I whispered naively, shivering in the cold: or was it from the words? I couldn't tell.

"I would never want you to," he whispered back, wrapping me into the warmth of his arms. I could hear his heart hammering against his chest, fighting to escape the pain it held inside.

I stayed with Oscar until he fell asleep, laying silently in his arms until I heard his breath relax. I carefully moved his arm from mine and tiptoed across the creaking boards and out in the twilight sky. I shuffled through the darkness, guided by the lights that illuminated the main house. I could hear celebratory voices reaching out to me across the long hallway as I padded my stockinged feet towards them. The chattering voices almost pulled me in and I had to fight the temptation to go and join them. I caught a glimpse of the happy bodies through the open door but if they spotted me they paid no attention. I crept up the stairs and through the silent hallway to my new room. The neat bed called out to me, and though the comfort was welcoming, throwing its warmth over my exhausted body, it still didn't feel like home.

Chapter 34

The attitude around the estate seemed to have changed dramatically since the news that the fighting had ceased reached us. I could tell they were giddy with emotion when I received countless smiles from people. Don't get me wrong, of course I was glad that the war had ended, I never understood the reasoning behind it, but if it hadn't affected me then, then why should it affect me now? I wasn't going to take away from anyone else's excitement though and I certainly wasn't going to complain about the change of behaviour towards me.

I stepped outside and gasped as the coldness of the morning hit me. My flimsy blue coat could not withstand these temperatures; it was more a tattered piece of material wrapped around me flapping uselessly above my knees. The mornings were now as dark as the night, silent and eerie as the last glimpses of the moon illuminated the grounds. Even the birds were still huddled together in their nests, sensible enough to stay out of the cold. I pulled my coat tight around me and trudged down the path, the sharp coldness stinging my cheeks. I could smell snow lingering on the air. Ben wasn't there when I arrived so I unlocked the shed door and huddled in the wooden shack to try and protect myself from the bitter cold. The key was like ice to my skin where it hung by my chest. I blew into my hands as I stared down the deserted lane, the warmth of my breath making my fingertips tingle. Eventually I spotted a figure walking towards me; head bent and body cramped.

"Sorry I'm late," Ben said sleepily.

"That's fine," I said, watching my frosted breath swim around me.

"I'll never understand why we have to be up at this hour when everyone else is snug in their beds. Surely I can change the hours," he mumbled grumpily, more to himself than me, as he crashed around the small shed gathering the tools needed for the day ahead. I didn't answer simply because I didn't know what to say, although the early mornings were hard during the winter months I had grown used to them and didn't feel as though I was in any position to complain. I stood there patiently waiting to receive anything that was handed to me like a good worker would.

"We had some visitors last night," Ben said out of the blue as we walked slowly towards the gardens.

"Well that's nice. Did you have a good time?" I asked politely. "I might have done if they were there to see me. But they seemed more interested in you and your father," he said peering across at me to gage my reaction. Though my heart was caught in my throat and I could feel the nerves thundering through my body, I somehow managed to keep my face free of all emotion.

"Oh really, who was that then?" I asked calmly, although my voice came out slightly more high-pitched than usual.

"He didn't leave a name, but he did ask where you were both staying now. I told him that you were now situated at the main house and that your father had to go away." I could tell by the way that he was speaking that he was now wondering whether he had done the right thing.

"Thank you, it's important that he can find me there." I couldn't risk Ben finding out about the secrets that I held, so I had to put a brave face on despite the fact that his words had been like a punch to my stomach. Ben smiled and let out a sigh.

"That's good then."

I could sense his relief so just decided to leave it at that. I balled my hands into fists to stop them shaking and had to force my head to stay straight ahead, fighting the urge to check the lane behind me.

I was on edge for the whole day, jumping at the slightest noise. Ben must have noticed my strange behaviour but he didn't say anything. I could feel his eyes on me as I worked but I wouldn't turn to meet his gaze because I didn't want the inevitable conversation. As my hands worked the soil, burying bulbs and patting down seeds, I wished that I could hide myself beneath that soil and not have to face any more problems.

The darkness that was starting to set as we were packing up set my nerves on edge. I found myself dreading the walk back to the house alone.

"Everything alright?" Ben asked, concerned.

"Yes," I choked. "Yes, everything is fine." The nerves were evident in my voice but he didn't ask any more questions.

"Okay, well I shall see you in the morning then." He made it sound more like a question than a statement.

"Of course."

He nodded to bid good day and turned his back on me leaving me standing alone in the impending darkness. I checked both directions on the path to make sure no-one was there and started to walk slowly thinking that this way I would be more likely to hear if anyone was approaching. I was wrong. My heart was thumping in my ears and my breath was as loud as ten voices as it escaped from my chest. This was what happened when you let your fears step into your mind like poison. You saw shadows when there were none; you heard a mouse and imagined a lion. Despite myself my legs started to work faster and I found that I was almost running. I could spot the lights from the stables up ahead and I immediately started to calm down knowing that if I could make it there then at least I would be safe. The way ahead looked clear so I slowed my pace to catch my breath as my steps brought me closer to that haven.

The next few moments seemed to happen in slow motion; my legs moved as though bricks were attached to them, my heart boomed one drum beat at a time and my eyes helplessly followed the three silhouetted figures that stepped out in front of me, blocking me only feet away from safety. My body stopped, one limb at a time, and I felt my chest squeeze as my brain registered the trouble that I was in.

"Good evening, Emily. You're a difficult girl to find." The voice had no face but memory told me that it belonged to Charlie Griggs.

"But you can't hide from us," another voice added. I guessed that it was owned by either Porter or Lambert but couldn't recall them well enough to tell.

"I wasn't trying to hide from you," I croaked, not wanting them to think they scared me.

"You may not be, but your father certainly is," Griggs said, stepping closer so that I could see his snarling face. "And if we can't get to him then we need to find you."

My breath caught in my throat and for a moment time froze. It had never even crossed my mind that once my father had gone they would want me. I had considered the possibility that they would still come looking for him but I had naively thought that when they couldn't find him they would just go away.

"We're still owed a lot of money, so I suggest you tell us where Thorne is," spat Porter or Lambert.

"I don't know where he is," I said confidently, knowing that I was telling the truth.

"Well you need to know otherwise we are going to have to get the money from elsewhere and since you're his own flesh and blood it looks like it will be falling on you," Charlie Griggs said spitefully. I had known that those words were coming but it still shocked me. There was no way that I could pay back that money and I knew they were also aware of that, making me anxious to know what message was hidden in those words.

"So, we will ask you one more time. Where is your father?"

"I told you, I don't know," I said, this time lacking some of the confidence I had mustered earlier.

"Then it looks like this debt is now yours to pay." They edged closer to me, making a semi-circle with their bodies so I couldn't escape through them. My only exit was to turn and run behind me but I didn't think I would be able to outrun them now that they were expecting it. My eyes twitched towards the barn to judge how close I was to it.

"Don't even think about it," Griggs sneered. "We will be on you before you can even finish screaming." Even in the dark he had seen the whites of my eyes move – I couldn't see any escape.

I felt my muscles loosen as the tension lifted and I started to give up. I couldn't run. I couldn't fight. They had me and we all knew it. I could take the risk and try to scream but I had a feeling that it would only make matters a lot worse. Charlie Griggs stepped forward to face me, not even an arm's length away. The close proximity of his body to mine made me feel sick. I had fought him off once, but we had been alone then. I was outnumbered. I felt my insides tightened as it dawned on me that this time he might be able to achieve what he had failed before. A cold hand was placed on my arm, his touch freezing my body. I gasped a sharp intake of breath and held it, not daring to make a single movement. The world seemed to stop; the swirling air paused, the racing clouds halted and there was no sign of life. There was only me and him, standing in a motionless pose: his hand holding me and his beady eyes piercing my soul. I slowly moved my gaze from the floor to meet his eyes, those eyes that reflected all the dark thoughts that he had hidden inside.

"I think you should get your hands off her," a voice spoke up out of the darkness, powerfully reaching out to us. Griggs turned to locate the voice but was faced with darkness. The pace of my heart quickened as I recognised the deep tones.

"Whose there?" he called out and I could have sworn that I could hear a trace of nervousness in his voice.

Stay hidden, I willed him, *please don't get involved.* But it was useless, even if I had shouted it out I knew he had made his mind up, and worst of all I knew that he was aware of exactly who these three men were.

"Get your hands off of her and then maybe I will think about telling you." He made it very clear that they didn't want to be messing with him and from the look I had seen in his eyes the other night I could vouch for that. I could see Griggs thinking about what he should do, the pressure of his hand on my arm softening slightly. His face told me that he knew it had all just been turned around and that what he had originally planned was no longer going to work; he needed a new plan and he needed one quick. As soon as his fingers lifted away from me he turned expectantly waiting to find the face of his intruder. I could hear the crunch of footsteps walking to join us and I held my breath dreading what was going to happen next. Dark hair and dark eyes joined the circle with a grimacing face, ready to battle for me.

"Emily, come over here by me," he demanded. I stepped back slowly, unsure if anyone was going to stop me. When they didn't I quickened my steps and anxiously hurried over to the protection of Oscar. He gently pushed me behind him and kept an arm held protectively across mine.

"From now on, if you have a problem then it is with me. You are not to lay a finger on her again."

There were still more of them than us but Oscar's tall, lean stature seemed overpowering in the darkness. Though if it was to come down to brute force, and I am sure that they were also smart enough to realise this, then they would have full control. I saw that exact moment when that realisation hit them, almost as though a light had switched on in their eyes.

"We do have a problem," the short one said as he stepped closer towards us. Oscar visibly tensed and he pushed me back slightly whilst simultaneously taking a step to meet the trouble.

"Go back to the barn," he muttered under his breath, all the while staring ahead and refusing to break the connection he had with the men.

"No, I'm not leaving you!" I cried outraged.

"Just go," he snapped, jolting his head round at me. The power in his voice made me take a step back and I edged into the shadows where I couldn't be seen, but where I could still see them. The wind carried their voices away from me so I could only read the situation by their body language. I watched them each take a turn in stepping closer to each other - the swift movements like a well-rehearsed dance – Porter and Lambert placing themselves on either side of Oscar. Even before anything happened I saw it play out in my mind, but when I tried to scream out in warning fear rendered me to the spot and cruelly stole my voice. The first crunch of knuckle against bone echoed painfully through the air until it touched me so hard I could feel the contact. I watched through blurred eyes as he was held down and beaten; hard boots thumping against his ribs and venomous hands hammering down on his face.

Oscar tried to fight against the heavy hands that held him down but it was useless. I saw the spray of blood that escaped his mouth as the fist lay him back against the gravel; his body motionless.

"NO!" I screamed out, the loudest noise I had ever made when my voice finally broke free. The three men stopped and stared at the spot where I appeared on the path and for a moment I was sure they were coming for me next. My entire body was shaking uncontrollably but I stood my ground, my need to save Oscar far greater than the need to save myself. It was only when I heard voices behind me that I allowed myself to breath. The three men scarpered faster than I had seen them move and I wasted no time in rushing over to Oscar's side. His eyes were closed as though he was sleeping, his pale face smeared with blood. His legs were curled up close to his chest as though he was still trying to protect himself, his fists grasped tightly together ready to hit back at the right moment. When I pressed my ear close to him his breath was faint; barely a whisper. I was unaware of the tears that were dripping off my cheeks onto Oscar's face, trying to wash away some of the blood that stained it. I kissed him long and soft, and when I pulled away I touched his mouth with my fingers. My hands were trembling.

Chapter 35

I couldn't feel anything. I was numb. I was informed that I had tried to fight Lenny off when he picked me up to carry me away from the body on the floor, but it is not something that I remember. I can vaguely recollect Lenny and Johnny carrying Oscar into the warmth of the barn, but it feels more like a dream than a memory. Everyone rushed around, using the limited knowledge between them to tend to the bruised and broken figure. I watched it all, sitting and staring from my place by the fire, but I took nothing in; the world was a giant blur before me. Despite the warmth of the crackling fire and the blanket that had been draped over me, I was shivering violently; the cold gradually seeping into every muscle. My face was ghostly white and I felt sick to my stomach. When I stretched my fingers out they were still trembling, traces of Oscar's blood decorating them.

I think that people came to check on me, but I couldn't be certain. I vaguely remember Lenny talking to me though what he said I would be unable to repeat. The minutes ticked by in a flurry, bodies bustling around all trying to help the injured victim, though for me it was painfully slow. I wanted to be next to him, to be able to hold his hand just to let him know that I was there. But I couldn't make myself, my eyes refused to see him like that again. Until I was certain that he was going to be alright I was not moving from this chair.

"Emily. Emily. Emily."

I heard my name being repeated in the distance, the rest of the words lost to my ears.

"Emily!"

The voice was louder this time and more urgent, gradually pulling me out of my daze. My eyes came to focus and I saw unfamiliar features forming before me, his hazel eyes searching my face. I watched his cracked lips form the next bundle of words.

"Hello Emily. It's David, I work down at the farm. My wife Mary is here with me as well. Would it be okay if she checked you over?" His voice was polite yet sincere and those features that had seemed new to me at first were now starting to seem old. I recognised the long sweep of his greying hair and the wrinkled lines along his cheeks. It felt as though I had heard his voice before. I didn't respond but he must have taken my silence as permission because the next thing I knew there was a cold hand grasping my wrist, fingers firmly searching my veins. The coolness turned my head toward its owner; soft brown eyes staring intently at my skin, making sure not to miss a heartbeat. Her controlled breath calmed me and I felt myself relaxing slightly as her exhales tickled my arm lightly.

"Did you get hurt at all?" he asked uniformly, his voice closer as I pulled myself back to reality. I shook my head.

"No," I said, my voice soft and wispy.

The farmer stood up when his wife gave him a reassured nod and me a soft, sympathetic smile, and they spoke more to Lenny than to me.

"I can't see any obvious injuries, I would just say that she needs to get a good rest. Hopefully it will be better in the morning."

"No, I'm fine. How is Oscar?" I asked, finding my voice. I glanced impatiently between the two men on either side of me, noticing the look they shared before answering me. It was only after a slight nod from Lenny that anyone spoke.

"He is sleeping at the moment. I have tended to his injuries as best I can but we shall be keeping a close watch on him overnight."

I knew that the lack of information was not a good sign, but I didn't push for more. I had learnt from previous experiences as a child that it wouldn't get me anywhere. Plus, I didn't want to hear that he wasn't alright. I pushed myself up onto heavy legs and steadied myself on Lenny's waiting arm.

"I want to stay with him," I stated, making it clear that no-one would be telling me otherwise. Lenny nodded and I knew that he had already been expecting that.

"Let's get you cleaned up first, there's a nice fresh bowl of warm water waiting for you." He gently guided me away from everyone and helped me to wash away the salty traces of my tears and scrub the night away from my hands. I watched the water turn red as my hands came out clean; how easily evidence could be washed away. He removed my blood stained coat and replaced it with a heavy blanket to wrap myself in. I slowly shuffled over to where Oscar lay, a make-shift bed set out for him on what usually served as their eating table. My breathing was shallow as I anticipated what I was to see next. His top had been removed so that the extent of his injuries could be seen; the majority of his torso had been bandaged up, bandages that already had splotches of fresh blood on them. I could see the faint purple colouring that was starting to appear on the parts of his chest that were exposed and the darker marks on his arms and shoulders where they had forcefully held him down. The blood had been washed from his face to reveal a large cut sliced across his forehead and one across his cheek that had already began to swell and colour from the impact of the punch.

I cautiously sat down in the chair next to him; scared to breathe in case it hurt him. My hand shook as I carefully brushed a strand of hair from the cut on his forehead. He didn't move. The gloves that had hidden his previous injury had been removed and his scar reminded me that he had survived this before, though I couldn't stop myself thinking that it couldn't have been so bad as this. His other wrist was discoloured with bruising from where his body had landed on it. I gently placed my hand into his, my unhurt palm against his perfect imperfection. I lay my head on the edge of the table, close enough to lean on him yet holding back.

My sleep was disturbed throughout the night as I constantly woke to check that Oscar was still breathing. I would hold my face inches away from him until I felt the soft touch of air graze my cheek. It was the early hours of the morning, about the fifth time I had woken, that I noticed he was burning a fever; beads of sweat gathering on his skin. I rushed to get some cool water and a cloth to place on his forehead, unsure what else I could do to help. I spent the rest of the night swapping the cloths that seemed to melt almost as soon as they were placed against his head, counting the seconds in between until someone would return.

I wasn't sure what time it was that Lenny came downstairs, having spent the night above the stables, to relieve me. All I know is that it was still dark outside and I was unwilling to leave Oscar's side.

"You have a job to do, Emily. I know you want to stay but we can take care of him," Lenny bargained with me.

"But what about your job?" I retorted stubbornly.

"There is enough of us to manage, plus we are only in the other room so I will be right here. You really must get going or you will be late."

"Ben will understand."

"You can't be sure of that, now get going." He shifted the chair I was sitting on away from the table and stepped in front of me to take over. His back faced me and I knew that was the sign I had lost so I dejectedly rose from the chair and set off into the morning without anything to protect me from the harsh winter air.

I was still in yesterday's clothes but I was hoping that would fall unnoticed, and thankfully the coat had soaked up all the blood leaving my mud-stained clothes untouched. My tired eyes were hallucinating the smears of blood on my hands even though they had been scrubbed clean. The darkness seemed to camouflage my ruffled appearance and the early morning disguised my sleep deprived face.

"Where's your jacket?" Ben asked when we met at the shed. "You'll freeze out here."

"I seem to have misplaced it," I lied. He shook his head at me then paused to think, his fatherly instincts battling to find a solution.

"Wait here one moment," he said before running back down the lane. He returned not long after with a coat slung over his arm.

"This is Ruth's old one, it is a bit tattered but it still does the trick which is why she hasn't thrown it out. Reckon it should fit." He held it out so that I could slip my arms in. The brown cotton coat was thicker and heavier than the one I owned, I could feel the warmth closing in over my fragile body.

"Thank you," I muttered as I buttoned the pegs up to capture the generated heat.

It wasn't until Ben met me after the lunch hour that he noticed my pale complexion and the dark circles around my eyes that gave away my sleepless night. I unsuccessfully stifled a yawn when I noticed him watching me.

"Is everything alright? You aren't looking too well," he asked with concern. I debated whether or not I should spin a lie but it seemed pointless and foolish considering he was most likely to discover the truth soon enough; I just didn't have to tell him the entire story.

"Oscar was attacked by a group of men last night, so I was awake through the night looking after him," I mumbled.

"Christ! Is he okay?"

"I'm not too sure, but when I left this morning he was still alive, so I am going to cling onto that." Infuriatingly, tears started to prick my eyelids and I had to try and swallow the emotion when Ben placed a comforting hand on my arm.

"I'm sure it will all be fine," he said politely. He glanced over the garden around me before continuing. "There's not that much more to be done so I reckon you will be able to leave slightly earlier. I think you are in desperate need of some sleep so that you are fit and ready for tomorrow."

I nodded gratefully, knowing that under those words it meant that I had to be back to normal tomorrow because he wouldn't be able to do this for me again. I got on with my work as best I could, trying not to think about Oscar and what was happening. The sky was gradually darkening, the evening was falling upon us, and I was sure that Ben wasn't going to follow through with his earlier statement when I spotted him walking towards me.

"I'm all done so I can take over here. Now off you trot," he said waving me off.

If it hadn't of been inappropriate I would have thrown my arms around him, instead I scurried off having to force myself not to run back to the barn.

I swung open the closed doors to find Oscar exactly where I had left him, the only difference being that the farmer was back there in place of Lenny.

"His fever seems to have set," David muttered when he noticed my presence. "You did a good job by tending to it so early."

"Has he woken up at all yet?" I asked timidly.

"He has stirred, yes, but the pain will be making him very tired, and really sleep is the best thing for him at the moment. I must insist that it is also the best thing for you. Mary said she can find something to help you, if you like?"

"Thank you, but I don't need it," I said, my exhausted body knowing it would have no trouble sleeping on its own terms.

"Very well," he said to me then turned to address Lenny. "I better get going; if you need any help then you know where I am." He left through the stables, leaving me to wonder how he knew how to handle the situation so well.

"He's right, Em. You really need to get some rest. You're not doing either of you any good by staying here," he said gently. I nodded; my body not strong enough to argue. I knew Oscar was in good hands and everyone was right when they said I needed to rest. I walked over to him and leant down to brush my lips against his unharmed cheek. When I felt him stir at my touch I believed, for the first time, that he would be alright.

I got back to the house earlier than usual which meant that everyone was still hurrying about. I got a few strange looks off a handful of the maids and manservants, but they didn't speak to me and I said nothing in return. I had nearly made it to the safety of the stairs when I was spotted from the kitchen.

"Emily, would you come here please?" Mrs Rook called out. There was no way that I could ignore it since she had seen me stop at the sound of her voice.

"Yes miss, how can I help you?" I asked politely as I walked into the kitchen. She didn't speak to me just looked me up at down, taking in the sight of my pasty skin, tousled hair and red rimmed eyes.

"Have you eaten anything my dear?" she asked, completely taking me by surprise. I shook my head, and then remembered my manners.

"No miss, I haven't."

She motioned for me to take a seat at the old wooden table when she prepared a plate of food for me. She placed a steaming bowl of fresh pea soup in front of me along with a clump of bread to fill my stomach.

"Thank you," I said with tears in my eyes, touched by her unexpected kindness. I let the warming, thick liquid slide down my throat, a sore reminder that I hadn't eaten in longer than a day. I wiped my bowl clean with the last of the bread and took it over to the sink to wash it myself. I placed the clean utensils on the side, unsure where they belonged, and went to leave.

"Thank you," I repeated, wanting to ensure that she knew I appreciated the act.

"Don't thank me, I can't let you starve can I!" she exclaimed, though I could tell from her sympathetic stare that there was more to it than that. However, I didn't receive the same sympathy from the kitchen maid who managed to follow me unseen.

"Don't get used to that, she only feels sorry for you," she said from behind me, making me jump.

"I'm not expecting anything," I mumbled sleepily, trying to continue up the stairs but she pulled me back and stepped in front of me to block my way.

"I know what you're up to and I don't like it," she continued, he jealous eyes boring into me. I ignored her comment, oblivious to what she was talking about, and tried once again to get up to my room.

"We'll see who wins at the party on Saturday though won't we, because I don't see how anyone would be looking at you when you're constantly covered in mud," she spat.

"What party?" I asked choosing to ignore the nasty comment.

"The end of war party," she said patronisingly as though I was stupid.

"Yes, right," I said casually, brushing the new information aside.

"Oh wait, have you even been invited?" she gloated, sensing a new source to play on. In fact it seemed to please her so much that she laughed to herself and went on her way.

I just shrugged, if I was honest then it wasn't something that I cared about at this particular moment; a celebration seeming completely inappropriate after what had just happened, I could see no reason to celebrate.

Chapter 36

I was trimming the grass that was growing over the lane – a long, tedious job that always caused my hand to form the shape of the gardening scissors – when the young stable lad came running up to me. His name escaped me, and I was too wrapped up in trying to remember it that I didn't stop to think what he may be approaching me for.

"Morning Miss Emily, Lenny told me that you're needed straight away," he donned his cap and smiled at me, the gap between his front teeth imperfectly charming. There was no real urgency to his movements but I knew that if I was being called away from work then it must be important.

"I just need to tell Mr Morton. I'll be as quick as I can."

"I will see you back there," he said cheerfully, his cheeks betraying a slight blush when I smiled back at him. I ran off to locate Ben in amongst the fruit trees staring up at the bare branches.

"Sorry to interrupt, but Lenny has sent a message that I am needed, is it okay if I go? I shall be back as soon as I can," I asked, slightly nervous about his response since he had allowed me to leave earlier the previous day.

"No problem," he said, continuing to stare up at the sky. I went to walk away but something about his confused expression pulled me back.

"Is everything okay?"

"Just wondering why there are so many fruit trees. How can they possibly get through it all?" he exclaimed.

"I think Mrs Rook makes a lot of pies," I replied through a giggle. "And I usually sneak the fallen ones to the horses so they don't go to waste."

"Smart thinking." He turned and smiled at me, waving me on my way. I ran off down the lane, curious as to what I was so urgently needed for. I had the answer before I had even set foot inside. The two men standing by the door, dressed in a smart blue uniform, said more than any words needed to. I unconsciously slowed my pace wondering if I had done something wrong, even though I was sure that I couldn't be held accountable for anything, even if I was feeling like I was entirely to blame.

"Hello," I squeaked politely when I reached them.

"Afternoon miss," one of them replied, though neither said anymore so they must not have known that they were looking for me. I quickly entered the barn and went in search of Lenny, oblivious to the absence of Oscar. I found him at the door of the stables watching over Johnny as he tried his best to tackle the extra workload.

"You asked for me?" I enquired.

"Yes. I'm sorry to do this but the police need to talk to you about the other night," he said looking down on me with sad, wise eyes. "And Em, I really think you need to tell them everything otherwise those men are going to get away with what they did to Oscar and I know you don't want that." I nodded in agreement, it was time the truth came out and if I was to be honest with myself then I felt nothing but relief over that fact.

"Is Oscar okay?"

"Yes little lady. He has been able to stay awake for much longer and has started to move around some."

"Have they spoken to him?"

"Yes, but I don't think he said anything you wouldn't want him too. So don't worry. Just go and do the right thing," he said in a fatherly tone. He walked me back over to the main doors, his hand resting lightly on my shoulder; either to guide me or to let me know he was there, I couldn't tell.

"Gentlemen," he called out to get the officers attention. "This is Emily Thorne, she's ready to answer any questions that you have for her."

"Is it okay to use your table again, Mr Hayes?" the taller of the two asked, even though it was clear they would be doing just that anyway. I once again walked back into the barn, this time sitting myself across from them at the table – only then taking note of Oscar's absence.

"Emily, we were told that you were there on the night of Wednesday the thirteenth. Is this true?" the small, dark one asked me. He spoke my name slowly as though he were rolling it off his tongue.

"Yes sir." I replied simply and shortly, apprehension starting to bubble up in my stomach. Lenny's words were echoing at the back of my mind, I knew that he was right but I was scared what would happen if I told the truth. I heard a delicate creak from above me and though I couldn't see anybody I knew that it would be Oscar; there for me like he said he would be.

"Could you please tell us, in your own words, what happened that night?"

I took a deep breath and on the exhale spurted out the events, sparing no details. The officers listened to me intently, exchanging sideward glances and knowing nods at certain elements of the story.

There was a short silence when I finished talking.

"Had you seen the men before?"

This was the question that I had been dreading. It was in this moment that I needed to decide what to do, but I had to make the decision quickly otherwise they would know that something was out of sorts. I closed my mind and answered with the first thought that came to mind.

"Yes."

One of them gave a short, sharp cough – I couldn't remember who was who – that caused me to jump my eyes up from my hands to his face.

"And how exactly do you know them Miss Thorne?" he asked in a more assertive tone now that they could sniff new information. His eyes latched onto mine so that I couldn't bring myself to look away.

"They had some dealings with my father so I have run into them on a few occasions." I kept it basic, I wasn't lying, and if they asked for more, then I would tell them. I just didn't want to go into it all unnecessarily. I couldn't find the benefits for either party to bring up information so far past.

"Do you know what those dealings were?"

"I couldn't be entirely sure, I do know they drank together at the local pub though," I informed them. When it came down to it I found myself unable to speak ill of my father to these strangers.

Luckily, they seemed happy enough with the response, having no reason to doubt the young girl of green eyes wide with innocence.

"Would we be able to speak to your father?" the tall one asked.

"He's not here anymore, sir. He left to go and live with my sick aunt. Somewhere in the Midlands, but I don't know the exact address." That lie came easily; practiced and perfected over time.

The two officers looked at each other knowingly; eyebrows raised and lips slightly pursed, obviously clued in to the fact that there was more to his disappearance but I don't think they suspected me of knowing the truth.

"I don't mean to be rude but I really need to be getting back to work," I confessed, worried that Ben would think I was taking liberties.

"Just one more question then we won't keep you any longer," said one, staring at me through squinted eyes. There was a long pause before the other one spoke, almost as though they were trying to worry me.

"Do you know their names?" the other asked eventually. I sighed inwardly realising that this is what Lenny had meant when he said I needed to tell them everything. On one hand I wanted to tell them so that they would suffer the consequences of what they did to Oscar, but on the other hand I was scared what would be said about me and my absent father. In the end it wasn't a difficult decision; Oscar had already suffered too much for me.

"There was a Charlie Griggs. The others went by Porter and Lambert but I never got their full names, sorry." I kept eye contact with them so they could see that I wasn't just feeding them fictitious names. There was a glint in their eyes that seemed to confirm that these were names that they already knew.

"Thank you very much miss, you've been a lot of help."

I slowly got up from the table expecting someone to stop me but when they didn't I dashed out the door. It was only when I stepped fully into the fresh air that I allowed myself to breathe properly.

I didn't waste any time informing Ben that I was back, I just went straight back to what I had been doing before. With scissors in hand my mind was dangerously wandering off course, busy trying to analyse looks and words that had been exchanged in the barn. It didn't seem as though they suspected me, and it wasn't like I had done anything wrong, unless me assisting my father to run away was a crime. I tried to force the worries away and just concentrate on the now; after all it was going to do me no good to worry myself sick over something that hadn't even happened yet. I buried myself so deep into my work that time flew by and it was Ben that had to come and find me to make me stop.

"I'm almost finished though, I can keep going," I insisted.

"No, Emily. The day is over, it will still be there tomorrow," he said, gently removing the tools from my grip. The grass was trimmed neater than I had ever seen it, almost though each blade of grass had been cut separately with utter precision.

We walked back in silence, I knew that he could tell something was up but I didn't want to be the first one to speak.

"Do you want to talk about it?" he asked finally. He hadn't pried and asked me what I had been wanted for earlier, he had just left me to my business and even now I could tell that he was only asking in case I was in need of a friend. I did want to talk but I was scared that I would break down and I definitely didn't want him to see that.

"I'm just worried about some things, but I will be okay," I replied, not wanting to reject his offer.

"Well if you need me then you know where I am," he said, and with that he was off home, not pushing me any further.

Now that I knew Oscar was making a recovery I was eager to go and visit; to see for myself that he was doing as well as I had been told, and mainly to apologise. As I pushed open the door I was suddenly overcome by nerves, afraid that maybe he wouldn't want to see me. I need not have worried though, for when I walked in he turned to greet me with a beaming smile.

"I was wondering when you would get here," he said happily. It was clear from the grimace on his face and the hunch to his walk that he was still in a lot of pain. I don't know whether it was seeing him like that or just the fact that I was actually seeing him that brought tears rushing to my eyes, but they flowed freely at the sight of him.

"Hey, what's all this about?" he muttered soothingly, reaching out for me. My bottom lip trembled as more tears gushed from my eyes. He tried to brush them away from my cheeks but couldn't keep up. I wanted to bury my head against him but I couldn't get the image of his bruises out of my head and instead found myself backing further away.

"I'm ... so ... sorry," I said through quivering gasps.

"You have nothing to be sorry for. I am the one that chose to get involved."

I just shook my head, unable to say anything more to him. He gently pushed my chin up to meet his eyes.

"I would have hated myself if this had been you. And I am getting better so please stop worrying and don't apologise."

He ducked his head and placed a tender kiss against my trembling lips. Gradually the tears dried out and I roughly wiped my sleeve across my face, tearing at my red, puffy skin. After my jagged breaths had eased from the aftermath of my sobs I finally felt able to speak.

"Did you know that they are having a party tomorrow?" I asked, eager to change the subject.

"Excellent, I'm a brilliant dancer," he joked. I stifled a laugh, not quite ready to join in.

"You should go, will give you a chance to get talking to more people," he added. I looked up at him with sad green eyes.

"I wasn't invited," I mumbled. "Not that I would have gone anyway."

"You forget I know you better than that, Em. But it is their loss for not inviting you. Don't you worry about them."

"I just don't understand why they don't like me, they just look at me like I am a stain on the carpet that they can't get rid of," I moaned selfishly.

He rubbed his thumb across the top of my hand and looked down at me with a knowing smile.

"Well you just have to make them like you then don't you!" he stated.

"I don't know how to do that," I sighed.

"You certainly knew how to do it for me," he said with a cheeky grin. "Just be you and they will struggle not to."

I gave up arguing and just focused on the fact that at least I had him. All I could do was try and if that wasn't enough for them then there was no point in me wasting my time.

Chapter 37

The disturbing kindness carried on into the next day where I found a slice of banana loaf waiting by the door for me, next to the brass key left to let myself out. This kindness may not have extended through the entire household but at least it seemed as though one person was on my side.

"Thank you," I whispered into the emptiness even though no one else was awake to hear me. I nibbled at my morning treat as I wondered through the early darkness. Winter was on its way and the stillness of the cold air warned me that snow could be expected; not something that I would look forward to. I noticed that Ben seemed unusually cheerful this morning but he didn't let on that there was anything in particular that was affecting his usually glum morning mood, so I didn't ask. His smile was infectious and I felt a new pleasure as we worked side by side; it was as though nothing had ever changed. I got lost in my work and I was grateful for the distraction that stopped my mind from running on overdrive.

"Enjoy the rest of your weekend," Ben said as we went our separate ways at the end of the day. It was only when I heard the wheels of a car approaching behind me that I remembered what was happening this evening. It hadn't even occurred to me that all the work I had completed today had just been preparation for the evening and now that I thought about it there was a slight feeling of resentment that I had helped to prepare for a celebration that I wasn't even a part of.

I didn't want to go back into the house but I knew that I needed to eat and wash before I could think about going anywhere else; I was caked in mud and there was a disagreeable odour rising from it.

As I stepped through the door and into the warmth the smells that greeted me were overwhelming: beef and wine and fruits stewing in their juices. If I wasn't hungry before, then the smell that tickled my nose made certain that I was now. I couldn't even sneak into the kitchens to try and make up some food as the flow of servants going in and out was continuous. Plus, I didn't want to risk a slapped wrist for getting in the way.

I rushed upstairs and out of the way to fill up my wash basin with water. I used the last of my soap to lather the cloth and wash away the smell of a hard day's work. As I watched the already murky water swirl around the mud that fell from me, and saw the additional marks on my already stained towel placed beneath my feet, I couldn't help but feel completely out of place in the clean household. I felt like every step I took tainted the immaculate floors; I would never belong here but I had nowhere else to go.

I dried myself roughly, not stopping until there were no longer drops of water falling onto my skin and I dressed warmly in thick tights and a woollen dress with a worn knitted cardigan pulled over the top. I located the pair of boots that I kept aside for my days off and walked out the door and away from this prison. I managed to escape without a word from anyone, but the smug look on Sarah's face as she watched me leave did not go amiss. I chose to ignore it, deciding that she wasn't worth my time – nor was anyone else that wasn't willing to give me a chance.

Being alone in the darkness still unsettled me, I couldn't stop myself from constantly checking over my shoulder; forever in fear of the shadows. There was more noise travelling from the barn than I was used to, many more voices there to make them audible to me from behind the closed doors. I almost turned away thinking that perhaps I was intruding on their plans, but either curiosity or fear pushed me forward. I crept up to the barn door, unsure though why I was creeping, but there was not a crack big enough for me to see through. The only way I was going to see anything through this door was to open it, but I had intended on looking without being seen myself. Instead, I made my way around the side of the barn and towards the stables that lay behind it in the hope that it would be vacated.

    I snuck through the large wooden door that had been left slightly ajar and into the horse-filled stables, their attentive ears picking up on my almost silent footsteps straight away. Most of the horses ignored me, smart enough to realise that I wasn't here for them, but Silver was different – he recognised me somehow, be it from my face or my scent I did not know – and he whinnied for my attention. I hurried over to him and stroked him lovingly to silence him, hoping that his cry out for attention had not been heard over the noise being generated on the other side of the doors. Silver nuzzled against me as I watched the closed door for any sign of movement. I stayed with him for a while, no longer curious now that I had the comfort of the horse beside me. As we stood there in companionable silence I couldn't stop my thoughts from wandering after the person I had tried so hard to push to the back of my mind; I hadn't heard any mention of the return of Thomas, and it was hard not to wonder how Edward was feeling about his brother's absence now that we knew the fighting was over.

I assumed that if the occupants of the house were celebrating then there had been no bad news, but in that moment I desperately wished that the past could be forgotten so I could ask my old friend if he was okay.

Silver let out a noise of protest as I backed away from him to go and peek through the cracks between the planks of wood. I couldn't make out much more than I had before, only the movement of a few more bodies which gave nothing away.

"Are you spying on us?" called out a chuckling voice. I jumped around, my body starting at the sound of being caught.

"No ... no," I stuttered before I recognised my captor. "How did you know I was here?"

"I saw you walking up the lane earlier and when you didn't come in I took a guess at where you would be. And may I ask why exactly it is that you are trying to pry the door open secretly?" Oscar asked.

"I wondered what was going on," I muttered feeling the blush starting to creep up my neck, once again embarrassed that I had been caught out.

"You know you could have just walked through the door, right?" he said jokingly. I nodded feeling ashamed even though I knew he was only messing around with me.

"It just seemed like you were busy that's all, I didn't think I should be intruding."

"We've been waiting for you, you goof," he said ruffling my hair playfully as he reached out to open the door for us. "Now are you coming in or would you rather stay out here with the horses?"

I looked at the beautiful man standing before me, his face still pale but not quite so sunken, and his dark eyes mischievously smiling. As tempting as the horses were I knew I couldn't say no to those smiling lips. "I'm coming in."

It took me a moment to register the changes in the barn; there were streamers and flags hanging from the high wooden beams and decorating the walls. The table — that had recently served as so much more — had been pushed to one side and a make-shift table cloth had been thrown over it which had then been finished off with an assortment of mugs, cups and a few plates scattered with sandwiches and the odds of whatever they had left. It would be no comparison to what there would be in the house but to me it looked a million times better.

"We thought we would have our own party," Oscar said with a smile even though he couldn't hide the strain in his face that gave away how much pain he was still in.

"But you were invited," I mumbled as I looked around at all the faces.

"I would never have gone without you," he said, bending his head to kiss the top of mine.

"Emily!" came a tiny voice, interrupting us. Lizzie came bounding up to me, wrapping her pudgy arms around my legs; her trust in me was endearing.

"Hello Lizzie," I said, bending down so that I was level with her.

"Are you enjoying the party?"

She nodded vigorously. "Mama and papa are here too. And Teddy," she said hurriedly, grabbing my hand to lead me over to them. As she pulled I nearly fell over, my feet all in a tangle beneath me, though I just about managed to save myself the embarrassment of falling flat on my face.

"I wanted to bring Anne but mama said that I couldn't in case I lost her. I wouldn't have lost her but she wouldn't listen to me," the little girl continued, her annoyance with her mother made apparent. It took me a moment to figure out who Anne was. I wasn't sure we had been formally introduced but my best guess was that it would be her doll, the one I had now played with on numerous occasions.

"Hello Emily," Ruth greeted me when we met up with them. Ben threw Lizzie up in the air and she giggled gleefully.

"Sorry lass, we didn't mean for you to be hauled over here but she ran away as soon as she spotted you," Ben said through the hands of his daughter that had been pressed against his face.

"Not a problem." I couldn't help but smile at the closeness of their little family, they looked picture perfect standing there; the beautiful daughter playing happily with her father and the wrapped bundle of the little boy peacefully sleeping in his mother's arms. I expected to feel a pang of jealousy over what I no longer had, but it didn't come; I could now appreciate what was there and not feel sad about it. The happy family weren't the only people here; Lenny was here with his wife who was sitting unsociably by herself, Johnny the stable boy was avidly chatting to the younger stable hand that worked with him and the chauffeur. Even some of the farmers that worked at the bottom of the estate had come to join in with the celebration.

"Did you know about this earlier?" I turned to Ben suddenly remembering his odd behaviour today. He smiled at me impishly.

"Oscar made me promise not to tell," he said. His eyes said more and when he and his wife exchanged a knowing glance I could tell exactly what they were thinking.

"Speaking of which, that certain young lad seems to be looking for you. Maybe you should go join him. You spend enough time with me as it is," he chuckled deeply.

I ruffled Lizzie's hair playfully and went to join Oscar who was standing with Lenny, both of them inconspicuously watching me walk towards them.

"So what do you reckon? I'm betting it's far better than the other one," Lenny claimed as he scanned the room. He threw his arm over my shoulders and gave me a little squeeze.

"You're a lucky girl," he added with a whisper before heading off to join his seemingly unimpressed wife.

"How did you manage all this?" I asked Oscar once we were alone.

"I just got some things together," he said humbly.

"But I only told you last night!"

"I had the time and I wanted you to know that there are plenty of people that like you," he shrugged.

"I like you," I mumbled in response.

He smiled down at me, a soft pink colouring his cheeks. He tucked his hand gently on the back of my neck and bent his head to kiss me; soft and gentle before a roomful of people.

Chapter 38

That night I spoke to more people than I had in months and my cheeks were sore from permanently holding a smile. I was surprised, yet touched, by how many people asked after my father; filling my ears with countless stories and memories that they had stored over the years of working with him. It was a pleasure that they had thought so highly of him and that he hadn't left in a cloud of shame as I had been imagining it. The hours ticked by happily and not once did I think about what I could be missing elsewhere because I knew that all I really needed was standing right here. I was sitting in the corner with little Lizzie curled up on my lap leaning against me, her soft sleeping breathes blowing against my chest.

"She looks really comfortable there," Ben stated as he approached with the intention of locating his daughter.

"I think she tired herself out," I muttered, it was nice to feel the comfort of someone so close to me.

"Shall I take her off you?" I think it's time we made our way back," he said, reaching out to gently to remove his daughter. There was an incoherent mumble when she was moved but she was straight back to sleep once she was nuzzled into his neck. I watched them leave, glad that Lizzie had the protection of her family surrounding her. Once they were out the door my gaze moved around the room until my eyes settled on Oscar who had propped himself up against the wall, lost in his own world. His eyes were downcast as though he was deep in thought and he was picking at the seams of his gloves as though he was trying to release a secret. It was only then that I realised that maybe all this wasn't a celebration for him at all; why would he want to celebrate a life he wanted to forget and the death of his friends? It may have been over for us, but for Oscar and the rest of those soldiers, the war would always live on.

"How are you feeling?" I asked, snapping him out of the world he had been washed away in.

"Erm, yeah, I'm fine," he answered, thrown slightly off guard by my abruptness.

I wanted to ask more, I wanted to know what he was thinking but I knew there were some lines that you couldn't get across unless you were invited over. I patiently waited for him to start talking but there was nothing, just a silence that helped neither of us.

The barn was quickly emptying out around us, a few of the slightly too intoxicated men being escorted out into the darkness by their quietly belligerent wives. When Johnny trundled up the ladder to bed and Lenny had been pulled away leaving us alone I knew that it was my time to make a departure.

"Thank you for tonight, I had a great time," I muttered politely, avoiding all the things I really wanted to say.

Oscar merely nodded at me in response like I wasn't even worth the effort of words. For a moment I forgot that he was rightfully upset and foolishly allowed my anger to take control.

"Goodnight then," I spat out bluntly, selfishly walking out leaving him to dwell in his sadness alone.

I didn't storm away dramatically; I just walked slowly; distancing myself from what I couldn't fix. Part of me was hoping that he would come after me, but I also knew that it was wrong of me to always be expecting that of him; there was going to come a time where it needed to be me that followed him.

The night felt ominous now that I was out in the cold; the dark sky littered with invisible clouds that masked the glittering stars. I was so busy searching the sky for a glimpse of those tiny balls of light that I didn't notice the hidden figure leaning casually against the garden wall; the faint wisps of smoke that clouded him more visible than he was.

"What are you doing out so late?" he croaked, the unexpected interruption making me jump for the second time that night.

I squinted into the darkness until my eyes adjusted to it and I was able to make out Edward's face. He pushed himself off of the wall and tried to take a step towards me though it was more of a stumble. His eyes were red rimmed and I had spent enough time around it to know that he had had far too much to drink. I was prepared for the stumbles, the stench and the slurred words but I couldn't prepare myself for how else it would affect him. It seemed that alcohol was a poison that had the power to turn the sweetest person into a monster and considering how Edward had been acting towards me lately I was not looking forward to what was to come.

"Are you going to answer me?" he slurred, confirming my suspicions.

"I'm just going back to the house," I replied, trying to take a sneaky step away from him.

"Where have you been?" he persisted.

"We had a celebration party at the barn, just like everyone else had," I said feeling as though I had to defend the actions of the night.

He was silent for a moment, perhaps struggling to think of another witty retort, or was he too wondering what we were celebrating?

"Look I'm going to get back, I didn't mean to bother you," I said as politely as I could manage whilst trying to take advantage of his silence. I started to walk away when his voice reached out after me.

"No, Em, wait." It was the smallest hint of the old Edward, the one that I had loved dearly, that made me stop; proof that he still had control over me. He waited for me to turn and face him before he continued speaking.

"I'm really sorry for everything I've said. I never meant it, it was just all for show. You know how it is. We had to keep up appearances Em." He slurred and stumbled his excuses, but it wasn't that which made me doubt him.

"Even when there was no one around to hear you?" I retorted sharply, unwilling to fall for his practiced charm this time.

"It was just in case. You've got to forgive me Em. We can go back to normal." He plastered a sickly sweet smile onto his face, his lips seeming too big for his cheeks, and waited for me to accept his apology as though I were idiotic enough to believe him.

"I love you too, I just couldn't let anyone know," he continued when I didn't speak. It was that false statement that tipped me over the edge. Trying to manipulate me with his charm and apologies was one thing but using my feelings against me was just pure malice.

He had shuffled closer to me so that his body was almost touching mine; the stench of alcohol radiating from his open mouth.

"How about a kiss to make it all better?" he suggested slimily as he tried to tilt his head towards mine, but I stepped away so that he was instead greeted by the empty air.

"No," my head shouted, but it came out as more of a whisper so either he didn't hear or he chose to ignore it.

"I know you want it," he spat and in that moment his eyes changed and I knew that the monster had been reborn.

"I don't want to, I just want to get inside," I hurried trying to get away from him but his hand was already on my arm.

"You can't tell me you don't want it now because you've already told me that you do," he said spitefully. "And I suggest that you do exactly as I say otherwise you may find that a certain group of men get told precisely where your father is." His blue eyes gleamed greedily down upon me as my head snapped up. He knew that he had my attention now and his smile reflected the image of the boy whom was used to getting exactly what he wanted.

"He's gone to stay with my aunt," I lied.

"No he hasn't, he is in Hertfordshire working as a road repairer."

"How would you know that?"

"I had him followed when he left," he stated as though there was nothing wrong with that statement.

I didn't know whether or not I should believe him, but I did know that I shouldn't put it past him. I didn't have time to appreciate the fact that I knew my father was safe because that knowledge only came with consequences that I now had to be dealing with. I wanted to speak, to defend us, but words failed me and instead my body succumbed to his force, allowing him to push me against the wall and into the protection of the shadows.

"No, I don't want to," I muttered trying to pull away.

"What, you don't want to protect your father? That's not very kind. I expected more from you," he sneered, keeping a tight grip on my arms. He moved a hand up to my face and grasped my chin, pinching my cheeks together. I closed my eyes and prepared myself for what was coming.

His lips were cold and hard against mine, the taste of his evening licking against my unresponsive lips. His free hand ravenously moved against my body, the feel of his touch making me sick to the stomach. I couldn't count the hours that I had spent imagining the moment when he would kiss me, but there was no loving touch or fluttering stomachs in this version of reality.

I stayed motionless, unwilling to give him anything that he was searching for, longing for the moment to end. But he didn't stop, his hand just kept edging closer and closer towards the bottom of my dress. When he grabbed hold of the hem in an attempt to pull it up I tried to throw myself in the opposite direction but the wall was in my way and it only made him press himself against me more; the hardness in his trousers telling me exactly what he wanted.

"Don't fight it," he whispered in my ear, his lust-filled voice making me cringe.

When his cold hand met my skin I shivered, unsure if it was caused by the coolness or his touch. His fingers crept across my stomach and up towards my chest. His distraction caused him to release his grip on me slightly and I was able to push him off of me before he could get any further. I stepped out into the open air so that I was no longer trapped by the wall. I now stood a fighting chance but Edward was clearly too drunk to realise this.

"Get back here, you know this is what you want," he slurred, tripping over his feet as he walked towards me. He stumbled slowly, unable to regain his balance and I ducked out of his reach as he fell flat on his face. I took the opportunity to run away from him into the darkness, oblivious to the figure that was walking in the opposite direction.

Chapter 39

The next morning I didn't want to get up, there was nothing that seemed worth getting up for. For the first time I had to force myself to get out of bed and face the world. I hunted through the drawers and found an old woollen jumper that I threw on; the cold already seeping into my bones and I was yet to step outside.

The wet drop that landed on my nose was too soft to be rain which left only one other option. Most would consider the pure white fluffiness of snow to be beautiful, almost magical, but to me it meant that my job had become twice as hard. The sleeping plants would now be buried beneath a blanket of snow out of reach to our nurturing hands and the branches would keep hold of the falling snowflakes; gathering them up as though they were sacred. My early morning footsteps were the first to disturb the fresh blanket of snow, leaving a perfect trail behind me. I tried to wrap my coat closer to me but there was no stopping the cold from creeping in. My flimsy shoes were no protection to my already frozen feet and the day had hardly begun. I heard the crunch of snow before me announcing Ben's arrival.

"There's no point in starting up yet, not in this sodding weather. Lenny said to take camp in the barn until there is at least a little bit of light," he said grumpily. Clearly the snow had no magical effect on him either.

We trudged through the deepening snow, grimacing as the icy flakes scraped against our faces, guided by the warmth of the glowing light ahead of us. We stomped into the barn and promptly closed the door behind us to hold out the snow and the briskness that followed. I stomped my feet repeatedly against the hard floor trying to bring some feeling back to them; the heavy moment only sending pain shooting up my legs. I shook myself like a dog fresh from a bath to free off some of the snow that hung to my coat. It was cold without it but colder still with it.

There was no greeting from the empty barn and the silence made the still air seem even colder. I assumed everyone was still sleeping so in apology for my earlier ruckus I tiptoed across the wide floor to sit by the table. There were logs in the corner waiting to be lit but I felt I should wait for someone else to do so, so instead I sat there shivering longing for the comfort of my bed. We sat shivering in the silence, either too cold or too tired to speak, waiting for anyone to wake and join us. Lenny's absence made me wonder if Ben's conversation with him had truly taken place and I started to feel like I was intruding. My leg started to unconsciously twitch as I became unusually nervous to be in such a familiar place.

A cold blast of air interrupted my thoughts and sure enough a frost-bitten figure appeared, grumbling and mumbling under his breath as he tried to brush off the snow.

"I don't see you getting much work done today, the weather is truly against you. But we could certainly use the extra hands if you don't want to be docked a day's wages," he suggested thoughtfully.

I nodded eagerly, not wanting to be stuck outside and I certainly couldn't afford to lose the money. Ben, however, seemed less sure – his face suddenly terrified by the prospect.

"I'm really not great with horses, I would be more of a hindrance," he mumbled sadly.

"No problem, there's plenty of other work that can be done."

Ben's face softened slightly at that and he too nodded his agreement. It must have been hard for him, torn by the opportunity to spend the day with his children but knowing that he needed his money. Unfortunately, money seemed to be an ever-growing necessity as the days went past.

Thankfully Lenny started up the fire and made us each a mug of hot coffee. Just seeing the glow of the flames and smelling the swirling steam was enough to send the warmth tingling back into my body. Lenny waited until the room had warmed up as much as possible before proceeding to push open the creaking stable doors so that the horses could share in some of our warmth. I scooted my chair closer to the fire to avoid the cool breeze that came with this act of kindness, scraping the legs against the floor with far more noise than anticipated. The commotion must have been enough to wake the upstairs inhabitants as the creak of soft footsteps could be heard overhead. The two young stable boys were the first to appear, chatting together sleepily as they made their way down the ladder. Their cheeks tinted at the sight of me so early in the morning, and I couldn't help but smile at their surprise.

"Morning," they muttered before scurrying off to the other corner. Oscar was the next to appear, but there was no sign of the expected smile and cheerful greeting that I usually received, instead I noticed his body stiffen and watched his face turn to stone. He nodded in our direction, though I couldn't help but notice it was more towards Ben than me, and then rapidly walked away into the stables. I was puzzled by his behaviour, true we had not parted on the most loving terms after the party but I hadn't thought that it would have lasted through till this morning. I tried to brush it off as a mixture of morning grumpiness and past emotions and pushed the niggling thought to the back of my mind. Anyway, I was too cold to worry about anything, I was certain that it would take some of the energy away from keeping my body from freezing in one position.

I drained the rest of my coffee then rinsed the cup out, wandering into the stables leaving Ben and Lenny engrossed in their conversation about who-knows-what.

"How can I help?" I said announcing myself. No one seemed as though they were going to be asking me to do too much; the two young lads looked up but quickly looked back at each other, not in the position to give me orders, and Oscar simply glanced at me before turning back to his work without a word. My eyebrows furrowed at his behaviour but I stopped myself from saying anything. If this was how he wanted to act then I would leave him to it, he could come to me when he was ready. Since I was given no instructions I headed to Silver's box and let myself in, hoping that I would at least be welcomed here. Sure enough the horse hurried over and buried his big head against me; his way of saying hello.

"Hello buddy," I whispered into his ear as I tickled under his chin playfully. I could feel Oscar's eyes on me but I chose to ignore them and instead started to clean out the box. I noticed a pair of gloves hanging against the wood, and since no one else was using them I happily snatched them to cover my hands. I grabbed the shovel and started scooping the old hay and other unwanted sewage into a pile ready to be discarded and replaced with the fresh substitute.

Silver stood watching me the whole time, gradually nudging closer to get my attention which only made my task all the more difficult. I laughed to myself as he pushed his face against mine, almost knocking me off my feet.

"That's enough now," I said gently. "I won't get anything done if you push me over."

The horse must have sensed my soft tone so instead of walking away he pushed his head against mine until my hand was up against his neck.

"Happy now?" I muttered as I stroked his soft mane contently.

"You're not much help are you?" Oscar called out snappily as he walked past the box. His comment shot through me, where there would usually have been playfulness to his words there was nothing. It was empty. It felt like I was no longer anything to him. I climbed out of the box and hurried after him.

"Have I done something wrong?" I asked, no longer able to hold myself back. "I'm sorry about last night but I didn't think it was that big a deal."

He turned round to face me, his face completely drained of all colour and blank apart from the painful look that haunted his eyes.

"If that's how you feel than there's really no point in talking about it." He dropped a bale of hay at my feet and walked off leaving me stunned and speechless. I paused, leaning my weight on the bale at my feet, wondering what it was about me that always seemed to drive everybody away. If I didn't know then I could never change it, but it seemed there was nobody left to give me an explanation.

I carried on with my task for the day, making sure the hay was perfectly scattered around the box and the feeding basket was topped up generously. I fixed the blanket around him securely, lingering for a moment longer than necessary to feel his heartbeat.

"See you soon," I muttered as the day drew to a close. The snow was now falling harder which made it almost impossible to see in front of me, that mixed with the darkness and the fact that I lost half a leg to the fallen snow each time I took a step, I knew that it was going to take me a long time to make it back into the warmth again.

My legs were frozen, my back painful from tensing, but I no longer felt the chill running through me; I had let the numbness become me. I could finally see the house its open arms reaching out. I made the mistake of quickening my pace only to find that my stiff legs couldn't handle the increase in speed. They tangled together and I dived head-first into a pillow like pile of snow. I struggled to push myself back up, my hands unable to find solid ground to support my weight. Eventually I managed to spin myself onto my back – with no ounce of elegance – and shuffled my back and bottom until I was sitting upright, finding the last ounce of strength in my legs to haul myself onto my feet. I tried to wriggle my face, with no luck; my nose was stuck motionless, my cheeks red and solid and my eyebrows were now covered in snow that was quickly freezing. My hair had managed to sneak away from the comfort of my hat and was either dripping down my neck or plastering itself against my face. I forced myself to keep moving. My eyes were watering from the cold but if anything tried to escape it was frozen as soon as the air hit it.

At first attempt the door wouldn't open no matter how hard I pulled and pushed. I was in the process of sliding down the door into the piling snow – an act of surrender - when it moved from behind me and I tumbled inside. I landed bottoms up at the feet of the butler, who probably could have caught me but chose not to.

"We locked the door to keep the draft out. There was no need for such a racket," he said patronisingly. There was no apology, no sympathy.

I didn't bother to reply, there was really no need. So I just brushed myself off, peeled my sodden shoes from my feet and padded away from him.

I was squelching up the stairs, wincing with every step as the heat started to battle with the cold, when I caught movement out the corner of my eye. I usually would have ignored it but a short, attentive cough caught my attention. I turned my head, a little too sharply, to find myself looking directly at the grazed and swollen face of a grimacing young lord.

Chapter 40

The month of March soon arrived, and the weather that surrounded us was a mirror reflection of my mood; cold, grey and miserable. The plants were slowly creeping through, but there was no sudden blossoming to brighten up the day. The past few months had been difficult, but I had buried myself into my work to try and stop the loneliness from putting me down. Soldiers had started to arrive back home and though I had seen none of them yet – be it because we were a small village or simply because no soldier had returned – I had caught snippets of newspapers that had been left behind and overheard conversations within the household about family members that were not the same person they had waved goodbye to. I had heard that Thomas had made it back home, but I was yet to catch a glimpse of him which made me wonder what damage he had suffered. In the past he would always be wandering around the grounds, ensuring that everything was running smoothly, and I was sure that if he was able to then he would have been out at every chance he could.

My thoughts always travelled to Oscar, and I ached to know that he was alright, but he didn't want me around him and it seemed there was very little I could do about that. This month also carried with it something else, something that brought jitters and unprecedented glee to everyone but me; Edward and Victoria were getting married. Luckily, I got to spend most of my time out of the house and away from all the merry preparations – just the smell of the wedding cake baking in the oven was enough to put me on edge.

We had been given very specific instructions on the layout of the gardens by no other than the soon-to-be bride herself.

"I want lots of pink flowers. And white. They will match the dresses then. And I want an arch, that one over there, to be covered in flowers also." She went on for so long that eventually I just tuned her out, mimicking Ben's nods of agreement. There was very little need for me to bother though as she paid little to no attention to me, apart from the scowl I received when her ridiculous list of commands had come to an end. I'm not entirely sure how she thought the process of growing flowers went but they certainly weren't going to just pop out of the ground in the colours she demanded them to be, and if the sun didn't start shining she would be lucky if there were any at all. It had taken months of preparation; seeding, turning the soil and caring for the mismatch of plants and flowers that had been buried in the ground long before spring had sprung.

Ben raised his eyebrows at me, a confirmation that he too thought she was out of her mind.

"We'll have to do the best we can, but unfortunately for her it's not going to be the monstrosity of pink that she had imagined," he said as he glanced around the garden helplessly.

"Let's keep our fingers crossed that it rains and then she won't notice," I suggested. Ben chuckled and leant against the thick trunk of the oak tree, sending a small swirl of leaves and petals swarming around him.

"I just don't know what she expects to happen in three days. Would have been more useful if we had received her demands along with everyone else," he sighed.

"Like you said, we just do the best we can. It's not like it is a terrible state out here," I reassured. Personally, I wouldn't change a thing. Though the buds were in the first stages of blossoming, they would be something spectacular when they opened; one would lead the way and the rest would soon follow, turning the garden into a harmony of colours. It would be far more aesthetically pleasing how it was now – bold colours complimenting the pale – making the eye want to take in every colour and shape. The pale girlishness that Victoria had suggested would just look dull and mundane, her petal filled arch simply drawing attention away from the magnificent oak.

"It's silly for her to change anything," I continued.

"We may agree on that but at the end of it all she will be another Lady to us, one who shall soon be helping to control the household."

He didn't need to say anymore, it was clear exactly what he was thinking. His fears may have been understandable but personally I had, had enough of cowering beneath the powerful when I was yet to see them experience a hard day's work. When it came down to it we were the ones that knew what we were doing, not them. But, unfortunately, Ben was right. They were the ones in control of our future. So, instead of standing up to the high and mighty as I so desperately wanted, I did as I was told and scanned my memory to remember where, or if, the white and pink flowers had been planted.

The next few days blurred into one as we woke earlier and worked until the sun set, later than we usually would in order to try and make something of what had been requested of us. Unfortunately for Victoria - though I must admit I was secretly pleased - there was an incredible lack of what she had requested so we had to make do with the little we had. The arch had been draped elegantly with vines and roses and we had reorganised the flower beds so the arrangement was more to her liking. Still, she wasn't pleased.

"This is not what I asked for! Did you not listen to anything I said?" she shouted out, stomping her feet like a spoilt child.

"This is all that we could do ma'am," Ben said calmly though the worry in his eyes was apparent to me.

"I wanted pink and white," she spat.

"The orchard has bloomed in those colours," I said without thinking that it would probably have been best if I had remained silent. She snapped her head sharply to look at me, her eyes narrowing as she took me in.

"It was you wasn't it. You did it on purpose to spoil my wedding day."

"Now, now, Victoria. There's really no need for that. Nothing has been spoilt," interrupted Lady Barrow who appeared at just the right moment. She took Victoria by the arm and gently guided her away.

"Mr Morton, Emily. The garden looks beautiful. Excellent work," she added before walking her sulking future daughter-in-law away from us. I could hear Victoria complaining in the distance but I chose to ignore it.

"He's sure picked one there," Ben commented under his breath as he turned back to the gardens. I smirked at the remark but remained silent. It was almost too late now anyway, tomorrow they would be wed and really there was nothing that could be done to stop it. There was no real reason why I would want it to fall through, other than the fact that I strongly disliked the girl. Perhaps there was still some part of me that clung to the thought that Edward, my Edward, was still hidden somewhere, but it seemed that the real Edward and this monstrous, spoilt brat were perfectly suited to one another.

"Are you going tomorrow?" Ben asked. The servants had been told they could go and stand at the back of the church if there was room, well I think the invitation only really extended to those house servants that worked closely with the family, but perhaps Ben had heard of the friendship Edward and I had once shared and had assumed I was welcome.

"I haven't decided yet. I might just wait until they get back here," I said unwilling to admit the real reason as to why I was so unsure; I didn't want to be standing at the back of a church watching the man I thought I had loved declare his love to another woman. It dawned on me that the reason I was feeling so upset about it was that it only served as a harsh reminder that I had lost the one that I had truly grown to love; that he was only metres away from me yet he always left me standing there at arm's length. That he would utter no more words to me than was essential, that the majority of the time he turned away when he saw me coming and that it had been months – long, hard months – since those dark eyes, that had once been so comforting, had come to rest upon mine. I missed him more than it hurt to say and yet I had no clue what I had done to make him leave.

The house was full of bodies and chirping voices, all there preparing for the big day; a day that would not involve them. It made me think that the bride and groom had really had nothing to do other than bark orders in every direction. I had hoped that I would blend into the background since my hands were of no use here – likely to cause more work rather than decrease the load – but I was spotted just as I thought I had made it to safety.

"Are you going to the church tomorrow?" The voice was a mixture of curiosity and a sneer, warning me to be on my guard.

"I don't think so, no," I said nonchalantly, turning to face Sarah even though I wanted to carry on walking away.

"You were actually invited then?" she said looking slightly aghast. "Didn't think you would be since you have nothing to do with them. Doubt they even know your name."

It was easy to ignore her nastiness simply because it was actually a relief to hear that not everyone knew about what had gone on between myself and Edward.

"I've been working here for some years, so I'm sure they know my name. Not that you have to worry though, like I said, I'm not going." I was fed up of listening to her, I just wanted to make her stop, but I was idiotic to think there would be any stopping her.

"I was just asking because Oscar and I are going together and everybody knows how you feel about him so I thought I would be nice and give you a warning."

Her sweet smile as transparent. *If you know how I feel then why are you going with him?* I wanted to scream at her but it was pointless.

"Thanks. Have fun," I settled for instead, taking the opportunity to leave.

Oscar had moved on then, from whatever there was to move on from that was. The news should have hurt more than it did but I think I had finally grown numb to the disappointment. As I washed away the evidence of my day, watching the dirt taint the fresh water, it was easy to see why I was alone; why would anyone love a poor, dirty girl who had nothing to offer.

Chapter 41

Despite my countless thoughts and wishes the sun was shining brightly; smiling down happily upon the nearly newlyweds. The bright sunshine had the opposite effect to what was desired on me, and I pulled myself out of bed sulkily. We had been ordered to stay out of sight – the exact words being that if you're not needed then then you're not to be seen. This didn't leave me with much choice of where I should go. I figured that the stables would be the most entertaining place for me and since Oscar was so kindly escorting Sarah to the wedding I wouldn't be invading his space; I could just sit silently with the horses and keep hidden.

I descended the stairs quickly and quietly, not wanting to be stopped. Luckily the kitchen was full and bustling and anyone that wasn't there was probably busy dolling themselves up or tending on the wedding party for breakfast. The thought of food made my stomach rumble so I decided to go to the village first to pick something up. Over the last few months I seemed to have been dropping weight, unintentionally, but I didn't have the money or the resources to keep myself fed. I could usually count on Mrs Rook to leave me out a plate for dinner when I got back in from the gardens but she had been so preoccupied with the wedding that I had been pushed to the back of her mind.

The village was eerily deserted for such a pleasant day but then again it was likely that everyone was busy anticipating the wedding of the year. I had enough money to buy myself some bread and milk and decided that I shouldn't have to be hidden away when I'd rather be outside. I walked back toward the estate, absentmindedly picking at the bread in my hand. I sauntered across the open field unnoticed and entered into the protection of the trees where I was led by the sound of water. The leaves were full on the branches, shading the path and blocking out the light, the soft breeze whistling through the gaps creating a harmony to my movement.

I stopped at the opening of the trees and stared at the figure perched on the rock staring out at the stream. The dark head turned to face me, disturbed by the sound of my feet. He wasn't quick enough to hide the sadness in his eyes, the troubled expression was easy to read, but it soon snapped back to a blank stare of nothing once he realised it was me.

"I was just leaving," he said before I could speak. He pushed himself up and started to walk away. I was prepared to let him go, simply because it was what I had now grown used to, but there was something that made me reach out and grab his arm as he stalked past me. I felt his body tense at my touch but I made myself commit to the action.

"What exactly is it that I have done to you?" I asked outright. He stared straight ahead unwilling to meet my questioning stare. His body stayed rigged but he didn't try to push me off; perhaps there was still a part of him that cared.

"Please, Oscar. You have to tell me," I pleaded, unable to fight off the tears that were creeping into my voice. It must have been this show of emotion that caught his attention because he finally turned to look at me. I allowed myself to pull my hand off of his arm now that he had acknowledged me.

"You really don't know?" he asked with zero sympathy. I shook my head and waited for him to continue. His lips pursed at my ignorance and he stared at me deeply as he tried to figure out whether I was telling the truth or not.

"I guess you're not going to the wedding," he said, more as a statement than as a question.

"No, but what has that got to do with anything?" I asked, confused by the knowing look on his face.

"It has everything to do with it. Were you not invited or could you just not bare to see him marry someone else?" he asked bitterly.

"I don't understand what you're going on about!" I shot back, my anger gradually rising. "I don't see why you should care anyway since you are taking Sarah." It came out sounding more jealous that I had intended.

"What?"

"She told me last night," I said, my confidence starting to falter under his stare.

"There's no chance that I would go to that wedding. She is lying to you. You should know that," he said.

"You still haven't told me what I did wrong."

His quick responses faltered as soon as I reminded him of that and he went back to brooding once more.

"I deserve an explanation. You just stopped talking to me, you suddenly hated me. It's been months!" I exclaimed, tripping over my words as they raced to escape now they had a chance to free themselves.

"I don't hate you," he muttered.

"Then why treat me this way?" I asked. He sighed and finally met my eyes.

"I saw the two of you together," he stated. Confusion swept over me, I was being offered another statement when I was hoping for answers. I tried desperately to rake through my memories and figure out what he meant but I was clueless.

"The night of the party. I came after you because I didn't like how it had been left. And I saw you kissing him." His voice was halted as he retold what he had seen. I knew now what he was referring to, unable to recall it previously because the actual situation was not how it must have looked to him.

"I know you probably won't believe me, but it wasn't what you think," I said with a sigh of relief, hopeful that there was a chance that I could explain this away and he would come back.

"No, I saw you kissing," he interrupted before I had the chance to continue with my explanation and I realised that it was going to be harder to change his mind than I thought.

"I understand that it must have looked like that but I wasn't kissing him," I emphasised. "It's a big misunderstanding, but if you let me then I can explain." I looked up at his blank face expectantly as I waited for a sign as to whether I was going to be given the chance or not.

"Fine," he said with a short nod, his arms crossed across his chest protectively as he waited to hear my story.

I suddenly felt nervous, my palms starting to grow clammy even though I knew everything I was going to tell him was the truth. Perhaps it was more the idea that he would ask for more information about the two of us and it would be then that I would have to admit to my earlier feelings. Or, perhaps the nerves were just a premonition to the fact that I was only setting myself up to lose him all over again.

"I, well," I stuttered, already off to a bad start. "After I left the party I was walking back home and Edward was there. He was clearly drunk but at first he was just talking to me and it seemed harmless. When I said I wanted to leave he didn't like it and started threatening me," I said trying hard to remember how it had all led up to that crucial point.

"What do you mean he threatened you?" Oscar interceded.

"He said that he knew where my father was and that if I didn't do what he wanted then he would tell them." There was no need for me to explain who that was referring to, he knew all too well. I noticed his face soften slightly but he didn't show any signs of giving in yet.

"He cornered me until I was pushed back against the wall. That must be when you saw him kiss me. I didn't want it to happen, I promise, but he had me pinned back and his hand was pinching me. I couldn't fight back. Please believe me," I begged.

"Did it go any further?" he asked promptly.

I remembered his cold hand creeping up my leg and fumbling with my dress.

"No," I answered truthfully.

He stood there silently for a while staring down at the floor as he mused over the new version of events.

"Okay. But why did he think he would be able to get that from you? And why would he go to the effort of blackmailing you?" I couldn't be sure if the questions were directed at me or if they were rhetorical but he spoke again before I had a chance to respond.

"Was the information he had about your father true? Did he go through with what he said?" he asked, echoing my own questions. It was a harsh reminder that my father could be dead and I had no way of knowing, but I also had no way of knowing that what Edward had said about him was even true.

"I don't know," I muttered sadly and I think it was then that Oscar realised he had made a mistake in asking those questions. He said nothing in way of an apology though, nor did he acknowledge that he had probably treated me unfairly in light of what he had just learnt. The mature response would have been to confront me about it, but I can't say that I wouldn't have reacted the same. Perhaps he thought he was in the right to be hurt and wounded, maybe that was what he needed, but I still couldn't make myself see it as an excuse; no matter what he had thought. It made me wonder whether things would be able to go back to how they once were between us, maybe now we had lost the easiness that had always been so comfortable.

"Does this mean that you're going to talk to me again now?" I asked.

"Yes," he said simply.

"So I don't have to sneak around the back to visit Silver," I said, an awkward attempt at a joke.

"I just said that things will be fine," he snapped. I immediately decided that it was best to no longer joke around and concluded that it would be safest not to push it too far. If I could even go so far as getting a hello in the morning then there would be a tremendous improvement.

"Well I should probably be heading back anyway. Thank you for listening to me, I'm glad we could get it all straightened out." I gave him a small, forced smile and headed back through the wooded sanctuary.

I was just emerging out into the open when I heard movement from both behind and before me. The fast footfalls informed me that Oscar was running to catch up with me and the loud volume of cheery chatter told me that I had left the woods at exactly the wrong time.

"Emily, wait," Oscar called out; I flinched despite myself, afraid that someone else would have overheard him. I stopped walking and waited for Oscar to catch up to me, hoping that he would also hear the voices and want to stay out of sight, or that they were generating enough noise that we would be barely a whisper in comparison.

"Emily, I'm sorry," he said slightly out of breath. "I shouldn't have treated you like that, I was just so hurt. And I thought that you didn't actually care for me so I wasn't sure how I was supposed to be with you," he said, blurting out the missing apology I had silently berated him for.

"It's fine, I understand." There was no point dwelling on the topic.

"I missed you," he said sheepishly.

I missed you too, I said to myself unwilling to step straight back into things. He moved forward and wrapped his arms around me in a strong embrace before I had the chance to argue it, just in time for Edward to see as he appeared at the top of the hill. He was slightly too far away for me to be able to make out his expression but I could feel the anger and hatred radiating towards me, making it perfectly clear exactly what he was thinking.

Chapter 42

From his position on the top of the hill looking down, he appeared very much the lord he already was; the stance was powerful yet terrifying. He had the power to do whatever he pleased and if he wasn't happy with me any longer then I could say goodbye to my home. I looked over Oscar's shoulder and held his stare, even though his eyes weren't visible to me. I couldn't let him know that I was scared; I had to try and stand my ground.

Someone must have called out for him because he seemed to reluctantly turn and walk away. I only realised that I had been holding my breath the whole time when I eventually exhaled, feeling the nerves rattle my body.

"Are you supposed to be working today?" Oscar asked, not seeming to notice the nerves I thought were radiating from my body.

"No, I was told to make myself scarce," I replied with a raised eyebrow.

"Do you want to come to the stables then? The horses tend to get spooked when there is a lot of people around and Lenny and I could use the extra hands." He made it sound more like a business proposal than an invitation to spend time with him, but I wasn't going to be picky about it, I would just take what I could get.

"Sounds better than sneaking around alone," I said as nonchalantly as I could muster. As much as I was looking forward to spending time with him again I could feel my stomach knotting, as though it was preparing me for something to go wrong. I had just about had enough of constantly living in fear and always expecting the worse – I needed to grab life by the reins and make it what I wanted it to be, not how others governed it. So, I chose to ignore that damning feeling until it eventually dithered, either that or I became so good at ignoring it that it would no longer be noticeable. It was proving to be a difficult task though since it was clear that neither of us had a clue what to say to each other.

"So … erm … have you been doing anything interesting?" Oscar muttered in an attempt to start up a conversation. It had always been so easy between us, it was hard to believe that we were now acting like we were practically strangers.

"Just working," I replied a little too curtly.

"Yeah, same," he said solemnly.

I resisted the urge to snap back a remark about Sarah, holding my voice to myself; sometimes silence was the best option.

When we entered the stables Lenny did a double take upon our arrival. I could tell that he was surprised to see me though it was obvious from the slight smile playing across his lips that it was not a bad surprise.

"Afternoon little lady," he called out loudly. "Nice of you to grace us with your presence," he said jokingly though it did make me wonder what, if anything, Oscar had told him to explain my absence. It wasn't as though I had ignored the old stable master, we had still spoken almost every morning when our paths crossed, I just hadn't been hanging around as much.

"I thought she could help with the horses seeing as she is good with Silver and everything," Oscar said before I had a chance to speak.

"Absolutely. Never going to say no to that!" Lenny exclaimed and I couldn't help but beam inwardly at the unspoken compliment.

I hadn't seen as much of the horse as I would have liked, only able to sneak round when I knew Oscar was busy elsewhere. It was a strange companionship that Silver and I shared being as he was a horse and couldn't respond to all my nonsense, but I had heard that some of the greatest bonds can be formed between man and animal; it was natural, it was easy and it was now one of the few moments where I could just simply be rather than dealing with the torrent of thoughts that gushed through my mind.

"I've let them outside whilst the ceremony is on, that way they can graze and get some exercise before the crowds return. They'll probably need bringing in soon though. Not sure when it's all over," Lenny rambled. "Saying that, why aren't you there? You and Lord Edward were always such good friends growing up." I saw a twinge of pain cross Oscar's eyes at the questions but he showed no other sign of emotion, nor did he say anything.

"We were, but we aren't children anymore," I replied starting to get irritated by the constant remarks and expectations over my absent invitation. I was starting to think that perhaps my father and Lady Barrow had been right when they had said that it was not proper and it would certainly not end well.

"I'd much rather be here anyway," I added. I quickly made my way outside so as to avoid any more conversation on the matter. My mass of curls bounded along with my purposeful stride. Silver and Arabella were nuzzling each other, noses so close it looked like they were sharing a kiss. I'm not sure if he smelt me, sensed me or just heard me approaching but as soon as I got a little closer he turned away from his female companion and happily trotted over to where I had stopped to now nuzzle against me. I felt bad for Arabella but it was warming to know that my horse loved me – not that it was my horse of course, he belonged to Edward.

Oscar eventually joined me after he had finished talking to Lenny – the topic I could hazard a guess at – and we just stood there in silence watching the horses at play. Neither of us made to speak, the silence more comfortable than an awkward attempt at conversation. I was enjoying the rays of sun beaming down on me now that I had forgiven the weather for brightening today. Spring was in full bloom and there was nothing quite so magical as that.

"Can you hear that? We better start rounding the horses up," Oscar stated. The church bell's chimes could be heard in the distance signalling that the wedding ceremony had drawn to a close. It meant that we now had the time it took to take the wedding photograph mixed with the journey back to the house to get the horses back into the stables; animals that were going to be none too co-operative in this weather.

"Is it really such a problem to leave them out? It seems such a shame to keep them trapped inside." I knew it wasn't my place to question the order but I just couldn't understand why they had to be hidden away – surely it would leave a better impression if the guests could see that the horses were happy and free.

"I understand what you're saying, but unfortunately orders are orders and not obeying them isn't worth the consequences." He placed his thumb and forefinger in his mouth and let out a high-pitched whistle. I was astonished to see all the horses turn their heads obediently in answer to the call, followed by the majority of them trotting towards us. Silver, the most defiant by far, and

Arabella were left behind. I would have expected her to follow the whistled order due to her bond with Oscar, but instead she seemed to be keeping watch over her stallion.

"Come on girl," Oscar called out to her but she uncharacteristically turned and walked in the opposite direction.

"Are you okay tempting Silver back in?" he asked looking perplexed.

"No problem." We both walked gently in opposite directions so as not to scare the creatures. Silver kept his head bent stubbornly in the grass feigning ignorance to my presence, though every time I changed direction his rear-end followed.

"Come on boy, time to go in now," I said calmly, for some reason thinking it would be that simple to coax him in. He let out a sound that bared a strange resemblance to a laugh and continued to ignore me. To be perfectly honest I hadn't really thought of a back-up plan because I had mistakenly assumed he would follow me, but it was now pretty clear that this wasn't going to be easy and I wasn't sure exactly what else I was meant to do. It was slightly reassuring, however, to hear that Oscar seemed to be having just as much difficulty as I was, that was until I turned to sneak a peek and saw that he had just made contact with the horse and she was now being far more receptive. The solution then was to do the same thing and hope Silver would listen to me. Somehow that didn't seem likely though and I found myself wondering if a horse could be open to some fake bribery – and it would have to be fake because my pockets were bare

"I've got your favourite apples if you come with me," I called out.

As ridiculous as it sounded out loud it was still worth a shot. My eyes could have been playing tricks on me but I was sure that I saw his head twitch slightly towards me.

"Do you want some apples? I tried again. This time his head popped up and he turned himself round to face me.

"Come on Silver. That's a good boy," I praised as he gradually made his way towards me. I took sly steps backwards towards the stables and we continued this way until we had almost reached the doors.

"Bribing a horse with empty pockets? Now that's just cheap tricks," Oscar whispered into my ear jokingly as he slipped some carrot cubes into my outstretched hands. I smiled to myself and led Silver the final few steps into the stables where Oscar took over. I brushed my hands and turned, hands on hips to look out at the sky, only to be greeted with Edward and his new wife stepping out the carriage – Victoria looking upsettingly glorious all in white with a smug smile plastered across her face.

Chapter 43

They were close enough for me to be able to make out the expressions on each of their faces, including that of Lady Meredith who couldn't have looked more pleased about her son's choice of bride. Victoria's lips were also turned up into that same smug smile that her mother-in-law was sporting but there was something else there that I couldn't quite read. It may have been that I was slightly biased in the way that I felt towards her but I could have sworn that it was a look of achievement that was hidden in her eyes, making me trust her even less than I did before. In most people's eyes, Edward would be deemed as a 'catch', but I couldn't see how it was an achievement to have won him over.

Edward on the other hand didn't look quite so happy, there wasn't that expected newlywed bliss radiating from him, instead he looked somewhat downtrodden as though it were simply a fate he had resigned himself to. The self-assured, cocky attitude that I had grown to associate with him was missing and the sadness that surrounded him almost had me feeling sorry for the Lord.

"The happy couple are back then," Oscar observed as he snuck up behind me.

"They just pulled up," I stated, not bothering to think up same lame excuse as to why I was watching them.

"Coming in?" he asked, showing no interest in the special occasion.

He placed his hand on my shoulder to guide me away from the moving picture. I stole one last glance at the new couple to find a completely new aura surrounding Edward; the sadness had been washed away, only to be replaced with a scowling anger that was directed at me for the second time that day. This time, however, I didn't stand and meet his gaze, I turned and walked away deciding that it would simply be easier to no longer have him involved in my life.

Lenny was already sitting there with tea made and cake served, waiting for us to join him. The company was appreciated but I couldn't help but feel restless being stuck inside, I wanted to be enjoying the fresh air. The fact that I had been told to stay out of sight probably contributed to the restlessness. Surprisingly it seemed as though I wasn't the only one thinking this as I saw both Lenny and Oscar glancing towards the door longingly.

"Do you think we are the only ones not out there?" Lenny asked, throwing his thumb in the direction of the open door.

"Probably. Though I know Ben was at home today. He can get away with not being seen in that cottage though."

"Let's all sneak round there," Lenny suggested mischievously – it was that mischievousness that had always made him seem much younger than he actually was.

"And how do you think his wife would feel about that?" I giggled, wanting to take him up on the idea.

"Ruth loves me, she would have me there every day if she could!" he exclaimed, playfully batting his eyelashes. It reminded me of my childhood when my father and Lenny would always play around with me like this; embarking on little adventures.

"We could probably sneak out to the village," Oscar added. He was walking back in from the stables where he had managed to disappear to unnoticed. My face must have displayed my confusion, as I looked from his empty chair to where he was standing, because he laughed gently at my reaction.

"They seem to be gathered in the house, I can't see anyone outside so I am sure we won't be seen."

"Really I shouldn't even be here, I should be at home with my wife," Lenny muttered more to himself than either of us.

"Does that mean you're going home to your wife then?" I asked, interrupting his thoughts. My voice came across as slightly disappointed, but I couldn't help it; I had selfishly wanted him there, partly because I wanted to relive more of my father but mostly just because I missed them both and at least there was still one of them here. Lenny had played as big a part in raising me as my father had and I didn't want to end up losing him as well. Not that he showed any signs of going anywhere, I was just being morbid – an unfortunate new character flaw.

"I never said that, I just said that I should be. So, we shall have to be sneaking past my window as well." He jumped up with a twinkle in his eye and walked off to start his adventure. "You coming or are you too scared?" he called back daringly.

Oscar and I shared a smile and hurried after him, feeling like rebellious children. Oscar poked his head out first, deciding it was safer than Lenny's eagerness to play truant, and signalled that the coast was clear. There was a long stretch of freshly cut grass that meant we would be left out in the open for about twenty seconds before we could make it to the safety of the tree branches that would keep us sheltered from any prying eyes.

"Ready?" Oscar's eyes were bright as he returned to check with us. We both nodded eagerly waiting for the next signal. Oscar took hold of my hand.

"Okay then ... GO!" he shouted as his legs bounded, pulling me into a run alongside him. The three of us tore across the open land giggling and squealing like children, not daring to slow until we were hidden.

Lenny pressed himself up against a tree trunk heavily and Oscar and I both bent over, hands leaning on knees to steady our own breath. None of us should have been in that state but I think it was probably more to do with the excitement than our general fitness levels. I watched as Lenny peered through a gap in the trees to check if we had made it without being noticed unable to stop the bubble of laughter bursting out of me.

"I know I'm old but you don't have to laugh at me," Lenny said with a false sense of hurt. I shook my head at him but couldn't stop myself from laughing.

"There, there." He patted me on the back with big hands as he walked past me and onto the next hurdle.

At the next checkpoint it was my turn to make sure that our getaway was still undisturbed. I snuck into the thickness of the trees, having to get down on all fours to poke my head out of the gap – much to the delight of the sniggering grown children watching me. If anyone had been watching us I'm sure they would have experienced some shock in witnessing my beaming face and mass of dark curls poking out from a line of unmoving trees, but luckily there were no eyes waiting to greet mine. I ducked my head to sneak back in, catching my hair on a hanging branch in my rush to get free.

"Ouch!" I cried out, muffled by the face full of clothing that was caught over my mouth. It was only then that I remembered I was wearing a dress and I anxiously tried to shuffle my legs under my bottom to preserve some dignity.

"Help?" I asked pathetically, but they were far too busy laughing at my misfortune to be of any assistance. In fact, although I couldn't actually see them, I was pretty sure that at least one of them was doubled over with laughter – my clue being that the sounds escaping them were becoming increasingly high pitched. I sighed and edged myself forward again so that I could free my hands. I managed to lay down on my front even though this caused the branch to pull my hair painfully, but at least now I was able to awkwardly untangle the captured strands of hair. I picked at the hair until I was able to loosen the grip so that it wasn't pulling my scalp so tight, but I was really struggling with the rest so I had no choice but to snap the tree, leaving the evidence in my hair like a hair accessory. I was just about to shuffle back out when my attention was caught by movement out the corner of my eye. I turned just in time to see a figure disappearing into the open stable door. I waited to see if they appeared again in search of us but there was no sign of them coming back, so I decided it was probably just one of the stable boys.

This time I made it out of my spy hole unscathed but something about my appearance set the calming hyenas off once more. It could have been the earth that was entwined in my curls, the twisted movement of the dress that had scrunched itself up, or even my mud stained elbows and cheeks – they had a choice.

"Want some help with that?" Oscar spluttered as he watched me struggle with the stubborn twig; lips pouted and eyebrows furrowed in concentration.

"Oh, NOW you want to help me!" I exclaimed indignantly. "Well, no. Thank. You." I stropped. But he chose to ignore my sulking and expertly unwound my curls. I readjusted the rest of myself then walked off purposefully down the lane.

We were crouched behind the bush opposite Lenny's cottage talking in whispered voices as the front window was propped open and his wife Dorothy could be heard walking around.

"There's no way we can get past unless we crawl beneath the window." Lenny spoke in hushed tones trying to calculate a plan.

"You do realise you're the only one she will be looking for, right? Which means that neither of us have to crawl anywhere," I said indicating Oscar and myself.

"No, because if she sees Oscar she will ask where I am and he is a poor liar." I nodded; he was right.

"Still doesn't mean that I have to though. So how about I walk past and you two can crawl under the window. You know as well as I do that she is unlikely to ask me anything, she has barely said two words to me my entire life!"

Lenny grunted in agreement and they both moved out of the way so that they wouldn't be spotted scurrying along the ground like insects. It was now my turn to try and supress a laugh as I watched them on all fours behind me – a desperate action to hide from Lenny's wife. I had to wipe the smirk off my face as I walked by the window because even if I didn't think she would talk to me it would be pretty obvious that I was in cahoots with someone if she spotted me grinning to myself like a maniac; after all I wasn't exactly known for being the happiest person around at the moment.

"Emily."

I was shocked into stillness, as were the two crawling figures passing me.

"Would you happen to know where my husband is?" Her spectacled eyes didn't look up from the knitting that she was holding, almost as though she already knew the answer.

"No ma'am, I'm all alone," I gulped completely giving the game away. I saw Oscar bow his head as the same thing dawned on him, but Lenny wasn't ready to give up yet and he nudged at Oscar until he started to move again and they were both clear of the window; the white-haired child smiling to himself triumphantly once reaching the other side.

"Good afternoon," I bid farewell as I slowly walked off again, consciously slowing my steps so it didn't look as though I were running away.

"Tell him to be back for supper," she called out after me loud enough for a shameful Lenny to hear as we ran off into the distance; three pairs of crashing footsteps clearly audible to anyone who was listening.

"Drinks are on me for assisting my escape," Lenny offered when we made it into the bustling pub; the whole village out to celebrate the matrimony of their favourite young lord.

"Why don't you go and find us somewhere to sit, there may be some empty tables outside."

I didn't see that being true, there was barely enough space to move, but I left the men to push their way to the bar as I battled my way back outside. It was the first time that I had visited the village when people were actually smiling at me, not that it was actually aimed at me, but their happiness was catching and I found myself returning the smiles. As I predicted there were no tables left but I was able to locate an empty spot by a tree that as an added perk was also slightly shaded. It was some time before they managed to find me leaning back against the old tree trunk with my eyes closed – for once not feeling any fear at being left alone. We sat in comfortable silence just enjoying the cool drinks, the warm sun and the refreshing breeze that rolled over us from time to time.

"Your father would be proud of you Emily," Lenny said as he gently grasped my arm. "You've been brave in a lot of difficult situations, more than most of us could handle. Just thought you should know that."

"Thank you," I muttered, looking up into those kind grey eyes. My father may have left but I had finally realised that I wasn't alone. He finished the last drops left in his glass then pushed himself up off the floor.

"I best head home to receive my punishment," he chuckled. "As much fun as it was to sneak off the consequences sure do make you wonder if it's worth it all." He ruffled my hair as he always did then sauntered off, running his hands through his thinning hair nervously.

I figured that this meant that we would be leaving now also but when I made to move Oscar pulled my shoulder back.

"Let's watch the sun set." So we sat together peacefully watching the sun tuck itself in for the night.

Chapter 44

The sky was darkening quickly as we made our way home, the warm breeze turning cooler as each minute ticked by. Our bare arms grazed against each other's as we walked down the empty lane, my fingers twitching to reach out for his every time we made contact. Whereas before the rustling of leaves or the chatter of the owls would have made my pace quicken and my heart race, I now felt safer just knowing that Oscar was by my side again. Love wasn't simple; life wasn't like the stories that you read about in books, it took time, patience and sacrifice. But I knew that we would be fine, simply by the fact that I could admit that I loved him. I had to believe that there was only so much bad luck out there for each person, surely meaning that mine was up now. I needed to believe that otherwise each morning would be too much to handle.

As we passed the clearing of the trees I instinctively looked to the left of me at the expanse of untouched land that surrounded us. The grounds empty with not a soul to spoil the sleeping earth. I turned back, smiling to myself at the serenity a silent night can bring when I noticed the sudden change of expression cross Oscar's face.

"What's wrong?" I asked, my voice an unintentional whisper. I watched as he strained his eyes to adjust to the distance, focussed on the spot that I had been admiring only moments ago. He held his hand up to me, though it was not a rude gesture, only to tell me that he needed to focus for a moment.

"I think I can see ... It can't be ... but I am sure that's Silver." His voice was a mix of concern and confusion, making me waste no time in following the direction his finger was pointing. There was no doubt in my mind who that horse was; his mane glowing a mesmerising silver in the light of the moon. However, the worrying question was how he had gotten there. There were only two plausible options, neither of which boded well: the first was that the box hadn't been secured correctly and he had escaped, or the second being that someone had purposefully let him loose. But I had watched Oscar lock him up, hadn't I?

"The locks on the doors are getting old," Oscar mumbled as though he was reading my thoughts, but there was still something in his voice that made him seem hesitant.

"Is he okay?" I knew that it was a stupid question but I couldn't stop myself from asking. He didn't even bother to offer me a response, just shrugged and started to walk onto that untouched soil beckoning for me to follow.

"He's probably going to be pretty scared, they're not used to being out alone or at night," he whispered as we got closer. He waved his hand slightly to signal for me to stop where I was. "Be careful, okay?" He looked me dead in the eye to make sure that I understood. I nodded my agreement for the first time feeling the inkling of fear at the damage this creature was capable of.

"He trusts you, Em. You probably have the best chance of calming him down. Just be gentle, keep calm and don't get too close unless he invites it." I could tell that Oscar was reluctant to let me do this by the sigh his words made, and it seemed that even he was nervous about the situation which was completely out of character for him. It didn't help to settle my own nerves that were currently bubbling to the surface, but I gulped them down and tried to focus; telling myself that fear was an anchor.

"Silver?" I called out softly expecting him to jump away at the intrusion but instead he locked his eyes onto me as though he was grateful for my arrival. He let out a low, nervous call and started to head my way without any further encouragement. I was slightly thrown by his behaviour having prepared myself for defiance but I wasn't going to complain. When he reached me he nuzzled his large head straight into my shoulder and as I put my arms around him for reassurance I could feel his strong body shaking beneath my touch.

I didn't say anything to Oscar, not until we had led Silver safely back inside and he had checked the door about ten times.

"He was shaking," I muttered as I threw in some extra hay for the horse. "I've never seen him like that before."

"You don't need to worry; he would have just been scared. He must have been out there for some time."

I could almost see the cogs turning in his head as he tried to figure out what had happened, looking back in confusion at the door that barricaded the horse in.

"You were great though, it's something special to watch the way he is with you. He isn't like that with anyone," he said still glancing across the room as if to check that the horse was still there.

"He will be fine. You have checked the door," I said, placing my hand on top of his – now my turn to reassure.

"Even so, I think I'll sleep down here tonight just to keep an eye on him."

I knew there would be no point in trying to reason with him and I couldn't offer to stay as well so I bid goodnight, kissing him softly;

my lips pressed to his concerned brow. As soon as I stepped outside the fear of the night crept in now that I was alone once more.

I thought that the commotion at the house may have started to quieten down by now, but as I neared the house I soon realised that I had been very wrong. Lights were blaring from every which way and my ears were greeted by laughing voices and the soft chatter of those celebrating. The atmosphere downstairs wasn't quite so celebratory though; the smiling, expectant faces I had left behind this morning had been replaced with scowls, apprehensive glances and hot flushed cheeks.

"Where have you been?" I was snapped at, quickly dampening the naïve thought that I could have got back in unnoticed.

"I was told to stay out the way," I replied in the general direction of where the question had come from, not entirely sure of who had directed it at me.

"That doesn't mean that you couldn't have stayed and helped us! We're swamped," said a red-headed maid who stepped out into my eye line. I couldn't even be sure that she actually knew who I was as I was almost certain I had never spoken to her before.

"I would only have been in your way," I retorted. It was true, my hands were made for the garden. I had little to no experience in anything they would have wanted me to do and they would only have wasted more time in trying to explain it to me than just doing it themselves. Plus, I really couldn't see how one measly person would have made the difference to the commotion that had been created. I didn't bother to wait for a response, just turned on my heels and walked away; they were too busy to be going at me and if she kept on then I was sure she would be the one ending up with the punishment, not me.

"She probably snuck down there to try and stop the wedding," I heard Sarah whisper not so quietly, making no attempt to try and keep her opinion of me hidden. But I didn't bite, it was obvious that she only wanted to get a reaction from me and I refused to give her the satisfaction.

"It's ridiculous that she is so hung up on him. He'd never even look twice at someone like her." The comment was clearly meant to hurt but what she didn't realise was that I had heard it before and it was that time the damage had been done.

I could have offered to stay and help with the tidying up, and I probably would have done had it not been for the unnecessary comments. So more out of principle than anything else I went and shut myself away in my room; away from the constant flow of a world that I did not fit into.

I woke early the next day despite it being my scheduled day off and headed on over to the stables with the rising sun accompanying me.

There was something ominous about the silence that followed; even the birds seemed only to be watching rather than filling my ears with their morning song. I decided to walk round the back and straight to the horses so as not to disturb anyone else. There were no heads popping over stalls to greet me as they were all still nestled into the comfort of sleep. I tried to unlock the squeaky bolt as quietly as I could but the rusted metal seemed to echo through the silence like a lone gun shot. It was as I shut the creaking door that I noticed Oscar propped up against the entrance to Silver's box, his head flopped to the side as he gently snored; soft dreaming breaths. My plan had been to go and check on Silver then head off before anyone noticed but I had forgotten that Oscar was going to be right there. I resigned myself to the fact that my plan had backfired and made it back out the door before I heard a voice calling after me.

"You don't have to leave." His voice was filled with the huskiness of sleep and there was something about it that made my insides somersault. He stretched his arms up behind his head to work out the aches of the night and I couldn't help but notice the definition of his muscles as he unknowingly showed them off. I shook my head to rid myself of the thoughts and stepped back in.

"I just wanted to come and check on Silver."

"Ah yes, the escape artist. He didn't try to make a run for it again in the night thankfully," he said through his stretch.

I peered over the box to find him lying in the corner, the slight rise and fall of his chest the only thing that signalled he was still alive.

His large, dark eyes were staring unblinking at nothing and it was that which worried me. Silver was as good in the mornings as I was, so much so that it was unlikely that you would ever catch him resting.

"Can I go check on him?" I asked, my hand already resting on the bolt.

"Be my guest," Oscar replied, scooting out of my way. Even as I stepped in Silver made no movement, not even to lift his head to check who had entered.

"You not getting up?" I asked, already anticipating the silence that answered me. I gradually made my way closer to the animal, careful not to move too fast as I knew that his temperament could change at any moment. I was practically standing over him, watching his shallow breathing anxiously when I spotted something on his front right leg; it was a red so dark that it was almost black but it was easy to spot that it was out of place on his light coat. I knelt down beside him without thinking that I was putting myself directly in the line of his hard hooves, and leant closer to inspect that imperfection. When I got close enough I noticed that the dark lump was surrounded by thin trickling red lines, the sinking feeling in my stomach only confirming what I had suspected; Silver was wounded and had been bleeding through the night without us noticing. It must have happened the previous night and it was that which made me anxious to call out for Oscar – he was already blaming himself for the fact that he had escaped so when he found out that the horse was injured he would be inconsolable.

"Oscar," I called out warily, fighting the urge to scrape the blood clot off his leg. Unfortunately for me it was that moment that Silver decided to take note of Oscar entering, his legs kicking out as he attempted to stand meaning that my arm took the force of his effort.

I was knocked clean off my feet and landed with a thump on my back. I think that the pain would have rendered me motionless had it not been for the immediate danger I was facing by laying on my back beneath an injured horse. I tried to roll over but a fiery pain shot through my arm as a cry of agony escaped, tears welling up as the pain overwhelmed me.

"Sorry about this." I just about heard Oscar whisper as he tucked his hands under my shoulders and pulled me out of the box. I opened my mouth to scream out but no sound could be heard. My head grew dizzy as I was dragged along the rough floor, flecks of light dancing before my eyes before finally the room went black.

Chapter 45

"It looks like her shoulder is dislocated. Probably best to get it back in place whilst she is still out." I heard through closed eyes. The voice sounded familiar but I couldn't place it, though everything did seem a bit groggy at that moment.

"Won't that hurt her?" asked a voice thick with concern; unmistakably Oscar's even through my haze.

"Yes it will. But it is going to hurt less than leaving her shoulder like this. Would one of you hold down her legs and the other hold her other arm tight please? Make sure you hold her down." I seemed to drift in and out of consciousness as they placed themselves around me, not noticing anyone's touch until cold hands took hold of my right shoulder.

"No matter what, hold her down," the voice stressed, and there was something about that seriousness that made me want to throw my eyes open but they wouldn't budge – it was almost as though they had been glued together.

The next part ran in slow motion though it could have only lasted a few moments to get me from laying down to sitting bolt upright, gasping from the agony. All I remember is the pressure on my arm increasing which is when everything went black, though this time I could feel the pain creeping through my blood. Each breath I took was harrowing and agonising, every intake lasting a lifetime as it jolted my shoulder. I felt my arm get pulled out as though the strength of the force would tear the limb from my body, certain that nothing could hurt quite like this. That was until I felt a pop louder than a gun which caused me to start faster than a hunted fox. My shock, stronger than the hands that held me down, allowed me to break free and I was left staring at the culprit who had forced my eyes open.

The corners of the farmer's mouth, the same man who had cared for Oscar, twitched slightly as he greeted me, his light hazel eyes surveying me to try and gather some clue as to how I was going to respond. I didn't speak; it still hurt too much, so I just continued to stare waiting for someone to tell me what was going on.

"You dislocated your shoulder and you're going to have a nasty bruise from where the horse connected with you." As he said this I couldn't help but notice that there was a hint of disapproval in his voice. He stopped talking for a moment to stoop down and rummage through the sack by his feet, emerging with an old, grubby white shirt. He expertly ripped the seams so that it unwound into a long slither of material.

"I will strap it for you but you are going to have to try and keep it immobile for at least a few days so that it has a chance to recover," he stated politely. It took some persuading to edge my fingers away from my injured arm, but eventually he did and was able to proceed slowly, and sorely, in securing the arm. After all the difficulty in doing so it did actually take away some of the pressure.

"What about work?" I asked even though I already knew what the answer would be.

"Unless you can do everything left handed, I suggest that you just keep yourself rested until your shoulder is healed. That would be my recommendation, you don't want to risk hurting yourself more and prolonging the recovery." Even though the speech was directed at me I noticed the look that was shared between himself and Oscar as though they had shared some secret whilst I had been unconscious. I didn't see much point in arguing with him, especially since he probably knew best, plus I was too sore to try and put up much of a fight.

"How's Silver?" I asked as soon as Oscar made his way back to me. I wasn't concerned about what had happened to me, I knew well enough that it was my own fault for putting myself in that situation.

"Lenny is with him now."

"But is he going to be okay? The leg looked pretty bad." In that moment I forgot that I had been trying to shield Oscar from the truth of it all, I was too worried now to keep it hidden.

"I've been with you, Em, I didn't want to leave you." He gently took hold of my hand and started to trace my palm; the slight tickle of the sensation making me smile despite myself.

"Can we go check on him?" I asked sweetly, knowing that I was probably going to have to persuade him to let me do anything for the next few days. He looked at me with a smirk on his face, well aware of what I was up to, then just shook his head in defeat.

"Fine! But you're not to get involved and if the pain gets too much then you tell me and we come straight back here," he exclaimed. I could feel his arms tense as we made our way over and I realised that he was probably just as anxious to find out the severity of the situation.

Lenny was deep in conversation with who I assumed to be the vet when we approached; the worried wrinkles and pale demeanour telling us all we needed to know. The vet left and Lenny buried his head in his hands.

"It's not looking good. Harry said that he thinks the wound has got infected. All we can do is wait and see how he is, just hope that he gets better."

Nothing about him sounded hopeful and it was a struggle to get past that to think positively, but someone had to.

"He's a fighter though. I know he can pull through this," I said in an attempt to make us all feel better.

"I don't know how it could have happened," Lenny shrugged. I looked over at Oscar to see if he had told him anything yet but he just looked sad.

"I'm sure it must have been my fault," he muttered dejectedly.

"No, I don't believe that. You're always so careful. There must be another explanation," Lenny assured. It was clear that they had already had the conversation so I didn't feel the need to interject. We stood in silence watching over the injured horse, unsure of what we should say. His large playful eyes seemed empty as he slumped back; a mere version of the magnificent creature he had become.

I heard the sound of angry footsteps but I didn't bother to turn, nor did anyone else it seemed.

"You're supposed to address me when I enter a room," snapped the powerful young voice. We all turned to face him, the men far more urgently than myself, and not because I was hindered by my injury. His ice blue eyes flashed over me, showing no concern for my present state.

"What have you done to my horse?" he raged directly at Oscar who fumbled under his unforgiving stare.

"We're not sure m'lord. He must have got out somehow." Lenny spoke for Oscar who was clearly struggling to think of what to say.

"That's not good enough. Someone must have let him out and we both know whose job it is to check the horses," he yelled, accusing Oscar. It was the emphasis that he placed on that someone that made me remember the mysterious figure that I had noticed entering the stables the previous day. I couldn't believe I hadn't thought of it earlier. It was then that I noticed the inappropriate glint of satisfaction in Edward's eyes and it took all my strength to restrain myself from voicing my discovery in that tension filled moment.

"My horse is hurt and someone is to blame," he said turning on his heels and stomping away. "Someone will pay for this!" he threatened, his words aimed at Oscar and bouncing off to hit me.

We all seemed to breathe out in unison once the room was clear, Lenny and I both turning to look at Oscar.

"He doesn't know what he is saying, he's just upset," Lenny said. I choked on a sarcastic laugh, which luckily went unheard.

"You haven't done anything wrong so nothing can happen," I added. Oscar leant back heavily against the post and sighed dejectedly.

"He's right though. They're going to want someone to blame and the most likely culprit is me."

Lenny and I looked at each other, mirroring each other's worried expression. There wasn't much else that could be said to comfort him because everyone knew that what he was saying was true.

I made my excuses and slid out the door, they were too wrapped up in the present moment to really acknowledge my mumbled excuse so I was sure they wouldn't really notice if I was missing for a few minutes. I moved as quickly as I could, although the pain in my arm made it slow going as every time I stepped too heavily it sent jolts shooting through my body. I tried to ignore the pain telling myself it was too important to stop despite what my body was screaming out. It felt like an eternity before I spotted the shock of blonde hair sauntering casually ahead of me.

"Edward!" I called out, the short distance left was still too much for me to catch up to him. He stopped but didn't turn, obviously recognising my voice and deciding whether or not he was going to speak to me today. But that hesitation, that moment of stillness, was all I needed to close the gap and make him listen to me.

"What were you doing yesterday afternoon?" I demanded, struggling to regain my breath after the short walk at speed.

"At my wedding." He stated as though I was being an idiot. Of course I should have known that he was going to say that but I also knew that he was aware that was not what I meant. The heat of the afternoon suddenly became very apparent, sweat beading at the nape of my neck as I stood in the spotlight of the sun.

"What were you doing sneaking into the stables then?" I asked, getting straight to the point.

"I don't know what you're on about," he insisted but the flash of concern in his eyes gave him away. It had already been obvious from the way he had spoken to Oscar that he had thought he had gotten away with it, and for a moment perhaps he had because it took time for me to remember what I had seen, but I wouldn't let him get away with it now – I couldn't.

"You know exactly what I mean. I saw you!" I exclaimed, my voice sounding forceful even though my hands were clammy. He looked down on me, his eyes scanning my face for any sign that I was taking a wild guess, but I kept my eyes hard and lips stern to show I meant it.

"What were you doing there?" I asked bluntly, giving him the opportunity to confess and let me see a glimpse of the Edward I had grown up loving. For a moment I saw his eyes soften to the colour of the clear sky but the hardness snapped back as quickly as it had gone; so quick it was almost as though I had imagined it.

"I don't have to answer to you. Who do you think you are speaking to me like this?" he snapped. I knew that he was trying to scare me but I refused to let him succeed. True, he had all the power but he would only continue to think he could use it over me like this if I let him.

"I know what I saw and you won't get away with it!" I shouted back.

"What exactly did you see? Me walking into the stables ... and doing what?" he said smugly. I froze. I had been so insistent on standing my ground and saving Oscar that I hadn't actually stopped to think it all through. He was right, I hadn't actually seen him do anything wrong, just assumed that he had let Silver out; but making an assumption was the worst thing you could do because there was no evidence there to back it up. The sun no longer felt so strong and the sky seemed to darken over as I realised I had probably only made things worse.

Edward stepped close to me, bending his head so the tip of his nose was touching mine.

"I suggest you keep away from me," he whispered threateningly his cold eyes trained onto mine, the closeness making me go cross-eyed. He placed his arm onto my shoulder, knowing exactly what he was doing. The touch of his breath on my skin made my pulse quicken and I had to bite hard on my lip to keep myself silent. He turned and stalked off leaving me standing there to revel in the enormity of the mistake I had just committed.

Chapter 46

No matter how hard I tried I couldn't keep unwanted thoughts from running riot inside my mind. I couldn't understand how, just because he had made one snide comment, I was finding that I was now doubting myself, but worse than that I was doubting Oscar. Before this there hadn't been a second where I had questioned his innocence, but now I couldn't stop thinking that there was a possibility that he had left the gate unlatched; that perhaps he just hadn't checked it properly. The worst part was that I wasn't even really thinking that, the thoughts had just been placed in my head by someone who had no love for either of us. I had been so sure and now I realised that I never had a reason to feel that way.

I could hear footsteps pacing as I drew closer to the stables and I could picture Oscar walking back and forth, replaying the previous day over and over again trying to figure out what he had missed. Sure enough that was the picture I was greeted with; dishevelled hair and frown lines deeper than they had ever been.

"You saw him lock the gate right, Emily?" Lenny called out, giving no clue that he had even noticed my absence. He was standing watch over Silver whilst simultaneously trying to calm Oscar: it was hard to tell who he was most concerned about.

I opened my mouth to say yes but the word wouldn't come, that one simple word just refused to help me. The world seemed to stop as it waited for my answer; no breath could be heard, everyone and everything froze, even the wind seemed to stop knocking on the door. I somehow forced my head to answer what my words had failed to do and though it brought life back into the room I could tell by the heartbroken look in Oscar's eyes that he didn't believe me.

"I always lock the gate. Always. I wouldn't have done it any differently," his sad, dark eyes pleaded with me, drawing me in closer to him.

"I know," I whispered, regaining control of myself once more. "Go through it again with me." This was the perfect opportunity to hear him tell his story without having to be obvious about the fact that I needed to hear it. As he spoke the guilt tightened its grip around me. There was no chance that Oscar could have done this, he was always so careful. I watched him constantly switch between running his fingers through his hair and tugging at the ends of his gloves until eventually he pulled them all the way off; his hand lay there exposed and bare. I heard the catch in his throat and it was then that I realised this was more than just a job to him.

"I've lost everything once before, I can't do it again," he croaked. A single tear escaped down the slope of his cheek before he had a chance to wipe it away unseen. That one action – that tiny loss of control – tugged at my heart so hard that the words escaped me before I even had a chance to think.

"I saw someone walking into the stables when we went to the village," I blurted.

"WHAT?" Lenny shouted before Oscar had a chance to respond, his eyes desperately searching mine to make sure it was the truth.

"Why didn't you mention this before?" Lenny demanded, his face was pale from exhaustion but his cheeks were now flushed red with anger.

"I ... I ... I didn't remember before," I stuttered shamefully, suddenly terrified of this man I had been convinced didn't have the ability to be scary. Oscar grabbed hold of my shaking hand and pulled me onto my feet so that the angered man was no longer towering over me.

"Lenny, calm down. She has told us now and that is what matters." An inkling of his old confidence had been returned to him now that he could cling to the possibility that he wasn't to blame.

"Em, tell us what you saw."

I wished then that I hadn't said anything because what I had seen was really nothing to go on; in my head I was sure it had been Edward but looking back I hadn't noted any distinguishing features that would have made me jump to that conclusion.

"I was too far away, I couldn't really see properly. Just remember seeing someone walk in that's all," I mumbled sheepishly to the floor, too scared to look them in the eye.

"So you couldn't make out who it was?" Oscar asked eagerly interrupting Lenny's imminent rant.

"No, I'm sorry," I said shaking my head. "It was probably just one of the other boys," I said indicating the space around us.

"Johnny has taken the time to go and see his ma and Luke was in the village with his friends, I saw him there," Lenny said, the anger dissolving. "There's no way it could have been one of them. Must have been someone else. You're our only constant visitor though, the rest of the time it is just someone requesting a horse," Oscar said distractedly. I watched him intently as he considered all the possibilities; facial expressions changed along with the different ideas that surfaced – some plausible and some dangerous to even think. When his eyes met mine I knew that we had both reached the same conclusion but neither of us would dare to speak it so we simply stood there, eyes locked together, trapped by a dark secret.

A resigned silence eventually fell over us, even the other horses didn't so much as breathe out of turn in order to get our attention; perhaps they could sense something was wrong. When Silver's bursts of agony became louder and more frequent, Oscar summoned up the energy to let out the other horses so that the cries wouldn't spook them. I could see that the horse was becoming more and more agitated and it killed me that I couldn't do anything to calm him down, but Lenny was adamant that not only I, but no one was allowed to get too close to him unless it was absolutely necessary.

Time seemed to move excruciatingly slowly as we watched the magnificent horse deteriorate by the second; his majesty and beauty seeming to ebb away.

"I can't watch this anymore," Lenny stated before walking away, leaving us standing there shocked by his sudden exit. Oscar wasted no time in bringing up his earlier thoughts.

"You think it could be Edward then?" he whispered as though it had been my idea all along. We were huddled together for security, protecting ourselves from any prying ears. I could smell the anticipation on his breath.

"That's where I went earlier. But he said that I had no proof," I replied sneakily. He stared at me in shock, not quite able to comprehend what I had just said.

"That makes him seem guilty!" he exclaimed. I nodded enthusiastically; glad that I could now openly discuss this rather than just doubting myself. I was about to comment on the fact that I thought he had been acting very strange when I heard voices approaching.

"Like I said, he's only getting worse," Lenny's voice boomed; not storming off like we had thought but instead fetching help. He and the vet walked briskly back into the stables causing Oscar and I to jump apart suddenly as though we had been locked in an embrace.

Luckily the men's minds were too preoccupied to pay us any attention and the blush that had reddened my face slowly crept back down my neck.

The vet took over the position where Lenny had been stood all day; his dirty blonde hair was ruffled and his clothes were refreshingly marked by the day's work. He was younger than most of the experienced men around but he had a knowledgeable look about his soft, yet serious, face. He nodded solemnly then spoke to Lenny. Though we were close enough to hear he took no trouble in trying to disguise what he was saying.

"I will go and check the injury again but I can already smell that the wound has festered. And if that's the case then I am sure you understand what will be the best option for him."

Lenny nodded sadly and moved to let himself and Harry into the box. I found myself edging closer, sniffing at the air to see if I could see what that trained nose had picked up. I was mainly greeted with the familiar musk of horses, hay and animal droppings though somewhere in that mix I could vaguely smell the putridity of an infection. It was only a smell that I knew because of my late mother.

I watched in awe as he was able to keep the animal calm enough to be able to investigate the wound – it was clear by his face that it was not looking good. But then again it was easy to tell that simply by watching the horse throughout the course of the day. I gripped the side as I waited to hear the inevitable verdict, Oscar's knuckles white against mine as we stood there silently. They didn't need to speak, it was clear from their dead eyes and hanging necks what had to happen.

"Someone will need to inform the owner, I can't do anything without their consent. It's important they understand that the sooner the better. I think the poor creature has experienced enough pain," Harry informed us.

"Probably best if I go," Lenny muttered sadly. The three of us stood and watched him leave, a deafening sadness surrounding us.

"Would you make sure the other horses are as far away as possible please. Don't want them wandering in."

Oscar left to do as instructed, leaving me standing there alone with the bearer of bad news. I stared down at my feet unable to think of anything to say – my mind was a cloud of white noise.

"I'm sorry," he said, breaking the silence.

"Pardon?" I squeaked.

"It's clear how attached you are to him. It's always hard when this happens and I tend to find that it's the workers that are more affected than the owners. So, I'm sorry," he explained and I felt an odd sensation, not unlike an electric shock, on my heart – his sincere words the first to really reach me.

It wasn't long before Lenny returned with Edward in tow; rather it was more the other way round with Edward storming through the door indignant with rage.

"I demand that someone tells me exactly what is going on! This blithering idiot cannot seem to provide me with a proper explanation," he shouted, red in the face. His arms swung in all directions throwing accusations at poor pale faced Lenny and demanding answers from everyone else in the room. When he didn't receive an answer straight away he stomped over to Silver's box, roughly pushing past me – almost purposefully into my injured arm. I unwillingly let out a whimper and he wasted no time in turning on me.

"I don't want to hear a peep out of you, in fact you shouldn't even be in here! Get out!" he exclaimed, staring directly at me. I didn't move straight away because I thought that it was just a meaningless result of his anger and that if I ignored it then he would pass over me.

"GET OUT!" he screamed in my face, the shock making me jump to life and hastily scramble out the room. Three pairs of eyes followed me sympathetically, wishing they could have helped but knowing they were unable to defend me.

I hid out of sight around the corner of the stables, pressed up against the wall so that I could still try and hear what was taking place. For some time there was only shouts, muffled answers and desperate pleas to be heard. Then silence. When the shot sounded I could feel it ricochet straight through my chest. This time I welcomed the silence that followed as the tears flooded over me.

Chapter 47

Nothing looked out of place. Everything stayed the same as though something so drastic hadn't just happened. The invisible walls that surrounded this estate made it into a sanctuary where it couldn't be touched by the hands of death; monumental events didn't leave cracks here like the rest of the population. The stately beings were protected from the horrors of real life. The war would only change them artificially, not so deep as to leave scars like it had done to Oscar, yet they celebrated and cried as though it were as much a part of them. As I stood there staring out through watery eyes at the intricately designed house, I felt nothing but disdain for the place that I had always thought of as my home. I could now see it for what it was; fake, pompous and condescending. They held no love for me and I no longer felt the need to return it. There was no beauty in the carefully laid brickwork, there was nothing charming about the old wooden arch and the magic had disappeared from the colours of the flowers. It all seemed empty.

I was so wrapped up in this emotional epiphany that I didn't notice that there was someone else standing behind me.

"I thought I told you to get out of here."

I turned to face the blonde-haired lord, his face inappropriately smug. There should have been some crack of emotion over the unexpected loss of his childhood horse, the creature that had patiently let him learn to ride and forever been loyal, but instead there was only a not-so-hidden gleam of satisfaction. It was abundantly clear that the love I had felt for this person could never have been real because that person didn't actually exist.

"Is that really what's important right now?" I asked disbelievingly.

"Of course it matters, you can't keep disobeying me!" he snapped.

I didn't bother to respond, there was really no point in making the effort when I knew he would always have a pointless answer to throw back at me. I figured he would interpret my silence as me giving into him and just walk away knowing that he had won, but he stayed put. I could feel his eyes on me as I stared out at the empty land.

"Why are you crying?" he asked gently. Instead of feeling glad that he had finally shown a tiny glimpse of being human I was instantly on edge, waiting for what came after this bravado.

"Because your horse is dead. Sorry, am I not allowed to be sad now either?" This time it was my turn to snap as I fiercely wiped my eyes with the back of my hand. His ice-blue eyes turned softer as he took in the sight of my blotchy face.

"I'm sorry," he muttered. "Guess this is harder than I thought, I shouldn't be taking it out on you."

I could easily have fallen for the trick sadness in his voice, but it didn't take much to stop myself from giving in.

"In fact, I shouldn't have been acting the way I have, you don't deserve it," he sighed dramatically and looked at me woefully – an expression that once would have made my heart melt. But it was a heart that he had hammered on too hard until eventually it had broken.

"Perhaps I was just jealous. You know; you and the stable boy. You both seem so happy."

I stopped myself from yelling out that the stable boy had a name and instead forced myself to remain silent. If he wanted to keep talking then he could ramble on but he wasn't going to get a response from me.

"I guess what I'm trying to say is that I love you too Emily. I always have, I just couldn't say. Now of course you know that nothing can really come of this, but no one has to know. It can be our little secret." He stroked my chin provocatively and gave me a wink as though we had just made a deal. He had spoken like I had just announced that I still loved him, he was so full of himself that he had just assumed that I felt the same. He had a wife! My stomach churned at the notion that he had just invited me to be his mistress and I felt nothing but disgust as I watched the insolent boy stride away without a care on his mind.

I stayed outside until I knew they had moved Silver's lifeless body – it wasn't an image that I needed to commit to my memory. It was only when I heard the movement quieten down that I entered back into the sombre stables. Oscar was busying himself by cleaning the now empty box, scrubbing hard at the fresh blood stain.

"Is there anything I can do?" I asked feebly. He looked around as though he were lost and non-committedly shrugged his shoulder.

"Not really."

"Shall I get out of your way?" I asked when he returned to scrubbing at the floor that was now almost spotless. He didn't answer so I interpreted the silence as a yes and turned to leave.

"Stay," he said quietly once I had reached the door. He didn't look up at me; his eyes remained firmly on that invisible stain. For a while I just stood there and watched him scrub away at nothing until I realised that unless someone made him he wasn't going to stop anytime soon. I crept into the box and knelt down beside him.

"Oscar it's clean now, you can stop," I said softly, gently placing my hand on top of his, but he kept going. I opened my mouth to try and persuade him again but he stopped just as the words landed on my tongue.

He knelt on that hard floor, hands gripping the splintered wooden handle of the old scrubbing brush. The muscles in his arms were tense from the strain and I could see the deep blue of veins pushing against his skin. His hair was clinging to his forehead, damp from sweat, and his eyes glistened in the empty space.

"I'm going to lose my job. I have nowhere else to go," he said on a whispered sigh. The words sounded painfully familiar.

"You don't know that. It wasn't your fault so there is no reason for them to get rid of you." I tried to sound reassuring but my voice sounder squeakier than anticipated.

"Edward already said it," he stated.

"Despite how much power he thinks he has, I am pretty sure that decision still has to come from Lord Barrow."

"That's where he was going."

"Oh." The defeated sound escaped my lips before I had a chance to breathe it back in.

I managed to pry the brush from his hands and we sat there together, fingers laced, as we nervously awaited the news of his undetermined future.

Footsteps could be heard crunching up the path and we both jumped up, still hand in hand, to face the news together.

"What are you two up to?" Lenny asked, eyeing us suspiciously. We breathed out in unison at his sarcastic question and momentarily let ourselves relax. Sheepishly we unlaced our fingers and I felt that tell-tale blush creeping back up my neck. Lenny noticed, I knew this because I saw a small smile dance on his lips, but he passed no comment.

"Emily, do you mind bringing the horses in for me?" Lenny asked politely, and though he didn't say it I knew that he wanted to speak to Oscar alone. They waited until they knew I was out of earshot before they started talking and since I wouldn't have been able to turn back unnoticed I obediently started to round up the horses.

They were all too willing to follow me, almost a stranger to most, after their long day outside. Silver's dominant presence was already missed and I understood that some of the obedience could be put down to them noticing something wasn't quite right. They all followed me back to the door and each wandered in the direction of their own box waiting patiently to be let in and fussed over by the two men who were waiting for them with fixed smiles. This applied to all but Arabella who stopped at the open doors and looked around apprehensively as though she were searching for someone, then slowly trotted over to the stall next to hers and rested her head sadly on the gate, looking down at the empty box.

"I don't think you should be handling those horses, do you? One death is enough for today." Edward announced himself making all three of us jump to his attention. Oscar's face automatically paled when he faced the smirking face of the unwanted visitor.

"My father wants to speak to you," he directed at Oscar, his words dripping with victory.

"Well he can speak to me too," interrupted Lenny. "Because I'm not going to see my best worker leave, especially when he has done nothing wrong."

I stared at Lenny in shock. In all the years I had known him I had never heard him speak out of turn, he had always just accepted circumstances whether they be fair or not. There was a new defiance in him that made me proud – I wanted the things that were right to be fought for, but it was very difficult to make a difference when you were one small, insignificant person in a world full of the powerful. Even Edward must have held some respect for the man who had patiently taught him the art of riding because he faltered at the remark, unsure of how to assert himself over this older, wiser man who had been on his father's service since before he had been a thought in his parents' minds. He knew, as well as everyone else standing in that room, that Lord Barrow would not dismiss what Lenny had to say light-heartedly and the likely outcome would be that Edward would be the one made to look a fool. He didn't make any excuses for his behaviour, there were no humble apologies, there was just a sour look that told us he would not be cheated by the likes of us.

"Emily, I need to speak with you," he barked, storming away and indicating that I should follow. I joined him, unable to meet the questioning eyes that latched onto me in fear that my face would reveal all. Edward grabbed hold of my arm roughly, pain shooting to my shoulder at the contact, and viciously kept squeezing to ensure he had my attention.

"I'm not sure you fully understood me earlier so let me repeat myself to make sure that it is clear," he spat maliciously. "I get what I want and what I want is you. So, you have a choice to make; you can choose to stay with your dirty stable boy and risk losing your job, your home and his job or you can do exactly what I want. I know which one I would choose." He pressed his lips forcefully against mine, his slimy tongue leaving a trail across my clamped shut lips. As soon as his back was turned I wiped the mark from my face before I even dared to breathe. My arm was throbbing in its strapping but even the slightest touch made it feel like it was on fire so I resisted the urge to cradle it.

I was greeted by Oscar's unsmiling face and my heart sunk.

"It's not what you think!" I exclaimed half-heartedly because I knew that my second chance had been blown.

"It's exactly what I think," he stated bluntly. "I heard everything."

That added statement gave me a tiny ounce of hope; I hadn't done anything to make either of them think that was what I wanted.

Oscar walked over to me and placed his hand gently over my arm sending warmth into the numbness that Edward had left behind.

"You don't need to pick him. Don't give him what he wants." He threaded his bare fingers through mine and lifted my hand to his lips with dimpled eyes; suddenly a courtier. It was chivalrous and gentlemanly and it sent a shiver of anticipation running down my spine. I tried to remember every sensation, from the way all the colours around me suddenly came to life to the electric current that danced over my palm like lightening on a stormy night. I wanted to remember every detail exactly as it was in this moment. But before I could complete my mental photograph he wrapped his hand around the back of my head, drew me closer, and kissed me. It was like our first kiss all over again; though this time I felt my heart and body cave into him. I could feel the pressure of Oscar's fingers on my scalp and the scratchy wool of his sweater against my fingertips. My heart felt like fireworks must, when finally after being lit, all that gunpowder has somewhere to go.

Chapter 48

The next few days passed in a haze. My heart had made my choice for me but I was still terrified of having to voice this out loud. I had been able to avoid it since the last time we had met, made easier by the fact that he was busy, but I knew that couldn't last forever. My mind was still battling with my options; on one hand Oscar seemed to instil a new lease of life in me, but there was also the daunting cloud overhead that reminded me that I was risking not only mine, but his, job which would ultimately leave us homeless. But did this mean that I also had to lose the people that I loved? No matter how much I tried to convince myself that I was doing the right thing, there was still something rubbing away at me telling me that there was always the chance that this could all get a lot worse.

It was that evening, as I was making my way back to the large house and the empty room, that Edward pounced and turned all my thoughts into reality.

"Been avoiding me?" he sneered, and I could tell that he already knew what was going to be said before I even had the chance to speak. I knew I was treading on dangerous territory now so my best bet was to bite my tongue and let him play the wounded soldier.

"I find it very interesting that you have chosen that path particularly after I warned you what was at stake. Luckily for you there was no good reason for you to be dismissed, not when it seems you have all started fighting each other's battles," he grimaced. "But I knew that if I pushed it hard enough then my father would give in to me and I would still get what I wanted in the first place."

I stared at him in confusion over his contradicting statements trying desperately to solve the complicated riddle.

He chuckled at the desperate look on my face knowing that he had finally asserted his dominance over me. He bent his head and lowered his lips to my ear.

"If he's not here," he whispered. "Then you can't pick him." His evil grin spread from ear to ear as he bathed in the glow of my astonished eyes.

I didn't bother to grace him with a response, I didn't even care that it hurt to do so, I just ran like my life depended on it holding onto a very thin strand of hope that I wouldn't be too late. I burst through the old wooden doors to find an empty room. I ran through to the stables desperately searching each box in turn for those coffee-brown eyes. As each second ticked by and I was still alone I could feel that fragile strand pulling harder and harder. I hurried back into the barn and climbed the ladder as quickly as I could manage, ignoring the pain in my arm. That same old squeaky floorboard creaked beneath my foot but this time there was no one around for me to disturb. I was alone and the place was empty.

I flopped down onto his bed with exhaustion, my brain no longer able to think of what else to do. I buried my head into the comfort of his starchy pillow. His smell washed over me and I felt hot tears sting my eyes as they rolled like streams down my cheeks.

The tears must have sent me to sleep because I was stirred out of my dreamless thoughts by a gentle hand against my cheek.

"A tear, Emily?" the voice questioned lightly. "Don't cry. You should know that I never would have left you."

I threw my arms around his neck, the pain no longer important, and clung to him like I would never let go. I wasn't sure of much, I couldn't be certain what I wanted or what the future held for me, but there was one thing that I was certain of.

"We need to get away from here," I whispered into his neck. I breathed in that familiar scent of soap and horses and I knew that I was home.

About the Author

With a BA degree in English Language and Literature, Alex has always had a keen interest in literature. She has been an avid reader from a young age, enjoying a wide variety of genres which is what inspired her to start writing. The Rule Of Thumb is Alex's first novel, but she wants to continue her story with future novels.

Other fiction from Stanhope Books

When Dreams Converge

When the dreams of wealth, power and freedom converge, the nightmares begin. After a dramatic life changing event in the Dominican Republic, Luke, a keen amateur sailor, persuades his wife to abandon their life in England and set to sea to live their dream of freedom.

During their voyage they are thrust into a world of crime, terrorism and murder. In a web of deceit and intrigue they are pursued by ruthless criminal organisations. In a plot which covers three continents, who will win and who will lose?

Human Rights

Ed Bush lives with his family in the coastal settlement of Chelmsford in South Britain, one of the United States of Europe. Their way of life is dictated entirely by the government known as Europarl. Every year at a four day celebration of human rights the people coming of age are assigned to their posts within the country.

Ed is recruited to join a rebel group and plans are made for him to leave, when he is distracted by the arrival of his new stepsister, Suzie. Will Ed leave with the rebels or stay with his family and accept his fate?

Watermelon Man

Regaining consciousness late at night in a dark alleyway in a strange town, the man realises that he has been mugged and robbed of everything—including his memory

He begins a journey that turns from a dream into a nightmare as nothing is as he had hoped it would be. Forced to confront his demons, his problems collapse into a web from which there appears to be no escape

The Grays Anatomy

Twelve short stories from horror author Rob Shepherd, featuring vampires, zombies and things that go bump in the night. Not for the faint hearted!

Long Overdue

By his own admission, Philip is living a humdrum life in the Essex coastal town of Maldon. His new boss at the town library is a pain in the neck, making even the job he loves difficult, and he longs for something to kick start him out of what he admits is a bit of a rut.

Soon after a new and unexpected friendship begins he determines to make some changes. Then one day his routine walk to work has him finding a dead body, involved with the police and feeling he must help his new friend by investigating a mystery from years past.

As events following the death carry him along, an abandoned sailing boat, half a letter and a surprising alliance sees him seeking to unravel the mystery of a missing person. He quickly realises that dialling the emergency services that spring morning is leading to changes that will affect his life, his job and his future as well as having him travel abroad and make some surprisingly impulsive decisions.

www.stanhopebooks.com

facebook.com/stanhopebooks

Twitter @stanhopebooks